MARRIAGE AS ADVERTISED

Jerome J. McCarthy

the real life series publishing company. llc.

Inquires should be addressed to:
The Real Life Series Publishing Co., LLC
P.O. BOX 1896
Keller, TX 76244

www.TheRealLifeSeries.com
info@thereallifeseries.com

DEDICATION

This book is dedicated to my wife Marla. Words cannot convey the volume of respect and admiration I have for the strength you display on a daily basis. God blessed me with a gorgeous, discerning, intelligent, praying woman who loves me unconditionally and I don't take that blessing for granted. You are the reason I am!

I also want to extend this dedication to married couples who have hit a rough patch.

Therefore what God has joined together, let man not separate -
Mark 10:9 (NIV)

TABLE OF CONTENTS

Table of Contents

Table of Contents

CHAPTER ONE

Guilt

It was 3am when an unexpected call forced Jon to abruptly awake from his deep slumber. The volume of the ringer was on the highest setting, thus making Jon's heart beat so hard that he could feel it thump against his chest. *What in the world? Man what time is it? I don't even remember falling asleep. Where was I?* Jon fell asleep on top of his comforter wearing the same clothes from earlier that evening; a cotton ribbed tank and jeans. He lifted his head while still lying on his back, and focused on the alarm clock until it was visible. *3am? Who could be calling this early? This is probably bad. Early morning calls are always trouble. The last time I got an early morning call, my wife's aunt died.*

Jon fumbled through the dark, located the phone and clicked the talk button. In a groggy tone, he mustered the energy to talk.

"Yep."

"Um, hello, I am sorry to call so early. Is Jon Carter available?"

"Speaking. Who is this? Why are you calling my house so dag on early?"

"This is Sheriff Dale Malone. I am sorry Mr. Carter. I am afraid I have some bad news. She didn't make it. She is no longer with us."

"What do you mean she didn't make it? Who is she? What are you talking about?"

"I am so sorry Mr. Carter. She was pronounced dead on the spot. There was nothing we could do to save her. You need to get down here immediately."

"No. No. This can't be. We just spoke a few minutes ago."

Jon was taken back by this news, so he attempted to prepare a timeline in his mind to piece things together. *I don't understand. We were just arguing not to long ago, but how long was it? Was it before I fell asleep? I can't remember what happened. Dead? It wasn't supposed to end like this.*

Time elapsed, and Jon stood at the crime scene with cordless phone still in hand. As he looked around, he became hypnotized by the twirl of the ambulance light bar. Everything appeared to move in slow motion as the collapsible gurney transferred the body into the ambulance. *This can't be happening. What is going on? And why are all those flowers on the ground?* While Jon observed the surreal scene and tried to figure out the purpose behind the flowers which occupied a small section of the damaged concrete sidewalk, he turned around to be politely greeted by a law enforcement officer.

"Mr. Carter, I am sorry but we have to place you under arrest. You have the right to remain silent. Anything you say can and will be used against you in a court of law. You have the right to an attorney. If you cannot afford an attorney, one will be provided for you at government expense."

Jon refused to make eye contact when the officer read his Miranda rights. The neighbors stood with their arms crossed trying to figure out what happened. The contrast from the red and blue strobe lights on the police car danced across the clothing of the concerned residents.

"Do you understand the rights I have just read to you?"

"Yes sir."

"With these rights in mind, do you wish to speak to me?"

"I suppose, but I didn't do nothing."

The officer's partner leaned over and whispered to Jon, "Look, I don't know exactly what happened, but if I were you, I'd keep my mouth shut until I got to the station and spoke with my attorney. This does not look good at all for you kid."

Jon turned around to allow the police to handcuff him. While the officer secured the cuffs, a vehicle passing by slowed to a snails pace. The tinted window slowly rolled down, and revealed Jon's old boss shaking his head side to side in disgust. Jon made eye contact, and was embarrassed his ex employer saw this ordeal. The officer placed his hand on Jon's head and assisted him into the back seat of the police cruiser. While guiding him into the vehicle, the officer moved his hand and allowed Jon's head to hit the inside of the car door. There was a light thud as the sound of his skull echoed through the empty cruiser.

"Man, what the…"

"Oops, sorry kid. You are a tad bit bigger than I estimated," the officer said in an unapologetic tone.

Jon was upset, but so overwhelmed by the situation that he sat there emotionless. *This is bull. I would love to go one on one with this cop. I can't even figure out what is going on, now I have to deal with this on top of it?*

As his head throbbed with a burning sensation, Jon's hearing became hypersensitive. The voice of the dispatcher from the police radio grew louder. Every sound became more intense; from the ambulance gurney folding and doors latching shut, to the officer in the front seat scribbling something on a notepad. *Why does it sound like he is trying to drive that pen through the paper? My senses are going crazy. What in the world is going on here? What am I doing handcuffed like a criminal?*

Jon studied the mosquitoes as they congregated around the light which emitted from camera of the news crew that just arrived. The reality of what was going on started to sink in and Jon slumped his head in shame. A single tear trickled down his cheek and fell onto his lap. He stared at the tear as it saturated his jeans then slowly evaporated. *Man, I should have never quit that job. I should have just stayed there. Maybe none of this would have happened.*

The cruiser pulled into the station, and they took Jon in for questioning.

"So why did you do it Mr. Carter?"

"You don't know. You weren't there. You have no idea what happened. Heck sometimes I don't know either. This doesn't even seem real."

"Well, that is why we are here. My job is to figure out what happened. And trust me son, this is very real. I think it is time you start explaining. What do you mean you weren't there? What happened?"

"I honestly don't remember detective. I remember an argument, then I just remember waking up to the phone ringing."

"So are you trying to tell me you blacked out?"

"You can assume what you want. I am just telling you what happened. I have no reason to lie. I have never been in trouble before. I have no priors."

The detective took a sip of his coffee, then placed it back on the table.

"Look boy, it's late, and I don't want to be here anymore than you do. I have a hot piece at home I wouldn't mind crawling up next to right now. This is not personal. I don't have a problem with you. I am sure you are a good person, but I can't help you unless you help me."

"I am trying to help you. I just don't know what else you want me to say. I honestly don't remember. I shouldn't even be here. I need to get home. Why are you holding me back? I am just a normal guy. I am in college. I am just trying to protect and provide for my family."

"Well boy, you are in trouble now. You told Sheriff Malone that you just argued with her a few minutes before we contacted you, now you are telling me you don't remember anything that happened? You can lie to me all you want, but all the evidence points to you. She is dead and you beat him until he almost died. What's the common denominator? You! You are responsible for what happened to both of them. And oh yea, you will be facing a double-homicide charge because she was pregnant. So as far as college, you might as well forget about it. You just completely ruined your life. And as far as holding you back, no one is holding you against your will. That is in your head. As long as you think like that, you will never be anything. Everything you try will fail. You are going to end up being just like your father."

"Just like my father? What kind of interrogation is this? You don't know anything about me or my father. What are you talking about no one is holding me? She was pregnant? What is going on here? This is not making any sense."

"Look, I am trying to help you, but I need you tell me the truth."

"The truth? I told you the truth. What else do you want from me?"

"Do own any firearms Mr. Carter?"

"No, I don't believe in guns. I have a wife and kids at home and I can't afford to have an accident. Why would you ask me that? What does that have to do with anything?"

"I am the one asking the questions. Why are you nervous? Do you have something you want to tell me?"

"Man, I don't know what I have to say to get it through your thick skull, I don't know anything!"

"We found a Kahr K9 9mm pistol at the scene of the crime. We also discovered that it was registered in your name. Did you forget about that too?"

"Well, it must be another Jon Carter somewhere, because I don't own any weapons…except for an aluminum Easton baseball bat."

"Let me paint this picture for you. You got into an argument with this woman. Hours later, the woman ends up dead. She has several bullet holes in her car which match a pistol that is registered to you. And the kicker…your prints are all over the weapon. Now tell me Mr. Blackout, where were you at approximately 11pm? Or let me guess, selective amnesia again, right?"

"Man, I don't know. I can't remember. You can paint whatever picture you want, but I am telling you the truth!"

The detective slammed both his hands on the table and stood up.

"Look, my patience is wearing thin. I have three eye witnesses that say they saw you and this young lady arguing in the front yard. You were the last one to see her alive, and now we are here trying to figure out what happened. I have a dead woman on my hands and a baby who will never get the opportunity to grow into his or her purpose because you decided to play God and take that from them. How dare you sit here and play me for stupid. Her prints are all over your car window. Since you can't remember anything, can you tell me how they got there?"

"Who are you talking about? What woman? I don't know about any woman or baby…or pregnant woman, or whatever. Like I have said a million times before, I do not know what you are talking about. There are only two women in my life…my wife and my daughter. Well actually four because I can't leave out Momma or Grandma. Then you have to throw in my mother-in-law with her fine self. I love her dearly too, so that is five."

"Is this a joke to you? Son, don't play games with me. You know what, take him away. I am tired of talking to this kid. Take him out of my sight."

The officer stood Jon up, and squeezed to tighten his cuffs.

"Man, why are these so tight? I am literally feet from the holding cell. I mean really, where can I go?"

The officer ignored Jon and escorted him down the hall to the holding cell. Before they arrived at the cell, the officer took a detour and literally pushed Jon into another interrogation room. Bam. The door slammed shut and Jon took a blow to his abdomen from the officer's knee. The sharp pain caused Jon to physically curl into a ball, which gave the officer leverage to push him on the floor. He took the ball point of his billy club and buried it into Jon's ribs.

"Are you resisting arrest boy?" The officer kicked Jon while on the floor.

Jon grunted to absorb the force, then responded, "I bet you were a chick magnet in high school, huh punk? You know if you weren't hiding behind that badge I'd wear you out. You will get yours, trust that."

"Are you making threats to a law enforcement officer boy? You must not know how we do it down south Yankee. You best take that talk up north." The officer squatted down, and nudged Jon with his club. "But you know what, being a Yankee is the least of your problems. I think you need to work on yourself before you start making threats again. What kind of man are you anyways? You were supposed to be there for her and you weren't. You ruin everything you touch!"

The officer raised his club, struck Jon on the back of the head. Jon blacked out.

* * * * *

Jon opened his eyes, and squinted as the beam of light from the sun pierced through the window blinds. He sat up in his bed, heart still racing. Shirt soaked with perspiration, Jon sat motionless as he allowed his mind to adapt to his surroundings. It took a minute or so for him to realize that he was safe at home. *Did they let me go? How did I get home? Hold up stupid, that was just a dream. A dream, but man my head hurts. That was too real!*

This was not just a random dream, but a reoccurring dream that had haunted Jon on several occasions. He looked past the empty bed, at the alarm clock which said it was 6am. *Good, I am still on schedule. April is not in bed, as usual. Wonder if she has left already? Man, I have to get ready for work, but this joker will not go down. I am straight pitching a tent here. Maybe April will give me some if she is still there. She is so sexy in the morning, and I am in heat right now.*

Jon went into the bathroom, and saw his wife wrapped in a towel brushing her teeth. He walked behind her, and politely showed his interest.

"Stop J. Put that away and leave me alone. I have to go work. You know how my boss is."

"Come on Ape. Just real quick."

"Maybe later baby. What were you dreaming about? You were tossing and turning all night."

"Ape, I can't even begin to explain. I just need to stop eating that White Tower before bed."

"You need to stop eating that stuff altogether. Those little burgers aren't right. They tear my stomach up."

"Oh, that's just because you have to eat them in moderation."

"Moderation won't help J. Something is not right about that stuff. It probably ain't even real beef."

"It's not. It is actually kangaroo meat."

"Boy, shut up."

April laughed, then reached up and pulled Jon down to her altitude so she could kiss him on the cheek. Jon moaned in acceptance of his wife's love. As she entered their walk-in closet to select an outfit for work, Jon followed her in and continued his campaign to be a candidate for intimacy.

"So if I keep saying something funny, can I laugh that towel off you? Or how about I use my teeth to pry it off you?"

"Jon!" April said in a scolding tone. "Stop being bad. Go take your kinky behind and stand in the corner until I leave. You are on punishment. Matter of fact, just stand there all day."

As Jon leaned against the door, he smiled and fixed his eyes on April.

"Do you remember when this closet used to be our refuge from the kids? Remember how our kids broke the lock on the bedroom door, and how we would be in here going at it and would look up and see the door knob turning slowly…like a horror movie. No matter where we hid, our kids would always find our location and terrorize us."

"Yea, those kids have your genes. You tell them no, and they do it anyways."

"Remember we used to bring pillows and blankets in here, and stay in here for hours? How we joked that we should install a ceiling fan? How we liked it because you didn't have to worry about volume as the multiple racks of your clothes made it like a sound proof room and muffled your screams? Or how about that tote we have in the corner with your sandals in it, and how we were in position and you were clawing at it while I…"

"J, you are acting up!"

Jon walked over and grabbed his wife, and kissed the back of her hand. He took her finger, placed it on his lips, gently allowed it to glide in his mouth, then pulled it out and kissed her hand again. April dropped the hanger which was in her other hand.

"How about we do a little somethin' somethin' again for old times sake…like we used to. Let's see if I can make you hit that note again."

April was tired of Jon begging, so she awarded his persistence. She shut the door, dropped her towel, and allowed herself to join with her husband. After they became one, April lay in her husbands' arms. With careful attention to detail, she used the tip of her finger to trace the outline of his facial features. As her fingers walked to the unshaven portion of his face, Jon closed his eyes to enjoy the delicate touch of his wife.

"I love you J."

"More!"

"You are going to make me late, I have to go."

April kissed him on the nose, grabbed her towel, then walked back into the bathroom. When she flipped the light back on, she assessed the damage in the mirror.

"Boy, look what you did to my hair. See, that's why I run from you in the mornings."

They both laughed, which was uncommon as they had not been getting along lately. Jon watched as his wife cleaned herself and prepared to leave. He loved her deeply, in spite of all their problems. April loved him too, but things were changing in their household. This was one of the rare occasions the two were around each other without fighting.

In the process of admiring the detail April took in primping herself, Jon ended up dozing off. His quick nap on the plush carpeted closet floor was interrupted when he heard April honk her horn as she pulled out of the driveway. Jon slowly sat upright, and convinced his body to stand up so he could wash himself prior to work. He walked into the bathroom, splashed water on his face, and let it drip dry.

As Jon analyzed his reflection, he couldn't help but think about the events from his dream. *No matter how much I try to forget, these dreams are not going away. This guilt is eating at me. Why can't I get over it?*

CHAPTER TWO

Routine

Jon

Sitting in his pickup truck while on break at work, Jon decided to call his wife to see what they were having for dinner. He grabbed his Nextel and autodialed 69 – his better half. The phone rang briefly, and she answered. "Hey woman, this is Jon. You busy?…I am just checking to see what you want me to get for dinner. I think the kids want pizza since your niece is spending the night, but I know you usually don't like what we pick…Thai it is then. See you later…More. Bye."

Jon sat back in the custom bucket seat of his F-250 pickup truck, and let out a deep sigh. He exhaled to release tension, then staggered off into deep thought about his wife and their situation. As he focused on his silhouette, which was captured by his stainless steel coffee mug, he began to verbally let his frustrations out.

"Man, I am tired. I don't know what I am going to do. April and I used to be so close, but now we rarely eat dinner together. We developed a routine which is uncommon for us to deviate from. After work April is responsible for picking the kids up from her mother's house and my obligation is to bring home food, which works out as we usually arrive home near the same time. I am truly grateful that April's mother watches the kids when they get out of school and I also admire how she keeps her home. She cooks three square meals daily, but that was a trait her daughter apparently chose not to adopt as we always eat take out. Even though I would love April to cook more, that is a small gripe in comparison to our other problems.

"Today is Friday and like usual, we have nothing planned together. When I was growing up I used to get amped for Friday's arrival as it represented a fun day, or the beginning of an exciting weekend. Now I am at the point where I dread going home no matter what day it is. Days overlap, weeks blend together, years pass, but through time it seems like nothing changes. I feel like I am stuck in the movie Groundhog's Day.

"People on the outside think we have the perfect marriage, but that is because everything with us has become rehearsed. We have simulated the exterior image of a close knit family, but the interior of this relationship is falling apart at the seams. I love that woman, but sometimes I just don't think we are going to make it. I drastically wish something would change because I miss the old April. I long for the way we were, but I have to deal with the reality that we are growing apart. Our lives have no spontaneity anymore; sex is scripted, conversation is brief, and there is just this distance between us and the gap appears too wide to bridge. We are not united…we are just two strangers raising kids together.

"Outside of our marital problems, I am also unhappy with where I am in life right now. I currently work in construction, but I always dreamed of running my own real estate investment company. In my spare time from operating this venture, I planned on flipping houses with my son as a hobby to show him the business, and more importantly to jumpstart his entrepreneurial blood. I had no doubt this is what I would be doing by this age. It is hard looking back at decisions I made that may, or may not have kept me from fulfilling my vision, but what is even worse is the effect it has had on my family.

"Enough of that dream, I have to face the reality of where I am and decide what to do about this marriage. It seems like no matter what I do, it is never good enough. I feel like April does not appreciate my hard work and contributions to this family."

April

"I believe for the goals you are trying to achieve, the best return on a short-term investment would be our High Yield CD. You have the flexibility of a short term, a locked in APY, and all our CDs are FDIC insured. I know you are in a rush, so take this packet. It has all the information on our plans, and I also have my business card inside. If you have any additional questions, feel free to call me. Take care!"

April let her customer out, and walked back into her office. Buzz. Buzz. Her cell phone began to vibrate while isolated on her desk. Without looking at the display, April frantically rushed to answer the phone before the caller hung up.

"This is April…Not really. What's up?…Pick me up some Thai please…Love you…Bye."

April picked up her office phone, and dialed extension 1256.

"Jenna, can you inform the tellers that I am on break and that I won't be taking any new customers? Thank you!"

April placed the phone back on the receiver, and began to stare at a picture of Jon and her children which she proudly displayed on her desk. She picked the frame up, and talked to the photo like it was a therapist.

"Jon never tells me he loves me; he always says more. Sometimes I don't even know why I say it to him. I am tired of trying. He has changed so much over these past years that sometimes I don't know if this is even worth fighting for. I still love him, but at times he just makes me sick. I often wonder if we have what it takes to turn this around. Maybe I need to start putting some money away, and just leave. If I am consistent, over time I can have enough stashed to afford me some financial stability and provide a way for my independence. I would prefer not to be on my own, but there is just an indescribable level of ignorance that has grown between us and I don't think I can deal with it anymore. It's like we don't know each other anymore. I really don't want to leave, but maybe that will prompt him to change. I have so many things I try to say to him and they never come out right. There is no reciprocal communication, so I never really know what goes on in that head of his.

"Jon is a good man, it just seems like lately the contrasts that made us attract like magnets are starting to repel us away; almost as if our polarities changed. He likes to stay at home and watch sports or play video games, whereas I like to go out dancing, or shopping. Jon is real good with speaking with people, but in some ways he is introverted; whereas I am very outgoing. Jon is a frugal with his money, and of course I am a frivolous little diva.

Jon likes to eat at hole-in-the-wall establishments; dirty little grimy greasy spoon mom and pop diners. I prefer to eat in upscale, four star or higher restaurants. There is one more obvious physical difference between us; my man is tall, where I am a short fry.

"Ok, I am just rambling now. I love that man and am not going anywhere, I just don't understand what happened. All those differences never mattered in the past, and I don't even know if they really matter now. I truly love him, but I am just confused and searching for answers for where we went wrong.

"We married 9 years ago when we were in our mid 20s. If I could go back in time, I still wouldn't change that because not all of our years have been bad. God blessed us with a 7 year old son, Jon Jr., and a 4 year old daughter, Jordan. We even have a German Sheppard Collie mix named Trina. Jon and I have good credit, a reasonably healthy family, and a nice Victorian style home. We take on the guise of the All American Family, and boy we should win an Oscar for the way we act at public functions, family gatherings, and church.

"It is not entirely false as I have always admired Jon for his intelligence, hard work ethic and how good he is with his hands. My husband is very good at what he does, and highly respected in our community. He received an excellent deal on our Victorian style home, and he performed all the work on it himself. The exterior he did all the landscaping, replaced the trim, and restored the original wood shutters and colors. The interior he restored the hardwood floors, replaced all the plumbing and faucets, and put travertine down in the kitchen and bathrooms. I could go on and on about the renovations, but trust me when I say that our house is absolutely gorgeous.

"Our house is a perfect mix of classic and contemporary. I love our house, but it is not a home. Things just feel so cold between us. It is like Jon doesn't put forth any effort to spend time with me, nor is he affectionate like he used to be. The same effort that he put into renovating our home, I wish he would invest into me.

"Besides our relationship, I have personal life goals I always wanted to achieve. When I sit and think about this, it makes me bitter and resentful at times. What about me and what I want to do? Between this job and the kids, I am stretched thin. I know Jon is under a lot of stress too, but at least he gets to do what he loves. Me on the other hand, I can't. Due to life situations I was forced to put my dreams on hold. Don't get me wrong. I absolutely love my kids and husband, but I think a lot of times when women get married, our ambition has to take a back seat to our husband. Our dreams get put on the back burner. I wanted to be a nurse since my earliest childhood memories. That is where my heart is. No one seems to care about what I want to do. I am stuck here at this dead end personal banker job with absolutely no room for growth due to the micromanagement of my branch manager. I am grateful to have employment, but this is not my passion.

"I am just tired and frustrated. I pray things change because I do not know how much longer I can take this monotonous life of mine. It is getting so bad I am sitting here talking to a picture."

Sandwich Board

"Hi babe," Jon stated as he walked through the door.

"Hi hun," April responded as they pecked each other to conceal their problems from the children.

Jon turned on the Disney channel and prepared the plates for his daughter and niece to eat on the couch, then took the other pizza into the den to watch a replay of the Bears game with his son. April grabbed a Sprite out of the refrigerator, and took her Thai upstairs to her room to call and chat with her girlfriends.

This had become a routine for the Carter family; arrive home from work and find ways to avoid one another. Sometimes Jon would even sleep in the den to avoid confrontation. They noticed the less they were around each other, the less they fought.

* * * * *

The weekend passed and Sunday rolled around.

"Jon wake up."

"What?"

"Are we going to church today or not?"

"Yes, of course we are. I will be ready in a few minutes."

The couple took individual showers in preparation for church, then proceeded with the task of grooming their children. After the mental checklist of ironed clothes, tucked in shirts, brushed hair and adjusted ribbons, Jon and April stood side by side in the dual vanity mirror making sure they were presentable; meanwhile not speaking a solitary word to one another. Eventually the family was finally ready and loaded April's car, which Jon drove on Sundays.

While in the car, April placed her purse on her lap and dug in to retrieve her lipstick. She flipped the visor down and used the mirror to dress her lips while trying to avoid the bumps in the road.

"That is a nice purse. LV. What does that stand for? I am sure it is some designer purse."

"Louis Vuitton."

"How much did you pay for it?"

"Not much."

"What does not much mean April?"

"Not much means what I said. Not much. It was a little over $700."

"$700? April, you know we can't afford that right now! We are on a strict budget, and if we ever plan on paying these bills, then we have to stick with it. What is wrong with you?"

"I am really not trying to have this discussion right now. Let's just talk about this after church."

"After church?"

Jon bit his lip to refrain from talking, and his anger provoked him to gradually accelerate the vehicle. April tried to remain calm and not show she was bothered, however his weaving in and out of traffic made her heart race. "This boy better not tear my car up," April thought. As the vehicle speed increased, she secretly clutched the door handle in an attempt to brace herself for the worst.

The couple safely arrived at church, and Jon walked around to open the door for his wife as if no argument happened. She reached up to straighten his tie and performed the rehearsed kiss on the cheek prior to getting their children out of their seats. The couple put together a string of fake smiles and greetings as they walked into church holding hands. Once inside, they sat on the pew in their usual section and awaited the start of service.

Jon and April truly enjoyed worshipping at this particular church. They both stood up and clapped their hands and sang during devotionals, and when it was time to pray they held hands like they used to when they first met. The service was going well, and it was time for their pastor to preach.

Jon and April both daydreamed during the start of the sermon. They really wanted to be that couple in love that they portrayed. They wanted things to get back to where they were, but the problem was they didn't know where to start. Jon reached over and initiated the favor of his wife by stroking her hand with his thumb as this was his way of saying he was sorry. April looked at him and smiled. She truly loved him, and during these moments of his affection she realized why she stayed and attempted to make it work. As she tried to control the warm tingly feeling circulating through her body from Jon's touch, the Pastor's words caught her attention and reminded her she was in service.

"As married people, and especially Christians, you can't hang out at the same establishments you used to. You can't do the same things you used to do. You are an ambassador of the kingdom. You represent your Daddy's name, and his household. You also need to be leery of the company you keep and the signals you send. You have to be conscious of this because people, believers and non-believers alike watch. You affect the perception of the kingdom."

April and Jon both shook their heads in agreement. They knew they didn't have the best influences around them, but they continued to hang out with the wrong crowd because they were avoiding the issues at home.

"You know when I was little, my mother and father were big on family name. They always told us not to disrespect the Jones name, and how we represent character. Well, while my dad was at work, I was being a typical young mischievous boy. My mother warned me about the people I hung out with. There was one kid in particular in our neighborhood who used to always get into fights, and would curse like a sailor. I tried to vouch for him and argue that he was a good kid, but my mother saw straight through it. I felt I should have been able to make my own choice of my friends, but in my day you weren't allowed to make choices; Momma made them for you. What I loved about my mother though is she took the time to explain why she forbid us from doing certain things. She told me that we have a choice of who we keep in our lives, and sometimes you have to choose to eliminate certain people. My mom told me that even at her age she has to choose who she allows in her life and who she cuts off. I didn't understand why you had to remove certain folk from your life, so she gave me an example. She told me that she could sit down and hold a conversation with me, and by the time we are done talking, take the worry and fear from within her and transfer it into me. That words alone could change me by evoking fear.

"I am losing you, so let me give you an example; the billion-dollar pharmaceutical industry. They flood our televisions, radio airwaves and magazines with numerous ads which list all these symptoms, and they make it appear that you can't cope or function in life unless you take their medication. They use words to induce fear, and prey on our ignorance. My mother went on to say that is the same thing people do. They use words to plant seeds of fear and doubt in you, therefore you have to be careful who you hang around with and seek advice from because before you know it, you will start to act like them.

"When a man of God gives you his blessing, he transfers something to you…there is a transferable anointing. Well the same happens with your friends. Their words and actions have influence that can transfer to you. Your friend can disclose bad experiences they had in previous relationships, and before you know it you end up sharing the same feelings and biases that your friend spoke to you. You can allow their multiple failed attempts at relationships ruin any chance you have at happiness. What you need to realize is most people like to see you fail. True, not all people want you to literally fall off the face of the earth, but they do want to limit your success to what they deem acceptable; and ironically that is usually one step below where they currently are. They can't handle you doing better than them because they feel it is not fair. A lot of people approach life like a race, so soon as they see you making progression towards your goal, they will tell you things to hold you back…and before you know it you will subconsciously adhere and become complacent like them. How does the old saying go…birds of a feather? If you let them, people will talk you out of your calling and your purpose. What I am trying to say here is that you need to learn how to move yourself into different circles. Put yourself around people who are at where you want to be. People that will help you grow spiritually. Overcomers who will expose you to a different way of thinking.

"When my mom gave me that speech, I thought she was just nuts and old and wasn't cool and didn't know what she was talking about. But you know what? She was absolutely right. My mom told me to stop hanging with him, but I didn't. I was disobedient and would sneak and play with him without her permission, and low and behold don't you know my mouth turned sour? I mean I put together curse words that didn't even match…just crazy combinations. I even got into a few fights. I used to think to myself, *Was Momma right? Was he changing who I was? Was he getting me off the path I was on?*"

"I didn't understand the significance of what my mother was trying to teach me at the time until I got older. The true revelation came to me at a much older age. You see, sometimes our need to be socially accepted puts us in a position where we compromise our righteousness. I think the problem many of us face is we feel like we can influence them to change, but the reality is they will change us before we change them. When I was younger, my sister used to date this guy who was just as wrong as wrong could be. He was an older man who used to sell drugs, and do Lord knows what else. I played football with this guy and knew he wasn't about anything, but she would not listen because she felt it was her responsibility to save this man. I kept trying to explain to my sister that that you can't help someone who doesn't want to be helped. I used to get so frustrated because it appeared that my sister couldn't function in relationships unless instability presented itself. She would pass the good guys up because she was accustom to abusive men and dysfunctional relationships. This happened because she allowed her morals to be corrupted. She knew better and was raised right, but my sister chose to hang around with immoral people. She allowed them to alter her character.

"Now this was just an example, but I don't want you to think that these negative influences are limited to intimate relationships. They can also be friendships, co-workers or even family members. The Bible warns us in 1 Corinthians 15:33 about the company we keep. Let me read the text from the amplified version. It says *Do not be so deceived and misled! Evil companionships, or communion, or associations, corrupt and deprave good manners and morals and character.*

"These are not my words. It says it right here. Associating with the wrong crowd can affect your character. Communicating with certain people, hanging out with certain folks, or even chatting via e-mail can cause us to compromise our moral principles.

"Do you remember in grade school science class when they took a balloon and rubbed it on the carpet, then static charged it so that it would stick to your shirt? How sometimes you think the balloon is gone, and turn around and find that it is stuck to your back? You don't even recognize it because it is so light, and subtle. Well that is how it is when you hang with negative influences. Things you may think are light or subtle end up sticking to you."

Halfway into his sermon, Jon received a tug on his arm from junior.

"Daddy, I have to go to the restroom."

"Come on boy," Jon responded with a strong, agitated whisper.

Jon was annoyed that he had to take his son to the restroom, but the alternative was an accident on the church pew. He held his son's hand firmly, and walked him through the foyer to the lavatory. While his son relieved himself, Jon stared at his reflection in the mirror. *Lord, I need to hear a word from You. I need some direction. Things have got to change.* Jon Jr. finished, then the two headed back inside. Jon placed his hand behind his son's head and navigated down the pew past various size church members, all the while trying to avoid stepping on toes and tearing stockings. After inhaling a strong diverse blend of perfumes and colognes along the way, the father and son finally returned to their seat. As Jon positioned himself, he adjusted his hearing to listen to his pastor, who was now speaking on marriages.

"There are some people in this service right now who are experiencing severe marital problems. Some couples in here right now argued all the way to church, then got here and acted like everything was ok. There are couples in here right now that are only staying together because of the kids, and plan on separating after junior graduates from high school. There are couples in here right now that married just because they conceived a child together before they were married. Some couples in this service will leave here, and the husband will go home and beat on his wife. Some couples in this service will leave here, and the woman will verbally abuse her husband. Some men in here right now have a mistress attending the next service. Some women in here right now have a man they are having an affair with. Some couples in here right now married someone they knew they were unequally yoked with because they were too eager to wait for the person God had for them. Some people in here right now married because they wanted to mask their insecurities, and marriage provided the perfect cover. Some people in here right now married because they felt the clock was ticking, so they jumped on the first person that gave them some attention.

"I know Christians don't want to talk about these issues, but it is the truth. These are realities for people sitting right next to you. You have no clue what that person sitting in front of you is going through! Abuse, lost trust, communication failure, financial difficulties, validation issues, attention issues, and infidelity are just a few of the many marital problems couples are facing and we need to deal with them. Can I get an Amen? We have to address these issues because we have couples that are hurting. Look, some of you right now are daydreaming and allowing your mind to wander because you are in denial. The enemy doesn't want you to receive this because he knows what will happen if you get delivered. There are couples that are missing out on the numerous blessings that occur as a result of being in a union ordained by God because they don't understand the purpose and intent for marriage. These couples are in love with the image or idea of marriage. They are more concerned with how their friends and family perceive them as a married couple, than growing together and fixing troubled areas.

"You know when I was a young teenager, I used to work a part-time job carrying a sandwich board. You do know what sandwich boards are, right? You ever drive by and see a person standing outside wearing an advertisement like a clown? Well, that clown was me. Hey you laugh, but there was no shame in my game. My family needed the money so I worked through the humiliation. Anyways, I was a young lad at the time, and I was strutting up and down the street like a little walking billboard for this company; smiling even though deep inside I hated my job, and what this company represented. I had the two boards on either side of me so everyone driving by could see from every angle. These message boards are attached with these straps that resemble suspenders. These straps allow the weight of what you are carrying to be evenly distributed to your shoulders.

"Well this is how some married couples are. They wear a sandwich board saying this is the perfect marriage in public, then return to the weight of trying to sustain a broken home. They take all this time to create this façade of what their marriage is, meanwhile trying to camouflage their deep rooted problems. They smile making you think everything ok, but you have no idea what pain they are experiencing deep within. Most people advertise marriage as this perfect union with minimum problems. This could not be further from the truth.

"What do you do when you are caught in a marriage that is going sour? How do you replace the bitterness with the sweet love which drew you two together? I do not know who I am speaking this to right now, but you need to listen to me closely. You need to know that all marriages have ups and downs. Do you hear me? All marriages. It is a part of life. There is nothing too great for God to deliver you from, but you need to understand that you must do your part. You have to realize that there will be high times, and low times. The key is learning how to balance the lows against the highs.

"The story that comes to mind is Joseph and the famine. Now I know you know this story, but since most of you haven't been to bible study since Halley's Comet last appeared, I will just tell you again. There was a famine in the land of Egypt which lasted seven years. Joseph predicted the famine was coming, so during the seven years of plenty, he stored up grain. Since the famine affected other countries, Joseph opened the storehouses and sold grain to them. Joseph didn't panic and give up at the first glance of trouble. He was cerebral about his situation. It wasn't that the situation was insurmountable, but it took someone willing to be proactive. Joseph predicted the famine and stored up during the seven years of plenty so that during the famine not only did they survive, but they prospered. Prospered in a time of lack! You need to apply this same principle to your marriages. I think a lot of times we come into marriages and think everyday will be like a walk in the park. I am sorry to burst your bubble but trust me, I have been married 24 years, and there will be some straight up funky days. We need to start being smart about this thing, and understand that in life, and especially in marriages, famines will come. There will be a low point in your marriage, but you can't just throw in the towel at the first sign of trouble. What you have to do is be proactive and take from the plenty to sustain you through the famine. Hold on to those memories and special things from your favorable periods during your marriage, and use them during the famine, or low periods."

Pastor Jones continued his sermon, then shortly afterwards service let out. April and Jon prepared the children to leave while attempting to absorb the message they just heard. As they sat prior to starting the automobile, they both realized that they pulled off another stellar performance advertising the perfect couple. Jon did a double check to make sure everyone was ok before he started the automobile and drove out the parking lot. As the family traveled home, he unloosened his tie and let it drape around his neck.

"You know April, sometimes Pastor Jones is all over the place with his sermons. I mean he can start talking about one thing, and end up clear on the other side of town. But you know what? He makes some good points from time to time. I like that part when he mentioned marriage as advertised. That hit a little bit close too home."

April looked at Jon, and with no facial nor audible response, turned her head and continued to stare out the passenger window.

CHAPTER THREE

The Company You Keep

Date Night

Every Thursday April's mother watched the kids to give April and Jon quality time together. That was the expectation. The reality was this young couple was using this time to distance themselves even further. Jon arrived home prior to April, and immediately took a shower to prepare for the upcoming evening. After dressed, he headed towards the kitchen, grabbed the orange juice from the fridge and took a drink directly from the container. While chugging from the carton, the telephone rang and startled him. *Man, I keep forgetting to change that stupid ringer.* Jon reached for the cordless on the counter, but was unable to exchange a greeting with the unknown caller due to the liquid that accidentally went into his trachea. He placed the phone away from his ear to clear his throat, then responded, "Excuse me. I am sorry. Hello."

"Sounds like you were drinking out of the container again. How many times have I told you…"

"I know Grandma. I know. How are you doing?"

"Doing good I suppose. I was calling to check on my great-grandbabies. Where are they?"

Jon loved his grandmother dearly, but knew by her intrusive questions where this conversation was headed. He still remained respectful and tried to address her concerns.

"Well Grandma, April took them over her moms. You know Thursday is our date night."

"Oh, that is nice of her. So, where are you taking your lovely wife? You have a restaurant picked out, or are you two just going to spend a quiet night at home alone?"

"Well actually, I am going out with the guys and she is going out with her girlfriends," Jon said in a regrettable tone as he knew his grandmother was about to scold him.

"Jon, baby, I am not trying to fuss at you. You know granny loves you, and what I say I say out of love. Listen to me carefully boy, you need to spend some time with your wife and leave all those worldly friends of yours alone. You a saved man now. You can't do the same things you did before you got married. You keep hanging out at those spots and with those people, you are not asking for nothing but trouble. Now you have been married long enough that I shouldn't have to tell you that. Take care of your woman and spend time with her. Trust me sugar, if you aren't giving her attention, someone else will!"

Jon heard the garage door open as April was arriving home from work.

"Ok, April is home. I'll talk to you later. Bye."

Jon, relieved that the conversation was over, sat on the barstool as he watched April wind down from work.

"Who was that? You look relieved to be off the phone."

"That was my grandmother. I love that woman, and I know she means well, but…oh, it doesn't matter. How was your day?"

April sighed, "Ok I guess. I am just ready to get these clothes off and go eat. I didn't have lunch today."

Jon exercised his nervous habit of playing with the plastic lid of the orange juice container. While staring at the cap in the palm of his hand he asked, "So, what are you ladies getting into tonight?"

"Well, Jassmine is supposed to pick me up in about 45 minutes. She volunteered because she wants to show off her new sportscar that her man bought her."

"Her man, or her grandfather?"

"J, don't say that. He is just a little bit older than her."

"It is not a little, he is at least 20 years older than her. Why do you always take up for Jassmine? I don't like that woman April. She married that man just waiting for him to croak."

"And I don't like your raggedy friends either, so what is your point?" April walked towards Jon, snatched the orange juice, and proceeded to pour herself a glass.

"So, like I was saying. Jassmine is coming to pick me up, then we are heading to O'Hare. I have an old high school friend, Tiffani, flying up from Atlanta. Once we pick her up, then we will probably go to the Cheesecake Factory. We have a lot of catching up to do, so don't wait up. Mom said the kids can spend the night."

April began to drink her orange juice which was slightly tainted with Jon's backwash. He chuckled under his breath thinking about how irate she becomes when she catches him drinking from the container.

"I took a short shower and saved some hot water for you. I will go up and start yours."

"Thanks baby," April responded as she watched her husband walk up the stairs.

Thirty minutes passed, and the doorbell rang. Ding, dong.

"Jon, can you go get that. It is probably Jassmine. Tell her that I will be down in five minutes."

Jon opened the door, and Jassmine greeted him by extending her arms for a hug.

"Haven't seen you in a while stranger!" She hugged Jon tight, moaned as if the hug was revealing a hidden agenda, then gave him a kiss on the cheek. "You are looking good J. How is life treating you?"

"Good I suppose. And you?" Using his peripheral vision, Jon noticed her new sports car. "A white Maserati, huh? Apparently you have been doing well financially, so why did I even ask? Of course financial security is the only important thing in life, right?"

"It is not white, it is Bianco Eldorado. And regarding security, well you know how it is. Some people go after the things they want, while others standby, watch and complain." Jassmine said in a flirtatious manner.

"There is a cost to everything Miss Jassmine."

"Some things are worth the cost J," as she looked Jon up and down inappropriately, "and believe me I would be willing to pay it."

Picking up on her vibe, Jon tried to politely end the conversation. He looked down at his watch, "I suppose so Jazz. Look, I really have to get ready to go."

"Guys night out, huh? Well you be good!"

"You too," Jon responded sarcastically.

By this time April was coming down the steps. "What are you two kids talking about?"

"Nothing. Nothing at all. I was just leaving." Jon leaned over and kissed April on the cheek. "You ladies be safe! April, call me so I know you are alright."

"Ok, I will. Bye babe. Love you."

"More. Bye"

Bulls & Wings

Every Thursday, Jon and a few of his friends hung out together. Sometimes, if they received permission from the ladies, they would rotate homes and take over the den. The majority of the time they went to the local sports bar. Jon was looking forward to watching the Bulls game and playing pool, so he jumped in his truck and headed towards the bar to meet his boys.

Jon befriended a lot of people, but only hung out with 3 guys; Aaron, Dana, & Gordon. Aaron is April's older brother. He is married, real laid back, and doesn't talk much. Dana is like a little brother to Jon. They grew up in the same neighborhood, and Jon always looked out for him. Dana is a romantic engaged to his high school sweetheart. They lost contact for years, met each other at a grocery store and rekindled their flame. Then there is Gordon. Self-nicknamed "G," he was the player of the group. Gordon married fresh out of high school, and entered the Navy to support his wife and child. However while at sea, he couldn't keep his ship at bay. Once he completed his military term, his wife left him. Ever since the divorce, Gordon has been against marriage and monogamy.

The sports bar had a decent gathering that night as most people were there to watch the Bulls play. You could hear the periodic cheers, drunken slurs, and faint conversations. Through the dense smoke filled sports bar air, Aaron claimed, "This game is mine. Eight ball, side pocket."

"Man, pool is like therapy. I love the sounds of the balls hitting each other. I like watching how they move. I love the physics of the sport." Gordon recited after one too many drinks.

As Aaron missed the shot, Dana watched the Bulls bring the ball down the court. "This has been the first time I have been excited about the Bulls since Jordan left. I like the chemistry of our team and think that we are legitimate. Hinrich & Nocioni, then you have Duhon, Gordon and now Big Ben? Give us a year or two, and I see us with our seventh ring."

Gordon, a long time Pistons fan, responded, "Man, are you kidding me? The Bulls will never win another ring because they are wack. We gave you Ben because we felt sorry for you. The Bulls winning another championship? You'd have a better chance calling back Rush Street Reggie. It's all about Deee-triot Baaa-sket-baaall."

Dana turned to the others in the sports bar who began to boo at Gordon's infamous Detroit Pistons chant which became popular when they beat the Lakers in the 2004 Finals. "You have to excuse my friend here. Poor thing came out at the shallow end of the gene pool."

The men sat and laughed as the attention fell upon Gordon.

"Seriously, I love Detroit like I was a native. How could you not like the Tigers, Lions and Badboys? And let's not even talk about the women? Whew. I tell you I have been all over the country, but there is something to be said about Detroit women. I have received some unbelievable favors from the women I met there. Maybe if my ex wife was from there, or learned some tricks from the natives, we'd still be together."

"Man that is not right. Why you playing her now? That woman had your kids, and stood by you. It seemed like you had a good thing with her. What went wrong?"

"What went wrong? What you talking about J? What went wrong was I married her for the wrong reasons. She was high school tail, and we were trying to play grown up. You know, do the right thing for our kids. I had no business marrying that woman. When I came back from sea, she was just a different person. Look, I really don't want to talk about her. What's up with you? Everything cool at home?"

"Man, I couldn't begin to tell you. I just don't know her anymore." Jon stared at the monitor as the Bulls passed the ball around, but it was apparent he was not paying attention to the game. He paused for a second, then released his thoughts. "I don't know G. We've grown apart. I still love her, but nothing is good enough for that woman."

"April?" Dana said surprisingly.

"Yes, me and April. Things just aren't going good. We always fight, and she has just changed so much."

Gordon was antsy to respond like he had some reserved atomicity awaiting its opportunity to be released. "That is just women for you. They paint this picture of the woman you want, and do anything in their power to get you. When you are dating, they are nice. They cook, they clean, and the sex? Whew. The booty is a thing of beauty. Once you get married all that stops. It is almost like they say *Oh well, now I don't have to do all those freaky things. Throw my slutty side out the window. I am a good girl now. Won't be needing that anymore. Who needs to cook? Pick some food up. Clean? Do I look like your maid?* Of course they will never admit that they changed because they have this wholesome church girl image where they have to act like they never participated in premarital sex. I guess they forgot about all the photos they took and videos they starred in. I swear, I don't know why half these women wear white when they get married. They should start wearing burgundy!"

Dana was becoming agitated by Gordon's remarks. "You can't base all women on the experience you had, G. They ain't all bad. And you know what? We need to man up and accept some responsibility. Men need to hold ourselves accountable, and admit that we contribute to the way they are. We paint this picture of what we want in a woman, then distort it. We are confusing them. We say we want a wholesome good girl who has not been around, but then we turn around and manipulate women to get them in bed. They feel like they have to do it to keep our attention, then we have the nerve…"

Gordon interrupted Dana before he could finish his sentence, "This spoken from a man who has not married yet. Man, save that speech for someone who cares. I can tell you are still wet behind the ears. That girl got you whipped. It is apparent you still don't really understand females. Let me school you guys on women." Gordon leaned back in his chair, and allowed his foot to prop on the end of the pool table "See, women have us fellas. They look into our eyes, and stroke our egos using their hands. They make us feel invincible by using seduction. That is a trap. The truth is women lie to manipulate and get what they want just like us. The only difference is they are smarter. Yes, they are smarter. How are they smarter Gordon, you ask? Well, for two reasons. The first reason why women are smarter is because they keep their mouth shut. You will never catch a woman doing dirt unless she wants you to know! But men, on the other hand, we have to run and tell our boys. Then when we do dirt, we never have good alibis. Women have like an underground social network. Their girl knows to lie immediately if they get a call from their girlfriend's man. They are trained well. We could learn something from them."

"Gordon, you are a plum fool sometimes. Where are you going with this?"

"Well Jon, I am trying to school this young boy on the art of war. This is no game; we are at war with these broads, and they are winning. So let me get back to my lesson. Now, you may want to take notes on this. The second reason women are smarter, and this is really a sign of sheer brilliance to me; they only tell us what we directly ask. If you don't ask women specifically what they were doing, where, and with who, they will not tell you. This is the kicker though…you have to be specific down to the words you use.

"I will give you an example. You run into a guy your girlfriend dated years ago. You ask her if they messed around, and what does she say? *Well, we kissed.* Now in her head, she knows she slept with him and did all kinds of tricks and favors for him, but since you didn't ask her directly, she manipulated the term 'messed around' and convinced herself that it just meant kissing. At this point her logic is that she technically didn't lie, and if you can believe your own lie, then you are ahead of the game. It is lying by omission, but since we ask in a round about fashion, they find a loophole and justify not telling us the truth. Now if we would do the same thing, we would be liars and cheats and dogs. If we don't reveal something we are dirty and good for nothing, but if they don't reveal something we never asked or didn't ask the right way. Do you feel me? Now this is just one example, but trust me they lie to us all the time fellas. My all-time favorite is the 3 guy lie."

"I am sure I will regret asking this, but what is the 3 guy lie?"

"Aaron, where have you been bro? I know you haven't been shackled that many years. The 3 guy lie is when you ask a woman how man men they have slept with, and they tell you 3 men because they feel that is what you want to hear. If they say more then 3 then they look like a whore, and if they say less than 3 they seem too inexperienced. The crazy thing is the way these women are nowadays, it is probably like the 20 guy lie. You know I was talking to my baby cousin the other day, and he was telling me how these young girls so loose now that they go down now before they even kiss you. Those lucky bastards. In our day, you would almost have to marry a broad before we received that kind of love."

"What is your point? This art of war, and lying stuff. Where are you going with this?"

"J I am disappointed. I would have thought you, of all people, would understand where I am going. My point is this there is a double standard so we as men need to start thinking before we get caught up with these women, and protect ourselves. Dana you may ask why I am telling you this? Well, I am going to tell you why. For one, because you are like my brother and I love you. For two, it is highly likely that you don't really know your woman like you think you do. You don't even know the right questions to ask. Like I said, you are still wet behind the ears."

Dana was becoming aggravated with Gordon, but he tried to keep his composure.

"I hear what you are saying, but you don't know her G. You don't know her at all. And like I said, everything in your little speech is based off the chicken heads you messed with, and failed relationships you had. My girl is different. It is not about sex, it is much deeper with us. We talk about everything, and our relationship is good. She is like my best friend. I have known this woman since high school. She doesn't lie to me, so I don't care what you say. You have no clue at all. We are completely open with one another."

Gordon began to snicker. "Open is right…your nose is wide open. Dana, you are a cool dude, so don't take this the wrong way when I say this. I am just trying to look out for you. Learn from my mistakes. Your fiancée is an intelligent, attractive woman, but don't do it. You don't know what that girl has been doing since she been out of high school. No telling what kind of baggage she accumulated. You really don't know anything about her. Hell, you don't even know if she pees in the shower. Back out now while you have the chance bro. Lifetime of misery, I am trying to tell you. I promise you will regret it! I know you think you have all the answers because you think you are in love, but you will end up like me. And once you sign your name on the dotted line, you better not break the agreement. It is definitely cheaper to keep her! Do yourself a favor and move her in first. That way, you will get a glimpse of how it will be to have your closets stolen and constant nagging 24/7. It will also buy you some time because women act like moving in is a sign of commitment. While she is staying with you, just use the excuse of limited finances as a reason for not purchasing a ring, or giving her the wedding of her dreams. That always works. In due time you'll see that moving her in will temporarily stop the marriage conversation, and it also leaves your options open. If it doesn't work out, or someone better comes along, then sever the ties and move on. Just make sure your name is on the lease, or mortgage."

Jon laid his pool stick on the table, "You are out of bounds G! Stop giving that boy advice. Getting married is not that bad. Dana reminds me a lot of myself years ago. April and I were like best friends as well. Not trying to sound soft, but we used to talk for hours. We'd just talk about anything. Yes, she is attractive, but our conversation turned me on more than anything. She was like one of my boys. I could share dreams with her, and she seemed excited about me fulfilling them. I even shared things with April I never told anyone. It is like anymore, there is very little talk between us. Now it seems like all we do is argue. No matter what I do, she always has a smart remark to say, or something to complain about. I swear sometimes makes me not even want to come home. It is like I fight all day long, and the last thing I want is to battle on my home turf."

Gordon was eager to submit a rebuttal. "Like I said before. That is just women for you. They all the same. All women nag nonstop. They have serious issues my man. They don't just have baggage; they have Samsonite grade luggage; that tough stuff. I think drama and stress is embedded in their chromosomes. That is why I am single never to travel that road again. Preserving my blood pressure. Not the kid. I don't have time for that stress."

"All women ain't like that," Aaron said breaking his 20 minute silence.

Jon, agreeing with his brother-in-law, spoke up as well. "I agree Aaron. You act like you are the perfect catch G? Get oudda here. You got just as many issues as some of the women we speak of. If not more." Jon drunk the rest of his cola, then continued. "Something has to change with us. I just don't know what to do. Man, it was not always like this."

Gordon rested his forearms on his thighs as he leaned forward. Jon's words sunk in and made him realize his friend was in need. "Jon, look, I am sorry bro. I don't mean to be negative, and I know I have been hating on your relationship. To be honest, I think part of it is I am envious I didn't have what you two have."

"You had it G, you just chose to have *it* others as well."

"It's not like that Jon."

"Well if it's not like that, that what is it?"

"It's more complicated than that. I just can't explain."

"Whatever man."

Gordon was hoping Jon would probe more so he could tell his story, but Jon did not bite. In a last attempt to get it off his chest, he blurted out, "Ok look, here is the truth. What really happened. Listen now because I will never tell this story again. We dated, if that's what you want to call it, my junior year in high school. She was the girl all the guys wanted. The thing is, after I landed her I lost interest. She was cool, but I think it was just the thrill of the chase that excited me. So fast forward. My dad got that job in Michigan, and we moved. This was like in May. I pretty much lost touch with her. I ended up coming back in town in September and ran into her at this men's clothing store. She was getting a gift for her dad's birthday, so I helped her pick out a nice tie, then we hung out afterwards. We clicked and ended up spending the entire evening together. After that, she stayed in contact with me, and would come to visit me on the weekends. Things progressed and we got a little serious I guess you could say. One thing led to another, and bam. I came home to surprise her Thanksgiving weekend, and she surprised me telling me there was a bun in the oven. We were trying to do the right thing, the family thing, so after we graduated, we got hitched. I called myself being a man, so since college seemed farfetched at the time, I enlisted in the Navy to support her and our child. I moved her out to Chesapeake, VA, and went to sea shortly afterwards. We split up three times, and went to several counseling sessions. God knows we tried to make it work. I believe me going out to sea was hard on her, and my newborn."

"Come on, you can be real with your boys. It was more than just going out to sea. Remember, I know you. You must have forgotten some of the stories you have told me about those port visits. Shall I bring up Palma, Spain? The beaches in Mallorca? The three ladies in one night? I remember some of those stories about those Spanish women and what they did under the table. Or how about Broward County Navy Days? Want me to continue?"

"The Navy was more than just women and partying. That was my family. It was like a brotherhood." Gordon's eyes glazed over as he reminisced about his service time and he began to smile. "Man those were the days. You just don't know. We used to get hammered. Broward was cool, Palma was off the hook as well, but my favorite port visit was the time we had a 4 day stay at St. Thomas. Prior to that trip, I didn't even know it was possible to make women that looked like that. Those women in the Virgin Islands were ridiculous. Not only that, but the place was just beautiful. The water was crystal clear, and there were Yachts all over. It was just a different experience for me; a young boy who hadn't seen anything outside of Illinois and Michigan. And oh did I mention, it was a serious party town. There were a lot of tourists from cruise ships, and desperate women willing to leave their inhibitions behind. But you know what, I never cheated on her. I mean, if you don't count favors."

"I could have sworn that you told me you stepped out on her. People always want to tell their side of the story trying to be the victim. You know you did that girl wrong."

"Yea, and you do the same thing. Sit here and cry about April like it is all her fault. Like you didn't do anything wrong at all. *Look at me. I am Mr. Perfect and I did nothing wrong. She is just different. Pity me. Give me sympathy because I'm the victim.* Man up bro and stop whining. Your problems are no where near as bad as you are making them out to be." Gordon slammed his empty shot glass on the table. It was obvious his liquor started to take root. "Ok, so what if I did step out on her? That is besides the point J. Yes, I cheated one time, and we worked through it and she said she forgave me. When I got out the Navy, everything was cool at first. She was happy I was home and whatnot. Then after a few days, her true side came out. She kept bringing up the past and what I did. If you say you forgive someone, then do it. Stop rehashing the issue, and let it die. Once she stopped nagging about my infidelity, then she started complaining about what I didn't do for our family, and how she felt like she was a single mom. Then she started doing little petty things. Like she would make my lunch for work, and I go to eat my sandwich and the bread slices would be in opposite directions. Or my favorite, she'd make my adored sandwich; mesquite smoked turkey and cheddar with a hint of Dijon. I am at work hungry, ready to get my grub on. I go to take a bite out of my sandwich, and discover that she accidentally forgot to take the plastic sleeve off the cheese slice. You know what I am talking about? How they have the little individually wrapped cheese slices…"

The group of men began to laugh at Gordon as he used his hands and facial expressions to animate his story. Gordon smiled as he continued.

"I am trying to be serious here. I can laugh about it now, but it was not funny then. That chick was off her rockers. I truly believe she was trying to kill me. After a few of her lunch stunts, I would just throw her lunches in the trash, and I stopped eating at home too. Heck knowing her, she probably tried to put some crushed glass in my food or something. I'd just have the ladies I work with make lunches for me. You know how I do. I used to have a three chick rotation. Every day a different one would bring me a dish. I used to have this one chick that used to make me banana pudding. Man, if you only knew. Ok, so back to the story. I ignored her little games, and tried to be supportive of her regardless. I stood behind her when she wanted to open her own catering business. In my opinion, it was a dumb decision and it really hurt our relationship, but you couldn't tell her anything. She worked there all day, and we really didn't get to do anything together. It was extremely frustrating. The situation grew worse, tempers flared, and I pretty much developed an attitude like if she is going to accuse me of cheating and not being supportive, then I might as well. So I just did my thing, we ended up separating, and we decided to call it quits. Now, I told my life story never to revisit there again. New topic?"

At this time, an attractive waitress came by and asked the men if they wanted any refills. Jon raised his glass, and watched as the waitress smiled while pouring his beverage to the brim. The guys paused for a second as they admired the young, perky attractive waitress walk away.

Jon looked at his friends with that glare, and stated, "Ok new topic. Sex. This is an issue with us as well. It has just changed. I don't know if it is because I am getting older, or what. Why is it so different when you get over 30?"

"Do you need some Viagra? Let me know because my dad always

keeps an extra stash in his sock drawer." Gordon asked.

"No, I don't need Viagra, and I am quite disturbed that you know where your father's personal stash is." Jon stated as he chuckled. "For the record, no I don't have any problem in the impotent area. There are other areas of our relationship which are impotent, but I assure you not the sexual part. I can't explain it. It is like such a chore now to get her in the mood. Maybe this is just how life is when you get older. I just miss the old spontaneous April. The April that would go to the back of the movie theatre with me, and…"

"Bro, that is my sister. I am not trying to hear all that," Aaron said while shaking his head in disbelief.

"Man, you spoke twice tonight. You are at your quota today." Dana replied.

The group of men all burst into laughter.

"I am just saying. We used to have such chemistry; in and out the bedroom. We would go at it like wild animals during mating season. Now the rules have changed. What is up with foreplay? Who invented that? We are too old for that. It is like I used to be a stud back in the day; now my sex drive has crashed. She wants to lay there for hours kissing and touching, and I just want to cut through the red tape. We are too old to waste hours and hours kissing and holding like we used to when we first dated. I am so consumed with life's time constraints and just the stress from being over a family now that I can't relax and let go. I feel like that is time I could be doing something to move our family forward. Everything I do feels like I am rushing. Maybe I am just getting older, but I have run out of the luxury of time. I feel this desire to just move and do something."

Aaron decided to add to the conversation.

"Tell me this fellas. When you are boyfriend and girlfriend, you get some all the time. Why does it change when you get married? Now I know the stereotypical headache excuse men get, but I can't say that is the case with my old lady. My wife is not stingy by any means, but it just seems there has been a decline. Why does it seem like we don't get it that much when we tie the knot? Is it because we can get it whenever we want? Is it a subconscious thing maybe?"

"Where that come from bro-in-law? You having problems at home too? Is there something in the air?"

Aaron chuckled.

"No serious problems, just real talk J. When the old lady and I dated, I will say in a 30-day period of time, we used to go at it at least 45 to 55 times a month."

"45 to 55 times bro? Come on now."

"You know what I mean. Now that is an average of course. Some days we went at it multiple times, and some days we rested. I mean seriously, there were some days I had to call of work. I even lost a job because the sex was so good. It was like she just depleted me. Like my soul was empty, and I was completely drained. Why are things different now?"

"My main man Aaron, I tease a lot about rules changing, but all jokes aside I have a theory on that. You want me to break it down for you?"

"Please do brother-in-law."

"Ok, here is my stance. I think the decline in sex once married is two fold. For one, we aren't young like we used to be. We have to face the fact that we are old now, and have more responsibilities as an adult. These stresses of everyday life wear on us."

"I can feel that J. I am definitely getting older."

"Age is the first point of my two fold theory. The second part is God's plan."

"Aw man, here we go again," Gordon said in a cynical tone. "We have a good conversation, and then he has to go get all philosophical on us."

"Just let him finish his point," Dana replied.

"Thank you. Now we all know that God tells us not to have sex before we get married, but none of us listen. We are hard headed. One day I was meditating and reflecting on life, and it just hit me. I was sitting there wondering why sex feels so good, and why we can't just do it? I mean, it is not as bad as some other sins. It is not murder. Then I really started thinking about the act, the union, and tried to create a scenario to explain it."

"You are losing me man."

"Try to follow me. God has a plan and a reason for everything he does. With that in mind, I thought about sex, and how it would be if we followed his plan. I mean, it was pretty deep. I sat and thought about how things would be if I took away all the women on my resume, and started fresh."

Gordon began to laugh. "Started fresh? Yea man, we all have some that we regret and want to take back. I have quite a few."

"No man, not like that. Aaron, you may want to stick your thumbs in your ears on some parts. Call it a parental advisory…or should I say sibling advisory, because this may get graphic."

"I can handle it bro. Just don't get too crazy."

"Ok, I am a visual learner, so I had to paint the scenario. Say April and I were both virgins when we got married. We take our clothes off, admiring each other's bodies since we never been with someone else naked before. We kiss and touch and explore one another. You remember that curiosity you had when you first were intimate with a woman? Well imagine that, but God basically looking down at you giving you the nod that He approves. You don't even have to feel bad about what you are doing. So after exploring one another and doing all that good stuff, we are finally about to become one for the first time. I feel around, and find where I am supposed to be. I am excited, and really don't last that long before I climax. Now April on the other hand, it is painful for her, and not enjoyable. The next time we become one, I learn a little bit more about what I am doing, and it becomes less painful to her. The more we become one, the more we learn what pleases one another, and the better we get. It is sort of like a teeter totter; things eventually balance their way out. Pretty soon we are hitting our stride, and going at it like some monkeys in heat."

"I can feel that. I am sure that experience would be unbelievable, but what does that have to do with bad sex in a marriage? The reality is most people aren't virgins when they get married."

"That reality is the point of everything I am trying to say. I believe most of us, since we went against God's will, burnt ourselves out. We slept with all these women, and used all the energy and creativity and freakiness that was in us for our wives on some flings. I think that is the problem with sex in most marriages. By the time people get married, they have already done everything sexually you can think of. Most just cover it up and lie about it, but you can't deny that your sexual past has an effect on you. I guess my point is if we would have waited, do you think we would still have these conversations? That's all."

"You know brother-in-law, I can agree with that. That was pretty deep. I never really thought about it like that."

"That is not deep, that is stupid," Gordon responded. "And it is definitely a lot easier said than done. Since you wanted to go all religi-fied on me, let me break this down for you. See, God created women from man. They came from our ribs. Now I think he was trying to give us a sign. How many ribs we have? Like 12 per side, right? I think that was a message that we weren't supposed to at least have 24 women in rotation."

"Gordan, shut up man," Dana said.

"No seriously though, Abraham had more than one wife, King David had multiple wives and concubines, King Solomon had like 700 wives and 300 concubines, shall I continue? And yes, I used to go to Sunday

School when I was younger, what? Seriously, I don't see what the problem is with multiple women? The law now prevents me from marrying all these broads, so I just give them what they need. It is just natural. Men are not constructed for monogamy. We weren't made to deal with one woman every day for ever and ever. And it is just sex. Hell these days, women are on board and make booty calls just like us. Casual sex is more common, which makes it a lot easier for us. We don't have to lie and tell women we love them anymore to get some. Plus, it is just too hard to resist a hot piece, so why not just release and relax?"

Jon removed the toothpick which had been resting in the corner of his mouth. "Well Mr. Sunday School, you should also know that God doesn't put more temptation on us than we can bare. We act like we can't resist, but the truth is, we can."

"Women were put here for our pleasure J. And shoot, I was put here to pleasure them. Gordon makes 'em scream like Mike Jackson in the U.K. You know, that is just something I do, so I can't speak for y'all."

The men began to laugh at Gordon's arrogance.

"Seriously though fellas, women need us. Without a man's pleasure, women get cranky and evil. Besides, sex is harmless. Well maybe not harmless, but aside from STDs, it is actually good for your heart, and emotional well-being. Sex is exercise, and exercise is good for your mind. It helps to alleviate stress and it alters your mood due to the release of endorphins. Not only that, you wouldn't like me if I don't get any. Call me Dr. Bruce Banner because when I get backed up I turn green. While in a drought, I may end up back handing someone at work or throwing a table or something. I need it regularly, and no I can't resist. We weren't built that way. J, you trying to tell me if you had a fine woman half naked pulling on you, you could say no?"

"Gordon truth be told, yes I could. The battle starts in our minds fellas. Since we are visual, we have to filter what we are exposed to. You have all these sexual images on TV or e-mail that seem to put us back to a warped mindset. I don't know, but I want more out of life. I have been down that road of tossing women to the side, and it gets tired real quick. And don't give me that mess about you can't say no because you can. Ok, say you have a fine half naked woman pulling on you, and right before you were going to put it in she said she had HIV, and she pulls your last condom off and throws it on the floor. You trying to tell me you would still sleep with her?"

"That is different J."

"No it is not different. That is my point. We have the will power to stop if we chose to."

"Man, why are you trying to Dr Phil that fool? Not like he is listening to anything you are saying." Aaron said.

"Ok, let's flip this. What would you do if you caught April cheating?"

"See what I mean? That brotha is just plain ignorant. We are talking about apples, and he goes and brings oranges into the conversation. He just likes saying stupid stuff." Aaron responded.

"I will entertain your question G. I'd probably just walk away; with my kids of course."

"Yea right J. Like the courts would allow that. I been stroked by the courts during my divorce. They don't care about men's rights." Gordon had been argumentative all night, and awaited a response.

"Who said anything about the courts? April knows that our kids would be an exchange for the pardon."

"The pardon?" Dana asked.

"Yes, the pardon. The pardon that releases the man she had an affair with from physical harm for touching my wife! These guys out here need to know it is not safe to mess with a married woman. Call it a crime of passion."

The guys laughed again, as Gordon prepared part two of his scenario.

"Ok, hypothetical situation. Say you passed away, and I was helping April bring some groceries in the house."

"Man, don't play. I come back like homeboy in that movie Ghost, and bust you in the head with some pottery," Jon said in a joking manner.

"I am just making a point. I mean, she is fine and all." All the guys laughed again. "So why don't you hook me up with April's friend Jassmine?"

"You two together? That would not be a good idea. Besides, Jazz is married."

"Married? All the better. That just means no commitment for me. And it is a known fact that she is still putting out."

"I know. The truth of the matter is I really don't like April hanging out with her, but what can I say…I hang out with you!"

"Come on Jon. Plug me with her. I know she can get us some box seats at Soldier Field. Besides, I know that old man she has can't know what to do with all of that. He only has another couple years left in the tank anyway before his engine fails anyways."

"Forget Gordon. Next topic. Where and how did you meet my baby sister?" Aaron asked.

Jon stared at the big screen TV and watched as the Bulls brought the ball down court, "That is a long story my man. A long story."

Cheesecake & Gossip

Every Thursday the ladies all got together to shop, eat, and talk about fashion, men and relationships. None of April's friends were married except for Jassmine; and she was not necessarily the poster child for a virtuous woman. Jassmine was a childhood friend who was slightly older than April. Whether it was lying, deceit or infidelity; there were no holds barred when this woman saw something she wanted. Jassmine married a man 25 years her senior, and everyone under the sun saw that it was strictly because of his affluent family. Her husband works in the front office for the Chicago Bears organization and comes from a lineage of wealthy real estate developers.

Alicia is April's interior decorating, overprotective older sister. She is not a diva like April, but is quite the drama queen. April loves her dearly, and appreciates how her sister gives sound advice. Alicia was a married, but her husband passed away when his plane, American Airlines Flight 77, crashed from one of the terrorist attacks during 9-11. He was on his way to DC for a conference, and April was going to surprise him and tell him she was pregnant when he arrived home. She is still grieving, and has not been in a relationship since his death.

Tiffani is a high school friend who moved to Atlanta to go to college. While in school her father passed. Tiffani received a healthy life insurance check, and she was careful to invest it wisely. When she graduated, she decided to reside in Atlanta as she was offered a position with a Fortune 500 company. After a couple years in corporate America, she started her own bookstore and novelty gift shop using capital from investments she made throughout college. With the implementation of eBay, her store took off, and she has been doing quite well for herself. She hasn't been home in years, but recently her uncle got sick; thus prompting her return.

And then there is Myra. Myra is just Myra. She is one of those people you can't describe, you just have to experience. She always says off the wall comments at the worst times, but she means well and has a genuine heart. Myra's mannerisms resemble Rose from The Golden Girls. She is book smart, but lacks common sense. She recently received her master's in Counseling Psychology, and is currently working towards her doctorate.

All these ladies went to high school together, and have been friends for years. A reunion was inevitable, and long awaited. The girls received a call from Tiffani explaining her flight was delayed, so April and Jassmine proceeded to the restaurant. They met Myra and Alicia there, and selected a secluded booth.

"Girl, I can't believe that Tiffani is coming to town. How long has it been?" Jazz said.

"Hmm. It has had to be at least 10 years because I don't think she has seen my kids, nor husband." April responded.

Midway into the conversation, Tiffani arrived. The girls screamed and tap danced in circles as they made up for lost time. April got up and hugged her long time friend, then pushed her away at arms length to look at her.

"Hey girl? You looking good! Man, it has been years!"

"I know. April, look at you. Two babies, and still the same figure as high school."

"How did you get here so fast?" Myra inquired.

"Well, when I called, I was at the President's Club changing my attire. I wanted to surprise you girls."

Jassmine appeared to be a bit annoyed. It was apparent she wanted to show off her new car, and this surprise entrance ruined her plans. In an antagonistic tone, she took a sip of wine then asked, "So, how long are you staying?"

"My business partner is running the store for me in Atlanta, and I will do what I can remotely. I needed to come up here and spend some time with my uncle. He is getting pretty bad, and I they think they may bring hospice in. Enough of that sad stuff, I really don't want to talk about him. How have you ladies been? Fill me in on all the details. What have I been missing?"

"Tiffani, I understand you don't want to speak about your uncle, especially since his condition resembles your father's passing. In my honest opinion, you shouldn't avoid and compartmentalize what is going on right now. It is perfectly ok to mourn. I believe you are going through a process of complicated bereavement."

Tiffani looked at Myra, but did not respond.

"You have to excuse Myra. She uses that psychobabble and overanalyzes everything," Jazz said in an attempt to steer the conversation.

"Ladies I am sorry, but I haven't eaten today and I am starving. Would you mind if I put my order in?" The table agreed they should place their orders before becoming too involved in conversation. As the waiter returned, April placed her order, "I would like the Fettuccini with chicken and sun-dried tomatoes."

While awaiting their orders, the girls made up for lost time and held two separate conversations simultaneously. As the women laughed, their volume received the attention of the surrounding patrons. After the food arrived, the conversation simmered down as the women satisfied their appetites.

Tiffani took a bite of her salmon, then placed her fork down. "So Alicia, are you still doing interior design? How is business? What's new with you girl?"

"Yes, I am still doing design. I have built a nice clientele base, and have seriously been thinking about stepping out on faith and starting my own company. I may need to siphon some entrepreneurial knowledge from you. Maybe you can help me start an online store, and figure that eBay thing out. Other than that, nothing new. As far as personal life, no man still. But hey, not like we can all be happily married like April."

April knew her sister didn't mean any harm. She often teased her about having the perfect family. Usually, April never responded, but this time she just wanted to get things off her chest. "Looks can been deceiving. I don't know Alicia. You know Jon. He is a good father, a good provider. I just don't know."

"Know what? What is there to know? What is wrong baby sis?"

"I don't know Lish. It is like the passion between us is gone. He doesn't even look at me the same way anymore. It is like that fire in him has died out."

Jassmine had a Freudian slip and spoke under her breath, "Well, I would love to light that fire." Her words were loud enough to hear, and all the women looked at her to show their disapproval for her disrespect. She attempted to clean up her words, "I didn't mean it that way. April, you know you my girl. I do have boundaries you know, and would never cross that line. I am just saying. He is a fine man, and if you aren't lighting that flame, someone else probably is."

Alicia and Jassmine have never been friendly towards one another. Even in high school, Alicia did not care for how this upperclassman was hanging out with her younger sister; influencing her to date older men.

"Jazz, don't make me come across this table and beat you senseless for my sister. Boundaries? You act like you have ever had any boundaries in your life. We all know your history. That poor man was married 33 years, and you come along and ruin a happy home? Do you know how long 33 years is? What all they been through together? All the pain they went through? Watching their children grow? All those memories they made together? You are wrong for it and trust me, you will reap what you sow. You will never be happy stealing another woman's man!"

Jassmine was apparently disturbed by truth hidden within Alicia's words, but as usual she masked her emotions and attempted to justify her actions. "See Alicia that is your problem right there. That is why you are single. You are cute, but you get caught up in this romantic idea that a man in shining armor is going to come along. Chivalry is dead, so get over it. Life is not like it was in the 60s. You have to be aggressive, go after what you want, and use what you have to obtain it. God gave me this gorgeous face, and this unreal body, and I intend on using it. Plus, I know how to please my man to the fullest. I really don't care what anyone thinks about it. I don't have to respond to your little simple self, but to humor you I will clarify the story for you. Yes, he was married, but he hadn't been happy for years. When I worked as his admin assistant, he would confide in me and tell me how she was not fulfilling his needs sexually, nor mentally. I explained to him how my needs weren't met financially. We came to an agreement, and 2 years later, still standing."

"Your contractual agreement sounds like you are a middle age hooker to me. And the sad thing is you are bragging about it like you accomplished something? Like making a man's toes curl is a life time achievement for you? What is wrong with you? Have you no decency? That man has kids your age. You were wrong, and him confiding in you was inappropriate from the beginning."

"Well since you have all the answers, tell me what was I supposed to do? Where can you find a good man these days? I honestly don't believe there are any good men left. They are either self-absorbed with their appearance, selfish, or have six kids by five baby momma's. I got tired of that mentality where I sat there waiting for something good to happen. Sometimes you have to be proactive to get what you want."

"I have to agree, sometimes it is hard to meet men because no one tells you on the first date that they live with their pregnant ex-girlfriend slash common law wife, and they have an open relationship where they want to experience others. You just have to find out when you are preparing a romantic dinner for your man, and while he is taking a shower his phone rings and he tells you to answer it and some woman is screaming talking about tell Reggie I am in labor," Myra stated as she stared at her plate while twirling pasta around her fork.

"See Alicia? Even someone as sweet as Myra gets used. That is messed up girl, but I got one to top that. I few years ago I met this guy at the shoe store on my lunch break. We made eye contact, or should I say he made eye contact checking me out. I pay him no attention to see what kind of moves he had. A few minutes pass, and he approaches me and asks me some questions about shoes. I forgot how he said it because all I remember was his smile. The only thing I could hear was him murmur something about buying shoes for his mother. We flirted in the store, and he asked me out for dinner that weekend. Playing hard to get, I said no thank you. Well the next day at work, there were some flowers delivered to me from him. I thought the gesture was cute, but a tad bit scary since I never told this guy where I worked and just met him. I paid it no attention since I assumed he just read my work badge, so I called the number on the card to thank him. Conversation went well, and I agreed to dinner with him. We met at a neutral location because I don't allow men to know where I live. Dinner went well, and he started looking more and more like a catch. He had a nice car, wore clean shoes, went to church, and even had a good job as a Unix Administrator. Don't know what that is, but it is something dealing with computers. In any case, dinner went well, and afterwards I followed him back to his house. He had a nice little home, but my instinct told me something was wrong. This house was a too nice to be a bachelor's pad. There was a hint of a feminine touch, but I ignored my instinct and just enjoyed myself with him. When I was leaving, I found a purse sitting in the rocking chair. I asked who's it was, and he said he let his brother use his place from time to time. Well, you can see where this was going. He walked me out, and we had a small kiss, and I drove back home.

"The next morning I get ready for work, and as I go to start my car, I see a note pinned under the windshield wiper. Thinking it was a flyer or advertisement, I didn't think anything of it. I got out of my vehicle to retrieve the letter, and it was a card from this guy. He basically said he enjoyed himself, and looked forward to our second date. Now at this time, I was a bit worried. How did this man find where I lived? What made it worse was he was this sprung and I hadn't even given him a taste yet. I ignored my instinct again, and go on a second date with him. I met him over his house and as he was getting ready in the bathroom, I saw some mail on the counter. Me being nosy, I looked, and there was a female name addressed on the envelope. At this point I am pissed because I know he is lying to me and has some chick living with him. We went to dinner, and I kept asking questions until I trapped him in his lie. Long story short, this guy lived with his mother, and had been house sitting his brother's place while he was out of town. The chick on the envelope was his brother's fiancé. So not only was this man a stalker, but he lived at home with this momma."

April began to laugh. "I don't understand why men lie so much. Like why couldn't he just tell you that he lived with his mother? I don't know. I know him living with his mother was not the ideal situation, but aside from that, how did he treat you?"

"He treated me decent I suppose. The problem I had with him was he lied to me. How can you trust someone when they start off lying to you as soon as they meet you? I tried to give him a chance, and even opened the candy shop for him a few times. I don't know, there was just something manly missing. Something about a man providing for himself and having his own turns me on. Him living with his mother bothered me. Not only that, but he was a punk to me, and I needed someone who would stand up for me. I tell you ladies, it is hard to find that right balance in a protector these days. The men I have dated were either too sensitive, and make it so if something went down, then I would have to defend them, or they were a complete hot head who flew off the handle if a man even sat next to me at the coffee shop. Where are the good men that just know how to be there for you, and how to demand respect? The sensitive ones that will jump in front of a car to protect you? The ones who know when to hold you, and when to give you your space? I am not a bad person, but I just had bad luck in the past with dating men. And after so many failed attempts, I started to realize that it was not them, it was me. People only do what you let them do. I had to empower myself, otherwise I would keep getting stepped on."

"Well if you took some time to learn who they are before sleeping with them, then maybe you would find the one. The type of men you attract sense something on you. If you are loose and giving it up, then all you will attract are dogs. If you are a liar, then that is what you will attract. Your problem is you need to close the candy shop for renovation and work on yourself in the meantime. We act as if sex has ever kept a man. I know sometimes we feel trapped, like that is the only way to keep his attention, but the reality is that will only keep him momentarily. What about everything else? Sex does not help to answer questions, or determine if someone is the one; especially not sex with married men. And you know what, I get more calls from ex boyfriends from the past that I didn't give it up to, versus the two that I gave myself to in a time of weakness. Those guys that I didn't give into their sexual demands, I apparently made an impression on. Yea, it hurts at the time because there is the threat of the man you like not giving you attention anymore. If you say no, guys are going to cry, they are going to complain, and heck they may even leave. But when it is all said and done, you will be the one that they remember years later. We have fell so far out of the will of God that we allow ourselves to give in to all the perverted things these men selfishly want us to do, then get our hearts broken when they cheat, or move on. We act as if we do everything that they ask, that they will be there forever. They leave, then what?"

"Ok and your holding out got you where? Where is the man on your arm?"

Alicia stared at Jassmine, and responded, "You know, I have had about enough of this heifer. I should come across this table and…"

"Lish!"

"I am cool April. Don't worry, I won't hurt your little friend. I actually refuse to waste anymore of my breath on her. So back to you. This may sound like a dumb question, but have you tried to talk to Jon?"

"Yea big sis, I tried to talk to him, but he doesn't listen."

"He doesn't listen, or you don't listen? I know you April. You have a tendency to not see anything outside of yourself. You are extremely stubborn and rebellious at times. I am telling you April, Jon is a good man. You need to fight for your man; for your marriage. Heck, I wish I had a husband to fight for." As Alicia picked up her virgin martini, it was apparent she began reminiscing about her late husband.

As soon as there was a moment of silence, Myra introduced another one of her classic analogies. "Ladies, I think the reason many of us fail in relationships with men is because we don't understand the blueprints. You have to approach it like a house. All homes have a foundation. Then upon that foundation, there is the framing, or skeleton of that home. The skeleton tells you how tall you can go. Within the skeleton, there is the insulation which provides comfort, the roof that provides a safe haven, and brick and wood which shield the elements. A lot of times people have the cosmetics down, but don't realize that the most important thing in a house is the foundation. It may look good on the outside, but if there is a crack in the foundation, or if it is unsettled, it disrupts the entire home. Within time, things inside will fall apart. You will notice doors won't close properly. I guess what I am saying is work on the foundation before you worry about the other things. Without a solid foundation in your relationship, what can you stand on?"

All the ladies all looked confused and sat quietly as they wondered who would respond to Myra's words of wisdom. Alicia broke the silence.

"April, maybe you need to just switch me seats and sit next to Myra. Then by osmosis, her deep metaphors will penetrate into the voided cavity where your brain used to reside and your marriage problems will dissipate."

"Leave her alone Lisha. She doesn't mean any harm. I just don't know. Everything is so different. We are like strangers living together. We don't even sleep in the same bed anymore. Most of the time he falls asleep on the couch, and when he does come to bed it is just for sex. Speaking of which, is another area that has changed. We don't make love the same anymore. That man used to be so passionate. I promise I used to see fireworks. I am lucky if I even see a sparkler now. It is like lately he is not into me, and that doesn't make our intimate relations feel good at all. But what is the alternative? I just do it anyway because I don't want to cause any more problems than we already have. He just wants it hot and ready, and it is like he doesn't want to put any work in. That does not make me feel sexy whatsoever. It makes me feel like I am just a piece."

"That is men for you. Half of them don't really know what they are doing. If we honestly told them the truth, their little egos couldn't handle it. They'd start whining and crying and curse us out, then run to some other woman to validate them. I can't stand them at times, but hey, can't live without them either. What you need to do is find you a little something on the side like I do. It is not uncommon. There are numerous websites you can go to find someone with similar interest. As big as Chi-Town is, hell why not? Men have been doing it for years. And besides, all men cheat anyways. We might as well get ours." Jassmine lifts her glass as if she wanted to initiate a toast. All the ladies just stared at her.

"We have jobs Jazz. We don't have a sugar daddy to finance our spending habits. We can't spend all day cruising around searching for high school boys." Alicia said.

"They are not high school boys fool. And with the internet, who needs to cruise around? I had my nephew set me up with a MySpace page. Whew girl, there are some fine men on there. If you get a chance, check me out. It's missjassmine; and that is Jassmine with two S's. Stunning, sexy, spectacular, sensuous, something serious; take your pick. You know my grandmother named me. They said she had some moonshine prior to, but I think she was just prophetic. She knew that I would be a super-star."

"Girl, shut up. I have never been on MySpace, but I hear about it all the time. Isn't that a place for a bunch of little kids and pervs? And what is Miss Jassmine? How would I find you on there? Outside of work, I rarely use a computer other than checking e-mail."

"April, where have you been? You know how to pull up a website I assume? If so, just go to www.myspace.com/missjassmine. No, it is not just for little kids and perverts. There are some grown men there, and…"

"Don't listen to her Ape. You get into a fight with your man and the first thing women, or so-called friends want to do is try to break you up. They will feed you negative things so you will be lonely and depressed and miserable right alongside with them."

"It is not just one fight. I tell you though big sis, sometimes I wish it was. When we used to fight, our makeup sessions were so lovely. I remember one time we got into this big fight. I can't remember what it was over. I just remember how he had pitched tent in backyard. He prepared a fruit tray and had a bottle of chilled wine. We laid and talked and touched each other all night as the crickets and owls eavesdropped on our conversations; as Jon put it. I never thought that I would enjoy outdoors, but that is my baby. He could create romance in any environment. Or should I say he used to."

"Listen little sister. It sounds like all is not lost. I don't get why you are sitting here telling us. Why don't you speak to your man like that?"

April wanted to obtain a revelation from her sister and friends, but she became frustrated trying to explain, "It is pointless. He doesn't hear me when I talk. He has his own special way of thinking, and sometimes it just seems like a waste of time to even try. Besides, he is more concerned with spending time away from me. It is like his eyes light up on Thursdays because he is so excited to go kick it with his boys."

"That is because men are selfish bastards. All they care about is how they feel, or what they want to do. Their little Neanderthal brains can not fathom being considerate or supportive. They'd rather run the streets with their boys, and get into trouble, versus being a man and taking care of home. It was like something was lost with this last generation of men. They are weak. They say they love us, but they don't. If they did, they wouldn't treat us the way they do. All they love is the way that we make them feel."

Tiffani had been relatively quiet through most of the conversation.

Thinking of her failed relationships, she decided to add to the mix. "I never told anyone this, but one of the reasons I left corporate America was because I fell in love with this client. I had seen him several times before in passing, but ran into him outside of the work environment at the Underground, and his charm completely swept me off my feet. We went out a few times and he said all the right things, moved the right way, touched me how I wanted to be touched. This man was absolutely gorgeous. Everything from his eyes down to his feet; I loved every part of that man. He was educated, athletic, and didn't have any kids. This fool even liked poetry. Oh, and did I mention he was a musician? He had this keyboard at the end of his bed, and he would write me songs and serenade me to sleep. He had an incredible voice. I can't really describe the hold he had on me, but I found everything he did so adorable. There was just something about the way he talked to me, and how he put words together. By his choice of words, you can tell he was refined and educated. I was so stupid in love with him that I would have done anything he asked. Yea, it was like that. He put some serious love on me. It was like when I was around this man, my feet never touched the ground. We dated for about 6 months and I fell deeply in love with him. Truth is, I still love him.

"Anyways, we got engaged, then 2 months after we were married he changed. His expectations were ridiculous. He wanted me to cook, to clean, to be submissive. I swear he acted like I was his slave. Long story short, things didn't work out. That divorce changed something inside of me. It was like a part of me died. The only way I can really compare it, is the same feeling I felt when my dad died. After that, my personality changed from passive to aggressive, and I decided to take care of me for once. I opened up that store I had been talking about since high school, and I honestly say that if it weren't for the divorce, I wouldn't be where I am right now. I suppose I have to look at it as a good thing. Even though I have no man, I am completely content, and I have a better understanding of men. I date, but if they think I am going to sit at home and cook and clean, they have another thing coming."

"You know Tiff, there is nothing wrong with knowing how to keep a good home, and why do we get so offended now if a man wants a good meal from his woman? You don't give power away by doing nice things for your man. You are each other's counterpart. You are designed to bring the best out of one another. Besides, I am sure there were expectations that you had for him, manly duties, that he fulfilled as well. Why do we turn our nose down at roles, and want to be so independent, then criticize men for not being men? We are dealing with a generation of…well, I don't even know what to call them anymore. This era of the metrosexual man is absolutely ridiculous. You go into your bathroom and your man has used all your clear nail polish up. I am not saying there is anything wrong with a man keeping himself groomed, but I think there comes a point where we need to redefine these roles. Do we really want a man who has more hair and skincare products than us and stays in the mirror for hours? Or do we want a man who will cut the grass, change the oil in the car, fix things around the house, and be someone to protect us? You got men now that sit there wanting Epson salt to soak their feet, and lay there with a chemical wrap and cucumbers over their eyes while their woman is out getting estimates on car repair. She is out there doing things her man should take care of. Heck, most of these new age men won't even kill spiders or take care of rodents anymore. I don't know about you ladies, but I want a real man. If I find a real man, and cooking and cleaning is one of the roles I need to fulfill for our house to be kept together and operate efficiently, then so be it."

"Alicia, if I had a real man who fulfilled his role, then maybe I wouldn't have had a problem doing those things for him. The reality was, I didn't. He was semi-metro. Not as bad as you described, but the boy knew he was fine and loved the attention he got from women. And oh did I mention, we were making love and I felt welt marks on his back? Yes girl. He let some chick scratch his back all up, and had the nerve to come home and put me at risk. She probably looked like a wolverine in the face because his back looked like a wild animal got at it…or a wild ho I should say. I don't know if he used protection with her, or how many women he cheated with. Then with those women he was with, you have to factor in how many men they let enter their bodies. There is no telling what all he exposed me to. How could I trust anything he told me at that point? Words can't describe how that type of betrayal feels. I put my all into him, and for what? I don't have time to put myself at risk for a man who won't even respect my body. From the very beginning of our relationship, one of my biggest problems with him was the fact I absolutely despised the friends that he hung out with. All of them were unfaithful, so I knew it was just a matter of time. I should have read the signs, and maybe I could have saved myself from going through so much pain."

Tiffani took the cloth napkin, and wiped the food from the corner of her mouth. After she was done she delicately folded the napkin, placed it on her plate, and continued her thought.

"Look, I am not trying to take sides here, but the truth of the matter is most men are dogs. You know what they want, and they just have different ways of approaching us to get it. From that standpoint, I can see Jassmine's angle. We have to empower ourselves and use what we got to get what we need. Why can't we be selfish sometimes? Men don't even care about us. All they care about is getting off, or what they want from us at the time. They give us money to pacify us, but there is always an ulterior motive for their actions. Everything they do stems around what they want in return. Men are actors. They act like they are listening to us, but when it all boils down to it they don't truly care about our feelings and emotions. They are so selfish, and I am sick and tired of getting walked over. It is time for me to get what I need."

"Amen girl. Plus there are so many fine men out there, why not sample more than one until you find what you like?"

"Jazz, I am at the point where I don't care if they are fine or not. To me it is not about looks so much, but about stability. I want a man that is going somewhere. Someone with initiative. I think it is a fair trade off. I give him some, and make him feel like he is doing something. Then in return, I get a return. That return can be clothes, cars, a home. Plus, it is so easy. Guys are so vain and stuck on themselves that they have no clue. Like Jazz said, they really think they are doing something in bed. They bounce up all cocky like they just accomplished this great feat. Most don't even know the first thing about the female anatomy. Like hello, it is natural to exasperate air when there is pressure inside you. But whatever, if a little moan here, and some acting there will boost their ego, then so be it. I think the trade off is well worth it."

Jassmine sat in corner with a huge grin, "Thank you Tiffani. I am glad someone here is being real."

"I can not believe you women." Alicia said, "Where is your respect for yourselves and your body? I don't claim to have all the answers. Yes, I am not perfect. I am not going to sit here and act like I am a saint that never had premarital sex. I knew it was wrong, and I had to justify my acts to suppress my conviction…but what you ladies are talking about is so far gone that my brain can't even wrap around your logic. You wouldn't know true love or romance if it came up and smacked you in the face. You are so busy trying to manipulate a man and make him like you. Where is your tact? What ever happened to letting a man pursue you?"

"See, that is what I am talking about. You are stuck on this idea that if you sit there like a good girl with your legs crossed that the heavens will open up, and a man will just fall out of the sky."

"Maybe I am Jazz. I can't speak for you, but I am waiting for my Boaz."

"Boaz?" April asked.

"Girl, you never read about Boaz and Ruth?"

"I remember hearing the names, but I really don't know the story. I try to read my Bible, but sometimes the stories don't make sense to me. All that ye, thou, shalt, thy old English sounding stuff. Then on top of that, I really don't understand what was going on in their era. The laws of the old testament versus the laws of the new. What you could and couldn't do. All that stuff is confusing to me. If I had a modern translation or something, maybe it could catch my interest."

"Well let me try to explain it in modern terms. There was a shortage of food down south. A man named E, his wife Naomi and 2 sons decided to move up north in search of better opportunities. E dies, and his sons end up marrying northern women; Orpah and Ruth. Ten years pass, and then both the sons die as well. At this point Naomi is just distraught. She hears that things are changing down south for the better, so she decides to move back. Prior to going, she tells her daughter-in-laws that she was too old to find another man and have kids, so they need to go back home to their mother's. Now Orpah kissed her and said peace. I suppose girlfriend was like shoot, I need a man, so forget waiting. Ruth, on the other hand, decided to stay with her mother-in-law. She basically pledged herself to be loyal to Naomi and take care of her. Naomi kept telling her to go, but after Ruth's persistence, Naomi conceded, and the two traveled back down south."

"Cute Bible story, but can you wrap it up?"

Alicia rebutted Jassmine's rudeness by putting a hand up to block her face. With the stop sign in place, she went forward with her story.

"So like I was saying, Naomi and Ruth went back down south. As soon as they came back into town, people started talking and asking if that was Naomi. You know how people do when they haven't seen you in a while? Well, Naomi responded that she wants to now be referred to as Mara; which means bitter. As you can imagine, losing all the men in your life, then living in poverty as they did. She was just going through some things, and becoming weary because of what had happened in her life.

"Anyways, Boaz was like a wealthy distant cousin on Naomi's husband's side. Naomi and Ruth needed food, so Ruth went out to glean in this field."

"Glean? What does that mean?" April asked.

"It is when people collect crops which are left after a field has been harvested. Most farmers left those for the poor."

"Ok, I get it. Continue."

"So it turns out that Ruth was working in the field owned by Boaz. He noticed Ruth, and told her to only glean in his field. He also instructed his workers to leave extra food for her. Ruth asked why he was extending such favor, and he advised that he heard of what she has been doing for her mother-in-law.

"Naomi noticed that Ruth was obtaining favor from Boaz, so she instructed Ruth to clean herself up, put on perfume and her best clothes, and ask Boaz to redeem her. Ruth did as instructed and Boaz was interested, however there was a catch. By law back then, Ruth had another relative of her late husband who was obligated, or next in line, to marry her.

"So she went to Boaz, and sat at the end of the bed while he slept. Once he woke up and saw her, he told Ruth - *I would love to make you the wifey, but he has dibs. It is like the guy code. I tell you what I will do though. I will go chat with him tomorrow. Meanwhile, sneak out the back and don't let anyone see you. We don't need any unnecessary drama.*

"The next day Boaz confronted this relative to see if he wanted to exercise his right. He went to the man, and asked if he was going to marry Ruth. Homeboy saw that the mother-in-law was part of the package, so he backed away. *Naw man, you can have her. I'm straight.* Since the guy declined his obligation, Boaz married Ruth and gave her a child…which Naomi raised. Now there is more to this story, but that is a quick run down of it."

Jassmine browsed through the dessert menu in an attempt to act like she was not paying attention. She closed the menu and placed it on the table. "Now I didn't catch all of that but the end. Let me understand this correctly. You are basically reinforcing the point I have been trying to make all night. What you are saying is we need to dress up, and go after the man we want. See, that is what I am talking about."

"No Jassmine, that is not what it meant. According to the law of that day, the widow seeking the marriage had to initiate it. She went in and laid at his feet until he woke from his sleep. Ruth basically positioned herself for Boaz to notice her, thus he was led to marry her. So to address your statement, yes she was proactive in that she positioned herself. But when it was all said and done, it was still Boaz who made the decision and moved forward. Just read the story. It really is good."

"I am going to have to read that Lish. Sounds interesting," April said.

"I love the book of Ruth. If you study the meanings of the names, it is pretty neat. From Elimelech and sons, to Boaz; each of their names have meanings which are significant to the story. I really think that is neat. I also like the testimony of Naomi. She had a tough life, and through her story you can see that sometimes God has to allow certain things in your life to happen to push you towards your purpose. Naomi raised a child and through his linage came King David."

"You know Lish, I needed that. Sometimes I look at my situation, and don't understand why certain things happen. It is reassuring knowing others have been through things, and that God actually hears our prayers. Sometimes it just gets hard. It is hard trying to be the bigger better person all the time. It is hard not conforming. Why can't I just snap sometimes, and go act a plum fool sometimes?"

"That is the thing April. We have free will. You have a choice. You can do whatever you want, but there are consequences for your actions. For everything you sow, you will reap. That is another reason I really love that story because of the message of character. You remember how daddy used to always tell our brothers that the measure of a true man is not what he does in public, but his character when no one is looking? Well, the same applies for us women. Look at this story. Ruth was a woman of character, and she didn't run away to search for a man when her mother-in-law tried to send her away. She stayed and was loyal and believed in God.

"Now you have to understand this was a hard time for them. Her husband, brother in law, and father in law died. I am sure there were some times she wanted to snap. Her mother-in-law was growing bitter, and she had to hear her mouth. No telling what things she was saying. All that has to have a toll on you. Through it all, she displayed character when no one was looking, and because of her acts Boaz took notice of her and she received favor from him. God rewarded her faithfulness with a kinsman redeemer. I just try to think about this story when I am alone, and tempted to do wrong. It let's you know that your good works don't go unnoticed. I just try to work on myself, and trust that when it is time, God will bless me with the man of my heart's desire."

"I admire your courage for standing on what you believe, but I already have my Boaz. He is rich and successful. If I would have sat there and not went for what I wanted, I'd be single right now driving a sedan."

Alicia shook her head. "You completely missed the point of the story. Why do I even try with you? You are content on doing things your way, and you won't be satisfied until everything you attempted to build comes crumbling down around you. Look, this is my sister's husband; not some cheap, uncommitted boyfriend she picked off the street." Alicia paused and made eye contact with Jassmine, "and definitely not some unconscious older man willing to leave his inheritance to any young tail that is nasty enough to lay down with him."

"Anyways, at least I have a man. One who can buy his own Boeing jet, and not fly commercial."

Alicia lunged at Jassmine, but April anticipated her sister's reaction, and grabbed her arm.

"My goodness, will you ladies please stop? You two are acting like we are in high school again. People are watching." Myra was embarrassed by the attention their table was receiving because of the commotion. "We are supposed to be helping our girl April."

"Why you say it like this is an intervention and I am an addict? Like help poor April, the girl with all the issues," April responded with a hint of sarcasm in her tone.

Myra became apologetic. "I am sorry. I didn't mean it that way. I was just saying that your situation seemed to be the major topic, and…"

"I know Myra, I was just teasing you."

"Oh. You know it takes me a while to get jokes sometimes."

The table sat in silence for a couple minutes before Myra decided to fill the dead air with conversation.

"What I don't understand is what happened along the way to set you guys off track? You guys appeared to be so in love. April and Jon, the All-American couple. You were the standard for how I wanted my relationship to be. From the outside, it looked like you guys had the model marriage. Hey, tell Tiffani how you met. I love that story!"

April grabbed the dessert menu that Jassmine placed face down on the table.

"I think I may have to order a slice of cheesecake first. That is a long story."

CHAPTER FOUR

Laws Of Attraction

The Pothole

When Jon and April met, neither were looking for love at the time. Both were hurt in previous relationships, so they were preoccupied with staying focused on their careers. That focus quickly shifted once their paths intertwined. April was driving to work, and reached over to change the radio station. As she focused back on the road, there was a pothole which was now unavoidable. April did not have enough time to brace herself before her car hit the sizeable hole. *Shoot. That sounded like it ripped the tire from the car.* After the loud thud, her car cut off. *Oh Lord, what's next??* She reached into her purse to grab her cell phone. *Batteries dead and I left the charger at home. This is just great!! I told daddy this car was junk.*

Jon was working on a project nearby. He and his co-workers spotted a 1969 Corvette stalled on the side of the road and noticed there was a female driver in distress. Without an ulterior motive, Jon instinctively went over to assist the woman. As he walked towards the automobile, his eyes scanned over the petite, well-dressed woman who was leaning inside her trunk examining the contents. *My, my, my. Look at that! About 5'4 ish, professional attire, and an hour glass figure which brings that outfit to life. She is sexy, I will give her that, but I wonder what she is about? Naw, hold your cool Jon. You been down this road before. Just help her like you intended, then walk away. You don't need any extra drama right now, especially given your track record with women. Just stay on your path.*

"Excuse me miss, but I noticed you are having car problems. You probably won't find the problem in the trunk. It's the other end."

"Very funny. I was looking in my gym bag to see if I had a spare cell phone battery."

"Would you mind if I took a look under the hood?"

At first April was apprehensive, but feeling her options were running out, she conceded. "Be my guest."

Jon proceeded to check under the hood, meanwhile April sat back and admired his physique. *He has a nice body on him. Has a cute butt too. Nope, all guys are full of it. Same drama, different package.* She stopped her romantic thought before it took root.

"So what happened Miss?"

"I don't know. I hit something. A pothole I believe. Then the car just turned off. Look, I am not trying to be nasty, but I am late. Do you have a cell phone where I can call a tow truck?"

"Ma'am, could you just try to turn it on again please." April attempted to turn the car over with no results. Jon continued to inspect under the hood. "Well, your serpentine belt looks fine, so it can be several things. Could be electrical. Could be bad motor mounts. Timing chain could have skipped some teeth. Let me go grab my tools, and I will have you on the road shortly."

Jon walked to his truck and retrieved his toolbox, then walked back to the automobile to make the necessary adjustments. While working on her car, he attempted to draw up friendly conversation. "This is a very nice car. Just needs some minor body work, and some work under the hood. Other than that, this is classic American muscle. I wouldn't picture a lady like yourself with '69 Stingray? Very nice."

April thought it was cute how Jon was infatuated with her car. *Now he sounds just like my father. Daddy bought this car for me at one of those auto repo auctions. He was excited the same way. He might as well have bought the car for himself because it is junk to me.* "I suppose so. This car has been nothing but one problem after another. There is more than a little body damage, and I absolutely hate this blue interior. I am actually thinking about selling it."

"Selling it? Take some advice from me, hold on to this. Hey, try to turn the car over again."

April tried and the car still wouldn't start.

"Would you mind if I took a look under your dash? I need to look under the console to check the safety switch."

While watching Jon move, April had a brief fantasy. *I wonder what he looks like with his shirt off?*

Jon extended his hand to assist her in exiting vehicle, but she refused his hand. "I will stay right here," she stated still trying to hold her standoffish position.

Even though April was not giving ground, she was impressed by Jon. *He is quite cordial, I will give him that, and I like his attempt at southern charm. I have no clue what he is doing, but he appears to be good with his hands. He has some pretty teeth too. Stomach looks nice through his shirt. Whew, he is a bit too close to my legs. Definitely some pheromones circulating around here. He is very attractive, but I can't let myself go down this road again.*

Since the switch was located on the right side of the shift lever beneath the console, Jon had to enter through the passenger side. This worked out since April would not move anyways. While Jon inspected the console, he was hoping he could come up with something witty to say prior to his departure. He caught a glimpse of April's legs and fought every urge to allow his eyes to wander. *Her legs look so silky and smooth, and she smells so good. It has been a long time since I was with a woman.*

Jon returned to look under the hood of the car, and started checking the electrical lines. After a few minutes, he asked April to start the vehicle again. This time, it started.

"Thank you so much. How much do I owe you? What was wrong?"

"You don't owe me anything ma'am. My guess was pretty close; an electrical problem. The main battery supply connection broke off of the starter lug."

"I have no idea what all that means, but thank you. I really appreciate it."

"I also noticed that you are a quarter low on oil, and have some bad spark plugs. May want to get those replaced."

"Who you telling? I haven't had a spark in a long time!"

Jon tried not to assume he heard what he thought. "Excuse me?"

"Nothing. I was just talking to myself."

Jon stood up and looked directly into April's eyes. "Excuse me, but I never asked what your name was?"

"April."

Jon wanted to just walk away, but there was chemistry there. It was apparent that there was an attraction between the two, so he dismissed his preconceived notion, and acted instinctively.

"April, my name is Jon." He reached into his pocket, then grabbed a rag to wipe the perspiration from his brow. "Forgive me for being so forward, but you are quite an attractive woman. I don't have any fancy pickup lines. I am just a good ol boy, and find you intriguing. I want to learn more about you. If you don't have any plans this weekend, I would love for you to accompany me to dinner and a movie."

"That's ok" April responded fearing his gentleman role was an act, "I am sure you are a nice guy, or you at least pretend to be one, but I am a busy lady. This is just a bad time for me."

Not to be deterred, Jon responded, "I understand. I tell you what. I may never get a chance to ask out such a beautiful busy lady, so could I borrow a pen?"

April retrieved a felt tip pen from her purse. Jon gently grabbed the pen, took a $20 out of his pocket, and began to allow the ink to permeate the currency. "I won't get any sleep tonight if I don't provide you with some avenue to contact me." He finished writing on the bill, and handed the pen back to April. "Here is my number just in case your workload permits."

April inspected the $20. On it he wrote DINNER ON ME and listed his number underneath. She laughed inside thinking about taking his gesture literally, and using the $20 to get herself some dinner.

As Jon shut her door, he stated, "And might I add, your car smells good inside. I don't know if it is your car, or the fragrance you are wearing. It smells like Thanksgiving."

April did not know how to take his comment. *What kind of comment was that? Was that in insult, or a stupid pickup line?* Before she could reason anymore, she ended up breaking a smile.

Jon smiled back. "Of course it doesn't smell like Thanksgiving. I just wanted to say something off the wall to see that beautiful smile of yours. You smell very good. It compliments you well. And hey, if you ever want to sell this car, now you have a way to contact me."

"I tell you what," April reached and grabbed a napkin and wrote a number on it, "if you seriously want to buy this car, call this number and ask for Mr. Black."

"Mr. Black? This is your father I assume?"

"How do you know it is not my husband?"

Jon smirked, "I saw you checking me out. I paid attention to your mannerisms, so just call it a hunch."

"Oh really? What makes you think I was checking you out?"

"Well maybe you were just interested in my pants, but I saw you looking at my butt."

April started to laugh, "Anyways, if you are interested, call the number."

"Don't worry, I will make sure I make a good impression on him before our first date."

April smiled in response to Jon's confidence, and bit her lip as she watched him walk away.

The Green Mile

Like a kid at a middle school dance that just got rejected by the popular girl, Jon walked the long green mile back to the construction site. He was not disappointed however because he had a feeling in his stomach that he would meet this young lady again. As he returned to the worksite, his friends were anxiously waiting to find out the results. Jon's co-worker, also named 'John' but spelled different, was the first to promptly ask, "So, did you get her number?"

Jon knew this co-worker for years prior to this job. They used to hang out together, but once Jon started attending church their friendship diminished and now they only talk at work.

"Naw man. She was not interested. Or at least she acted like it. Something about her though. I felt something."

"It is called being in heat. You backed up. How long has it been bro? I know you are not gay with all the women after you. I just don't get the celibate thing. I understand church and religion and all, but you can't let that rule your life. Now listen bro. My sister has this one friend. Whew. I mean I don't even know how to explain it but whoa. This girl's body is ridiculous. I am trying to tell you all you have to do is feed this chick and she will be down for about anything afterwards. It doesn't even have to be a fancy place. Just get this girl a burger and she will be good to go. Just let me know, and I can call and…"

Annoyed by the conversation, Jon cut him off, "She was attractive, don't get me wrong, but it is not that. I just felt something with her in that small interaction. I liked her personality, and how she has this guard up. It was cute. Not to mention, she is very intriguing. I want to know more about her."

"Well, whatever you felt, it is not as much as you could be feeling. Man, don't take this the wrong way, but you need to get over Diane. That was a long time ago. Just let it go man. It was not your fault."

Not really wanting to discuss Diane, or the events of the past, Jon raised his voice and replied, "Somehow you feel that because we have the same name it gives you permission to pry into my personal life? I did not ask your opinion, nor seek your advice. This talk about Diane, and my personal life ends right here. We used to be cool, but that era has passed. We are co-workers, not friends!"

As Jon was walking away, he heard his co-worker say, "I am sorry man. I didn't mean to…" as his voice faded away.

* * * * *

Seven weeks go by, and Jon was at home unwinding from his busy day. He sat on the edge of the couch, and arranged the magazines on the coffee table to bring about some order. As he was straightening up his area, a cute little girl came running around the corner wearing a long pink Minnie Mouse t-shirt and matching house slippers. "Come give me a kiss, then get ready for bed baby," he instructed the pony-tailed 5-year old girl. He picked her up and allowed her arms to wrap around his neck. Her head rested securely on his shoulder while he carried her off to bed. He gave her another hug and kiss prior to saying he loved her, then tucked her securely in next to her raggedy plush baby gorilla he won for her at a local carnival. Jon shut the door, grabbed a beverage from the fridge, and stretched out on the couch to watch ESPN. Thirty minutes into Sports Center the phone rang.

"Who could this be calling at this hour?" Jon thought.

He reached over, grabbed the phone, and pressed talk.

"Hello."

The Wrong Number

A few weeks passed, and April ended up taking the same route where her car stalled. This time, she was driving a different vehicle since she whined until her father sold the Corvette. She got near the location and slowed down hoping that she would see Jon again, but to her disappointment he was no where in sight. *It's been weeks. Girl, what are you doing? You stalking this man now? It must not be meant to be. Just let it go.* Discouraged, April took him not being there as a sign and continued to run her errands for that day.

Later on that evening, April set the mood for a relaxing environment. She put on her favorite DVD, grabbed a glass of Merlot, and sat up comfortably on her queen sized bed and newly purchased comforter. While fumbling through her purse searching for her cell phone, she noticed a $20 bill folded and stuffed in her billfold. As she opened the bill, she remembered her interaction with Jon, and began to smile. *Ok, I tried to not think about him, and found this. Maybe this is not irony. Why can't I stop thinking about him now? Maybe I should call and give him a chance? No April, he is probably no different than any of the others. Besides, he probably forgot who I was by now, and has some other girl laying up in his bed.* After staring at the $20 on her bed, and wrestling with her thoughts on whether or not to call, she picked up the phone to call her girlfriend. *Maybe Tiffani could help me decide what to do. I forgot to tell her about this tall dark and handsome man who helped me a few weeks back.* April dialed the number, and as she was listening to the phone ring, a man answered.

"Hello?"

April was caught off guard as she did not anticipate her single girlfriend having company.

"I am sorry. Is Tiffani there?"

"Tiffani? I am sorry ma'am, but I believe you have the wrong number."

April recognized his accent. She immediately pulled the phone away from her ear, and looked at the phone display. She covered the receiver as she realized she contacted Jon by accident. *April, how could you be so stupid?*

"This wouldn't be April, would it? The beautiful young spunky lady I met a few weeks ago?"

April froze up and said, "Let me explain. I was trying to call my girlfriend, and what happened…"

"A Freudian slip?"

"Don't flatter yourself Mr James. Or George. Whatever your name is."

"It is Jon, but thanks for your attempt to butcher it. And may I ask, why do you have up such a guard? I don't bite. Unless you want me to."

"See."

"I was just playing April. So how about dinner? Did you think about me at all? I know you have been on my mind."

"Well you know…" April's sentence was interrupted by a screaming kid in the background of Jon's phone. "Is that your kid?"

"Hold on for a second." Jon stated.

April sighed. *Every time I think I have a winner, it is always too good to be true.*

"Ok, I am back. I had to tuck babygirl in. She was having a bad dream."

"So why didn't her mom tuck her in?" April responded sarcastically.

"She is out of town."

"Ok, I get it. So when the cat's away, the dog will play, huh?"

"I suppose. We are having fun while mommy is gone."

April was becoming furious at this point. "So this is funny to you? I don't get guys. Why even go through all that? Don't you have any respect for her? If you want out, just leave her. Don't you love her?"

"I love her very deeply with all my heart."

"So why…"

"April, can you let me explain please?"

"Why didn't you just let your intentions be known? We are too old for games. But you know what, humor me. I need a good laugh."

"You know, you really need to learn how to trust folks and stop being so standoffish. Every man is not bad. Every man does not cheat. For the record, I am a celibate, Christian man. And the woman I profess my deep love for is my sister. My niece is staying with me this weekend."

April felt embarrassed. She held the receiver on her chest and called her self stupid several times before she put the phone back to her ear. "Oh my goodness. You must forgive me. I am so so sorry."

"No need to apologize. Make it up to me. Dinner Friday night. You can pick your face up then."

Elated Jon put forth the offer again, April felt she had been playing hard to get long enough. "Ok, I don't see what dinner could hurt."

"Well April, it is getting late and I am exhausted. I didn't formally ask, can I have your telephone number?" April recited her number.

"Friday night it is then. 7pm. Good night April."

"Good night George."

The two chuckled prior to disconnecting the call.

CHAPTER FIVE

Chivalry

Dinner

It was 15 minutes prior to the agreed upon time, and Jon eagerly showed up to escort April to dinner. April heard his car pull up so she peeked through the blinds and grinned; admiring his timely arrival. He confidently strutted to the door, and politely knocked. She stood on the other side of the door and hesitated so that she would not appear too desperate. After a minute of gathering her composure, she opened the door to be greeted by a handsome man with a warm smile holding a single long stem rose. He extended his arm and advised, "This is for you."

"Thank you, that was nice of you." April responded. "Just let me grab my coat, and I will be ready."

As she turned and walked away, Jon admired her figure. April had dimples and a smile that could warm a cold heart. Jon helped April put on her leather coat, which matched her ensemble. April wore a stretch NY & Co. button up shirt that accented her curves, and gently rested past her hips; concealing a portion of her form fitting jeans. To make up for her height, she wore stiletto Gucci boots with a matching purse. Her clothing was stylish, and her cleavage almost made Jon forget his vow of celibacy. Her fragrance was one of a woman who pampered herself; a feminine aroma that Jon had craved and missed.

"You look nice," Jon stated.

"So do you!" April responded.

April admired Jon's attire as well. When he moved to open the door, she caught a glimpse of his gold necklace sneak up past the all white mock turtle neck shirt which hugged his torso. He wore a nice blazer which fit comfortably over his muscular frame, with jeans and casual shoes. No name brand garments, but very clean and he smelled incredibly good.

Jon escorted her to his '69 Chevrolet Corvette, which was a surprise as April was not aware Jon purchased her old car.

"So you bought my car, huh? When Daddy told me he sold it, he mentioned it was some short guy, so I assumed…"

"I had one of my co-workers pick it up because I was out of town. But I did speak with your father on the phone. Sounds like a nice guy. I already asked him for your hand in marriage, so at least that is out the way."

April smiled, but did not comment. *This boy better stop talking about marriage before I believe he is the real thing. I could picture him as my man though.*

Jon escorted April to the passenger side and opened the door for her. It was apparent to her that Jon had put some work into the car. He changed the interior color, and replaced all the paneling and gauges. It looked like a completely different car. The interior was very clean, and smelled like wild strawberries. Through the car fragrance, she caught a glimpse of Jon's masculine cologne.

"You did a nice job with the car."

"Thanks. I plan on painting it white. I think it would really make this interior pop. I just need to do some minor body work on it first, and get some things running smoother under the hood."

The couple pulled off, and Jon pressed play on his cassette player.

"Coltrane, huh? I wouldn't figure you as a jazz man."

"Well, my grandfather introduced me to it. He was a jazz musician. Plus it calms me down. Helps me to unwind. You must know a little something about jazz too. I am impressed. Most people our age don't have an appreciation of this type of music. I don't think they really understand the history."

"As much as I would like to take credit, I have to be honest with you. I only knew because my father listens to jazz all the time."

"Well, it is an acquired taste. You hang around me long enough, you will like it."

"I see." April paused as she watched Jon maneuver the vehicle through traffic. She looked him over once again impressed with how well he cleaned up. "You smell very nice by the way. Almost like Christmas dinner."

Jon began to laugh.

"Hey, I said I was just messing with you. You were giving me the cold shoulder. I had to say something out there to catch you off guard. Trust me, I am not that lame."

"Sure, you were just playing. Yea right. You know you probably try that sorry game on all the women you see coming past that construction site."

April was in a playful mood, so she continued to tease Jon, and decided to mock his mannerisms. "So where are we going for dinner, Sir?"

"Well the WWF has this wrestling match tonight, and I scored us two tickets."

April was not happy with the direction the date could possibly go. *Lord, I pray he is just playing. I know I did not just get all dressed up and cute to be going to some funky wrestling match. Just try not to get smart with him.*

"Oh really. And this was your idea for a first date to get to know me, huh? That is definitely not lame. Real smooth."

"I was just playing with you. Loosen up girl. I am taking you to a little pizza parlor I been going to for years. I am sure you will love it… Ma'am."

April was relieved they weren't going to a wrestling match, but was still apprehensive of this mom & pop pizza parlor. She envisioned their first date being a nice romantic Italian restaurant; now her dream was tarnished. She painted a mental picture of a hole-in-the-wall establishment with grime on the tables, dirty glasses, spotted silverware, and a cook wearing a white greasy apron. She tried not to throw a tantrum, and held her disappointment in.

When they arrived at the parlor, April was surprised to see it was not as bad as she thought. They entered, and immediately it was apparent that Jon was a regular, and well liked. The owner came out and shook his hand and gave him a hug.

"Jon my boy. It's been a while. How have you been? How is that niece of yours?"

"We are doing good Adriano. Not bad at all."

"Who is this beautiful young lady accompanying you tonight?"

"This is my friend April."

Adriano and April paid respect to one another.

"You want the usual Jon?"

"Well, let's see what the young lady wants."

"I trust your judgment. I am fine with what you choose for me J."

"There you have it Adriano. I will take my usual. Can I have an extra blanket of cheese, chunky toppings and additional seasonings on it? I would also like to have a nice bottle of Chianti while we wait."

"Anything for you my boy Jon. Be right out."

April admired the relationship Jon had with this restaurant owner. The couple took their coats off, and sat down in an attempt to get comfortable. There was a moment of silence when the two stared at one another.

"Why are you staring at me April?"

"Just curious, why did you pick here?"

"I wanted to see you get messy." Jon thanked the waitress as she brought the chilled wine to the table and poured them a glass. "I could have taken you anywhere, but I don't want a facade. I want to learn about the real April Black. The one that gets messy when she eats, and licks her fingers. I want you to relax, and talk to me. If you grant me a second date, then I will take you to my favorite Sushi & Hibachi restaurant. Since we can't engage in premarital sex, the way you order will be an indicator of how adventurous you are."

April smiled. She liked the way Jon spoke to her, and how witty and quick on his toes he was. Even though this would not have been her choice for a first date, once she absorbed the ambience, it was very romantic. The restaurant was dim and each table proudly boasted a flickering candle as Italian music saturated the environment.

"I love the music they play at Italian restaurants. I know this sounds stupid, but it makes me feel like I am in a movie."

"This is Domenico Modugno."

"How do you know that? You listen to Italian music as well as jazz?"

"Well, I suppose I could act like I am well rounded in an attempt to impress you, but I will be honest with you like you were honest about you dad. This place plays the same songs over and over."

April began to laugh.

"April, you have the sexiest dimples I have ever seen!"

"Wow. I can't say that anyone has ever referred to them as sexy, but thank you."

"I didn't mean it like that, but you know what I mean. You ever see someone so attractive to you that you just blurt out something stupid? It is like the girl in high school that makes you nervous and intimidates you because she is so beautiful. The girl that is out of my league. That is how you make me feel. I am not trying to make you feel uncomfortable, but you are just stunning to me. I love your smile, and those dimples, and how warm I get when you look at me with that curious face."

"Curious face?"

"Yes, curious face. That face where you are trying to figure me out. Trying to figure if I am legit, and if my intentions are sincere. That face where you think you may fall for me, but still are waiting for me to do or say something stupid."

"You think you know me?" April responded in a mischievous manner.

She used her laughter to steer the conversation away from her. "So they play the same songs every single day?"

"Not everyday, just on the weekends. That is usually when Adriano's grandparents come in. You see, this was their restaurant, and they handed it down to Adriano after his parents passed. He tries to honor their traditions, and he knows how much they love Domenico Modugno, so he plays what they like on the weekends. Usually he mixes it up during the weekdays to attract a diverse crowd."

April fixed her eyes on Jon while he spoke. As the date matured, confidence continued to ooze from his pores, and he grew sexier to her. He opened doors, paid as a man should, and had good conversation. April began to relax, and enjoy his company.

Jon was also intrigued by her. He noticed her apprehension upon entering the restaurant, but sensed that she would change after she opened herself up. He often caught himself staring directly into her eyes, and it excited him to see her blush in return.

Conversation

The waitress brought the deep dished pizza over to the table. Jon grabbed a slice, and placed it on April's plate. They both atttempted to eat the messy pizza while trying to be cute. By the time they were done, they were both laughing and licking their fingers.

"Jon, I have to admit. I didn't know what to think prior to coming here, but I am pleasantly surprised. This is very good. So, other than having good taste in food and clothes, tell me more about you as a person. What do your parents do for a living?"

"I am glad you liked it." Jon took the napkin from the table and wiped his mouth. "To answer your question, my dad owned a custom homebuilding company that he built from the ground up. Due to some bad decisions, and a ruined partnership with my uncle, he lost everything. Him and my uncle to this day still don't speak on it."

"What happened?"

"My dad was an architect, and my uncle was over the construction. The company ran smoothly for years, but over time it started to erode. They began to have disagreements about upcoming projects, and little feuds led to big power trips. There were some bad investments along the way, and lack of communication. Then you had the wave of these big commercial homebuilders. It pretty much put us under. That was a hard time for our family; financially and emotionally."

"I could only imagine. I am assuming you are not from Chicago because of your accent, and mannerisms. Do you have any other relatives here?"

"I was raised here, but I guess you can say I am not from here. I guess you can call me a southern mutt. A little bit of Louisiana, a little bit of Carolina. As far as family that lives here, just my sister, niece and paternal grandparents. My grandfather was an engineer, but quit to pursue his dream as a jazz musician. He moved from Louisiana to Illinois, and my grandmother supported him. She was originally from Carolina. Heard him play in a band when he was on the road, and met him after the show. Been together ever since. I spent a lot of time with my grandparents, latched on to some Cajun colloquialisms."

"Cajun, huh?"

"Yep, I gaar-won-tee. You can't get crawfish or gumbo up here in Chi-Town like down south."

"Can't say that I am a crawfish fan. Yuck. So tell me more about your father. An architect? That sounds very intriguing to me. It has always amazed me how people have the ability to visualize something on that scale, and bring it to fruition."

"Yes, it was intriguing to me growing up as well. I would sneak into his office late at night, and look at the blueprints for his current contracts. One night he got up to check on something, and caught me in there. I froze like a deer stuck in the headlights as I just knew I was in trouble. My father just laughed, then he sat me on his lap and began to teach me how to interpret them. He was a stickler for seeing things through to completion, so when he taught me about the business, he instilled that principle in me."

"That had to be cute…you sitting on his lap. I bet you learned a lot from him over the years."

"My father was an excellent teacher, and loved to share his work with the family. He frequently took my mom, sister and me to different job sites to see his projects. When I was younger, business was doing well, so we traveled a lot. Dad took us to Spain to visit Santiago and Barcelona. He also took us to Prague, Venice, Buenos Aires & Athens. Those trips help to refine my thinking, and allowed me to appreciate various architectural styles."

"Wow, a well traveled man. What did your mom do for a living?"

"My mom was a journalist, so as you can imagine she was tough on me about enuciating my words, and articulation. She always stressed that to be successful, I had to be effective in communication."

April was amazed at how well-spoken Jon was. April assumed construction workers were high school dropouts who couldn't find a better job; a nasty stereotype that Jon quickly erased. She admired how he talked about, and treated the women in his family.

"You look pretty fit. I am surprised you aren't a professional athlete."

"I used to play a little in high school."

"A little? What, you rode the pine? What sport did you play?"

"I played baseball and basketball, but football was my love. Me sit the bench? No, not likely."

"Where you any good?"

Jon let out a stifled laugh, then sighed. "I guess you could say that. Some people thought so. I won a couple awards at the Nike and Adidas basketball camps I attended. Football wise I was on the USA Today's Super 25 list, was Gatorade Illinois Football Player of the Year, and..."

Speaking about the past appeared to bother Jon as he stopped in the middle of his sentence.

"I don't like to really talk about it because it makes it seem like I am bragging, and that is not what I am about at all. I am probably one of the most humble men you will ever meet. Let's just say I was highly recruited by a few universities, and planned on going to Penn State. I never had any major injuries throughout high school, but my senior year I tore my ACL playing a pickup game of street basketball. Go figure."

"I am sure my brothers probably know who you are. They are sports fanatics. Sorry to hear about your injury. Look at the bright side though, if you didn't get injured, you wouldn't be sitting here with me. You'd probably be on a beach with some hot model."

"I take the first option...to be with you. I am quite content where I am right now."

A blushing April attempted to keep the conversation moving.

"So where do your parents stay, if you don't mind me asking?"

"No, I don't mind. After my little sister graduated, my father, after a failed business attempt, retired and moved to Florida with my mom. He has RA and they say the warm climate helps. That is my family in a nutshell. I am pretty well-rounded, love music, love art, love architecture, love your smile."

"Love yours too!" April responded as the couple exchanged flirting glances.

"This entire conversation has been about me. Your turn. Tell me more about this beautiful woman across from me. Did you attend college?"

"For a little bit. I did 2 years, and…" April paused trying to change the subject. "It is just a long story. I did 2 years, I didn't do so well, and my scholarship was pulled. I was having medical problems, and there were family issues. I didn't have financial aid, so I sat out a quarter. That was 5 years ago. The story of my life."

"What were you going to school for?"

"Nursing. That is my passion since I was a little girl. Nothing else seems to feel that void. I know that is what I was created to do."

"Why don't you pursue it?"

"Oh, it is too late now Jon. I am so far behind, and with work and all. Just don't have the time."

"You could make the time. You know there are adult night…"

April cut him off. "I am not trying to be rude, but can we talk about something else? I, like you, sometimes don't like talking about the past."

Sensing the uncomfortable tone, Jon attempted to change the conversation. "Understood. Ok, then tell me about your family?"

"Oh, they are not as interesting as yours."

"All families are interesting if you dig deep enough. Might uncover some things you don't want to know, but interesting nonetheless."

"Well J, there are secrets in my family. I just don't know about my family. Like why my mother gave me up? I never really knew my real mom. My step mom was not all there. Definitely one fry short of a happy meal if you know what I mean. I have no idea what Daddy saw in here. She thought she was Evita, and when I was 11 she ran off with our Mexican gardener Javier. My dad went crazy after she left him, and so they put him in a nut house. And from there, I kept getting tossed around in the system. Landed in several group and foster homes throughout my childhood. And the guy you called, Mr. Black, he was my foster parent. I took his last name because he was the only father I knew."

Jon, hoping it was a joke, kept his poise. "Was not expecting that. Don't really know what to say."

"Just messing with you boy. That is for that wrestling stuff in the car."

"You got me on that one. I didn't know what to say. That was a good one. I like a woman with a sense of humor. So tell me about your real family."

"My real family, huh? Seriously J, my life story is pretty boring. My dad worked for the FBI for years. One midlife crisis day, he just got up and quit." The tone changed as April paused to take a sip of wine. She placed the glass down, and rubbed her finger around the edge while deep in thought.

"No one knows why he quit. My mom was a stay-at-home mom, but returned back to work as a professor at the local university. My dad would just take the car, and go out Lord knows where during the day. He would arrive back later on, and fall asleep early. I don't know what he was doing, or who with. I really don't want to know. All I know is he was exhausted afterwards. I don't know what to say about that. My dad is really introverted. He never speaks his opinion, and keeps to himself. The most he ever speaks is when he watches sports with my brothers. Our conversations never went past how I was doing in school. He is a smart man, and I love him. I don't know. Our relationship is just different. My dad is just a special character."

"How many siblings do you have?"

"There are 6 of us including me. I have 4 older brothers, and 1 older sister. Adam, Aaron, Anthony, Alicia, Adrian and then me April."

"All those A's. How did your mom keep the names straight? What are the nicknames?"

"Some have no rhyme or reason to them. Adam we call pooter. Don't ask. Aaron we call Pluto because he doesn't talk much."

"Pluto?"

"Yes, Pluto. Mickey Mouse's dog. The one that doesn't talk. I told you they were silly. Anyways, Anthony is Tony of course. Adrian we call Chubbs, which is a wordplay on Chicago Cubs. Chicago, Chubbs, get it? Then there is Alicia who we call Lish, or DQ; short for Drama Queen."

"I see you left one off the list. What do they call you?"

"Spoiled brat. Babygirl. Ape. Small fry. Mine changes depending on their mood."

"Cute. Well Ape, you ready to go?"

"As a matter fact sexy, yes I am."

First Kiss

Jon and April initially intended on going to the movies after dinner, however after talking so long in the restaurant, they ended up missing the show time. April suggested they rent a movie, and go back to her place. Jon thought it was a good idea, and they proceeded to travel to the local video store. While they walked the aisles, Jon held her hand as if they had been together for years. April felt warm and secure in his tight grasp. She loved how his thick fingers encased her hand. April thought it would be funny to pick a movie she thought Jon would not like, so she grabbed a chick flick to see his reaction.

"How about this movie?" April said with a devious grin.

"I am open to new things. You never know. I might like it." Jon responded.

"Ok then. Next time, we will pick a guy movie and watch it over your house. And maybe I will like it."

"Oh, you will like it." Jon said with a smirk.

"Are we still talking about the movies J?" April giggled.

Losing track of all time, the couple finally arrived back at April's place. Prior to opening the door, April looked into Jon's eyes and became caught in the moment. She paused, and in an attempt to open the door, began to fumble her keys. Jon took his left hand and caressed her jaw line, and placed the other hand in the small of her back. She felt the strength of his fingers pull her body towards his. It was the most gentle, sensuous kiss. April's eyes slowly opened as her lips retracted from the familiar kissing position they were in.

April didn't want the kiss to stop there, nor his hands. Like a cobra and a snake charmer, she followed his lead. *Whew, that boy got me all hot and bothered. I can't believe as fine and strong as this man is how sensual and soft he kisses. If he only knew what he could have right now! No April, be good. I don't want him thinking I am loose or anything. His hands just feel so good on me. I haven't felt this way in years.*

Jon was also overcome by a wave of emotions. *I have to restrain. I am really into this girl. Don't want sex to complicate things. I have to know if this is real. I need to back up and give myself some room. Can't put myself in that position because this woman is smart, funny and sexy. I can easily see myself justifying my actions, and giving into my desires. I need to clean this up. I don't want her to think this is all that I am after. I tell you one thing, when I leave here I am straight taking a cold shower.*

Trying not to ruin the moment, nor his standings, Jon responded, "I am sorry, but you looked so cute trying to unlock that door."

April responded with a seductive smile.

"I am serious April. I am not like that. I am not trying to sleep with you. I have just really enjoyed myself tonight, and you are just so radiant inside and out. I had to see how you tasted. Disappointed?"

April continued her silent flirtation using her bedroom eyes, then she pushed the door open. "Forgive me for the house, it is a mess. I was not expecting company."

"My attention is not focused on the house April."

April entered her town home excited about her new love interest. She asked Jon if he wanted a drink, and he requested an ice water. She asked Jon to prepare the movie while she provided the popcorn and beverages. As the popcorn cooked, April went and changed into a t-shirt and jogging pants. By this time, Jon finally figured out how to work her VCR. He returned to the couch and was pleasantly surprised to be greeted by a relaxed April sitting with her legs tucked under her. Jon liked that she was becoming comfortable in his presence, and he found her to be very sexy in her leisure clothes. April welcomed Jon to take off his shoes, and sit next to her. Jon sat down, and positioned himself to hold April. Secure in his arms, April relaxed as Jon stroked her hair. She allowed his comforting touch to soothe her to sleep.

Breakfast

April woke up and realized she was in her bed. With no recollection of what happened, she searched her memory bank for the last events prior to her retiring last night. *Did I drink that much wine? How did I get in bed?* As her vision cleared, she looked over and noticed Jon's mock shirt laying next to her with writing on it. She picked it up, and noticed a slight hint of his cologne. She placed the shirt on her nose and took a big sniff. Then she pulled the shirt from her face so she could read the message. It read:

My Dear April,

As much as I would have loved to continue to watch you sleep and drool on me, staring at your angelic face for a prolonged period of time would have provoked me to react in the flesh. I truly enjoyed my date with you, and hope this is one of many.

The chivalrous part of me wanted to awaken you this morning with breakfast, however that would imply that I spent the night. I don't believe my resolve is strong enough to resist you. When you ascend from your slumber, give me a call and perhaps we can go out for lunch…or brunch.

Yours forever,

Jon

April grinned. *How often do you see a man that refined, with those hands, and good penmanship?* She picked up her phone and called Jon.

"Hello." Jon answered.

"Morning handsome."

"Hey sexy!"

"I received your message. So why did you write on a shirt?"

"I figured that was the safest way for you to have my scent in your bed. Besides, you looked so peaceful. I didn't want to disturb you."

"You could have stayed. I trust that you are a gentleman."

"Well next time I will bring some pajamas."

"How about boxers?"

"Well Ape, if things work out the way I want, you will have me to embrace in the mornings permanently. You can dress me how you want then."

April smiled from ear to ear. At that moment she was so giddy that if she lost a limb, her adrenaline would have kept her numb from pain. April experienced that warm, tingly feeling that a new romance provides. She was glowing in anticipation for what was to become of their relationship.

"I can hear your grin over the phone. I wish I could see those dimples." Jon walked to his fridge and leaned on the door as he stared at its empty contents. "Listen, I thought about staying and making you breakfast in bed, but I didn't want to rummage through your fridge without permission. I know a quaint little French bistro which serves the best brunch. What do you say? My treat."

"Sounds like a plan J!"

CHAPTER SIX

Courting

Chicago

Over the next few months of courting, Jon and April's relationship advanced. They enjoyed each other's company and traveled a lot together, however out of all the places they went, their most romantic dates took place within the architectural gem; Chicago. The monetary value of their date was not as important as the time they spent growing closer together.

"What do you want to do today Ape? You want to go to the zoo? Or we could take the L to the museum?"

"I really don't care baby. You pick. What sounds good to you?"

"I didn't have anything in mind. I wonder if anything is going on this weekend?" Jon asked.

April looked at her calendar before responding, "Why don't we go to the Blues Festival?"

"Aw baby, do you know I completely forgot it was this weekend? That sounds good. Blues Festival it is."

Jon and April's dates varied. Sometimes he would pick her up, and they would go spend the day at Lincoln Park. The two would walk around for hour's visiting women accessory stores, specialty boutiques, and trying new restaurants. Aside from window shopping on North Michigan Ave, one of April's favorite places was the aquarium. Holding on tightly to her man and walking through the aquarium made her forget about all her problems. The peace and tranquility of the living corals seemed to set her mind at ease. From hanging out at the Waterfronts and taking walks along the pathway, to listening to Jon explain the architecture within Millennium Park, April just enjoyed being in the presence of her man. Time appeared to stand still when she was with him. She loved Jon unconditionally, and even though she never brought up marriage, she often wondered if their relationship would go in that direction.

Since April's passion was to be a nurse, she often volunteered time at a local nursing home. To keep their theme of spending time together, Jon would make it a date and tag along to help out. He admired his woman and how she interacted with the elderly patients. Her genuine heart was attractive to him, and he loved her tender spirit. While watching April interact with patients at the nursing home, Jon knew that she was the woman he wanted to spend the rest of his life with.

Male Baggage

Jon planned a weekend getaway with April to Indianapolis since he scored free tickets to the Pacers versus Lakers. April was not a huge sports fan, but she loved traveling with her boyfriend and enjoyed her time with him when they attended games. The couple had good conversation during the 3 hour trip, and when they arrived back in Chicago, decided to go to Jon's place to unwind. Jon began unpacking his luggage, while April lay on his bed staring at the ceiling fan.

"Baby, I love just spending time with you. I had so much fun this weekend."

"I did too April. Hopefully we can have these moments for the next fifty years or so."

"Only fifty? You can't die on me, you have to live forever, ok? You promise?"

"Yes Ape, I promise. As long as you promise that you are mine and only mine."

"Of course I am only yours boy. I will always be yours."

"You know Ape, I want what my grandparents have. I admire my mom and dad, but my grandparents were the most influential couple to me. I remember when I was little my cousins and I would play in the backyard, and my grandparents would sit on the back porch while putting together a jigsaw puzzle. They were the sweetest couple, and always did cute things. Things I really didn't admire until I grew to be a man."

"Things like what J?"

"Just how they treat one another. They are still so passionate after all these years. I tell you one thing I think is cute is their tradition on holidays. My grandparents believe in saving money, so instead of buying cards for one another on birthdays, anniversary's and whatnot, what they do is go to a Hallmark store, and find a card for one another. After a few minutes, they exchange the cards with one another within the store, kiss, then attempt to put the card they received back in it's proper place. When I was young I thought it was stupid, but as I grew older, I appreciated how they expressed the love they had for one another. Watching my grandmother wrap her arms around my grandfather's neck and kiss him like she is in her 20's is something to see."

"Yea, I love your grandparents. They are adorable to me." April rolled over on her stomach, and kicked her feet back and forth like a little kid as she watched Jon unpack.

"Jon, what are your dreams? During the trip you asked me a million questions and made me pour my heart out regarding my nursing aspirations. Where does your ambition lead you? I know you love architecture. What are your dreams? Why didn't you go back to college?"

"I have so many real estate aspirations April. And college? I just don't know."

"What don't you know. What is stopping you?"

Jon held his suit case up in the air, "Baggage. That is what is stopping me. Baggage."

"Boy, stop being silly. I am being serious. I could help you if that is a problem. I want to be here for you, and support you like you support me."

"I have a past April. A past that haunts me sometimes, that's all." Jon threw his suitcase on the floor and walked to the bathroom, which was adjacent to his master bedroom.

Fearing his tone and mannerisms, April's heart rate sped up. Her life had met so much disappointment that she had anticipated this moment. The moment where something would reveal that Jon was not her knight in shining armor. "Baby, what are you talking about? What kind of past? What have you done that can't be corrected?"

"Ape, I'd rather not discuss it right now."

"Jon, do you have some kids out there somewhere? A wife? What are you talking about your past? Please open up to me."

Jon shook his head no as he was sparring with internal thoughts.

"Baby, open up to me. What is wrong? You on probation? Been in prison before? What is up? Talk to me."

April blurted out the sentence not expecting a response. To her dismay, Jon's body mannerisms changed.

"Oh my God. You have a record? You have been locked up before, haven't you?" April said in a panic.

"Ape, it is not what you think. It is more complicated than that."

"So what did you do? Sell drugs? This is freaken unbelievable. We been dating how long now?"

"If you would just calm down, I will explain."

April was hurt, but prayed that Jon would tell her something to ease her mind. At this stage in their relationship, April let down her guard and invested her heart *Maybe he was just an accessory? Maybe he was just standing by? Or maybe it was a case of mistaken identity?* She juggled several scenarios that would clear Jon of the charges.

"It was an assault charge a couple years ago."

"Assault?" April grabbed her purse, and attempted to leave. Jon ran to the door to stop her, and grabbed her arm to prevent her from exiting.

"What are you going to do? Assault me too?"

"Look April, you have every right to be mad. But I love you, and can't lose you. Please just sit down and let me explain. Then when I am done, I will have no choice but to respect your decision to where we go from here. Just please hear me out."

April walked over to the couch to sit down, and crossed her arms in a pouting manner. "I'm listening. You have 5 minutes."

"I was once enrolled in college. I didn't know what direction I wanted to go in, so I chose civil engineering. I actually completed two years, and was returning for my third. My sister was in eleventh grade, and had been dating this older punk for a year or so. This was also the period of time where my father's business started to decline."

"Can you please get to the point?" April said. Her leg twitched from a combination of fear and resentment.

"Well, my father's rheumatoid arthritis became worse, along with other medical problems. There were things that needed to be done at home that he couldn't do anymore. His money was flying out of his hands faster than he could count due to this business failure, and he had to liquidate a lot of his assets. So I decided to put school on hold, and come back home to help out. I obtained a 9 to 5 gig, and helped with groceries, utilities, medical bills and household maintenance. I basically did whatever I could do to help out. My goal was two-fold. One, to alleviate some of the pressure my father was experiencing at the time, and two, to get my sister into college."

"Jon, that is all very nice what you did. Everyone knows you are a giving person, but where are you going with this?"

Jon was starting to become annoyed with April's tone. "April, you don't have to be nasty. Just give me my 5 minutes, then you can do as you please."

"I apologize. Continue."

"With me being home, I could keep a closer eye on my sister; something I was unable to do from college. I had my ear to the street. Well, I came to find out that my sister's little boyfriend had been beating on her. He wouldn't hit her face, but would bruise her body in places clothes concealed. Irate, I confronted her, and she denied the allegations. I confronted her boyfriend, and he denied he ever touched her. I threw him up against the wall, and threatened that if I ever caught him doing anything, or if she told me anything, that I would break his neck. He had already graduated, and I didn't feel comfortable with my younger sister dating this older guy. There was no reason for a junior in high school to be dating a guy his age, but my family was stressed so they turned the other cheek. It probably wouldn't have made a difference anyways because you can't tell a young girl in love anything or she will rebel."

April sensed where the conversation was going, and her body mannerisms changed.

"So long story short. I was working a 9 to 5 at this office building. I never liked being confined to a desk, and I was very unhappy. There is something to be said about stress in an office environment. The mental exertion of working in an office outweighed any physical stress that I experienced when I worked in construction with my uncle when I was younger. I was frustrated because I was so close to completing college and never did. I prayed for change, but nothing happened.

"I remember they would have these potlucks at work. You know how you always work with that one woman who has cats, and you try to be nice, but you refuse to eat any of her food for a fear of cat hairs. You know how cat lovers are. They let their cats use their paws to stir the food when they are preparing it. Anyways, they would have these potlucks, and I would just distance myself and be anti-social. I would go stare out the window like a kid watching his friends play outside. I felt I was on punishment because I knew that I should be doing something else. I often asked God why my life was so stagnant? Why was I stuck in this rut? The office environment was not for me. I loved construction and I belonged outside. Nothing is better than having your work setting vary based on the project. I love the smell of lumber. I love the empowerment of grabbing raw materials and machinery, and creating something. Working with my hands is my passion.

I love coming home from work, and watching as the dirt swirls down the drain in the shower. There is something therapeutic, and rewarding, in a manly sort of way, about that moment."

"Baby, I am not trying to be smart, but you are getting sidetracked. You are all over the place with your story. What happened Jon?"

"I am sorry. I just got caught up in the thoughts I had that day. So let me fast forward. I went to work and something inside me just told me it was time to move on. I politely went into my manager's office and told him that I was putting in my 2-week notice. I explained to him my desires, and why their company was not part of my plan. He understood, and let me go that moment. Two weeks paid, so I did not complain. That day was a roller coaster of emotions. Waking up that morning, I would have never imagined that one single event would change my life forever. Like a railroad switch; I transitioned from one guided rail, to another. The situation forced me into my calling. I just never knew my prayers would be answered in that manner."

"I don't understand J. What you are talking about?"

"Well, after I quit my job, I was driving home wondering if I made the right decision or not. My thoughts were interrupted by spotting this young punks car parked around the block. The kid was trying not to be obvious, but it is hard when you have a tangerine Nissan with Radio Flyer wagon tires and rims that cost more than the car itself."

April chuckled. "Stop being stupid and trying to make me laugh. I am mad at you, and shouldn't be laughing. Finish the story."

"I parked my car near his in a manner that blocked his, and walked to the house so they couldn't hear me coming. As I approached the back door, I heard screaming upstairs. This wasn't the string of fake moans that women orchestrate to please their man, but this was a woman in distress type of scream. A scream like she was fighting for her life. I run through the backdoor and up the stairs. Two seconds before I reacted I absorbed what was going on. This guy was on top of my sister without her permission. His shirt was off, and his khaki pants were hanging around his knees. After I looked back at the situation, I assume they were being frisky, and she told him to stop and he took it too far. At the time, it didn't matter if she wanted him in her or not…that was my baby sister. I came in, and I remember seeing him forcefully work his way inside my sister as she was screaming for him to stop. I saw her face, and tears running from her eyes." Jon shook his head as he revisited the story and his eyes began to tear up.

"Baby, I am so sorry." April said as she attempted to comfort her man.

"I grabbed him by his neck, and threw him head first into the wall. His body dented the sheet rock. Like a fighter knocked against the ropes, he pulled up his pants, got his bearings and came back at me swinging. I dodged his punches, and landed several severe blows to him. I don't like to brag, nor talk about this. No one outside of my sister and parents knows this story."

As Jon sat on the edge of the couch, April crawled behind him, and rested her chin on his shoulder. She gently kissed his neck, then placed her arms around his waist.

"When it was all said and done, they told me that I broke his nose, jaw, orbital socket, cracked two ribs, and ironically his neck."

"Dang boy. What did you hit him with?"

"Let me finish the story. As he lay there, I went to comfort my baby sister. My eyes were red with tears of anger. I was so hurt that my beautiful young sister was violated. Hurt because I was not there to protect her. I did not know what to say to her. Trembling from emotional pain, I reached for the phone to call the police. As soon as I connected to an operator, this fool got up and lunged toward me. His arms locked around my waist like a high school wrestler as he tried to take me to the ground. I dropped the phone and struck him in his back. We wrestled around the room knocking lamps down and pictures off her dresser. My sister was crying hysterically in the background. The room looked like a whirlwind when we were done. I clinched his body around his sore ribs, and he released his grasp long enough for me to toss him off me. I threw him with such force that he stumbled over my sister's stereo on the floor. He was unable to regain his balance."

Jon stood up breaking April's grasp around his waist. He walked to the living room window and looked out as he recalled the events from that day.

"The combination of stumbling over the stereo and his loose pants provided enough momentum to carry him out of the second story window. He survived, but barely. I walked over to the window numb to what just happened. I look down and see his chest subtly elevate as he inhaled, then decline as he exhaled. His breathing was disrupted by choking, but he was still alive. There he lay on our back lawn on my mother's flower bed with multiple lacerations due to the shards of glass from the double window pane. He also had injuries from my punches to contend with, along with the fall to the ground; which broke his tibia. I looked out the window, and saw his broken leg buckled underneath his body in a contorted fashion. The fall also broke his neck. With a smorgasbord of feelings feeding my emotional appetite ranging from redemption to remorse, I attempted to do the right thing and not just let him suffer. I picked the phone up and instructed the operator, who ironically was still on the line, to send the police and an ambulance over."

"Oh my goodness." April was overwhelmed and didn't know what to say.

"This guy pressed charges on me. He said I threatened to break his neck, and that the sex was consensual. They had one of those SANE nurses take a look at her."

"Sane?"

"Yea. I forget what it stands for. Sexual Assault Nurse something. I can't remember what the E is…maybe Examiner. In any case, they performed a rape kit on her and gathered evidence; fingernail scrapings, semen, and whatnot. That was enough to charge him with third-degree criminal sexual conduct and force him to do some time. Me, on the other hand, I still had this assault to deal with. Since I had no priors, all they gave me was probation."

"Baby, I had no idea. I am so sorry. When you weren't saying anything, I thought…"

"It is ok Ape. That is not all of the story though."

"There's more?"

"Yes. Probably the biggest blessing to come out of this chaos. My sister was impregnated when he raped her; thus my beautiful niece was born. Because of what happened, I feel an obligation to be there for my niece. I know her father was a bum, but she did not ask to be here, and I try to provide her with a positive male role model. She knows who he is, but we have not told her what really happened. She is too young. Maybe when she grows to be an adult."

"I don't blame you J. If I were in your shoes, I'd probably do the same thing."

"This is why I haven't applied for college. You have a criminal record, you might as well save your application fee. Even trying to explain it, they don't care. That stigma of a record prevents you from doing a lot of things. But like I said, that day was also a blessing. It was the last time I worked in an office building. When they took me in, I was sitting in the back of the cruiser speaking with the officer. He was explaining how he shouldn't tell me this, but he probably would have done the same thing. We talked on the way to the precinct, and somehow got on the topic of construction. I discussed my background working with my father, and what I wanted to do with my life. Long story short, he stated that his cousin Gary owned a construction firm, and they were looking for a new foreman. In the midst of all that chaos, a door was opened for me. That got my foot in the door with construction. I called the guy, explained my situation, and he understood. I been at his construction company ever since."

Female Baggage

A couple weeks passed, and April had planned on surprising Jon with a romantic evening. She called him early that morning, and caught his voicemail.

"Hey baby, this is April. Call me soon as you get a chance. I have something I want to ask you."

Time elapsed with no call from Jon. It was early afternoon at this point. She called again, and got his voicemail. Upset, April hung up. A couple hours pass, and still no call from Jon. Sitting on her couch shaking her leg in a nervous fit, she called again. Voicemail. April grabbed her purse and keys, and proceeded over Jon's house.

When April pulled up to the house, she saw Jon's car out front. Disturbed at him not answering either phone, she used her key to let herself inside his house. She walked quietly, but no one was home. Not knowing what was going on, April plopped down on the couch and stared at his figurines on his fireplace mantle. *What is going on?* She immediately went to his bedroom, and inspected his sheets. *Hmm, nothing out of place here. Doesn't smell like perfume or sex.* She rummaged through his drawers, and didn't notice anything out of place. Frustrated, she went back downstairs and waited for his arrival.

Time passed, and April heard a car pulling into the driveway. She peeked out the window, and saw Jon in the passenger seat. He leaned over to kiss the woman on her cheek, then stepped out of the vehicle. As the woman pulled away he waved then headed towards the front door with one shopping, and two grocery bags in his hands. Soon as he came through the door, April swung and punched him in the arm.

"Where have you been? And who was that?"

Jon chuckled as he leaned in to give her a kiss. "Well hello to you too.”

"Jon, don't play with me. Who was that, and where you been all day? I saw you kiss her. I am not going down this road again Jon. I just can't.”

"This road? What did I…”

"My dad used to do that crap to my mother. Just be gone all day. No one knows where he was, or how to reach him. Probably out with some whore. I will not stand for that!”

"April, I truly love you, but listen to me. I am not your father. If this is going to work between us, you are going to have to learn to trust me.”

"Trust J? Where were you? I been worried sick all day. I been trying to call you and you haven't called me back.”

"Baby, my phone was broken.”

"Phone broken? Come on. You are smarter than that. You owe me the decency to at least come up with a better story than that.”

"Girl listen to me. I dropped my phone at the construction site yesterday. My sister knew a guy at the cellular store who could get me a replacement. She didn't necessarily want to deal with this guy, so I made her a deal. If she got me a good replacement deal, then I would buy her groceries. I felt it was a fair trade, and plus I just wanted to spend some time with my baby sis. Not to mention, she wanted to show off the new car she worked so hard to get.”

Jon placed the bags down, and shut the door behind him. "We dropped my phone off, then my sister, niece, and I took the free trolley to the museum. I didn't think about checking my messages because you told me you and your sister were going out today. I picked up something for you today…" Jon reached into his shopping bag, and handed April the newest cell phone she had wanted.

"Thank you for this phone. I am really trying to trust you J. You have to understand where I am coming from. My mother used to sit there looking stupid while my dad was gone all day. She would just zone out. I have been with such trash in my life. Guys just using me for sex. Not interested in me as a person. Guys in the past have always just used me for instant gratification. Like I am a receptacle. I just don't know. With not being able to reach you, my brain just snapped.”

"April, I love you sincerely. On behalf of the men who did you wrong, and because I used to be one of those guys, I apologize. But trust me, this is a new day. What we have is something special. I would never do anything to put this love in jeopardy. I love you more than anything. I need you. I find myself thinking about you all throughout the day. I never approached you about sex like that, so you can't categorize all men that way. I am interested in who you are as a person. I love who you are, not what you give. I want to know you. I want to be with you. Day and night. And regarding sex, we have the rest of our lives to make love. You are worth the wait."

"I love you too baby, and I hear what you are saying. I just don't know if you want to be with me sometimes. Why would anyone want to be with someone like me? With all the issues I have?"

"We all have issues. I know I have my fair share. Problems are needed. They cultivate you into the person you are right now. All you been through has shaped this beautiful woman in front of me. Aside from beauty, you are very intelligent, and witty. I love your sense of humor. I love to just sit and watch you read. I love to sit and watch you sleep. I love how your body reacts to my hands when I stroke you while you are deep asleep. How you smile in your dreams. I love the way you make me feel just by touching my chest and kissing it when my shirt is off. I love the way you look at me. How you speak to me. How you cook and take care of me. I could go on and on."

"J, you are all I have right now. I am putting my all into you. Please don't hurt me. I opened up to you about my dad. I never told anyone that before. I shared a lot of things with you I never shared with anyone else. Please don't hurt me."

"Only if you promise to do the same April. Promise to do the same." Jon hugged his weeping girlfriend, and kissed her on the forehead.

The Proposal

Months went by, and April and Jon continued to grow closer together. In route to Jon's house, April grabbed her keys, and walked out the front door of her town home. She was shocked to see a group of family members and neighbors all staring at her like she was on a hidden TV show. *What is going on here?* Rose petals laced the steps of her town home, and created a path which led to the middle of the street where a royal chair resided. April walked closer following the rose petals, still oblivious to what was going on. Jon came around the corner and grabbed her arm to escort her to a chair which sat in the middle of the street. It had a red velvet seat, and was dressed with all the jewels which adorn a chair of royalty. *Where did he get this chair from? He steal it from Medieval Times?*

She looked around and tried to absorb her surroundings. In the middle of the street were 5 bobcats in a semicircle with their buckets full of roses. Once April sat down Jon gave a signal, and like uniform soldiers, hundreds of roses fell from the Bobcat buckets onto the street. The roses formed a barricade and circled the chair where April sat.

Jon went down on one knee, and you could hear the small audience react with oohs and ahhs.

"April, I am not a slick talker, I am not Mr. Romance, and I am not filthy rich. But what I do know is that I am a man of my word and I promise I will take care of and protect you. I vow to keep the spontaneity between us, and my love and respect for you is rich and worth more than any dollar amount man can throw our way. I am positive, without a doubt, that I am the man God created for you. I knew that from the first time I interacted with you. Soon as we spoke, I felt something. Ever since I worked on your car, there has not been one night that I have fallen asleep without thinking about you, nor has there been a morning that I woke up without you on my mind."

April began to tear up. Jon took off his shirt and the ladies outside screamed. On the left side of his chest, there was a tattoo with 'April' written in cursive. This was a surprise to April as this sign of affection never existed on Jon's body prior to.

"Baby, I don't want to wake up to an empty bed, then work through the constraints of work schedules and time to see you for a small portion of the day. I want to watch you sleep, and wake up next to you. I want to cook for you, and bathe you, and hold you. I want to help you fulfill your dreams. I want you to proudly display my last name, and to bear my children. For the seeds of life that God embedded in me to grow in your stomach. I want to grow old with you. To take long walks on the beach together when we are in our 60's."

Jon grabbed the shirt that he took off, and laid it at April's feet like a servant giving royalty a gift.

"On our first date, I left a shirt with you. This shirt is symbolic. I want to exchange this shirt I left with you, for me. I want to lie in the bed next to you. I want you to be my wife. Will you marry me?"

Jon lifted construction hat off the ground, and it revealed a ring box. April's tears started to flow.

"Yes, baby. Of course I will marry you."

The scene was surreal to April as neighbors and family members clapped and cheered. Jon had prearranged for a few of the neighborhood kids to come by after April accepted, and throw rose petals up in the air.

It was truly a beautiful scene. April was experiencing so much joy that the sounds from the city and murmurs from people were all drowned out by her adrenaline. This demonstration of his love muted everything surrounding her, and all she could focus on was her future husband. Her body was warm as she admired his effort, and she began to tear up again as she looked down at the stunning marquise diamond which fit her perfectly.

CHAPTER SEVEN

Lost In Translation

Alarm

Beep. Beep. Beep. Jon reached over and literally punched the alarm clock to symbolize the beginning of another monotonous day. *Well, at least I didn't have that stupid dream again last night.* He rolled over to a cold bed, which was no surprise since April had a habit of leaving before he woke. Jon rolled his body over to the side of the bed, and sat upright to clean the sleep from his eyes. As he looked at the damaged alarm clock, he grabbed the nearby phone and attempted to call April.

"Hello."

"Hey baby, you at work yet?"

"Nope, still stuck in traffic."

"Quick question."

"What?"

"I know this is Friday and you probably have plans, but they are having this retreat at the church tonight, and I thought it would be cool if we went. I don't know too much about it, but they are having individual classes specifically for men and for women. I been out of it lately, and I think some spiritual food may fill me up. Maybe afterwards we can go get a milkshake or something?"

"I have to see how I feel later on J. I have to be in the mood to deal with those church folks. They are extremely nosy and try to pry into your personal business. I won't even speak on how judgmental they are. I swear they act as if they never sinned a day in their life."

"It is not therapy April, it is just a class. You don't even have to talk; ignore them and see what you can get out of it. I just thought it may be good for us to be around other positive people for a change, and get some insight. Seems like these classes will be good."

"Good for what? Tell me. What will it change?"

"Why do you have to be argumentative about everything? I just asked you a simple…you know what, forget it. It is early and I am not trying to go there with you. You can just do whatever, but I am going tonight regardless. Maybe it is best I go alone since I am the only one with issues in this relationship."

"What is that supposed to mean?"

"It means exactly what I said. Bye April."

"Jon, you better not hang up on me! You want to be Mr. Holier Than Thou Christian Man on me, then explain yourself. Be a man and speak up."

"Be a man? You know April, it is pointless with you sometimes and right now I don't have the energy to even put up a battle. No one was trying to be holy, I just thought that we were both in a rut and probably could get something out of it. Like I said, whatever April. You are just a spoiled brat and always have to have your way so I concede; you won this argument. Can I go now?"

"Spoiled? Spoiled? What do I have to make me spoiled? I can't even buy a nice suit without you talking about our finances and what we can and can't do. You act funny if I spend too much on groceries, or lunch. I can't even buy personal toiletries without you trying to make me feel like I overspend."

"Here we go again. You know our situation, but somehow we end up going around this same mountain over and over again. You know Ape, just go ahead and cuss, scream, say what you must and let me get off this phone so I can salvage the rest of my day."

"Sometimes, I truly hate you J."

"Bye April."

April screamed at her phone, and threw it into the backseat of her car.

Finances

Jon met Dana at the church later that evening. Dana had really been turning his life around after he married a few months back. Even though Dana didn't have longevity in his relationship, he reminded Jon how things used to be with April. Jon also liked watching Dana's character transformation as he became more active at the church. He was one of the few friends that kept Jon focused on the right path.

They gave each other the masculine one hand shake-hug combination, then proceeded to walk down the corridor to the room where the host just started the session.

"Today, we want to speak on financial stability."

The men in the room responded to the host with a subtle "amen" in agreement as he continued the introductions.

"This is an open group discussion, but we are blessed to have an extraordinary panel today consisting of…"

While Jon was taking his seat, he blocked out the introduction of the deacons, elders and financial specialists which were on the panel, and examined the room. Men ranged from their late teens to early seventies. The session started and the men offered several questions for discussion. Midway into the class, a man near Jon's age raised his hand.

"My name is Ron. I am fairly new here, but let me just say I am truly enjoying this atmosphere. Just look at this setting. A bunch of men on a Friday night helping one another grow spiritually with no women around. That being said, men can I be real here?"

The host responded, "Yes Ronald that is what we want. You can trust what is said within these walls stays here. I think this is good and healthy, especially for you men with ladies. We want you to be able to honestly share your concerns without feeling the burden of attempting to explain your inner most thoughts to your woman. Before we go further, let me clarify before I start getting letters from wives and girlfriends; I am not telling you to stop communicating with your lady. I am referring to the feedback we receive sometimes when we open up, and things are constantly held over our heads. Now that I went on record, back to you Ronald. Yes, we are here to be real and help one another out. What's your question?"

"Ok, my question. I have aspirations, but it seems sometimes I can not obtain any favor. It is like every time I get on the road, I start cruising a nice speed, then some roadblock occurs. You see I was raised in a single family home, so I seen first hand how hard it is for single mothers out there. My dream was to open up this daycare to provide these women with a safe, affordable childcare solution. The problem is, every time I get something done, or it feels like I am one step closer, then something huge always comes up that knocks me back. It is not that I don't have faith, I just get frustrated at always trying fight through these obstacles."

Jon decided to chime in, "I can certainly understand what Ron is saying. I have ambitions and dreams as well. I believe every man does. You see, I work in construction and I would love to take the talents I have, and the relationships that I have with others to form my own real estate investment and construction company. Like he stated, I have faith that God can do anything, but sometimes it seems like the cards are stacked against me. It is like when I try, I fail miserably."

One of the elders, Brother James spoke up, "Well young men, faith without works is dead."

"What does that mean?" Jon responded.

Dana leaned over and whispered, "He is speaking about James 2:17."

Slightly distracted, Jon nodded acknowledging Dana using the mannerisms of a parent ignoring a talkative child, and adjusted his attention back to Brother James.

"What I am trying to say young man is you can't just sit there on your hands and expect to be delivered from your situation. You have to do the works part to initiate the favor, and activate your faith. If it is within His will, it will be done. See, the problem is you have to move out of that state of complacency. Get out of that comfortable place. If you do what you've always done, you'll be where you've always been. If you want a change in your life, you have to do something different. People who refuse to change commit to fail."

The host shook his head in agreement, "Amen. I agree. You know, my grandfather used to always tell me that fear tolerated is faith contaminated. Jon and Ron, you both sound like gifted individuals, and you men need to understand that your circumstances will never abort the will of God. Now we all have faced some loses, but in order to win, sometimes you have to lose. Always keep in mind that there is a lesson to be taught in defeat. Pray that God opens your eyes so that you can recognize the gifts that he embedded within you. Once you guys get to that point where you know your worth and allow God to use you, then that gift within you will bring you before great men."

"That's Proverbs 18:16," Dana whispered.

I appreciate Dana's willingness to give me these passages, but something about him reciting these scriptures is agitating me. Is it rude to tell someone to shut the hell up in church? Ok, let me calm down. I know he means well, but I think I am just irritated because he knows His Word more than I do, and I am envious.

"I can't speak for anyone else," Ron responded, "but in my case, my dreams are often put on the backburner because of my financial situation."

One of the guys who had been silent the entire night raised his hand.

"Forgive me if too intrusive, but what happened to put your finances in such disarray? That is important because you don't want to revisit bad spending habits. We have to learn from our mistakes so we don't repeat them. There shouldn't be anything you can't recover from. If it doesn't kill you, it only makes you stronger."

Jon was somewhat offended by the tone of this gentleman. *What is wrong with this guy? If it doesn't kill you it only makes you stronger? What is that supposed to mean? Wonder if he has ever lost anything. People who haven't been through anything always have some stupid comment to say. Calm down Jon. He meant well. Remember you are in church. Maybe I am just in a bad mood because I am still upset at April from this morning? I shouldn't take it out on others. Put yourself back in line soldier.*

"Ron, if you don't mind I would like to respond. There is a possibility it had nothing to do with bad spending habits. In my situation, it was the birth of our daughter. She was born 4 months premature, and was only one pound. I could literally hold her in the palm of my hand. Don't get me wrong; I love my wife and kids more than anything and would not trade them for the world. It is just that this child completely depleted our savings, and put us into a hole. I have been trying to restore our finances to where they were, but something always comes up. Whether it be house repairs, auto repairs or medical; something always happens. Prior to my daughter, we were doing quite well. Afterwards we just incurred medical bills that put a dent in our wallets. It changed the entire dynamic of the household as I was forced to work 16 hour days, while April was off work using maternity and FMLA. Medical bills piled up with one income and it was very hard to adjust. Now she is back at work, but we still haven't truly recovered. Can you see how things could go wrong? I don't want to sound like I am crying about everything, I am just confused and feel like I am running out of mental resources. It almost feels like I am going crazy at times."

Ron shook his head in agreement, "I completely understand what you are saying. Boy do I understand."

"Jon, do you tithe?" Brother James asked.

"I do sometimes. Depends on how bills are that month, but I attempt to. I love the Lord, don't get me wrong. I know that it is important to give, and I try to give what I can. I always give something though."

"I see you young men have a common problem with your finances. Let me give you a piece of advice son. I determine my economy by my giving." Brother James sat his Bible on the floor as he continued his thought. "From experience, I know that those holes in your pocket won't be sewed up until you align yourself with the Word of God. Tithing is not about money, it is about trust and discipline. What you need to understand is the provision is already there, but you have to do your part to release your blessing.

"Now practical advice. How do you turn things around from this point? You have to sit down, be honest with yourself, and assess your situation. Then from there, you have to plan. You young people today want everything instant; quick grits, microwaves, TV dinners. Getting out of debt is like losing weight; it doesn't just happen overnight. When you get a chance read Proverbs 6, verses 6 through 9. This is a parable about the ant. The ant has no body telling it what to do, yet it is proactive and stores up so it can have a harvest at winter. The passage warns you to wake up. In other words, you have to be a man and stop hiding behind that blanket of lazy excuses. You need train yourself to think ahead; to store for the winter. I encourage you to start thinking in terms of decades, then develop a plan for your life. Go home, take out a piece of paper and a pen, and write out a plan."

"I understand what you are saying Brother James, and thank you for your wisdom. That definitely makes sense longevity wise, but what do I do about the present? Right now this issue is poisoning other areas of my relationship, and it seems that everything is falling apart at the seams. I am distant from my wife, and don't give her the attention and affection she deserves. I know and recognize this, but I am just so stressed with trying to keep things in order that I just don't have the energy. I have good intentions, but soon as I walk through the door, I don't even get a moment to decompress before I am hit with nagging and constant arguments about petty stuff. Women don't understand the stress we deal with, and how that affects us in so many different areas of life. They don't get that if a man is not providing how we feel we should, how it eats at us. They take our silence for us being oblivious to what is going on."

"Young man, listen when I tell you that I understand. Something similar happened to me when I was younger. My daughter had a near fatal car accident riding home with her gymnastics instructor. Rehab and medical bills put us under. It strained our relationship, and I didn't want to admit it. I was working two jobs to keep food on the table. I didn't understand why has this happened to us? I was confused and hurt. These are the parts of marriage no one explains. What do you do when there is something traumatic that happens to the family? These are confusing parts of our life that we can't avoid. You just can't act like these issues don't exist; eventually they have to be confronted. I had to be honest and talk to my wife about my frustrations. Once I talked to her, and determined I would do right by God and give according to His Word, that is when things started changing for us. We made a turn around but not one day sooner."

"I appreciate your testimony Brother James. I needed that."

After the session, Dana and Jon sat there as the room cleared out.

"Jon, I can't act like I know what you are going through. I can only imagine how this could put a strain on your relationship. But you know, sometimes you have to focus on what you are blessed with, versus what you lost. Let me ask you a question. Do you still tell her that you love her?"

"Man, I show my love daily by going to work everyday and raising my kids. Show my love with coming home everyday. I don't know. This situation is stressful and I don't think she understands. She acts like I don't care."

"Bro, I remember something you said to me before I got married. You said *Dana, my only advice to you is to not start something you aren't willing to do for the next 20 years*. I didn't realize what kind of gem you gave me there. But you know, sometimes the advice we give to others, we need to heed ourselves. If you opened doors, then continue to open doors for her. If you told her you loved her, then continue to tell her you love her. If you guys went for walks, then continue to go on walks with her. Don't start anything you are not going to consistently do. These are words coming from your own mouth."

"You are right man. I just don't know what to do at this point. I feel like I am trying to put together one of those 1000 piece jigsaw puzzles, and all the edge pieces are missing. Like I can't hold this together. Tell me, where do I even start? I have never been the one to endorse complacency, but we just fell into this rut. A rut where we learned, or should I say managed, to live with one another, and during the process we slowly grew apart. I still love her, but I just don't know how to get back on track? Sometimes she is just so rebellious. It is like she just picks fights sometimes, and won't listen to me, even if she knows I am right."

"Bro, my dad shared something with me before. I was frustrated because my lady and I kept getting into stupid arguments. It could be something as simple as driving somewhere. It could be a place that I have driven to numerous times, but she would sit there and argue with me, and our navigation system. I thought she was going nuts, so I spoke with my pops and he broke it down for me. He told me that sometimes we do things and don't take into account women's feelings and opinions. Then what happens is later on, they will rebel against something that we care about. In other words, we can't expect them to care about our feelings if we continue to discount theirs."

"What is wrong with women? Why do they act like that? I can feel what he is saying, but there are two sides to that story. Yes, I know sometimes I can be insensitive, but what about her? What about the times I open up to her, and then she uses that against me later?"

"Well bro, I don't have an answer for that. That is definitely something women need to work on. It is already hard for a man to let down his guard and reveal himself, but when he does so and then the woman comes back and uses that info for leverage later on down the road, that makes a man completely want to shut down and not communicate."

"Amen my brother. Amen."

Attention & Affection

"Alicia, Jon is mad at me. We got into an argument, and I went off on him earlier. He was telling me about this women's class at church he thought I might like. The truth is I wouldn't mind going, but I was just…I don't know what I was. I guess I was just being confrontational. Would you mind going with me?"

"No, I don't mind at all. I didn't have anything planned tonight. Do you want me to drive, or you?"

"I never pass up a chauffeur"

"Ok, I will be there in an hour."

Time passed and the sisters were running late. They arrived and sat near the back so they wouldn't disturb others. As they took their seats, they saw that Sister Valentine was teaching the class tonight.

"You know ladies, my husband and I had a discussion one time about a man's needs, versus a woman's. We talked about how a man has a need for sex, whereas a woman can live without sex. This blew my husband's mind, but what I had to explain to him is we like sex, but don't need it; what we need is affection and attention. Therefore today, we are going to address this issue of a woman's need for attention and affection, and how we go about obtaining it.

"For this session, I would like to speak about Leah, and her desire for attention. For those of you who don't study your Bible until you come to church, the text I am referring to is Genesis 29:14-35. For times sake I will summarize, but I encourage you to read the entire 29th chapter.

"Jacob came to visit this land, and fell in love with a woman named Rachel. In order to marry Rachel he had to work seven years for her father Laban. Jacob worked these seven years, then Laban tricked him into marrying his older daughter Leah by swapping sisters on the wedding night. Jacob asked his father-in-law why he was deceived, and Laban responded that it was not custom to give away the youngest daughter first. He told Jacob if he worked an additional seven years, then he could marry Rachel as well. Jacob was so in love that he took Laban's offer and after the first week of marriage to Leah, married her sister Rachel. Jacob had children with Leah, who bore six of the 12 tribes of Israel, but his heart still belonged to Rachel.

"I read this story once when I was younger, but as I grew into womanhood I looked at the story from a completely different perspective. The thing that stands out to me was how hard Jacob worked to get Rachel. My question to you is do you position yourself to even allow men to court you, or are you proactive thus eliminating their ability to hunt? I will leave that one alone until later.

"Let's get back to the story. The Word says that when Jacob came into the land, there was a huge stone over the mouth of the well. If you read on it says that the shepherds would roll the stone away to water the sheep. Since this took a few men to move, we can infer that this was probably a nice size rock. Continue to read on, and you will see where Jacob is introduced to Rachel. It was apparent that Jacob was trying to impress her because the Word says that he rolled the rock away by himself to water the sheep. Jacob's courting impressed me. I mean who in here wouldn't want a strong man? But what impressed me more in this story was Rachel. Notice, she didn't do anything to gain his attention other than present her meek spirit. This man was willing to work seven years for this woman. I want you to think how long seven years is. Ask yourself, what have you ever waited seven years for? Jacob works these seven years, then gets to the end, is deceived, and agrees to an additional seven years. He dedicated fourteen years of labor for one woman. Let this serve as an example ladies; if a man wants a woman he will work, or do whatever it takes to get her. The key is if he truly wants her.

"Let me revisit this meek spirit again. The Word says that a woman should have a meek spirit. Read I Peter 3:3-5. This passage should be our blueprint, so read several translations until it sinks in. I am going to quote from the NIV: *3 Your beauty should not come from outward adornment, such as braided hair and the wearing of gold jewelry and fine clothes. 4 Instead, it should be that of your inner self, the unfading beauty of a gentle and quiet spirit, which is of great worth in God's sight. 5 For this is the way the holy women of the past who put their hope in God used to make themselves beautiful...*

"Now I am not telling you to go out and dress like a bum. You still need to carry yourselves with dignity and class. What I am saying is that you shouldn't let your clothes be the only way beauty shines. In other words, you shouldn't be showing all your goodies trying to get the attention of a man. You can dress nice without having your skirt being so close to the candy store, or your cleavage all hanging out. A woman should have a quiet spirit and like Rachel, have an inner beauty which radiates through.

"Some of you women are looking at me with blank faces, so let me just say it plain. You should allow men to hunt you, versus the other way around. Half the problem is women nowadays try to think for a man. We make comments like *Oh he loves me, he is just confused right now,* or we make excuses for his behavior. Ladies, a man knows what he wants, and doesn't need us to tell him. We don't have to manipulate, or think for him. Men are hunter's instinctively.

"I see I am alone tonight, so let's go back to the Word and look at the other side of this story. Leah, on the other hand was in a situation. Leah's eyes were described as weak and dull looking, whereas her sister Rachel was described as lovely and beautiful. Think about the issues she had from her sibling alone? I want you to put yourself in Leah's shoes. Your younger attractive sister gathers the attention you so long for. Then on top of being the less attractive sister, you have a father who has to trick men into marrying you. I understand this was the law of the land, but maybe she willingly went along with it because she felt this was her way out? Maybe she was tired, and thought this man would rescue her and provide her with the attention she apparently lacked? Whatever her thinking was, once she married Jacob it sparked a thirst for his attention which was never quenched. The Word speaks on how Leah prayed for her husband to love her. She deeply craved his attention, and even through conception of his children, his love never changed towards Rachel.

"So where am I going with this? Well first, you can't make a man love you. You can't force or leverage a man to love you with children or other acts. Even deeper, you need to find out what it is inside of you that is making certain men gravitate to you. If all you are meeting are dogs, then maybe there is something emitting from your spirit that they can sense. I am not trying to be mean ladies, but speak the truth out of love. In order to discover why you are attracting certain men, you have to heal from your old wounds. You have to look within, and do an assessment. Do I have issues with my father that lead me to act out? Do I have baggage from previous relationships that have damaged me more than I'd like to admit? You have to be honest with yourself. Ladies, we have to get this under control, before we end up getting in situations where we are miserable like Leah. Instead of spending years in misery seeking the attention of men, we need to learn how to first allow God to validate us…"

While the class was going on, there were some ladies sitting in front of Alicia and April who were holding their own conversation outside of the class.

"Look what Sister Pryor has on. She is just asking for it. You know she has slept with half the usher board."

"Well I heard that is a two way street. Rumor has it her husband spends a lot of time with the youth choir director, Sister Karyn. I won't mention any names, but a reliable source told me they saw his car parked in front of Sister Karyn's house when Sister Pryor went away on that woman's retreat."

"Shut your mouth. If I am not mistaken, Deacon Pryor and Karyn's husband are first cousins, right? You know, now that you say that, Karyn's oldest child's head is definitely shaped like Deacon Pryor. That little rascal does favor him. How could he not know that child is not his?"

One of the other older women chimed in, "Oh shut up Gayle. Just like you didn't know why your man left you 20 years ago, huh? Why don't you stop gossiping, and try to pay attention. There are actually women in here trying to learn."

April snatched up her purse, walked out the class, and cried as she walked down the hallway. Alicia was in the bathroom at the time. As she walked out, she saw April walking down the hallway with her arms crossed approaching the exit. April went outside towards the parking lot, and the exit door swung open shortly afterwards as Alicia went searching for her little sister.

"What's the matter baby sis? Did one of those old bitter women say something to you?"

"Alicia, I don't want to end up like those women. I don't want to be in the middle of some scandal. I don't want to be a bitter old single woman."

"Girl, what are you talking about?"

"Oh, it don't matter. Nothing matters anymore."

By April's tone, it was evident that something was bothering her.

"Ape, you have done this since we were little. You get hurt or upset about something, internalize it, then you just start talking and reciting sentences from the middle of your thoughts. You start rambling and I have no clue where you are coming from. I want to help you, but I don't know what you are talking about."

"Then Sister Valentine's message? I don't know Lish. Yes, I want his attention, but I don't think I am Leah. He used to love me like Rachel. What happened? I just don't understand. He was so considerate and giving. Where is the guy in the video store willing to try new things? Where is the well-traveled, spontaneous man who took me everywhere? I was the center of his world. What happened?"

"Well Ape, I am sure you changed as well. Do you do the same things you used to when he was pursuing you? What do you give to him? Do you still encourage him and give him compliments? Do you still get dressed up and make yourself presentable just for him, or do you only dress up when you going out with your girls? And as far as traveling goes, you are older and have kids and more responsibilities now. You can't just drop everything on a whim and get on the road like you used to. When are you going to grow up April, and stop acting like a spoiled little brat? You can't have your way all the time."

Alicia saw how hurt her sister was, and felt bad for how she spoke to her. She lowered her tone, and approached April to give her a hug.

"Look, I am sorry. I know you are going through a tough period right now. I never try to hurt you intentionally. Everything I say to you I always say out of love."

"I know Lish."

"I tell you what. If you really want to go out, I will keep the kids for you. Better yet, why don't you plan a small trip or vacation together? It would be a nice surprise and I can take care of the kids for a few days."

April pushed away from her sister.

"It doesn't matter because he doesn't even appreciate me Lish. Why go through all that if he doesn't care? He'd probably just go off on me about the amount of money I spent."

"You don't give him an opportunity to appreciate you. All I hear from you is he don't do this, and he don't do that. What do you do? When are you going to stop feeling sorry for yourself and trying to be the victim, and fight for your marriage? I am not singling you out, this goes for both of you. You can keep pointing the finger for ever at one another, but that will never change the situation."

April leaned against the car and blotted the tears from her eyes with a tissue as her older sister spoke the truth.

"I just want things back how they used to be. I remember I'd be on the toilet and he would open the door and come in and talk to me, or open the door just to tell me he loved me. It was like no boundaries; he loved me unconditionally. He would write that he loved me on the bathroom mirror so when it fogged up from the steam of my shower, I would see it. Or sometimes I would go to work, and there would be an e-mail waiting for me that would say something like *Baby, it is 1am, and I could not sleep. I sat and watched you sleep for an hour. You are so beautiful. I just wanted to let you know I have been kissing all over you while you were sleep. Have a good day my love! J.* Now, I am lucky if he gives me any compliments outside of those rare periods of time when we are having sex."

"Well at least you have someone to have sex with. When you have a child, it is so hard to find someone. You have to put your child first, and how many men really want to settle down with a woman…a widow at that…that already has a child? I don't know April, I know your situation is rough, but it is nothing you can't get through. Trust me, you have it a lot better than I do on my end. Do you know how hard it is preparing to go to sleep every night knowing that a cold bed is waiting for you? You don't know how bad I miss the reassuring touch of a man in the middle of the night. How I long for that protector and provider to be present in my home. That man that is strong enough that he will make love to me the way I need, but spiritually grounded enough to cover our family in prayer. You don't know how it feels when you don't have someone's arms to lay in. How it feels when you had a bad day and try to cope telling yourself everything will be alright, but the reality is no one is there to comfort you. How empty that feels just wishing you had someone at all to be there for you. Someone to talk to and confide in. Someone to open stubborn jars and fix things around the house. The little things you take for granted when you have a man. Be thankful you have someone girl. I would welcome bad sex as a problem."

"Alicia, you are beautiful inside out, you are wise, you have a genuine heart, you are an excellent mother, and you are strong woman. Then talent wise, girl there at not too many people who are as creative as you. The way you can completely transform the interior of a home or office has always amazed me. You are just…I can't even describe what I am trying to say. I just admire so many qualities about you, and wish that I possessed them myself. I have always looked up to you, and am so thankful you are my sister. I know that there is someone out there for you."

"Thank you April. That was sweet of you. Still doesn't make the situation easier."

April looked up at the stars in the sky. She had a million thoughts running through her head.

"And you know what Lish? As far as sex, yea it is pretty bland at the moment, but you are right…I guess I shouldn't complain. I know back in the day, whew. When we used to make love, my God! That man did things to my body that…umm. Let's just say he made me feel like nothing I have ever felt before. Jon would have me saying things my lips have never uttered. And girl, he has made me cry several times while making love. We would go at it anywhere too! Oh my goodness…the bathroom at Momma's house, our kitchen counter, it didn't matter. He was so spontaneous. His calm demeanor made me comfortable and his eyes could convince me to do anything. I can't explain it, but the way it used to feel when he would…"

"April, shut up! Dang, girl. Remember I am trying to walk the straight and narrow, and all this sex talk is not exactly helping. Maybe you missed what I just said. I do not have a man to put it on me like that, and it has been quite some time since I took my vow of celibacy. Now some days are better than others, but you are not making this one of those some days. I am not trying to leave church and go home horny because my sister keeps bragging about some good sex she is having, has had or whatever. How messed up does that sound? You are not supposed to leave church in heat."

Both the sisters began to laugh.

"Seriously April, back to what I said regarding communication with him. Do you ever tell him this? Have you ever sat down and talked to him about how you feel about everything?"

"I don't know Lish. I live with him, but sometimes I feel like I am a single woman. I just crave his love. I desire his touch. I need his attention. I just feel he doesn't want me the same way. The old Jon would greet me when I got out the shower with a thick Egyptian cotton bath towel, dry me from head to toe, and lotion my feet. Or sometimes he would jump in and wash my hair, then take the time to brush it for me after it dried. This new Jon won't even take a shower with me anymore, and if he enters the bathroom, he never speaks."

"April, I think…"

"What is wrong with men Lish? Why don't they talk? Why do they sit there looking stupid? How am I supposed to know what is going on with him if he doesn't open up?"

"How is he supposed to know if you don't open up? You have to be direct and tell him instead of throwing tantrums."

"But he used to…"

Alicia was becoming exhausted listening to her sister whine. She interrupted, "Baby sister, I get the point. He was Mr. McDreamy and was romantic and wonderful and the sun shined brighter when he was around and the birds sang louder. I get it. Everyone knows that Jon is a good man, I am not discounting your feelings, but you are not listening to me. Talk to him."

"You just don't understand Jon. You don't understand."

April walked around the vehicle and entered to signal she was ready to depart.

CHAPTER EIGHT

Temptress

Carmen

There was a local mom and pop diner which was Jon's preference for his lunch hour as the home cooked meals provided comfort food. While sitting at the counter playing with the salt shaker, he heard the ringing of the bell which signaled someone was entering the diner. When the door opened, the patrons greeted the new guest; a young woman dressed in an expensive business suit. She walked to the counter, placed her purse down, and swiveled in the bar stool towards the menu. Deep in thought, Jon glanced over and made eye contact with the young woman. He politely nodded, and turned back forward as he proceeded to drink the rest of his cola.

The young woman, apparently new to the diner, leaned over and asked Jon, "So what is good here?"

As Jon turned towards the young lady, he had a chance to look her over. He did not notice how attractive she was. *Whoa, where did she come from? Looks like she is in her early 20s, tight skin, body appears firm, and she has the whitest teeth.*

Jon crunched the ice which was in his mouth, then responded.

"Depends on what you are in the mood for. I am not a soup fan, but people love it here. All the sandwiches are good. Burgers good. Really can't go wrong with the daily lunch special, or anything on the left side of the menu."

Preoccupied with thoughts of his personal problems, Jon got up from the bar stool.

"Pardon me. I don't mean to be rude. It has just been a long day."

"No offense taken," the young lady replied.

Jon looked over to the lady, "Enjoy your meal," then slapped a tip on the counter.

*　*　*　*　*

Two weeks later, Jon went into the same diner and got a booth with a window seat. He stared at cars going by while he daydreamed about where he was in life. He thought about his marriage, his kids and his dreams for his own business. The familiar bell rang from the diner door, and something compelled Jon to look up. It was the same young lady from a couple weeks ago. Jon made eye contact and nodded to acknowledge her. The young lady waved, then approached the booth.

"Is this seat taken?"

Jon extended his hand. "Be my guest."

"I didn't get to introduce myself last time. My name is Carmen."

"Jon."

"Nice to formally meet you Jon." Carmen reached for the menu. "You know, I took your suggestion last time. You were right. Good food here."

"I am not trying to be impolite, but what is a pretty young lady like you doing in a place like this alone? You don't seem like the type."

"Why do you say that? What is the type? Oh, is it because of my attire? Looks can be deceiving. Don't let the exterior fool you. This girl right here likes to eat, and I have no problem getting my hands dirty."

A part of Jon's brain thought she was flirting, but being the humble guy he was, he ignored his ego driven thoughts. "What do you do for a living Carmen?"

"I am a paralegal. I love what I do, but it is very stressful. The attorney I work for is a prick, so every now and then I go to lunch solo and try to unwind. I heard through the grapevine this place was decent, so I decided to check it out."

"I do the same…come in here to unwind. Comfort food here."

"So, I am fairly new to Chicago. Are you a native?"

"I suppose you can say that. I was born in Louisiana, but been here most my life."

"A Cajun man. Interesting. Do you go back often?"

"Not as much as I would like."

"Did you know anyone affected by Katrina?"

"What is up with the twenty questions? You working for the feds or something?"

"I apologize. I guess that is just the future attorney in me. Inquisitive nature you could say."

Jon shook his leg in a nervous fit while he looked out the window of the diner.

"I didn't live in New Orleans."

"Oh."

"To answer your question, yes I knew a family affected. We moved when I was little, but over the years I kept in touch with this one kid. We were neighbors, and his family ended up moving from Baton Rouge to New Orleans shortly after we left. We continued to write each other throughout the years, and even played against one another in some AAU leagues when we were in high school. I still speak with him from time to time, but you know how neighborhood friendships fizzle as you get older."

"Yes, I understand. That Katrina was something else. It has been how many years now? That was in what…2005? That was so sad."

"No, the sad thing is I don't believe most people in this country realize how bad it really was. Either they don't realize, or don't care. Then for the survivors, just imagine having your home uprooted…all your family heirlooms, photos, everything…and having to start all over again. I can't begin to imagine the psychological effect that has on you. How something as simple as rainfall to most can trigger fear and emotions within these people. Little things we take for granted. I went down to help, and it was so traumatic I don't even like talking about it. Don't get me wrong, I love this country, but our government's response time was unacceptable. I don't understand how we are this powerhouse of a country, and have people on our own soil that were unable to get the aid they needed. Lives were lost for what? Logistics? Man, I need to stop before I get mad."

"I agree 100% Jon. That was ridiculous. I was not there, but I spent many nights on the couch watching the news in tears. Is your friend ok?"

"Depends on what your definition of ok is. He saw his mother go underwater, and to this day they have not discovered her body. I talked to him a couple times since, and he says he can't find peace until he can put her soul at rest. I tried to speak to him about…well, let's just say he is struggling with his faith right now, so it is hard to witness to him."

"J, I don't know what to say."

"What can you say? Sorry to damper the mood, but that whole situation is still a bit touchy to me."

"No need to apologize."

Jon continued to gaze out the window, and watched as a man attempted to hail a cab.

"Carmen, are you a Chi-town native?"

"Actually, I am a Georgia peach"

"Really? A southern belle. Interesting. What brought you here?"

"That is a long story. In a nutshell, my fiancé moved me here, but then decided to play for another team."

"O-k, I will leave that one alone." Jon replied.

The waitress took their orders, and they sat and prepared their next round of questions.

"So Jon, tell me about yourself. What do you do for a living? What do you like to do? What is your passion?"

"Well that is a loaded question. I guess that is the lawyer in you, huh?"

"No, this has nothing to do with my profession. I am just curious. And I am not a lawyer yet…I am a paralegal."

"I work in construction. I love building houses. That is what I like to do, so I guess you can call that my passion. My dream is to own my own real estate and construction company."

"A man good with his hands. I assume you are married?"

"Why would you assume that?"

"Well, you seem too good to be true. And I know this is cliché, but the reality is all the good men are taken."

"Yes, I am."

"Am what? A good man, or married?"

"Both. I am a good man I suppose. I come home every night, and I don't have a wandering eye."

"Yet," Carmen responded under her breath.

"I have been happily married for 9 years," Jon raises his left hand to expose the back of his naked hand, "can't wear my ring at the job site."

"So modest. I know you are making some woman very happy. So, do you have any kids?"

"Yes. A boy and a girl." Jon reached into his wallet and pulled out photos of his children.

"What are their names?"

"Jon Jr. and Jordan."

"Your little girl is so adorable, and little man is handsome like his daddy. Must have gotten his looks from you."

"Carmen, if you keep giving me compliments. I may have to treat you…"

"Treat?"

"Yes, treat." Jon waived the waitress over. "May I have a cherry cobbler with ice cream for the young lady."

"Sure thing sugar," the waitress said as she winked.

"Cherry cobbler. Trying to negate my workout?"

"From what I have seen, you will be fine. You are young enough that you can burn calories in your sleep. How old are you anyways?"

"I am 24."

Jon's ego boosted through the roof. *A 24 year old woman trying to seduce me? I still got it.*

"Jon, I have only been in this city for a few months. What is there to do here? What do you do in your spare time?"

"There is plenty to do here, but I am probably the wrong person to ask. My schedule is full with projects. When I am not at work, I am overseeing the construction for the expansion of our church. I do side jobs here and there. I assist relatives with maintenance and do various projects. I try to go out at least once a week with the fellas, but we just hang out. Nothing to write home about."

"A church man too? They don't make men like you anymore."

Embarrassed, yet flattered, Jon responded, "Oh stop it…keep going."

Carmen began to laugh. Jon watched the young woman pull her hair behind her ears while continuing to tease him with her body language. It appeared like everything was moving in slow motion. He knew that this interaction with Carmen was wrong, but loved how this beautiful woman made him feel young again. During their flirtation, the waitress brought over the cobbler with two spoons piercing the crust.

"Why are there two spoons?" Carmen took out a spoon, put it in her mouth, then spun it upside down as she pulled it out. "All you need is one."

Man, this young girl needs to stop it. Why is she throwing it at me like this? Maybe I am on one of those reality shows or something. This seems like one of those Gordon setups. "So tell me Carmen, why are you wasting your lunch talking to this aged man? Do you know how old I am?"

"Your age does not matter to me. And whatever it is, you don't look old. Besides, I prefer to say refined."

"Refined, huh? More like ancient. I remember when I was in my early 20s like you. I had so much stamina. So much dexterity. Now I can just get off the couch, and crack a bone or knock something out of place just by walking. Signs you are getting old."

"Stamina?" she responded. "The way you are built, I bet you could keep up!"

"I am sure it would be fun youngen."

Approaching a dangerous crossroad, Jon tried to end the conversation before it went any deeper.

"Look, it has been fun flirting with you, but I have to get back to work. Maybe I will run into you again?"

As Jon walked out the diner towards his truck, Carmen watched him through the window.

"I'm quite sure you will Jon…if I have my way."

CHAPTER NINE

Nostalgia

Charles

April was sitting at her desk finishing her paperwork when a teller called her line.

"Mrs. Carter, there is a gentleman out in the lobby. He wants to open a business account, and get some information about investment options."

"Send him in."

April turned in her chair away from the door to grab some forms from her file cabinet.

"Excuse me miss, but I was told that you could assist me."

April, recognizing a familiar voice, turned around in her chair. "Charles?"

"Well, are you going to sit there all day, or get up and give me a hug?"

Oh my goodness. What is Charles doing here? I feel sick to my stomach.

April felt like her heart dropped into her stomach. Reluctant to revisit past feelings, April fought the queasy feeling and attempted to give Charles a plutonic hug. "So how have you been? You look like you have lost weight."

Charles stood back and looked at April while shaking his head. "Wow. It has been a long time. Thanks for noticing. Actually I haven't lost too much weight. You know I used to be pretty husky. I just learned how to eat right, and started weight training. Chiseled some of that baby fat off. So tell me, how have you been?"

"Life is good. I can't complain." April stared at Charles, and suddenly she was hit with a wave of emotions. Charles glanced over and saw the photos on her desk.

"So is that your man? Married, I assume? I know someone had to secure a catch like you."

"Yes, that is my husband, and two children. Are you married now?"

"Wow. All married and grown up. Look at you. You look good April."

"I see you avoided my question."

"I didn't necessarily ignore. I was hoping that I could entertain you to lunch. Then we can catch up."

"I don't think that is such a good idea Charles. I am a married woman now."

"And I am a married man. April, I don't want anything from you. I just want to catch up and talk. It has been a long time. How long now? Over a decade?"

"Yes, it has been a long time, but I don't think…"

"Just lunch. That is all. Lunch on me."

April decided lunch was safe enough. "Let me grab my purse." She took her cell phone, and cut it off so she wouldn't feel guilty if Jon called. "Ok, I am ready."

April walked outside and Charles escorted her to his white Range Rover. "Looks like business is good."

"Well, I can't complain. Remember that business I had in college? Well it took off."

In college, Charles created a very popular, proprietary tutor software program. He took the profits and invested in additional equipment. Charles always had something going. If he wasn't selling his program, he was building and repairing computers. He ended up dropping out of school, and partnered with an old college roommate. Together they formed a consulting firm named BPS, which stood for Business Productivity Solutions. He grew the company to a team of 25 consultants, and he is doing quite well for himself.

Charles pulled into a popular Italian restaurant. As they entered, Charles continued to give April compliments.

"I can't get over how good you look girl."

"Italian, huh? Very original."

"I thought you may like. Remember last time we came here? Prom night."

"Charles, please let it go. So what have you been doing? How is your wife?"

"We can talk about her later. I am here with you. That is all I care about right now." Their conversation was interrupted by their host as she placed a basket of hot rolls on the table.

"Hi. My name is Erin. I will be your hostess. Can I start you with an appetizer?"

"No thank you. I think we are ready to order. I would like the Five Cheese Ziti al Forno, and my lady friend here will have the Rigatoni con Pollo. A Coke for me, and a Sprite for her."

The waitress gathered the menus. "Good choice. I will have your drinks right out."

April and Charles told the hostess *thank you* as she walked away.

"So you took the liberty to order for me? What makes you think I wanted that?"

"I don't know what you like anymore April. I know you used to like pasta, so I guess I just assumed. I am sorry, I was just trying to recreate the moment."

"That moment has come and gone Charles."

"April, I have a confession to make. I didn't accidentally stumble upon you. My cousin Jassmine told me where you worked."

"Oh did she? Why doesn't that surprise me?"

"Did Jazz tell you that I ask about you often?"

"No, I told her that if we were going to remain friends, that she was to no longer mention your name, nor relay any messages from you" April paused. "A lot has changed Charles. I am not the same little naïve, gullible April that you once knew."

"I see. You are all grown up. And may I say, you matured quite well."

"So, where is your wife? And do you have any kids?"

"My wife is back in Seattle. I have one child; a daughter. So, where is the Mr.?"

"Working on this metropolitan park project. They are renovating recreational facilities and parks for children."

"How is that for irony? He is working on sandboxes, and I am here trying to play in yours."

"Sorry Charlie, but only one person plays in this sandbox, and it is a private park not open to the public."

"Come on Kitten. You know I was just joking with you. We had something. What happened?"

"What happened?" April became upset Charles was playing dumb. "What happened was you wanted me to stay at home while you went around hunting for anything that moved with two legs. I put my all into you, and you went out and put your all into every other female."

"That was years ago. I am sorry. I am a changed man."

"For your wife's sake, I pray you are."

"I did love you April. I did then, and I do now. You will always have my heart."

"And you are also married. I am sure your wife…"

"You are trying to tell me that you feel nothing?"

"Whatever Charles. Next topic. What are you doing back in town?"

"My company landed a 3 month contract with a firm here. Since I know the terrain, I volunteered to come back and pioneer the project. Now that I am here, I am seriously thinking about relocating back to Illinois."

"Please don't. Stay right where you are."

"Why you say that? You know April, just being honest with you…"

"Honest. That's a concept."

"I love your spicy temperament. Always have my sexy high school sweetheart."

"My nothing. I am not yours."

"I will be transparent with you April. I know that I was not the best boyfriend. I know I hurt you, but seeing you now? I don't know. It is bringing back some feelings I have been trying to suppress for years. If I could only go back in time…"

"But you can't, so it is pointless to talk about it. The damage is done. We were not meant to be. I am happily married, and you," April paused to try to say something nice, "well, I just hope that you are treating her right. I don't know her, but no woman deserves to go through what I went through."

"I will leave her for you Kitten. I will leave everything. Just say the word. Let's just get up and go. We could move to Florida. I have a beach house there."

"Yea, that would be great. Then we could visit my in-laws in Orlando."

"April, I have thought about you for years. I do love my wife, but what we had was so different. I just can't explain it. She can't love me like you can, and I know that he can't love you like I can. I always felt you were the one."

"Fool, shut up."

"And we had so much fun. Do you remember when I stripped for you in the kitchen and your dad came home? I had to run out the back door half naked. Or when you were holding on to that tree, and those kids caught us…"

"Charles, please stop!"

"We were so wild."

"And stupid! I am married now. A married, Christian woman with kids."

"Dang, why did you say *Christian* like that? I am saved too Kitten."

"Then act like it."

"Ditto."

"What is that supposed to mean?"

"I saw how you looked at me when you turned around in your chair. Your smile told it all. I felt your body react when I hugged you. I will always be your best because I was your first.

Lord knows I wish I could take that back. Hindsight is 20/20. I will never forget how he took my virginity, and how I laid there wondering if that was sex. He didn't even care about me, he was just trying to get off. The worst part is he is still the same ol arrogant Charles from when we were younger. My little world revolved around him, and I never got anything in return. I gave my body to him, even though he sucked. I just wasted years of my life not being fulfilled. I guess I did it because any affection from him was better than none at all, but if he knew how I really felt, it would probably crumble his little world.

After thinking about their past, April rolled her eyes. "Whatever Charles. Don't flatter yourself. I was young and stupid."

"Do I still make it twitch?"

"Nope, but Jon does."

"Jon is not here. So you telling me you didn't feel anything? I can't accept that."

"Charles, I am not trying to be mean, but I don't sit around thinking about you, or what we had. That was the past and I left it there. Nostalgia is not always thoughts of good times. It sometimes resurfaces pain. What is the point of this?"

"Like I said Kitten, I didn't want anything from you. I just wanted to apologize."

"No more past talk. Let's just enjoy lunch."

April sat regretting that she came to lunch with him. *Even though I hate him, something makes me gravitate towards him. He has not changed, but is compelling; in a shallow sort of way. Definitely not a catalog model, but he does have excellent taste in clothing and looks sharp. Aside from church, Jon never dresses up just for me. I know I shouldn't be here, but heck why not? Lunch shouldn't harm anything. As long as Jon never finds out, then it shouldn't change anything. Besides, not like I am cheating or anything. No April, this is not right. Don't forget what he did to you. Just keep this civil and finish lunch.*

"I haven't been home in years. I hear Jassmine landed herself a sugar daddy."

"Well, you know your cousin. Nothing has changed much since we were younger. She is a beautiful woman who cashes in on her looks. I just pray she finds someone she truly loves and stops playing games with these men."

"You know April, I total agree. But there are some things that you don't know about Jassmine. Reasons why she acts the way she does. I don't want to tell all her business, but just keep in mind usually when people act out a certain way, it is because someone they loved hurt them deeply. We have some serious issues within our family."

"Don't we all?"

"How are your mom and dad doing? How about that tribe of siblings? What's up with that spicy sister of yours; Alicia?"

"Mom and dad are good. Alicia is good. Sure she would have some choice words for you right now."

"Alicia never did like me. I couldn't understand why."

"Charles, shut up. Her baby sister's boyfriend tried to hit on her. Why would she like him? You know, thank you for lunch, but this is a bit too much for me. Can you please take me back to my office? I am running late."

"I am a changed man April, but I understand if you need time to see that." Charles signaled over to the waitress requesting the tab.

April remained silent while Charles drove her back to work. He attempted to make small talk, but she muted him out and stared out the window. Her thoughts were divided between thinking of Jon, and how Charles hurt her in the past. They arrived at the bank, and Charles leaned in and kissed April on the cheek. April did not react to his affection, and politely thanked him for lunch prior to shutting his door.

Charles rolled down the window and asked, "Do you think we can see each other again?"

"No. I don't think that would be a good idea. Goodbye Charles."

"Bye April."

Charles sat in his car and smirked as he watched April walk back into the building.

CHAPTER TEN

Salsa

South of the Border

On the way home from work, Jon called April to see what she wanted him to bring home for dinner. She told her husband to just come home because she decided to cook. A few minutes later Jon arrived home. Exhausted from a tough day at work, he was relieved he could finally leave the stress from the war he fought all day at the door and walk into peace. While Jon was taking off his work boots at the door, he was delighted to be greeted by the aroma of fresh garlic and onion. He used his senses and followed the trail of spices and seasonings. When he stepped foot into the kitchen, he crossed the border as their Bose Wave radio used Latin music to transform the environment.

"What's all this for?"

"Well, I never cook, and since it was Mexican night, I suppose I went a little overboard."

"Smells good. What did you make?"

"Ve bañate, then I will tell you when you return."

"I am rusty on my Spanish, but it sounded like you told me to go take a shower?"

Jon laughed, and went to take a shower as his wife instructed. He lathered in the shower and temporarily allowed the weight of life to roll off his shoulders. When complete, he returned to the kitchen to fill his appetite and enjoy the south of the border atmosphere April created.

"Sit down and relax. I will be your waitress for the evening."

Jon watched in admiration as his wife prepared items on a tray. She grabbed a huge frosted glass out of the freezer which she prepared while Jon was in the shower, placed it on the tray and walked closer to her husband; all the while maintaining eye contact.

"Here are your chips and your choice of pico de gallo, or queso fundido. The Sangria Swirl Margarita is compliments from the sexy woman in the kitchen."

As April turned to walk away, she made sure she twisted her hips in a seductive, exaggerated manner.

"Girl you better stop before we end up missing dinner." Jon stated flirtatiously. "Seriously, thank you for all of this. What did you make?"

"First let me apologize if you don't like. I got these recipes from Teresa at work, and I couldn't decide what to make and went a little crazy. I figured I'd start you with chicken tamales as an appetizer, for the main course Carne Asada a la Tampiqueña, then Chocolate Banana Chimichangas for dessert."

The couple ate dinner, and for a brief moment forgot about all their problems.

"April, thank you. This was incredible."

"I am glad you liked. Mi sexy esposo, vamonos a bailar salsa esta noche!"

"What?"

"I said that I want to go salsa dancing with my sexy husband tonight."

Jon was reluctant to ruin the moment, but before he could open his mind he spoke, "I am sorry, but I must pass."

"Andale mi Papi, te prometo voy a comportarme de lo mejor!"

"April, I am sorry but I never paid attention in Spanish class."

"Spanish is the romance language. Come on baby, let's go. Salsa is so sexy, and no telling what it could possibly lead to afterwards. Si bailas conmigo, mis labios bailaran en ti despues! Trust me, it will be fun." April walked near her husband and stood him up. With stretched arms, she rubbed his head and allowed her fingers to delicately massage his ear lobes; which was his weak spot. When Jon closed his eyes enjoying his woman's touch, she turned around and backed into him; allowing her arms to reach up and grab the back of his head. Jon kissed his wife on her neck while her hands gently welcomed her husband. While her body was next to his, she did a provocative dance to entice him to her offer. "I said that I promise I will be on my best behavior."

"Sorry Ape, just not in the mood."

"Not in the mood? You are never in the mood for me, but you make time for what you want."

"April, what is that supposed to mean? The things I want are free.

Everything you suggest has a price tag associated with it. We can't just splurge every time you get an impulse to do something."

"These are Salsa lessons, and they are at the YMCA. The first class is free. Let's just try it out. Why don't you ever want to try something new?"

"April, I said no and that is the end of it."

April picked up the pillow from the edge of the kitchen nook and threw it at Jon.

"Fine then!"

She stormed out the front door and slammed it to add an exclamation point to her exit.

Relax

Jon picked up the phone to call his buddy Dana.

"What's up man. This is Jon."

"What's going on man? What's new with you?"

"Same ol same ol. Hey, I was checking to see what you were getting into tonight. Thought maybe we could play some cards or something?"

"Sounds good J, but I had already promised my old lady I would take her to the movies. Where's April? She go out with the girls tonight?"

"No, she left here mad at me though. I have no idea where she went. Probably went over her mother's house so all the ladies could sit over there and talk about what kind of dog I am."

"Dog? What did you do this time?"

"Messed up as usual. Long story man, and I don't want to hold you up."

"I got a little time before the flick starts. What happened?"

"Long story short, I got home and the Mrs had this nice Mexican spread laid out for me. I mean, the girl cooks like her momma when she wants to. She was dancing, and being seductive and just doing everything right. She looked so good, and that just really turns me on when she goes through all that effort for me."

"I don't get it. Sounds like you guys had a good time?"

"Well we were flirting and whatnot, and I was about ready to take her upstairs and lock her in there until the morning; that was until her proposition. After dinner she asked me to go salsa dancing, and I wouldn't go. We got into a little dispute, then she stormed out the house."

"Why didn't you go?"

"Dana, you have to live with April to understand. She just likes to splurge on things, and I don't think she understands how bad things are financially sometimes."

"Well bro, splurging may not be a bad thing if you are investing it in your relationship."

"Man, honestly I wanted to go, but I just can't think about playing when we got so much going on. We have bills to pay. Life doesn't stop just because you want to have fun."

"J, you need to relax. You are going to end up pushing her away."

"Hard to relax with that in the back of your mind."

"Well, it will be worse if you have to think about her with another man in the back of your mind. If you aren't giving your wife attention, eventually someone else will. What is it going to take for you to open your eyes bro? This is what we signed up for when we married. It goes beyond sex and having children. You have to talk to her. You have an obligation to sow back into your wife man."

"Yea, I guess you are right. Well look, I don't want to hold you up. Enjoy date night with the Mrs, and tell her I said hello. We'll hook up sometime next week or something."

"Alright bro. Hey, keep your head up J."

"You too my man."

Jon picked up the phone to check on April. He hit the talk button, then hesitated. *You know, maybe I will just let her let off steam. Besides, if she is at her mother's house, and her sister is there, I know that is nothing but trouble. I am sure my name has been pulled through the mud. If I call, I would have to listen to her mother and sister scold me, and I am really not trying to hear their mouths right now. I will just sit here on the couch until she gets home, then apologize.*

After a couple hours, Jon ended up falling asleep on the couch. April entered the home quietly, and took her shoes off at the door. She looked at Jon sleeping on the couch, and shook her head. As she skipped up the stairs, she let out an exhilarated "Whoo hoo" as she was still riding the excitement from her night.

A groggy Jon woke up when he heard the sound and sat upright in an attempt to adjust his eyes. He thought he saw April dancing up the stairs, but after a few seconds he laid back down assuming it was just a dream.

Caliente

April was so upset and hurt that she left the house and drove off without her purse. Her eyes became wet as her car radio played the slow song CD that Jon prepared for her. April placed it in her player earlier that day when she was grocery shopping to get herself in the mood. As she winded through the neighborhood trying to see through her water stained eyes, something snapped and her brain went to a special place. *You know what, I don't even care anymore. This boy doesn't care, and I don't know what is going on in his head. I need to start taking care of me. Here I am all dressed and cute, I have slaved in that kitchen all day, and all I want is a few minutes to enjoy with my husband and he says no? I am about to go right down to this class by myself, flirt, and have myself a good time regardless.*

April encouraged herself to go to the class alone. After a few minutes, she arrived at the facility. She walked to the door and saw all the couples inside. *This is a mistake. Look at all these couples. I need to go.* No sooner than she turned around, she was greeted by a handsome Latin man in his late 20s.

"You're not leaving on me, are you?"

"And you would be?"

"I am the instructor, Isaias. And what is your name?"

"This is a mistake. Look at all these loving couples here. My partner chose not to come, and I thought…"

"Hey, no use driving all the way home now. You made the effort to come out here, so enjoy the class. I tell you what…how about letting me be your partner tonight?"

April looked the young man over. *He is a little cutie pie. I shouldn't but hey, Jon should have come with me tonight. I might as well enjoy myself.*

"Well, I did have my mind set on coming tonight. But you have to teach the class, and I don't want to distract you.

"You will not distract me. Trust me."

"You sure you won't mind?"

"A beautiful lady like yourself? Why would I mind? What was your name again?"

"April"

"April. A beautiful name for a beautiful woman. Did you know that the name April has Latin origins?"

April smiled in a flirtatious manner. "No, I did not know that."

"It means to open. They named the month *April* because in spring, that is when flowers bud, or open. I tell you what. I will be your partner tonight, but you have to promise me one thing. Promise me that you will let your inhibitions go and open up to me tonight?"

April responded by blushing, then allowed the instructor to hold her hand as he walked her into the classroom. When they entered the room, the combination of the brass instruments, cowbell, bongos, timbales and Congo drums set the mood and subconsciously April began to move her hips and get into the rhythm. She loved the attention the instructor gave her, and she stood to the side and watched while he started the class.

"Welcome to Salsa For Beginners. My name is Isaias and I will be your instructor this evening. As many of you know, Salsa dancing is very sexy, and exciting. It is a combination of Latin and Afro-Caribbean rhythms; therefore you will find variations from region to region."

April enjoyed learning something new, and liked the charisma the instructor had. He was very patient, and April picked up on the moves quick. During one of the steps, Isaias looked directly in April's eyes and in his exotic broken English stated, "Wow, you don't need beginner class, you need to come back for advanced. My Latin flower, you are blooming."

April smiled as the instructor twirled and gyrated and allowed her to temporarily forget about her problems at home.

After the class dispersed, April was the last to leave as Isaias began to teach her some advanced moves.

"You know April, you are very good for a beginner. In the 3 years I taught this class, I have never seen anyone pick up on the moves that fast. I hope that I will see you in more classes. Maybe you can even help me teach these classes one day."

"You are a very sweet man Isaias. Thank you for being my partner."

"No problem beautiful. You bring your husband next time?"

April was glowing so much that she temporarily forgot she was married. She came down from her cloud when Isaias mentioned Jon.

"Only time will tell. Who knows with him?"

"Let me pack up, and I will walk you to your car. It is dark out there, and no woman should have to walk out there alone."

April allowed the young man to escort her to her vehicle. When they arrived at her car, he walked up on April and attempted to hug her. April was caught off guard, but since she didn't see any harm, there was no resistance on her end. Their bodies had been on each other all night dancing, so there was a familiarity there. While holding on to her, Isaias allowed his lips to graze her cheek and follow her jaw line towards the corner of her mouth. April felt he was attempting to kiss her so she pushed him away.

"Isaias, no. I am married, remember."

"I am so sorry. I was just captivated by your beauty. Hey, I know a nice Latin club. The night is still young. What do you say?"

April paused as she seriously pondered going out with the young man. *No April, you need to go home. You are already weak and mad. You do not need anything else to tempt you to act up. If you continue to be around him, you are just asking for trouble. Just go home!*

"As much fun as that sounds Isaias, I can't. Out of respect for my husband, that would not be right."

Isaias put his head down in disappointment. "I understand. I will see you again, right?"

"Like I said, we will see. Thank you for tonight. I needed it."

April shut the door to car, and smiled. She was flattered she was being pursued by this young gentleman. She started the car and proceeded to drive home. Back drenched with sweat, April knew that she was dehydrated and needed some fluids. Since she left her purse at home, she rummaged through the ash tray for some loose change, and found a $10 that Jon left in there. He folded it and hid it under her change. Jon had a habit of going in her car without her knowing and leaving money in her ash tray. He always told her that it is wise to stash money in various places just in case you lose your wallet or purse. April smiled thinking of the thoughtfulness of her husband, and was glad she didn't go out dancing with the instructor. She pulled into a gas station to purchase a juice, then continued home.

When April arrived home, she attempted to not wake her spouse, so she removed her shoes at the door. She looked over at Jon sleeping on the couch, and shook her head. One of the rhythms was still in her head, and as she walked up the stairs, her adrenaline motivated her to perform some new moves she learned. As she skipped up the stairs dancing, she let out an exhilarated "Whoo hoo" as she was still riding the excitement from her night.

April had a wonderful night, but once her high wore off in the shower, she regretted her husband was not there to experience it with her. *I wish my baby was there, but oh well.*

After her shower, she crawled into bed with a smile on her face and allowed her exhausted body to rest.

CHAPTER ELEVEN

Baseball

Flirt

It was a Saturday, and the Carter's were running late for Jon Jr.'s baseball game. Junior had been playing in this league for a couple years now, and it had become one of the few times the family would come together, outside of watching television and church. Sometimes April and Jon's friends would come to support their kids as well.

"April, are you ready yet? Come on."

"I just have to do my hair."

"You had all morning to do your hair. Girl, just put a hat on. It is a baseball game. You already cute."

"I am not a man. I can't just splash water on my face and go. All you see here takes time. It doesn't come pre-assembled."

Jon was becoming frustrated with April and the time it was taking for her to get ready.

"Ape, you have 10 minutes."

"Ten minutes? Whatever. If it is that serious, just go and I will drive there myself. We have two vehicles. As a matter of fact, just do that. Go, and I will take Jordan and go pick my mom up."

Jon walked out irate that April took up so much time. He grabbed his son's equipment, loaded the truck, and peeled out the driveway.

* * * * *

Time passed, and April finally arrived at the game. She went and sat next to her sister and mother. She recognized Jassmine across the bleachers and waved for her to come sit by them. Jassmine saw Alicia and really didn't want to be bothered, so she sent April a text message - *I am waiting for someone. I will give him until the 4th inning, and if no show I will come down.*

April responded back - *Ok girl.*

While Jassmine was reading April's response, Gordon walked up behind her.

"Hey, what's up sexy? Didn't expect to see you here."

"Boy please, what do you want?"

"Why you acting like that? Would you mind if I sat here, or were you waiting for someone?"

"Free country. Be my guest. Just don't try nothing. I know what you are about Gordon."

"What's that supposed to mean?"

"Means what I said boy."

"Well, I know what you about too. And trust me, I am no boy."

"Whatever. G can you leave me alone, I am trying to watch my godson."

"Well don't forget he is my godson too Jazz," Gordon responded in a contemptuous tone.

"How can I forget? Every time I buy him something, his godfather comes behind and tries to buy something bigger. Napoleon complex maybe?"

"Get your mind out the gutter. I just love him, and want to spoil him." Gordon pulled out his cell phone which was vibrating, checked the caller ID display, then slid his phone back into his pocket.

Jassmine rolled her eyes, then after a fifteen second silence she blurted out, "One of your little hoochies, huh?"

"What does it matter? You said I wasn't about anything, right? Besides, you told me to leave you alone and watch the game, so that is what I am trying to do."

"Oh, did I hurt babyboy's feelings?"

"Jazz, let's cut to the chase. I know you want me, and that is perfectly ok. We are both adults, and both have needs. No need for us to play games."

"Oh my. Where this courage come from? Boy have you forgotten I am married?"

"First of all, stop calling me a boy. Second, what is your man doing for you that I can't do?"

"What is he doing? I should be asking you what you could do for me. You can't even afford to get my car detailed. Trust me, I am out of your league."

"Well, that is an opinion. You know sometimes men from the minors get pulled up to the majors. It is all about what kind of game you put on that night. So how about this. I cook dinner this evening, and you cover breakfast in the morning. If you don't like what I give, then I will issue a refund."

"Wow, I have heard some bad pickup lines, but you? You are a plethora of foolishness. I'm speechless. All I can say is that you are really trying. Have to at least give you a C - minus for effort."

"C- minus? That's not barely college credit. See, now I have to go to the vaults."

Gordon scooted closer to Jassmine. His lips were close enough to her ear that it tickled the little hairs on her neck. He spoke in a voice slightly above a whisper as he proceeded to recite his one-liner serenade.

"Did the sun come out, or did you just smile at me? Since I am new to the country and you are the prettiest site I have seen thus far, can I tour your body? I melt in your mouth, not in your hand. I lost my bed, can I borrow yours? Do you have a quarter? My mother told me to call home when I meet the girl of my dreams. Why don't you come sit on my lap and we can talk about the first thing that pops up. If you were a tear in my eye, I wouldn't cry for fear of losing you. I'd like to name a multiple orgasm after you. I think your clothes would look good in a crumpled pile on the floor next to my California queen. Want to go half on a baby?"

"Boy stop," Jassmine chuckled.

"Want me to stop? I can keep going. I got lines for days."

"No please don't. Spare me. Are times that bad where females actually fall for those lines? I can't believe those actually work."

"You know I was just joking with you. I am not that cheesy…I heard them on this comedy show I was watching. Seriously though, you know we have chemistry. We are cut from the same branch. I think you know that I am wild enough to tame you. If you ever need to have that urge satisfied, you know how to reach me."

Jassmine stared at Gordon with a smirk, and allowed her mind to entertain the thought of the possibility of a relationship with him. "Like I said, I am watching the game. Please change the subject, or stop talking to me all together."

Gordon knew his words sunk in, so he smiled and turned his attention back to the game. Time passed and Gordon ceased his pursuit of Jassmine.

"Jazz, do you want something from the concession stand?"

"No thank you."

Gordon walked away, and Jassmine continued to watch the game. Soon as he was out of sight, she gathered her belongings. *This is my chance to move. I am going to use the restroom, then change my seats.*

While in route to the lavatory, she saw Gordon speaking with a young boy. She discretely stood around the corner to satisfy her curiosity.

"So why are you crying lil' man?"

"I lost my money pouch. My mom allowed me to come to the game, and she gave me money go get us food, and bus fare home. Now I have no way home, and I can't reach her at work. My mom works real hard. Even if I reached her, she can't afford to lose any days at work."

"Us?" Gordon asked.

"Yes, us. Me and my two younger brothers. They out there watching the game."

Gordon admired how responsible and considerate this child was of his mother's provision.

"Stay right here son. I will be right back."

There was innocence about this young boy that touched Gordon's heart. He walked to the concession stand, purchased three hotdogs, 3 slices of pizza, 3 fries, 3 Icee's, then walked the boxed items over to the young boy. "I would give you a ride, but I am sure that your mom taught you not to go anywhere with strangers, so here goes $20. This should cover your way home. I also have some snacks for you and your brothers. Here you go."

As the young boy reached to accept the box from Gordon, his eyes began to tear again.

"Thank you so much sir. You don't understand how much this means to me. I was not expecting this at all. I don't know how I could ever repay you."

"I tell you how you repay me. When you get to be my age, you help someone else out the same way. Look, I tell you what. Here is my business card. Tell your mom to call me, and I will send all you guys to the Wrigley Field. My treat. She appears to work hard, so I think it would be a good get away for you guys."

Gordon handed the card to the young boy and tears began to stream down his face.

"Are you ok lil' man? What's the matter? You should be cool now."

"Sir, you just don't know what you did."

"Oh, it was no problem. I am sure you would do the same thing if you were in my shoes."

"No, you need to know how much of a blessing you are. You see, our family doesn't have much money. Our dad died after my younger brother was born, so we have been struggling ever since. I cut grass, or do whatever I can to try to bring some extra money in. My mother never gets to do anything with us, and her sending us to these games is her way of treating us. The thing is, she never does anything for herself. Most of the time when she sends us here, she will skip her lunch at work. She always sacrifices to provide for her family. Well last night I prayed for something to happen. I prayed that God will bless my mommy to have lunch, and that one day we would be able to take her to a real baseball game. I prayed for a day where money wouldn't matter, and we could just go to the game as a family and see my mother smile. I prayed so much, and it seemed like God was never listening. I can't explain it this time, but it felt different after I prayed. Then today I lost that money, and thought about my mom…then I met you… I'm sorry, but I am just very overwhelmed at this moment. I thank you so much!"

"Son, you are very wise beyond your years, and have a good heart. I love how unselfish you are, and your desire to take care of your family. You make sure that you be safe going home. And hey, make sure you don't lose my card."

"Oh don't worry mister. I won't lose this!"

Jassmine watched and smiled as she saw a different side of Gordon. She walked around the corner and began to softly clap.

"That was sweet of you G."

Gordon was alarmed to see Jassmine. "Oh, you weren't supposed to see that. Now you can't tell anyone about this. You know I have a reputation."

"Gordon, stop being silly. You know, sometimes you are a sweetheart. You just mask it with ignorance. It is like you have this fence built around you. Like you have this façade you put up to try to conceal who you really are. Appears that you have been hurt before and you try to put up this guard."

"You know Jazz, I could say the same thing for you."

Jassmine was not expecting that response, so she paused before responding, "You know what, you are right. That is how I recognized it. I will be honest with you, that side of Gordon I could fall for."

"Well let me be honest with you as well Jassmine. Don't get me wrong, I am attracted to you, and given the right circumstance, whew. But if I am honest with myself, I think the main reason I pursue you is because you are something I can't have. I tease a lot, but if you were to ever give me the time, I'd probably run. I do have boundaries. I never mess with married women."

Gordon telling Jazz he was no longer interested sparked her interest. "We will see about that," she thought.

"Look, I am going to try to find April. I told her I would go sit by her."

"That is cool. I need to find Jon as well. Hey, it was nice running into you. Look forward to seeing you again."

"You too G."

Thirsty

Jon couldn't locate April at the game, so he ended up sitting near the dugout. After a few innings, he received a text message from April – *Meet me by the concession stand. I am thirsty.*

As instructed, Jon immediately went to meet his wife. He approached the concession stand and walked behind April.

"What you want to drink?"

"Well hi to you too. I know you aren't still mad about this morning?"

"It is deeper than that April. Look, I am missing the game. It is almost over. We can do this at home. What you want baby?"

"Don't baby me. I swear sometimes you talk to me like I am stupid."

"I don't mean to April, I am just trying to make sure I don't miss our son playing on account of us arguing. We can argue at home."

"Just get me whatever. I don't even care anymore. I just wanted to see you and I was going to tell you I was sorry, but forget it now."

"That's great April. Very grown up."

"You know, if there weren't kids around…nevermind, I will just keep my mouth shut."

"Say what you got to say. Not like these kids never heard it before."

"J, I tell you sometimes…"

Mid sentence April was distracted when she looked over and saw Jassmine and Gordon talking, and apparently flirting with one another.

"J, look at that."

April and Jon looked over and saw their friends body mannerisms favoring one another.

"Oh hecks no. I know they didn't…"

"Let's just hope they didn't J. You need to talk to your boy."

"You need to talk to your girl!"

Jon looked over and made contact with Gordon, and waved him over. April walked away as Gordon approached.

"Hey April."

"Bye Gordon."

"What's up J?" Gordon's tone suggested he was in a playful mood. The two clasped hands, and gave each other a one-armed hug. "What was up with April? Did I do something?"

"Who knows. Don't take it personal. Bro, I know you…and Jazz? Please tell me you aren't messing with that woman."

"Naw man, not at all. We were just talking. And she ain't that bad man. You just need to know her."

"Stay away from her Gordon. Nothing but trouble."

"Man, enough of Jazz. What's up with you and April? Why she roll her eyes at you like that? Or was she rolling her eyes at me?"

"Man, I don't know G. Probably both. We got into it again today."

"What happened this time?"

"Bro, her just being a woman. I just don't understand women sometimes. They know we have to be somewhere at a set time, and seems like they still can't get ready in time. Little J almost missed the bus over here because she was sitting there trying to be cute. What makes it so bad is after she makes us late, then tells us we can go on without her. Like if you knew that before, why didn't you just say that? She already knew she wanted to go pick her mom up and ride solo, so why did she play around all morning?"

"Bro, I don't have any good advice for you. You know me. I say you have two options. A, you suck it up and try to make it work. Or 2, you find you a piece on the side."

"A or 2? I thought it was supposed to be A or B?"

"Well, you know I have family from Arkansas. Blame it on first cousins. You know they can smell fresh DNA there. Had a flight out of there before, and they had two terminals; A and 2."

Jon burst into laughter.

"Boy you got no sense whatsoever. Thanks. Sometimes laughter is the only thing that gets me through some of these days."

I know I shouldn't be listening to Gordon since he is always talking about stepping out, but he is funny to me. It is like when I hang out with him and my friends, the humor helps me through these hard times. A male bonding type thing I suppose. My marriage has this open wound, and laughter sometimes is the only anesthesia which temporarily numbs the pain. The problem is this provides a temporary solution. I don't need a band-aid, I need our wounds to be sutured.

Friends Like You

After getting into the small argument with Jon at the concession stand, April went to talk with her girlfriend Jassmine.

"Hey April. What's good girl?"

"So is that who you were waiting for? Gordon?"

"Just leave it alone April. It was not like that."

"What did that old tired pimp want?"

"Nothing."

"Jazz, please don't sleep with him. You only asking…"

"I am a grown woman April. Trust me, I can handle myself."

"Just watch out for him."

"It was not like that April. We were just talking. And furthermore, I think you have enough trouble of your own than to be worrying about Gordon and myself."

April didn't appreciate Jassmine's words, but she knew they were the truth.

"You are right."

"What is up with you and your man? Why aren't y'all sitting by one another? What was that little spat about?"

"Spat?"

"I saw how you just looked at him. Something is going on between you two."

"J has been acting really simple. I don't know what got into that man lately, but he has just changed."

"Well, you know where I stand on that. Hey, not to change the subject, but you know Charles is in town, right."

"Yes, please don't remind me."

"Oh, so he came by to see you already?"

"You knew, huh? I bet you set it up."

"I would never," Jassmine said with a devious grin. "I just wondered how it went with you guys?"

"It went. Nothing more to say about it. I am a married woman, and that was the past. Please don't bring this up around Jon, or anyone else for that manner."

"Girl, you know me. I will go to my grave with one million secrets. I know how to keep my mouth shut. Hey, I just want to put this out there. If you ever get that urge, and you need an alibi, you know I am here for you."

"Thanks Jazz. What would I do if I didn't have a friend like you? A woman who, during a weak time in my marriage, tells me she will be my alibi. If I need a body hid, she will help me to bury it and hide the evidence. That's why we have been cool for so many years."

"Hey, what are friends for?"

April shook her head. "Girl, you are a mess. You know I am not even built like that. So enough of that. Are you going to come sit by us? Alicia won't bother you. She is actually in a good mood today."

"I would love to, but I have to run. My old man has something special planned for me tonight. Then tomorrow we are flying out to LA, so I have to buy some new clothes so I can look sharp."

"Well have fun."

"I will try. Kiss Junior and tell him Auntie Jazz enjoyed watching him hit the ball."

"Ok girl. You take care."

April hugged her friend, and retreated back to her seat next to her mother and sister. She tried to shrug off what Jassmine said, but her need for attention opened her mind to the possibility of a tryst.

Trust

Doubt

Years ago when Jon got into trouble by assaulting the man raping his sister, the arresting officer advised that his cousin Gary was looking for a new foreman. Jon didn't realize it at the time, but Gary was also Gordon's uncle. He contacted Gary a few days afterwards and immediately received favor and was offered a position on the spot. Over the next few years, Gary was Jon's mentor in construction, and often times they would discuss personal matters.

"J, when I was your age, man I had all the women. You want to know a sure fire way to break the ice with a new woman?"

"Not that I have any reason to use it since I am a happily married man, but go ahead and tell me."

"The best way to initiate a conversation with a woman is to have a puppy. Chicks dig puppies, young blood. It never failed when I had a puppy, I would come home with a pocket full of numbers. Now I knew this years ago, but there are actually studies out now that show a higher percentage of women would be willing to spark a conversation with a man with a puppy, than without."

"I am sure you get your statistics from a reliable source," Jon laughed. "Ok genius, what do you do when the puppy grows up?"

"Man, do I have to spell everything out for you? You sell it, and buy another stupid."

"You have absolutely no sense whatsoever. Just like your nephew."

"On a serious note, J you remember that one broad that we saw when we had that contract bid back in June last year?"

"Vaguely. It was a retirement community, right?"

"Yes, but she was no old woman. Well, long story short, I seen her at the gas station. I offered to buy her a drink at the local bar. After a few drinks, we went to the hotel and I put something on that woman."

Jon knew that this was not the best person to seek advice from, but something about this adulterous co-worker offered Jon a shoulder to confidently place his indiscretions on.

"You keep messing around like that, one day the old lady is going to find you and we'll be watching you on the news carried out on a stretcher."

After sitting in silence for a second, Jon decided to share personal information with Gary.

"All jokes aside, can I tell you something in confidence?"

"Yea man, sure."

"I was at the diner the other week, and I met this young lady. Man, she is something else. I feel bad…almost like I am cheating on April."

"I am going to tell you like I told my nephew when he got married. He had that girl up in that house all alone, and thought she didn't have company. You can't leave a female alone. You see when Adam left Eve alone in the garden, she got into trouble."

"What in the world are you talking about Gary?"

"Look youngen. Don't take this the wrong way, but you actually trust April? One thing I have learned in life is that women can be so manipulative. They make us feel like we are king of our own domain, then come to find out they are making another man feel the same way. And they are so slick about it because women learned the fine art of keeping their mouth shut."

"Now I see where Gordon gets it from. Trust me, April is not out there like that."

"Maybe not. All I am saying is just keep your eyes and options open. You never know until it hits the fan. Ask Gordon. He almost lost everything. Hell, he had to even sell his bike because the alimony and child support was raping his check to the point he could only afford Ramen Noodles. If he would have listened to me, and just stayed with her and kept some on the side, everything would have been cool. Hey, it's the American dream. Look boy, you have a fine young woman basically throwing herself at you. When we were younger, our mission was to pull down panties. Now women are pulling them down for us. Take advantage man. Take advantage. I know I would. Nobody knows but you, her, and I…and you know I am not saying nothing."

"You been married longer than me. What kind of advice is that for a young brotha trying to keep it together? You are a mess." Jon paused as he attempted to filter what Gary told him. "Besides, what would a young woman like her want in someone like me anyways? I am just entertainment. Something to pass the time."

"You know, my father used to tell me that a woman sizes a man up within the first 15 minutes. Within those minutes, she has already made up her mind whether or not she is going to give it up or not. It is just up to us to not say something stupid."

Jon didn't want to laugh, but he couldn't help himself. "Man, you need to stop."

"I wasn't trying to be funny J. I am telling you, you have to play the game. Let me share some wisdom youngen. Now we all hear the rumors of women faking."

"Rumors?"

"Yes rumors. I refuse to believe it," he stated as he chuckled. "No seriously, we all know women fake, but few women realize that men fake as well"

"Man, what are you talking about?"

"You know, fake. How we exaggerate when they are doing things for us. Give them a growl, or cuss and tell them how good it is. The things we say to pump their heads up to make them think it is better than it really is so we can get off. I tell you, if you make a women feel like she is the best ever, the sky is the limit. That is the key son."

"I suppose. You have the game completely figured out, huh?"

"Son you don't get to be this age and not learn a few tricks along the way. See you young boys are caught up in the myth that you are doing something. After I seen my wife deliver my kids, I realized I wasn't doing anything at all. So I went back to the lab, and studied women so that I could teach young knuckleheads like you and Gordon. You see, it is important that we, as men, understand women. I will give you a tidbit, but the rest will cost you."

"Well thank you for the coupon," Jon stated while laughing.

"See growing up, some women intimidate us because of their looks. You know how it is natural for us to fear rejection. Well there are two little secrets most men don't know. The first secret is confidence is sexy. Not arrogance, but confidence. There is a big difference and I don't have time to cover it.

"The second secret, and this is one of the most important points so take notes. Regardless of how they look, most women have low self-esteem. Even the fine ones J. Just look at that Girls Gone Crazy or whatever that thing is called. Not saying they are fine since they are minors, but listen to what I am saying. Those women are just screaming for attention and validation. Women like that don't know their worth, so I exploit it and use it for my gain. That is why I truly believe that any man, given the right circumstances and saying the right words, could be with any female. Why do you think you see all these ugly men with these fine women? They understand the game."

"So life is a game, huh? That was all cool in high school, but we are adults now. Heck, you are dag on near a senior. Isn't there a point where you say enough, and are ready to grow up? I mean seriously, women are crazy these days. You can't sleep around with every woman you see. Women will kill you nowadays. Wake up with a knife wedged into the passenger seat of your car…or worse."

"That is spoken like it came from experience. Look, you can't fear that youngen. You have to put the law down. Let a woman know you mean business."

"Thanks for the enlightenment. I never knew that," Jon said while teasing Gary. "Seriously though, can I ask you a personal question?"

"Rap with me youngen. What's up?"

"What happened with you and your old lady? I mean, what happened that made you just not care anymore?"

"Who says I don't care? I care J, it is just a lot to the story."

"I understand if you don't want to share. That is cool."

"No, it is not that." Gary took his steel toe boot off, and began massaging his foot. "Jon, one thing you need to learn about women is they never get over their old boyfriends."

"Why do you say that? I think I would have to argue that. I believe they can sever ties."

"See Jon, that is what I mean about your generation. So naive. You let your pride block any ability to see that your woman could be tied to another man. Women are twisted my man. Even since grade school, women are wrong. They either go for the older guys, or the men who treat them like dirt; meanwhile the good guy sits on the sideline and gets stepped on, walked over, and cheated on. Women will always think about their ex boyfriends. As soon as things get tough in the marriage, their minds wander to how life would be if they chose the other man."

"Sounds like there is a story behind that. You going to elaborate?"

"My daughter went out and bought us one of those Bell computers. Bell, Hell, whatever they are called. I never use the thing because computers are just stupid to me, but my wife does to communicate with the kids and sell her perfume. One day my daughter called me and said she e-mailed me some photos of my grandkids, so she walked me through using that dag on computer. Long story short, my old lady didn't log out. I believe that is what they called it; login or logout. Whatever she was supposed to do, she didn't and…well let's just say I caught her e-mailing her ex boyfriend. She had been speaking with this fool for months. I never said anything; I just ignored it and did my thing."

"Why didn't you say anything? It is not like you to keep quiet."

"Son, there are only two things a man needs in life. Three if he wants to be happy. Food, sex, and sports. As long as those needs of mine are met, I really don't care about too much else."

"Naw man, there is more to life than that. Marriage shouldn't have to be like that."

"Well Jon, you have all the answers so you tell me."

"I didn't say I had all the answers Gary, I just refuse to believe life, or marriage, has to be stereotypical ball and chain. There has to be a formula to a good marriage, we just haven't figured it out."

"There is no formula, this is life. The only formula is trying to understand the chemical imbalances of women, and how to co-exist with them."

"Since I am young and don't know any better, humor me and tell me what women need."

"To be honest Jon, if I knew that, then I would win the game. That is what I am still in search of. You see, I always thought that women need two things in life; security and comfort. Provide them with comfort, and stability and you good to go. The problem is I provided her with this, and she still chose to look outside."

"Bro, that is tough. I don't know what to say on that one. You know, you should check out my church. We have this real good men's ministry, and we sit there and have real talk like this. Well, maybe not so explicit, but it is not like how church used to be. There is a new movement where people are being real. What are you doing this Sunday? Want to come to church with us? I am sure your wife will like it as well."

"I would, but you know the Bears are playing my Dolphins. Not to mention, your pastor is longwinded."

"You can TIVO that game man. You should come check us out. You might get something out of it."

"Now you sound like my old lady. Hell, I can TIVO church. That way I can fast forward when he is asking for money, and pause when the camera passes a hot, single, desperate young lady. You know church girls are the some of the wildest in bed."

"Man, there is so much more to service than women."

"Like what? Don't get me wrong. I am no atheist and I don't believe in evolution. I believe in a God, and a higher calling or power or whatnot, but as far as church goes I just don't see the point. Half the people there go for tradition, or because their grandparents went there. Others go because they are brainwashed into putting money in the pastor's pocket. Plus, half those women at your church are the ones I see at the bar on the weekends."

"Don't generalize and say that man. We all fall short bro…you included. You can't judge a body of believers based off a few members. There are tons of people in the world that claim to be Christian, and have never picked a Bible up in their life. Your comment is like saying you won't buy a particular car model because you knew one person who had problems with it. You never read the manual, you never checked out the manufacturer, you never opened your eyes to the good reviews…but you just automatically assumed, based off that one incident, that they all must be bad."

"I think you are missing my point Jon. I am not saying all people in church are bad, but the reality is most are hypocrites. I just don't believe in organized religion, so why should I waste my time going?"

"Because it is not about *religion* man, it is about your *relationship*. We can talk all day about who did what in the church, but all that is irrelevant. When the dust settles at the end of the day, you are responsible for you. Their actions have absolutely nothing to do with your salvation. If you rob a bank and get caught, you can't turn and tell the cops that you did it because you saw Jesse James do it. The police will hold you accountable for your own actions, not what Jesse James did. Look, I am not trying to preach to you, all I am saying is that you can't let some bad experiences you had build a fortress of pride and deter you from forming a relationship with Christ."

"And where has your relationship got you? If it is working, why isn't it helping your marriage? Why are you even thinking about that young lady if you are really getting something out of that church you go to?"

"It is deeper than that Gary. I am trying to do right, and I am by no means a saint. I have a desire to do right, but sometimes…I just can't explain." Jon stood up to end the conversation. "The invitation still stands. Call me if you change your mind."

Jon walked away, and let his words sink in. *Why is it I feel so blessed in some areas of life, and in others it seems like God is ignoring the caller id when I call? I try to seek advice, but it seems no one around me understands. Everyone around me is from where I used to be, versus where I want to be going. This period of time hurts, and it is extremely stressful and frustrating.*

Insecurity

April wanted Tiffani to meet her family. Unfortunately Jon couldn't make it due to work obligations. They met at Dave and Busters so the kids could play.

"Tiffani, how is your uncle?"

"Not good. I don't want to talk about him. Can we talk about something positive? Your kids are so adorable. You have such a beautiful family. I wish I could have met Jon. You landed a man that even works on Saturday's. You did well for yourself. I am lucky to land a man that works at all."

"Thank you. I know I am blessed. My children are healthy, and I have a husband. I know some women would kill, literally, to have a man; and he does work very hard." April gave her children some change, and instructed them to go over to the arcade so she and Tiffani could engage in an adult conversation.

After the kids ran off, April looked down at her plate deep in thought. She used her fork to play hockey with the croutons from her salad. "Tiff, I try not to take that man for granted, but my marriage has been on the rocks for some time. He has been so distant. I don't know."

"Guilty are we?"

"Guilty?"

"Yes guilty. I heard Charles is back in town. Rumor is he is doing quite well for himself. You guys hook up?"

"Charles?"

"Girl, stop playing dumb. I know he found you. I don't know what kind of hold you have over him. And vice versa."

"He just came in to say hi. Besides, I love Jon. Charlie was old luggage. This has nothing to do with him. I just don't know what is going on with Jon. Sometimes I just wonder if there is someone else. I am almost looking for any excuse to leave."

Tiffani began to give April advice, but April didn't hear her because she was busy tossing thoughts back and forth in her head. *Just ask her. No April, that is psycho. Don't do that. But girl if you don't ask, you will never know. No,*

I can't. I don't know what to do. Oh forget it.

After a minute or so of rationalizing, April blurted out, "I need a favor."

"A favor?"

"Yes, a favor. And I wouldn't ask you unless I really needed you."

"April, what?"

"Monday morning, go down to the job site, ask for Jon, and flirt with him. Tell me how he reacts. He has heard of you, but never seen you before. Just use an alias name."

"What? Girl, are you crazy? I don't feel comfortable doing this April. Plus, I don't even know what he looks like."

"Just ask for him. Look, I am not asking you to sleep with him. Just hit on him, and tell me how his mannerisms are. Please. I need this. I have to know."

"I don't think this is a good idea April. Most men flirt, that is a given. What would this prove?"

"That may be the case, but I am interested in how he handles himself. I need to know if I can trust him or not."

"Girl, if it is that serious, why not hire a P.I.?"

"I don't want to go overboard and get more people involved into this than necessary. Girl please. You the only person I can trust with this."

Tiffani wanted to appear like she was not eager, so waited before she agreed. "I don't know if this is a good idea, but I will do it for you."

Just Like Daddy

Monday came, and April was nervous all day anticipating Tiffani's report. She arrived home from work, and saw Jon sleeping on the couch. *Wonder why he is home earlier than usual? I always beat him home. And why is he sleep?* Not realizing the pain she felt was transference from her relationship with her father, she immediately became upset.

Trying not to make a scene over it, April walked into the kitchen, and put the tea kettle on to boil. As the water was heating, she went on the back porch to call Tiffani. The phone rang, and went straight to voicemail. About this time, paranoia was settling in. *Where is this chick?* No sooner than she grabbed her phone to try Tiffani again, her cell phone rang. Before she could check the display, she anxiously answered.

"This is April"

There was no response, but April heard a faint sniffle on the other end.

"Hello. Is anybody there?"

Immediately Tiffani began apologizing.

"I am so so sorry April. I didn't mean for it to happen."

"Didn't mean for what to happen? What are you talking about?"

"Please don't be mad at me. I slept with Jon. I didn't mean this to happen…"

"April hung up and dropped her phone in disbelief. Her heart fell into her stomach. She saw the image of Jon sleep on the couch, and she immediately thought about her father. Rage consumed her, but she wanted a confirmation first. Deep down inside, she didn't want to believe it, and was hoping to find some evidence to exonerate her husband. In an attempt to gather this information, she picked up the phone, and called the construction company Jon works for.

"Is Jon there?"

"No, he has been gone all day. He had an errand to run or something."

The guy who answered the phone snickered after he made his remark. This immediately made April see red. She calmly prepared her a cup of tea, and sat down at the kitchen table as her hand trembled from bad nerves. After 5 minutes of trying to absorb the situation, she walked into the living room, and tossed her remaining cup of tea on Jon. Awaken by the hot tea, Jon jumped up and screamed with a deep baritone lion roar.

"What is your problem?"

"You screwed Tiffani? My best friend?"

"Tiffani? Who in the world is Tiffani? Ouch. Dag gone it what is wrong with you?"

"Don't play stupid with me."

"Girl, calm down. What in the world are you talking about?"

"How did you do it? Huh? Speak up! Why? What was it about her? Why did you do this to me?"

"I have no clue what you are talking about, but I tell you if you ever throw anything hot on me again…"

"You were not at work today."

"And?"

April walked up and poked Jon in the chest with her index finger, "And where were you?"

Jon laughed in a mildly insane manner as he took off his shirt, and blotted dry the tea which splattered on his jeans.

"Oh, so it is funny? What is so funny Jon?"

"Whew, I am trying to laugh this situation off before I do something stupid. You threw some tea on me because I was not at work?"

"You already did something stupid. Now I am going to give you one more chance to come clean. What did you do today?"

"Look, I took off today to help your mom out. I was repairing her back patio. I was there all day from 8am until 4pm. She even made me lunch with her fine self; leftover chicken casserole. I see why your dad kept getting her pregnant, but I assure you we are not sleeping together. I wish sometimes, but we aren't."

"Stop trying to be funny."

"Call her Ape. Better yet, give me the phone." Jon grabbed the phone, and dialed the number. April spoke with her mom, and she confirmed Jon's story. April was still confused, and felt betrayed. Not knowing what was going on, she called Tiffani back.

"Tiff, this is April. What happened today?"

"April, I am so sorry. It just happened. I went down to the site, and asked for him. He was on his way to lunch. We had too many drinks, and it just happened. But listen, he is still sleep if you want to come catch him in the act."

"Catch him?" April hung up. *This heifer has some nerve.* April laid her phone on the coffee table, covered her face, and fell back on the couch crying. When she confessed to Jon what she did, he hit the roof.

"So you had a woman try to seduce me? All I have done for you and this family, and you do this? I haven't given you any reason to think that I am stepping out. What has gotten into you lately?"

April pleaded for forgiveness. After the dust settled, Jon realized what happened.

"Baby, you said Tiffani said the guy was there now, right?"

"Yea, she said that Jon is here if you want to come bust him out."

Jon began to chuckle.

"What is so funny?"

"There is another John at the site. He was the one I told you about a while back. We used to hang out back in the day, but he just started getting on my nerves. He is always in someone's business. Short, bald and chunky guy. So your friend gave him some? Wow. Times must be pretty hard for her."

"Yes. Some friends I have. Regardless of who she slept with, the point is she thought he was you! I can't believe that slut tried to sleep with my husband."

"I think this is a sign. Maybe we need to reassess the people we hang around."

"Maybe we do baby. Maybe we do."

"I am so sorry Jon. Let me clean you up."

April and Jon hugged and kissed, but it was dry and emotionless. Later on that evening the couple sat down and watched a movie together for the first time in months. Jon replayed the events that happened earlier that day, and was hurt deep inside that April didn't trust him. *I never gave this woman reason to be insecure. Why is she acting like this?*

Even though they were civil for the remainder of the night, there was still unrest between the two. This incident didn't help their relationship, but rather acted as a catalyst for a series of events that began to erode their marriage.

CHAPTER THIRTEEN

Black Ice

Through Jon's Eyes

It was a Wednesday when Carmen walked into the diner. By her mannerisms, I could tell she was distraught. I positioned myself to be the shoulder she could cry on.

"What is wrong Carmen?"

"I messed up big time. I can't believe I screwed it up."

"Screwed what up? You are too hard on yourself. It can't be that bad."

"I didn't have the right documents in to the attorney, and because of me, this poor guy may not get custody of his son."

I did not know how to react to Carmen, so in an attempt to comfort her, I moved from my side of the booth, sat next to her, then placed my arm around her shoulder.

"It will be ok. Trust me."

This gesture had become common with us. Through time, we became more comfortable and our lunches ended with hugs. Conversation between us definitely grew to be more personal and intimate. We were becoming relaxed in each other's presence. So much, in fact, that sometimes the patrons often mistook us for a couple. The way things were going with April, sometimes I didn't even care. Carmen seemed to appreciate me.

"Enough of me and my drama, tell me about you. What are your dreams?" Carmen asked. "I remember you telling me you wanted your own business, and were into building homes. You never gave me details."

"Oh, you don't want to know about my boring dreams."

Carmen reached across the table, and grabbed my hand. Man, her hands were soft.

"Jon, if I didn't want to know, then I wouldn't have asked. You are such a sweet man, and have so much potential. I see great things in your future!"

I can't lie. I loved how Carmen encouraged me. I sat there and began to tell her my plans for various business ventures I wanted to pursue. Carmen advised that she could put me in contact with certain key people to get things in motion. Near the end of the entrepreneurial conversation, the waitress brought over the peach cobbler that I ordered prior to Carmen entering the diner.

"That looks good. Can I have some?" She bit her lip in flirtatious manner which sent my mind racing.

"Sure."

"Feed me Jon. I'd rather you be in control. I don't want to eat too much."

I drove my fork into the crusty part of the cobbler, and made sure I extracted little bit of everything; crust, peaches & ice cream. Carmen took a bite from my fork, and closed her eyes in delight.

"Oh my goodness. That cobbler almost made me have an orgasm."

"Girl, you are silly. Man, you cleaned the fork."

"Down to the last drop."

I prepared another bite, and fed it to Carmen.

"More like you pulled the enamel off."

Carmen covered her mouth to keep food from coming out as she laughed. At this point, I looked up at the diner clock, and realized the time.

"It has been fun, but I have to get out of here. You can have the rest of my cobbler."

"See you later sexy."

"Bye Carmen"

* * * * *

While driving home, I stared at the red light and rehearsed future conversations that I would have with the guys next Thursday. I wrestled with inner demons and struggled with my thoughts of indiscretion with Carmen. I must admit that I was committing an emotional affair in my heart, and in my mind I had lustful desires that I could not describe. Here I am in my late 30s, and I have this young, vivacious woman idolizing me like I am a pop star. It was well beyond flattering. She appeared to be attracted to me mentally, as well as sexually. I couldn't figure out what was going on with me. Was I going through mid-life crisis? Was I just acting out because I was unhappy with myself and where I was in life? Whatever it was, stumbling upon Carmen didn't make it any better. Having a young women attracted to you really boosts your self-esteem, however it causes you to lose focus. Talking to Carmen allowed me to forget about all my problems at home. Time with her was like an IV drop with morphine; with one press of the button I could alleviate my pain. I had control…or so I thought.

Later that night, I was helping my son with a report. I flipped through the encyclopedia looking for crustaceans and the page opened to *Carmen*. I remember my parents taking me to see Carmen the stage play when I was little, but the event slipped my memory. I was too young to fully grasp what was going on. As I continued to read on, it explained how this French opera was the story of a beautiful gypsy woman with a short temper. She managed to seduce many men with her looks and dancing, and ultimately was responsible for their downfall. This hit me like a ton of bricks. "Is this a sign?" I thought. At that moment, my heart was consumed with guilt and shame. I am supposed to be raising a young man to do right by women, and here I am being a hypocrite. I knew that I had to end this inappropriate behavior.

* * * * *

A few weeks passed and I foolishly ate lunch at the diner again. Even though I had been feeling convicted lately, I had wondered where she had been, hoping that I would run into her again. Once I saw her, I knew that I had to end this. Or should I say, that is what I intended. By the look on her face, I could tell something was on her mind. I walked over to our normal booth where Carmen was, and sat down.

"You seem distant today Carmen. Is everything ok?"

"Jon, what do you think about me?"

Whoa. That caught me off guard. It was apparent that she was fishing for compliments. Carmen had an outstanding body; firm, young and chiseled. She could also hold an intellectual conversation, and she was into sports. I found myself really admiring some of her traits, but I knew that I needed to keep my thoughts to myself and tread these waters carefully.

"Carmen, you are an intelligent, attractive, charming lady. Given different circumstances, no telling what could have come about. But I am a married man, and this is inappropriate. I apologize for sending you mixed signals."

"Jon, I know you are married, but I feel something between us. I am extremely attracted to you, and I know you feel the same way. I am tired of playing. I want to spend some time with you outside of this place. I am tired of hearing forks and knifes clank on plates. I want to hear you in my ear instead."

Carmen reached in her purse, and pulled out an envelope.

"I have this room 4 blocks from here. If you like that cobbler, I assure you that I am sweeter. Come by so I can clean your fork!"

When she got up from the booth, she slid a hotel key across table.

"Don't keep me waiting too long J."

Carmen leaned to kiss me on the cheek, then walked out. I wanted to stop her, but froze in the moment. Her words completely threw my game plan to end this relationship off. I knew this was wrong, but when someone pursues you it is so flattering. After rationalizing the act in graphic detail, I thought about the consequences and realized I had to end this immediately. Not next Wednesday, but today. I secretly battled with flesh thoughts as I knew I was about to flirt with disaster, but I convinced myself that I will be strong enough.

*　*　*　*　*

As I approached the hotel, I decided whether or not I should go through with it. Maybe I should end this the next time I see her at the diner, I thought. My flesh logic took over, and I slid the key in the door. Beep, click. The light turned green, and I entered.

I walked through the doors, and surveyed the room. Carmen's body was wrapped in the sheets like a sexy mummy. The only thing it revealed was her legs and shoulders. When she stood up and walked over to me, the blanket came unraveled and it revealed a matching bra and panty set underneath.

"I was beginning to think you didn't like me anymore. I almost got started without you."

Seeing her youthful body provoked my lustful loins. She stroked my chest, and navigated the terrain like she was reading Braille. While touching my body, she kissed my neck as she unbuckled my pants. I dropped the key card on the floor, momentarily closed my eyes, and thought back to the conversation Gordon and I had about his ex-wife. *You know, G had a point. Heck if she is going to accuse me of stepping out, I might as well. Plus, her body is calling me. It looks better than I could have imagined. This girl is dang near flawless.*

Carmen pulled my shirt down in an attempt to kiss my chest. When she did so, it revealed the tattoo of April's name. Carmen tried to kiss the tattoo, and in that moment I came to myself and grabbed her arms. At arms length, I asked, "What are you doing? You know I am a married man."

"She doesn't know how to treat what she has, otherwise you wouldn't be here."

"It is not that easy Carmen. I didn't come here to sleep with you."

She put her finger over my mouth, then allowed her lips to gently touch mine.

As I stood temporarily immobile by her seduction, my mind broke the spell Carmen had over me, and grabbed her arms to push her away.

"Seriously Carmen. The old me would turn you out right now, but I am a family man. A new creature. I am trying to live my life right, and I am definitely not leaving April."

"We can talk about that later daddy. Extinguish my flame. Put it on me like you know you can."

I couldn't believe I let things get as far as they did. *What is wrong with this woman? Why is she throwing it at me like this? I have never stepped out on April before. I am a husband and a father. What am I doing here? I have a wife and kids at home. Why am I here?*

"You know Carmen, as tempting as it is, I just can't. I know if I give in, I wouldn't be able to live with myself. I been down this road of having pointless sex and hurting women's feelings. I am not trying to do that anymore. You are a pretty girl that doesn't need to waste her time with an old married man. You are searching for a void that can not be filled by me."

"Then why did you come?"

"That is a good question. Honestly, I came to end this. This ain't me. We have to end this."

Carmen stood there crying, so I took it she understood my words. Or so I thought. Boy, men are stupid. Just when we think we know women, then bam; they do something that completely throws our mind out of whack. I really don't understand how a women's brain works, and today was no different. I walked out the hotel room, placed my back on the door and let out a deep sigh. At first I wrestled with flesh thoughts of knocking on the door and just doing it. Then that conviction really kicked in. I visualized April and my kids. I thought about all we went through as a family, and I physically felt sick.

While I stood there with my back to the door, Carmen was inside the hotel going wild. She screamed at the top of her lungs that she hated me and that I ruined her life. She started shouting obscenities, and throwing items within the hotel room. I heard something shatter, which I assume was either the lamp or the television. I decided it was time I left so I jumped in my truck, and to be honest I lost it. I sat there, broke down and wept. This situation stirred some emotions in me, and I felt so hurt that my life was going in this direction. *Why is my marriage falling apart? I still love April, but it just seems like she changed.* After I cleaned my face, I did the only thing I knew how to do; humble myself and pray.

"God please forgive me for my lustful thoughts and actions. Forgive me for committing adultery in my heart and mind. Forgive me for committing adultery physically. Help me Lord to sever this tie I created, and to mend my marriage. I love April, but I do not know what to do. I want this marriage to work, but I don't understand her. Teach me to be a better husband. A better father. Help me with my issues of pride, and always having to be right. Teach me how to see April's point of view. Help me to learn about women Lord so I can be a better man. In Jesus name I pray, Amen."

CHAPTER FOURTEEN

The Resort

Through April's Eyes

I continued to see Charles for the next few weeks. We would go to lunch, or he would drive me down Michigan Avenue to shop at Mag Mile. I have to admit, I loved the attention I was receiving. I also liked how Charles would spoil me, and buy me things I couldn't afford because of Jon's budget and our financial situation. Secretly, I wanted to get caught by my husband. I was becoming bolder and doing things to see if Jon would recognize. I wanted the old Jon to come back and like Jacob, roll the stone away from the well to impress me. I guess that Jon had lost interest, and since he hadn't noticed a change in me, my actions did not cease.

It was a Thursday, and I moved things around in my schedule to make sure Charles and I could have lunch again. Charles had instructed me to be prepared because he had a special surprise for me, and I was eager to see what he had up his sleeve. This particular day, I went to the break room to get some apple juice and overheard some female co-workers talking. It was a table full of married women speaking like they were part of a secret order, and the discussion topic was cheating on your husband. I took my time pouring my juice so I could eavesdrop. They talked about everything from sexual positions to get what you want, to alibis and locations, to ways to communicate with the other man. One woman said her lover purchased disposable cell phones for them to communicate, whereas the other said she merely disguised the lovers name in her cell phone as one of her girlfriends. Although techniques varied, there was one thing they all agreed on; that their husband's egos were so big that they would never suspect it.

I started to feel guilty for my indiscretions so I eased out of the room. I tried to forget about what I heard, but I couldn't get their conversation out of my mind. *Just how many married women are unhappy? What did their husbands do to provoke them to be intimate with another man? I wonder how their men are in comparison to Jon? I mean, Jon is not that bad of a man.*

I initially struggled with guilt, but that feeling quickly dissipated once my lunch date called. Charles started to become a regular at the branch, and since he opened business account no one was suspicious when he visited. One time he even took out a business loan just to make our interaction appear legitimate. In an attempt to misdirect any suspicion that may arise from my co-workers, I concealed our rendezvous by driving to a local shopping plaza, parking my car, then entering Charles's vehicle.

This day was no different as we followed the same routine. I parked my car strategically so it appeared I was inside shopping, and waited until I saw Charle's Range Rover. Once he pulled up, I quickly hopped out, set the alarm to lock my car, and jumped into his SUV.

"So where are we going today? And what is my surprise?"

"Just be patient April. You will see."

We drove for a few minutes while having general conversation, then we finally arrived at the destination; The Ritz-Carlton.

"What is this about?" April asked.

"They have an excellent Café inside which overlooks the lobby, and the food is awesome. I was going to take you to The Peninsula, but maybe I will save that for next time so we can stay the entire day."

I always wanted Jon to take me to the The Peninsula since Jassmine ranted and raved about it how excellent and accommodating the service was. She took the time to explain every detail of her visits there from the complimentary champagne and chocolate assortments you receive on your birthday, down to the bed side command console which allows you to control everything from the lighting, music, TV, even the privacy notice. I didn't see the big deal about the console, but she explained that when you are trying to unwind, it is surprising how much that little touch makes a difference.

At times, I thought Jazz was a saleswoman for that resort. I immediately ran home to tell Jon, and he told me we would go someday. In a sick twisted way, I was glad Charles took me to the Ritz instead. Even though I was in a resort with another man, I wanted to reserve The Peninsula for my husband. There was still an ounce of hope in my heart that our marriage would turn around. I was just hurt, and acting out.

We sat down for lunch, and I browsed through the menu. As soon as I saw the buttermilk fried chicken with mashed sweet potatoes, I immediately thought of Jon. *That is my baby. I know that is what he would have ordered.* I pulled my cell phone out to see if Jon called, and my caller history showed no sign of his concern. I turned my phone off, and proceeded to order the Lobster Bisque soup with the artichoke stuffed gougère. Charles and I had good conversation, and lunch was excellent.

"Thank you for my surprise. This was very nice. My lunch was delicious."

"The surprise is not over. Call off work."

"I just can't call off."

"Sure you can. You already worked 4 hours. Just say your kid is sick. Say you had some bad shellfish. Come on Kitten. Trust me, I think you will like."

Intrigued by what Charles had up his sleeve, I called work and told them I would be taking a personal day for the remainder of the afternoon. I closed my cell phone and slid it back into my purse. Charles took my hand, and instructed me to follow him. As we walked throughout this resort, I absorbed the ambience. The peaceful environment was contagious. It completely changed the way I felt inside. The place was absolutely gorgeous. The air that circulated about was fragrant, fresh, and revitalizing. While walking through the resort, I saw a concierge staff worker who resembled Jon. The music in my head abruptly ended with the scratching sound of a vinyl record. I instantly felt torn inside and disgusted with myself. *What are you doing? Look who you are here with April. But you know, I must admit this environment makes him look better. Or maybe it is his position that makes him a little bit attractive?* Charles's smile took me back to a special place, and I once again suppressed my feelings of guilt.

We walked into the elevator, and Charles pressed the key to 28th floor. Now I have never visited this place, but it took no fool to realize these were the executive suites. When the elevator doors opened, Charles fumbled in his pocket, and retrieved a key card. Soon as I saw that card, I hesitated. I been down this path before, and was not trying to let things go that far.

"What are you doing Charles? It is not even going down like that. I can't do this."

"April, just trust me. It is not like you think at all. Just come in, and see what I have for you."

I was skeptical at first because I had no intentions on sleeping with him, but I figured Charles would never hurt me. I don't know why I agreed, but I rationalized my behavior. *Since I got this far, I might as well see what he has planned for me.* I finally moved from my reluctant stance, and stepped out of the elevator. We approached the door and my stomach filled with butterflies. *What are you doing here April?* I went back and forth about leaving, but felt I couldn't cause any additional harm by just seeing what he had for me. Charles slid the key in, and opened the door. I walked in slowly behind him, and was greeted by a luxurious suite with two massage tables. Charles walked over to the phone, and dialed an extension that he had apparently memorized.

"We are ready. Thank you." Charles hung the phone up, and looked at me. "Go in the bathroom and change. There should be a robe there. I arranged us an aromatherapy massage."

I smiled, and went into the bathroom to change. While taking off my clothes, I looked at myself in the dual sink, Italian marble vanity mirror. I literally saw the movie depiction of the inner struggle of right versus wrong; conviction versus following my flesh. On one shoulder, I had the sassy April wearing a sexy form fitting red dress with red stilettos to match; and of course the stereotypical pitch fork. Then on the other shoulder, I had the sexy reserved April. Yes, both my sides are sexy! The sexy reserved side wore a nice white Chanel sweater, with a matching white ensemble. *April, girl put your clothes on and leave. What are you doing? No, it is not that bad. It is just a massage. But girl, you are married, and you are in a hotel with your ex boyfriend looking at your partially naked body in the mirror. This same guy who slept with every girl within a 2 meter radius of himself. Then again, at least he appreciates my body, and is trying to do things for me. I don't care. I am going to get my massage, and then be done. After this, then I will end it. I can't travel down this road with Charles again, and I don't want to send him the wrong sign.*

I walked out with my robe secured tightly with the belt, and noticed Charles took the liberty to undress and robe himself. While admiring the décor in the room, I saw his silk tie and designer suit straddling the chair. Knock knock. Charles opened the door, and the masseuse's entered. They instructed us to lie down, and they began giving us instructions.

"Hi, my name is Alex, and this is Kristen. We will be performing your aromatherapy massage today. Have you ever had a massage with us before?"

Charles was a regular here, but made every attempt to comfort me. "I had one at the Ritz in Key Biscayne. Could you please just explain to my beautiful lady friend?"

"No problem. We start with a traditional full body Swedish massage, then they move on to a deep tissue massage on a focused area. When complete, we do hand and foot reflexology, then end it with one choice of 3 blends of aromatherapy oils. We have Relax which has lavender and promotes relaxation, Refresh which is revitalizing and energizing, and Mobility which is good for stiff joints and muscle pains."

After the instruction, we chose the oils, and the massage began. I must admit, I became lost in the moment. The massage relieved so much tension that I temporarily forgot I was a mother and wife. My body was so relaxed I just let my reservations go.

"Thank you." Charles said as he held the door to escort the masseuse's out. He gave them a generous tip, and put the latch on the door behind him. I was so relaxed I almost fell asleep. I laid there and moaned for a while with contentment. Eventually I sat up, retied my robe, and let my legs dangle off the side of the table. Charles walked over to me, stood between my legs, and attempted to stand me up. He aggressively grabbed me around my waist, and kissed me. This caught me completely off guard. For a second I was lost in the moment. His hands roamed my body, and with his body movements, he suggested I lay down. I felt his excitement, but didn't want to go there. This was oh such a familiar place.

He picked me up, and laid me on the bed. My body mannerisms invited Charles, so he took off his robe, and climbed on top of me.

"Nothing you haven't seen nor felt before." Charles said with the look of love in his eye.

Kissing continued and Charles started to rub his hand up my thigh. I was so relaxed that I didn't stop him. During our escapade, the sitcom on TV we were listening to went off the air, and the local news came on. The first story the newscasters reported on was the metropolitan park project. *Oh my Lord. That is the project Jon is working on. What am I doing? What kind of woman am I? I love that man regardless of what is going on. I can't do this. This is not me. How did I get myself caught up like this?*

Immediately I felt guilty, and attempted to stop Charles. He was in that special place guys get to when the blood leaves their brain, so I firmly grabbed his wrist and told him to stop. Charles continued to grope, and try to maneuver himself inside of me.

"Charles stop!"

"Baby, just calm down. No need to yell. Just relax. I have learned a few tricks since we were kids. Trust me, you won't be sorry."

He proceeded to kiss my neck, and used his knee to pry my legs open. He became more forceful, and I felt a sick feeling knowing I made a huge mistake. Charles had a different look in his face that I never seen before, and it scared me. My eyes glossed over with tears like someone poured water in them…I just knew he was about to rape me and somehow I felt it was all my fault because I put myself in this position. *Lord, please give me the strength. I am sorry.*

"Stop I said!"

Charles was breathing harder, and there was a different spirit about him. While trying to force himself inside me, he licked the tears which raced towards my ear. Since Charles had been lifting weights he was much stronger than he used to be; therefore I was unable to move him off me. I felt so helpless, and it looked like my options were running out. I reached up and placed my thumb behind his mandible; right below his ear lobe. This was a pressure point Jon showed me while wrestling that hits the mandibular nerve and radiates pain down the lower part of your jaw. I applied my thumb to the pressure point, but Charles must have been possessed or something because it did not even phase him at all. He grabbed my wrists, pinned my arms down, and attempted to work his way inside me. His unwelcome presence touched my inner thigh and I moved my hips to keep him from penetrating me. Soon as his nose grazed my cheek, I opened my mouth and bit the cartilage part of his ear like I was Tyson. He let go of my arms, and I was able to take my right leg and kick him off of me.

My nerves were so bad at that point that I was trembling uncontrollably. I picked up the remote and threw it at him; aiming for his face. He ducked and the remote shattered as it hit the wall.

"What is wrong with you? Oh my God. Oh my God. What have I done? Oh my God. I have to go."

"No, don't go. Kitten, I am so sorry. I didn't mean it. I thought that is what you wanted? I saw how you looked at me."

"How could you think that is what I wanted Charles?"

"I am so sorry. I just got so excited. We have such a strong connection, and I thought you felt the same way. It has been so long since I had you, and my body is so attracted to yours. Please stay. I won't try anything. We can just watch a movie or something."

"I can't Charles. I just can't. Things have changed. I have changed. I am married, you are married. I have kids. We aren't who we used to be Charles. Get over it!"

Charles tone changed from soft and coercive to firm and demeaning.

"I didn't exactly drag you here. You came of free will, and I didn't see you complaining at all. All the money I spent on you? You owe me that much. I can't believe you are going to leave me like this after all I did for you."

"Leave you? We shouldn't even be here in the first place."

I couldn't believe the audacity of this guy. I grabbed my clothes and started to put them back on.

"Go home to your wife Charles."

"This is not right. I love you Kitten."

"Charles, no! I shouldn't be here. You are right, I shouldn't have accepted all this. All those items when we went shopping. I was wrong. I was dead wrong. I am wrong. You can have everything back."

"Kitten, don't do this."

"Charles, stop coming by the bank."

"Don't be ridiculous. I have an account there."

"There are numerous other branches you can go to. Don't play with me Charles. If you do, I will tell your wife everything. I need you to let this go. What we had is over…or should I say, it was over years ago."

"Why you got to be like that?"

"Because that is all you understand."

I put both hands over my face and sighed deeply trying not to cry in his presence. I did not want to give him that much power.

"My God, what is wrong with me? I have to get out of here."

Charles ran to the door, and tried to stop me from leaving.

"Look, I know you want this. I was your best. I was your first. I know your body better than you. No one can give you this like me. And I know you in a drought. Jassmine told me you guys don't even sleep in the same bed anymore. Why don't we just be adult about this, and satisfy one another. We have something special. No one has to know."

"Charles, don't flatter yourself. You were not all that, believe me. I faked like most women just because I craved your affection. You were actually awful. You had no clue what you were doing with that little ugly thing. Did you really think I enjoyed myself? How'd it go? C-H-A-R-L-E-S…I can't believe you sat there and made me spell your name, you vain bastard. And the more I think about it, I really don't know why I gave you a second look. You are tired. I wish you all the best, but I don't ever want to see you again. If you don't move right now, I will tell Jon everything. Trust me, you do not want him to come after you."

Charles stepped aside, and began his verbal assault as April gathered her belongings and walked out the door.

"Have it your way. I don't give a damn anyways. You weren't all that either. You didn't call it little and ugly when you were feeling it. And guess what? I used to think about your sister to climax. Yea, that's right. And you know what else? I don't even know why I wasted my time with you again either. I made you, and taught you everything you know. You were a nobody before me, and won't be anything without me. You were just a piece of a…"

I walked out while Charles was talking. I really didn't care about his macho tirade and rounds of verbal assault, but I was distraught and hurt I let it get this far. I was very disappointed in myself. I arrived at the elevators and tried to hold it together, but I lost it once I saw my face through the reflection of the gold elevator doors. The bell dinged as I reached the lobby, and I attempted to clean my face.

I approached the front desk to ask for a cab. The taxi pulled up, and I slowly slid across the backseat as I gave my destination. When we pulled off, I looked at my face in the cab's review mirror. I saw the traces of dried mascara like a road map down my face. I looked directly into my own eyes and I began to weep again. There was so much pain within my body that I went to the only place I knew. Like most people in trouble, I ran back to my Father. Not my earthly father, but heavenly one. I didn't care if I looked crazy in front of the cab driver; I sat there and started to pray.

"Lord, please forgive me. I repent. This is not me. I do not want to be with any other man but the one you gave to me. Forgive me for my adulterous behavior. Protect my mind and heart Father. Wrap your arms around me and comfort me. Help me to heal, and deal with my issues from my past. I want to make my marriage work, but I am so frustrated. I don't know what is going on in Jon's head, nor how he truly feels about me. I don't know what my future holds, but I know that You love me, and have my best interest at heart. Teach me to be a better wife. Teach me how to have a successful marriage. Teach me how to understand your Word, and your purpose for my life. In Jesus name, Amen."

Chapter Fifteen

The Separation

Selfish

A couple months passed since April and Jon had inappropriate relationships. April did not encounter Charles anymore, and Jon stopped eating at the diner to make sure he didn't run into Carmen. Even though they weren't practicing infidelity any longer, things still hadn't changed between the two.

It was a Saturday, and Jon woke up early to cook for April. The children were spending the night at Alicia's house, so Jon thought he would surprise his wife with breakfast in bed. April walked downstairs, and didn't speak one word. She opened the fridge to grab some juice, and ended up handling an empty container.

After she shook the carton, she blurted out, "Why do you always do this? If you are finished with the juice, then throw it away. What is wrong with you?"

"April, whatever. I didn't even do that. That was you."

April remembered that she was the one that placed the empty container in the fridge, but she was just looking for a way to initiate an argument so she could let out her frustrations.

"Every time Jon. Every single time. You are just so selfish. It is always about you. You never care about anyone else but yourself!"

"Whew, what is wrong with you? Somebody had a bowl of Cranky Flakes for breakfast. Why don't you go back to sleep? I will be up in a second."

"That is not funny, and sleep doesn't have anything to do with it Jon. It is you, and how you are so selfish and only think about yourself. And no, I don't want you to come upstairs for whatever you have in mind."

"Ape, I didn't want that. I was going to surprise you and bring you up…"

"It is bigger than orange juice J."

Jon knew this was headed towards a serious argument, so he started scrambling the eggs while gathering his thoughts.

"Bigger than orange juice, huh? Yea, I bet. I keep forgetting that I am the bad guy and it is always my fault. What did I do wrong now?"

"See, why do you have to talk to me like that? Was that necessary?"

"Umm, correct me if I am wrong Ape, but you are the one that woke up and picked an argument with me."

"I didn't pick an argument, all I said was that you were selfish and inconsiderate. Anytime someone tells you what is wrong with you, you fly off the handle and place blame somewhere else. You can not take criticism at all. God forbid if Jon has any issues. He is Mr. Perfect."

"Ok, please tell me who has given me criticism and I have not taken it well? Name one person."

"Me."

"Are you serious?" Jon chuckled. "Ape, not this morning. It is too early."

"That is what I am talking about…selfish. Everything revolves around you and what you want. It is like you think I am a joke."

"So I am selfish? All I do for this family, and you say I am selfish? All I sacrifice day in and day out? All I give, and not getting anything back in return, and I am selfish? I can't believe you. I work 60 hour weeks sometimes, and as tired as I am, I am in here trying to surprise you with breakfast. It is just a no win situation with you. It is like every time I try to do something nice for you, you end up picking a fight or just saying something off the wall."

"Oh, so now you going to throw working and providing for your family up in my face? You act like I don't work either. Besides, that is part of being a man. You don't get a medal for doing that…that is what you are supposed to do."

"You know what I meant. Stop trying to be stupid."

April walked up on Jon and poked him in his chest with her index finger.

"So I am stupid J? Huh? Is that what you are saying?"

"Whatever April. Back up out my face."

"Don't whatever me. Who are you? Sometimes I don't even know the man I have been living with for the past 9 years. How can you just tune me out and act like I don't exist?"

"I tune you out because all you do is yap yap yap and nothing comes out. You always pick a fight over something stupid, and sometimes I just don't have the energy to go toe to toe with you."

April attempted to smack Jon, but he caught her wrist in his hand.

"Look, you can be mad at me all you want, but I have never disrespected you, or touched you in any way. You will not disrespect me! That is something I will not stand for."

Sensing the anger in his voice, April retracted and her eyes began to water. Her voice cracked as she began to speak.

"Well what do you have the energy for? What is going on with you? Are you giving that energy to another woman?"

"Are you giving my attention to another man?"

"Don't try to flip this on me."

"April, shut up. I am not going there with you. This conversation is just plain foolish."

"Shut up? Who are you talking to? You do all this talk about disrespect, then you turn around and talk to me like I am some cheap girlfriend? I am your wife. I deserve better. How dare you disrespect me like that!"

"How dare you disrespect me in how you always come at me with these unwarranted accusations? Disrespect me saying that you don't care about me trying to provide for this family. Like my contributions don't mean anything?"

April sat for a second before responding. She felt bad for how she came across, but she was hurt and didn't know how to articulate what was bothering her inside.

"J, I am sorry. I didn't mean it like that. I trying to make this work, but I do not know what to say to get through to your thick skull. Am I doing something wrong? What did I do to make you hate me?"

"I don't hate you at all April, it is just sometimes you…look, I said I don't want to talk about this right now. Just drop it, please."

"See, I am trying to open up to you, and you just shut me off like I am a side piece. Like I don't even matter to you. The conversation always ends when you want it to end."

"Yep, pretty much. Like right now…it is over."

"You just don't get it Jon, and this is not working. I am miserable. I can't keep doing this."

"You know what April, you are exactly right. This is not working. I can't continue to live like this either. Maybe we need to separate for a little bit."

"If you want out, just say so. Don't be a punk about it. You want to leave me, don't you? Fine, I will pack my bags."

"Woman, what is wrong with you? Do you get off trying to stress me out? My God, I can't take this! You know what, I can't do this right now."

Jon slammed the skillet down, grabbed his truck keys off the counter, and shoved the door open on his way out the house.

April grabbed a tea cup from the table and launched it at the door. As the glass shattered, she started to cry. With her back against the refrigerator, she slowly allowed her body to slide down, knocking all the magnets off on her course to the floor. Once her bottom stopped her descent, she rested her arms on her knees, and buried her head to sob.

Wisdom from Grandparents

Jon drove around to get some fresh air. Not initially having a destination in mind, he decided to visit his grandparents since he hadn't seen them in a while. He pulled up to their house and saw his grandfather sitting on the porch slowing rocking in his porch swing. He nodded his head to acknowledge Jon, then pulled out his old oxidized saxophone and blew a short melody. Jon walked towards the porch, and his grandfather's sax sent him down nostalgia lane. *Man, grandfather has an unusual way to make that instrument sing. The way he plays, it feels like you can hear the saxophone recite lyrics. Ever since I was little, it has always placed me into a trance.* While Jon relaxed in the company of their nonverbal conversation, his grandmother came out to hug him.

"Are you hungry? Is that girl feeding you right? Do you want some fried gator tails baby?"

"Yes ma'am."

When she turned to walk away, Jon's grandfather patted her on her rear.

"Stop it Sonny," she chuckled.

The screen door snapped shut, then Jon looked over to his grandfather.

"Grandpa, how do y'all do it after all these years?"

"How do we do what boy?"

"How do you keep that spark? You guys are still going at it years and years later."

"First of all, don't say years like that. You will be my age one day.

Second, I have forgotten more than you will know. Your generation acts like you invented something."

"I know Grandpa. I wasn't trying to be disrespectful. I know you forgot more than I know. That is why I am asking you. Please. I need your advice."

He placed his saxophone on his lap, and looked directly into Jon's eyes, "Son, you look troubled. I don't know the source of your question, but if you want what we have, you have to work at it. Now there will be some rough patches, but when you hit those spots you need to learn how to look within. Most of the big disagreements between couples are because individuals won't address their own faults. It really boils down to being selfish."

"Man, there has to be something else to your spunk."

"If you desire to make it work, then you will be willing to do what it takes; even if that means changing yourself. Your grandmother and I have a desire to make it work. We do whatever it takes. We are completely honest with one another, thus the reason we have grown together and been together all these years."

"I know Grandpa, and I really admire your relationship, and try to imitate what I see. I just want that passion to be restored. That fire that I saw in her eyes when she used to stare at me. It is like her fire has blown out, and I don't know how to relight it. Heck at this point, if I get it lit I don't know what to put on it to keep it burning."

"Well, the one material that keeps this fire burning is the Word of God. You need to embed this Word in your heart. Meditate on it day and night."

"I read my Bible Grandpa, but…"

"There are no *but's* about it. You are head of your household, so act like it. You need to understand how powerful spoken word is. One word out of your mouth can completely change your entire situation! All it takes is one word Jon."

"It is not that simple Grandpa, see…"

"One word would show you are a man of character. One word would show her that you are listening. One word would prove that you intend on establishing stability. One word would provide comfort. One word would cease calamity. Wars begin and end with a word Jon. One word can change her entire world. It could build her up, or completely tear her down."

"I suppose. I can speak one word to her, but the problem is she doesn't listen. See Grandma is different. We deal with a different breed of women than your generation. With April…"

It was apparent Jon's grandfather was not interested in a rebuttal as he continued to cut him off and not let him finish his sentences.

"One word was good enough for God to speak creation into existence. You young people need to dig in that Word, and not just pick up your Bible on Sunday's. Would solve half your problems."

"I must admit, I haven't studied my Bible as I should."

"You are in construction, right?"

"Yes sir."

"You understand blueprints then. The blueprints to marriage are right here. Stop whining and read it." Jon's grandpa picked up an old Bible with a torn bind and faded letters, and handed it to him. "Take this."

"I already have a Bible Grandpa."

"Boy, just take it."

"Yes sir."

"You young people have the answer right in front of you, and hear it several times, but still attempt to do things your way. Your generation is so rebellious. You have the prescription, now it is up to you to take the medicine. Now go get your grandpa some of those gator tails!"

Our conversations were always short and to the point. Grandpa often made me self assess myself. After our talk, I thought about what he said. What was it that I was doing wrong? Am I a bad person? He is right in that I need to read my Bible more.

Jon walked into the kitchen to fix his grandfather a plate.

"Hey suga."

"Hey Grandma."

"Looks like you losing weight? That girl not feeding you?"

"I think my weight loss is more so from stress. We are having problems."

"Um hmm. I overheard. Pass me those breadcrumbs." Grandma proceeded to batter the gator tails with a mixture of flour, breadcrumbs, and various seasonings. No measuring cups were in sight; everything done by hand.

"Grandma, it is like I don't have anyone to talk to. No one understands. My friends…"

"That is part of the problem right there. Stop getting advice from single friends. They can't relate to what you are going through. And don't get advice from cheating men, or couples who are going through problems either because those words are coming from a bitter, frustrated person who doesn't want you to be happy. You have to watch who you listen to because people have a tendency to try to bring you down."

"I understand, and you are absolutely right. Since you and Grandpa don't fit that bill, tell me how you do it? You still have that spark. Everything with April and I is routine and dry. No spontaneity at all. Besides our kids, all other conversations evolve into arguments."

"Hand me 4 eggs baby." His grandmother continued to beat the eggs, and began to batter the gator tails. "Arguments about what?"

"Anything. It could be a Wednesday and the wind hit the left side of her face. She is so moody. I guess I just don't understand her. I don't understand women. It is like we can be talking about one thing, and she bring up some entirely different event from months ago."

"Jon, go out back and pull me up some garlic."

Frustrated because he felt his grandmother was ignoring him, he sighed, then pouted into the back yard garden to extract the garlic from the soil. He brought the garlic bulb back inside and allowed his grandmother to inspect it.

"Did you see the new flowers I planted out back? Your grandfather helped me plant the Butterfly Weed and Japanese Roof Iris. I should have called you to help. Your grandfather and I are getting too old to be bending down like that. Some days are better than others. Comes with age I suppose. Do you know anything about gardening?"

"No Grandma, I can't say I know too much. Doesn't seem like there is much to it though."

"Follow me outside."

Jon's grandmother walked to her flowerbed, and retrieved a plant from the ground.

"Why did you pull that up?"

"I wanted to teach you about gardening. The first thing you need to know is that the key to growing good plants and vegetables is fertile soil. You see these roots? These roots keep it planted in the soil."

"Grandma, I am not trying to be disrespectful at all, but I know what roots are. If you need me to help, I am more than happy. You don't have to guilt me. I am just having a bad day right now and…"

"Boy listen. This is your marriage. Just like this plant, without proper nurturing it will not grow nor mature; it will die. What I am saying baby is you have to stick your roots in some fertile soil. Nurture it with the Living Word."

Jon's grandmother tossed the plant on the grass, then wiped her hands on her apron.

"You and April are like that flower…uprooted."

"I think I get what you are saying Grandma. But what if one plant is rooted, and the other is not?"

"Boy, do you ever read your Bible? Do you know what your purpose is in the marriage? Do you understand your role in helping one another?" Jon's grandmother shook her head in frustration, and continued. "Look, when you are attempting to plant a garden, there is technique called companion planting. The idea is that some plants perform better when planted together. There are several reasons why. Some may add nitrogen in the ground. Some repel insects. Some enhance the flavors of others. Some attract beneficial organisms. Some serve as a protective shelter or shade. My point is you and April are companion plants. You guys need to get rooted in this Word, and learn how to bring the best out of one another. Learn how to bring the spice and flavor back. Learn how to protect your marriage and keep harmful things away."

I love how my Grandma teaches me. Some of her analogies are so simple on the surface, but heavy underneath. This is definitely April and myself. I can see my head is going to hurt by the time I leave here.

Jon assisted his grandmother back into the kitchen.

"Now I am never going to look at plants the same way. That was pretty heavy Granny. The thing is, I want to be her companion, but sometimes I don't know how. It is like she has these crazy mood swings. Like this morning, we got into an argument about some orange juice that she drank. It is like sometimes I wonder if she is just trying to make me go insane. Our arguments start over the dumbest thing."

"Son, let me give you some advice about women. You do realize that sometimes when a female is mad, there is a root issue usually completely non-related to your argument. Your lady can be mad at you for not noticing she cleaned the house, or recognizing the effort she put into dinner, or a new hairstyle, or an old issue." She paused as she placed the battered tails in the hot grease. Jon watched as his grandmother carefully orchestrated each tail in the hot cast iron skillet.

"Or a big one…maybe she is mad at you for not fulfilling a promise, or not adhering to your word. That was a problem your grandfather and I had our first years of marriage. If you say you are going to do something, then do it. Don't fill us up with all these hopes and dreams if you never intended on following through on your word. If you do this to a female, she will process it internally, but externally argue with you about taking the trash out. This is why some women grow to be bitter and resentful within relationships. Women like visionaries; men who can lay out a game plan, and see it through. Women like men who take charge, and will let them know where they are going in life. If you don't plan your life, someone else will plan it for you."

His grandmother paused again to allow her words to sink in. She grabbed a moist rag from the sink, and proceeded to wipe the counter clean from the ingredients that spilled.

"What you need to realize is that men and women communicate differently Jon. I remember when you were little, you used to like airplanes. When communicating, think of men and woman as airplanes. Men are like those planes on Navy aircraft carriers; they immediately take off. Women are more like commercial planes. We circle the runway several times before we take off; or get to the point we want to make."

"That makes no sense to me. Why can't women just say what is on their minds, instead of beating around the bush."

"We can go all day about the differences between men and women. You asked me how your grandfather and I do it, and I am trying to tell you. People who have successful marriages work at it. Some things may not make sense to you, but just work through it. Work meaning sometimes you have to do what you don't want. Sometimes you have to shut up and not argue when you think you are right. You have to be the bigger person. You also have to learn how to listen."

"But what about her?"

"We are not talking about her baby. We are talking about you, and what you can do on your part. Work on yourself first. You are head of that household, and very influential over her. Your spouse is a direct reflection of you, and how you run your house."

Grandma paused with that uncomfortable silence to let that point sink in; it worked. I never thought about that before, but I will never admit it because I don't want to sound stupid. It makes sense though. April and how she has been acting lately is a reflection of me.

"You know, when Sonny courted me, he didn't have a dime to his name. Money didn't matter because he still had expectations on how he wanted to be treated. The way he demanded respect really attracted me to him. He gave me a list of the things that he expected out of a relationship, and vice versa. Baby, people only do what you let them do. In other words, in every instance of life, you teach people how to treat you."

"I suppose so. But Grandma, these women are different than in your era. They don't want to hear all that submissive stuff. They make their own money now, and pretty much act like they don't need men for anything. They are so rebellious, and disrespectful."

"Women haven't changed baby, men have. Some women just adapted to your change. You start being the man that God called you to be, and you command the respect of your woman. The problem is, men don't want to do what it takes to merit the respect of women. Men are too busy being gigolo's, and trying to juggle several women. That is not what God created you to do. Women still have the same desire because God created us that way. It is just that through time, men have lost focus on the gift God gave them, thus these radical women were birthed. I think April is a beautiful girl inside and out; I truly love her. If she is not submissive to you, it is probably because you are not submissive to God."

"What is that supposed to mean?"

"You have to figure that out. I have already told you enough, and Grandpa gave you the blueprint."

Jon's grandmother took a fork, and gently extracted each tail from the hot grease, to a nearby plate draped with paper towels.

"Let me ask you a question. I know you go to church and participate, but what about at home? Do you pray with your family? Do you sow into your wife? Do you help her to achieve her goals? You know women do have dreams as well. It is not always about you."

In the middle of the conversation, Jon's cell phone rang. He looked at the display, and it was April's number.

"Wow Granny. Her ear must have been itching, because this is her right now. Excuse me for a second. Let me take this call."

Jon walked out on the back porch to get some air, and speak to his wife and apologize.

"Hello babe."

"Hey Jon, this is not April."

Jon recognized the voice, "Hey Mom. What is going on? Where is April?"

"Jon, I need you to meet me at Rush Medical."

"What? Why? What is going on?"

"I will explain when you get there, just hurry!"

Jon kissed his grandmother, and told her there was an emergency. He ran out the front door, jumped into his truck, and sped off.

Wisdom from Momma

April cleaned herself up, and drove to her mother's house. Her mom was in the kitchen standing at the island cutting up red onions. April walked behind her mom, and hugged her tightly; allowing her head to rest on her mother's shoulders.

"What's the matter baby?"

"Nothing Mom."

"Alicia tells me that Tiffani is still in town. I thought she was only staying for a couple weeks? How is her family doing?"

"Her uncle was doing pretty bad. They brought hospice in, and he passed shortly after. I don't really want to talk about her."

"What she do? She flirt with Jon too?"

"Too?"

"Yes too! Just like that little loose girl Jassmine. The one married to that old man. That one I told you to stay away from. That girl has been trouble since she was 16 years old."

"I see you have been speaking with Alicia. You gotta love older siblings."

"April, I understand you like your friends, but trust this old woman; you need to stop listening to all those bitter, resentful, married, and single, no good friends of yours. These women will plot and scheme to try to steal your man from you. They stand on the sideline while you have been in the game for 9 years; then try to come in and take all you built. That is why you really need to watch who you hang out with."

"Now you sound like Jon."

"Take it with a grain of salt April. You are going to do what you want to do regardless. I am trying to help you protect your marriage."

April walked over to the refrigerator, and looked at a photo of her mom and father at Disney World when they were younger. She tried to hold her emotions in, but couldn't and suddenly burst into tears.

"Momma, I need help."

"Do you really? Because you have a habit of not listening when someone says something you don't like. Just like you ignored what I just said."

"Mom, I don't know what to do. I am miserable. I have physically been making myself sick. I want it to work, and to have a family for my kids, but I don't know anymore. Our finances are just terrible, and Jon doesn't love me like he used to. Everything is just falling apart."

"That boy Charles got a hold of you, huh?"

"No…I mean yes….but no. This was way before Charles came back. Charles is married anyways."

"Babygirl, I usually stay out of your business unless you ask me some advice directly. But that Charles? I must be honest, I never liked that boy when you dated him. That is why I used to be so hard on you back then about spiritual ties. You young people have no clue what the consequences are for having sex. Here it is, how many years later? Nothing is casual. You about to let some old lust come between you and a good man. Let me be straightforward. Charles never cared about your well being. He was selfish and was an opportunist. Still appears to be. When he sees something he wants, he goes full force with no respect, nor regard for others."

"At least he has a vision…unlike my wonderful husband. Jon will probably end up being like daddy. Making me work."

"What is that supposed to mean young lady?"

"I am not trying to go through the same thing. Marrying a quitter. There are some things I want in life before God takes me from this green earth. I didn't sign up for being miserable. I don't know how you put up with daddy. He never talks. And how do you just get up and quit a job when you have a family to support??"

April's mother lunged at her and grabbed her jaw with a tight grip.

"Don't you ever disrespect your father again, do you hear me? All that he has sacrificed for this family? You will respect him! I will not have a disrespectful, ungrateful child in my house."

"Momma, I am sorry. I just don't want to have regrets like you."

"Regrets? Who said I had regrets? I love that man with every part of my being."

April was hurt about her situation with Jon, and her relationship with her father. This pain provoked her to say a sentence to her mom she had wanted to recite for years.

"But mom, you had to know he was stepping out on you. He would leave and go Lord knows where, and come home tired. Come on mom, do the math. You are an intelligent woman, so you had to see it. How could you just turn your back and ignore what he was doing? Did you stay with him just because of us?"

"Stepping out? Oh my Lord. Is that what you thought? You have been thinking that all these years?" Disappointed and hurt by her daughter's words, her mannerisms changed. "You have no clue what he went through Ape. No clue at all."

April's mother sat down at the breakfast nook in their kitchen. I am about to share something with you that goes no further than these walls. Do I make myself clear?"

"Yes ma'am."

April walked over and sat down in the nook across from her mother.

"Your father resigned from his position because of the results from his physical exam."

"Daddy failed a physical? Why? How? He used to run 4 miles every morning. He is in better shape than I am. How could that be possible?"

"April, I don't know how to tell you this other than coming straight out. Your father had prostate cancer."

"What? Cancer? What do you mean cancer? Daddy can't have cancer."

"I know this is a lot to digest baby, and I am sorry."

"Cancer? Why didn't anyone say anything?"

"At that time, it was like our family was spinning out of control. Everything happened at once. Your brother Adam and his wife had a miscarriage. Aaron and Tony were in that car accident. And Alicia? She always had some drama going on. It was just an overall rough period of time for our family, and your father and I felt it best not to add that stress on you kids. Your dad was tired and slept a lot because of the treatments. The doctor gave us an option for a radiation treatment called external beam therapy. The machine is similar to an x-ray, and it shoots a beam that destroys the cancer cells without placing radioactive sources in the body; like seed therapy. The only problem with the external beam treatment is it is extremely time consuming as it is administered 5 days a week over 7 weeks. He had no option; he had to quit."

"Oh my God. My daddy."

"He is better now. His last checkup, they saw no signs of cancerous cells. You just need to know that your father is a prideful man, and I trust you won't tell anyone. So prideful in fact that first few weeks of treatment he would not allow me to drive him. That is where he'd go during the days April."

"I don't know what to say Momma."

"Nothing for you to say babygirl. You just need to understand that there are things bigger than you and you and your feelings. And for the record, let me also set something else clear. Your dad loves you guys unconditionally. I am not making excuses for him, but he just doesn't know how to communicate with women. Do you remember when you were 8 years old and broke your leg falling off that swing? Well I do because I could not calm that man down. Your dad cried uncontrollably. He was so hurt. He always wanted the best for you."

"But he never said anything?"

"That doesn't mean he doesn't care Ape. Men are nonverbal."

"Men are just stupid. They act like knuckle dragging cavemen and just sit there and stare off into oblivion. Why don't those Neanderthals just say what is on their minds?"

"Ape, you need to learn that men and women communicate differently. And sometimes, we don't always make it easy for them. Sometimes we talk in circles because we are mad about something else and lash out, instead of just being direct and telling them what is bothering us."

"That can go both ways Momma."

"Yes it can, but you need to decide. Do you want to be right, or do you want to save your marriage? Marriage is about compromise and sacrifice."

"I guess you are right. You always have the right response. How do you know so much?"

"Do you think your father and I stayed together all these years because of you kids? I mean, he is a good lover."

"Mom!"

"I am just saying. We know each other well. Not to mention, your dad is an excellent dancer!"

"Mom, please stop." April's laugh temporarily stifled her heartache. As she sniffled, her mother grabbed her chin and raised it elevate her face to eye level, "April, look at me. Jon is a good man. A good Christian man. And it helps that he is easy on the eyes." April and her mother both chuckled. "Seriously April. Jon loves you, and those children. Support that man! Make him feel appreciated. There is a king within him. Trust me, if you don't support him, there are numerous women waiting in line that would love the opportunity to!"

"I guess so."

"I love you baby. If you don't hear anything else I say, listen close. This is the one liner for a successful marriage."

"What's that?"

"Keep God first in your marriage."

"What is that supposed to mean, and why does everyone say that? Everyone kept telling me that at our wedding."

"Baby, when you have seen the things that I have seen. Whew." April's mother put her head down and whispered *Thank you Jesus* under her breath. "I tell you Ape, there were times when we had nothing but God to rely on.

He is the key. Without Him as a foundation, you are headed for chaos."

"I pray. I tithe. I go to church. I am putting Him first."

"April, I am not trying to judge you baby. As a parent, all I can do it guide you in the right direction. You have to find Him for yourself. You have to develop a relationship with Him. If your relationship is not right with Him, then it won't be right with Jon. Read your Bible. Study it. Set aside some personal time to meditate on it. Everything you need to turn your marriage around is right there. He can restore. He can amend. He can loose."

"What if I read the Bible and nothing changes?"

"April, the Word has the ability to transform you and Jon, and it has the power to bring life back into the dead areas of your relationship."

"That sounds good, but how? How can words in a book turn our life around? And what do I read? Maybe I am just reading it wrong or something."

April's mother sighed in frustration.

"Baby, I can't hold your hand and walk you through this one. I can point out some passages for you, but it is you that has to make that determination that you want to live by the Word. Pray for direction April. He will illuminate your path. Everything you…"

April leaned over clutching her stomach, and belted out a deep squeal and cry. April's mom immediately sensed something was wrong.

"You ok baby?"

"Momma, I have been feeling this sharp pain in my abdomen." April screamed again, "Owww. It is pain like a cramp. I have been spotting. Been dizzy. I can't be pregnant. I had my tubes tied. What is going on with my body?"

"Let me get my keys. I am taking you to the hospital."

In route to the hospital, April's mother called Jon.

"Hello babe."

"Hey Jon, this is not April."

"Hey Mom. What is going on? Where is April?"

"Jon, I need you to meet me at Rush Medical."

"What? Why? What is going on?"

"I will explain when you get there, just hurry!"

Through the pain, April could hear her mother speaking to Jon. She replayed the conversation between her mother and herself. *Momma always talking that church talk.* April's rebellious side did not want to admit it, but something about her mother's words took root. She felt pushed into a corner, and figured she already tried everything else on her own, so why not try God? April determined right then and there that from that point on, she would start dedicating time to seeking God and developing a relationship with Him. *You know what, I am tired. I have been trying this my way, and I am desperate for some new results. I am going to set aside time I use for talking gossip on the phone for studying and meditating. If that takes cutting some folks off, then so be it! My marriage is more important to me.*

April closed her eyes, and began to pray. No sooner than she said amen, they arrived at the emergency room.

CHAPTER SIXTEEN

Crossroads

Jeremiah 6:16

Speeding and weaving in and out of traffic in an attempt to get to the hospital, Jon's acceleration was halted by a stubborn red light. He tapped the steering wheel frantically while staring at the stoplight; anxiously awaiting the color to change green. *Oh Lord, please have mercy. Not again. I beg you.* After a few minutes he arrived at the hospital, pulled into the emergency unit, literally ran through the automatic sliding doors, and received directions from the nursing station to the location of his wife. As he approached the room, he saw his mother-in-law standing with the doctor.

"Doc, this is April's husband. You need to explain to him."

"What is going on? Explain what to me?"

"Mr. Carter, my name is Dr. Sullivan. Your wife had a tubal ligation procedure, correct?"

"Yes, after our second child. She was premature, and we had her tubes tied after her c-section. All due respect doc, can you please just cut to the chase. What is wrong with my wife?"

"Mr. Carter, the lab results are back, and April was pregnant. The pain she was experiencing, and the vaginal bleeding are symptoms of what we call an ectopic pregnancy; also known as a tubal pregnancy. These are potentially fatal as they can lead to internal bleeding. Bleeding results from the rupture of the fallopian tube. The good thing is we detected this in time."

"My Lord. She was pregnant? How could this happen?"

"As far as how your wife got pregnant, that is something we can't tell you definitely. When these procedures fail, there are things to factor in like the timing of the failure, the surgeon's skill, and the method used.

There are several methods for the tubal ligation procedure, but essentially it comes down to the fallopian tubes being either burned, cut, or blocked. Your wife chose the burn method, or what is referred to as bipolar tubal coagulation. At the site where the sterilization procedure occurs, there is a healing process which results in the fallopian tube scarring shut. There is a possibility that a passageway may remain that is wide enough to enable sperm to pass through. In that case, the embryo could implant in the fallopian tube."

"I can't believe this." Jon looked over at his mother-in-law and shook his head, "So what is going to happen?"

"Usually we would perform surgery, but we feel that we caught this in enough time. We can treat her with an injection of methotrexate. This will dissolve the fertilized egg, and allow her body to reabsorb it. I am sorry Mr. Carter."

"What are the side effects?"

"It can cause headaches, drowsiness, skin rash & dizziness. This procedure has a high success rate, and low side effects. However I will advise that some patients don't respond to methotrexate. In those cases, surgical treatment is required."

"Thanks for all your help, and thank you for being honest with me. Can I go see her?"

"She is resting, but yes."

Jon slowly walked into the room, and as the door shut, his wife opened her eyes.

"April, I am so sorry baby."

"That is ok hun."

"You were pregnant?" Jon's eyes began to tear up.

"Yes, I know baby. I can't believe this either J."

"April, I didn't mean to leave like that. You know I love you. I love you more than anything. I can't lose you. I drove over here thinking about my life without you, and I couldn't imagine how I would maintain. Where did we go wrong?"

"I don't know, but that is the first time you have told me you love me in months J."

"It doesn't mean I don't. I show you how much I love you daily by going to work, coming home, trying to provide."

April laughed under her breath as she thought about her mom advising her men are non-verbal.

"Why does tragedy have to bring a family together?"

April reached to turn the TV volume down from the remote on her bed, "I don't know baby, but at least we still have one another. Things could be worse! I don't know how I feel yet about this. It is all too much right now. I don't understand why God allowed this to happen, but I know there is a reason for everything. He has our best interest at heart, I truly believe that. And even though we experienced a loss, I believe that we just gained a blessing."

"A blessing?" Jon asked in a confused manner.

"Yes baby, a blessing…a salvaged relationship. Now I know my husband still loves me. You don't know how much that meant to me to hear you say that. And on this trip over here, I made a decision that I was in this marriage for the long haul. I will do whatever it takes to make this work."

"Yes I agree Ape. Somewhere along the lines, we allowed dissention and distance to come between us, and I think a lot of it is my fault. We were killing each other, and I apologize for my part. We were definitely headed down the wrong road. I don't know what just happened, but I feel a shift. Almost as if we did a U-Turn in the middle of the road."

"Well I like to think of it as a crossroad. You know we were just at that place in life where we didn't know what direction to go in. But you know what, as long as I am on the same road with you I am at peace."

Jon leaned and kissed his wife on the forehead.

"I can feel that. I remember reading a story in the Bible…I think it was in Jeremiah…and it talked about the people in Israel and how they rejected the Lord's way. It spoke about them being at a crossroad, and refusing to take God's path. I think that is what happened to us. We were at a crossroad in our marriage, and decided to remove God from the equation and take our own paths."

Jon pulled up the chair to the side of the bed, and continued his train of thought.

"Look April, I have tried to go about this my way for too long. I let my pride take our family down that wrong path. Starting today, I want to recommit to God, and to you. I am sorry I have been distant at times, but that is just my way of dealing with things. I internalize a lot."

"A lot like what baby?" April said as she rubbed her husbands face.

"I will be transparent April. It is frustrating being the head of this family. When babygirl was premature, working those long hours did something to me. It broke my spirit something terrible. It bruised my ego because that was not how I planned on living my life by that age. I have this beautiful wife, and I want to spoil her and give her all these nice things, and I couldn't. It frustrated me that I couldn't provide for you. That I still can't give you the things you deserve."

"Jon, I don't need all those material things. All I need from you is you. I love just spending time with you. How you used to hold me. How we used to wrestle. Our long talks. I don't need to go out shopping to have fun. If I am honest with myself, I just do that to fill a void. The truth is we can go to a park and I will be content; as long as I am with you. I would much rather spend my time with you then going out with the ladies. I miss your attention. Jon, I love you, and I do not want to go anywhere. I am willing to do what you want me to do. I am sorry for how I have been as well. I know I am a brat at times, and not the best wife."

"God sent you in my life. From the time I looked into your eyes, I knew you were mine. I felt something different. I look in your eyes right now, and I still feel the same way. We have had some rough patches, and days we didn't speak, but there has not been one single day where my love for you has diminished. I am determined to make this work, and I am committed to change."

Jon stood up pushing the chair away, and in the process somehow stomped his toe on the hospital bed, thus provoking April to laugh.

"I am even willing to sacrifice my foot. Dang that hurt. All jokes aside though, I miss your smile."

Jon leaned over to kiss her again, then gently grabbed her hand which had the IV taped to it.

"What are you doing J?"

"Something I should have done a long time ago. Inviting God back into our lives. Or as the old folks would say it, putting God first in your marriage."

April smiled thinking about the conversation she just had with her mother. She saw a change in her husband, and her spirits were lifted as she realized that God was listening to her prayers. She closed her eyes, and opened her heart as Jon prayed over their marriage.

"Dear Lord, We come to you asking for forgiveness. Forgive us for not putting you first in our relationship. For not coming together as a family and praying. We thank you for covering us from day to day. We pray over these doctor's, Lord. Pray that they are knowledgeable and alert and are able to give April the treatment she needs so she can come home. We pray asking you for healing and recovery. I thank you for blessing me with this woman. We thank you for healing that is taking place between April and myself. Allow us to communicate better, and be able to understand each other. In the name of Jesus we pray, Amen. "

"Amen! Thank you J. I needed that."

The Accident

Weeks had passed, and April and Jon were talking about her stay in the hospital.

"Jon, I was just wondering. If something really happened to me, how long before you would date someone else? "

"Baby, I would be so distraught, I would have to at least give it 2 weeks."

April hit him on his arm.

"No seriously, that thought never crossed my mind. I didn't marry you with intentions on us getting a divorce. That is the last thing on my mind. Where did that question come from anyways?"

"Well, I know all these women want you. I just wondered. You are a catch."

April sat quietly as she prepared the initial question she wanted to ask.

"Ok, Tell the truth J. When we first met, you were acting like you were celibate. You can be honest with me and I promise I won't get mad. How many women did you have at the time?"

"None."

"Come on now. As fine as you are?"

"April I am being honest, none. I had a couple women interested in me. I dated for a little bit, and had conversations with others. Yes, I flirted with women, but I didn't go there like you think. I was saving myself for you." Jon threw a playful smile in the direction of his wife.

"You don't have to butter me up to get some. All you have to do is ask. I love to please my man."

"April I am telling the truth…I was celibate. I just needed to learn who I was."

"What was her name? Apparently someone broke your heart."

"It is not what you think. I just don't like to revisit that period of time."

What did you tell me in the hospital? That you would start talking to me. I thought we were being honest?"

Jon sighed. "Using my words against me, huh? Ok, if I tell you this story, please don't hold this over my head. I never really spoke to anyone about this before."

"Baby, I am not going to hold anything over your head, I just want to get inside."

"You don't want to get inside this head of mine. You may get lost like Alice in Wonderland. Sometimes I don't even know what is going on."

"Well there is only one way to find out. Go ahead and try me. What goes on in that sexy head of yours?"

"You can't call me unglued after I tell you this."

"J, just spit it out. Nobody thinks you are a nut job. You are one of the most intelligent men I know."

"April, I have these dreams from time to time. I don't know why I have them…I guess because I hold so much in, that it is my body's way of coping emotionally. To be honest, I really don't know why I have them, and they are hard to explain."

"Dreams of what?"

"They are like a mixture of the past and future. They are weird and some are hard to articulate. The best way for me to describe it is that parts of my dreams make me feel like I am experiencing déjà vu. Sometimes I can't tell what came first, reality or my dream…if that makes sense. Certain parts of my dreams I see vividly, and they end up coming true. Nevermind, you probably think I am off. What were you saying again?"

April didn't know if Jon was playing or being serious, but she anxiously wanted her questions answered.

"You know what I was saying. We were talking about your old girlfriends, and then you tried to throw the subject in a different direction to avoid my question. Was that the big story you asked me not to hang over my head?"

"Oh, I forgot about that," Jon smirked.

"Go ahead and tell me your story so I can get mad then beat you up afterwards."

"Ok, seriously, this is the story. All I was going to say was when I was younger, I was a playboy…"

"Oh my goodness, I think I am going to be sick."

"It is not that bad, just listen. So I had my fair share of women, but I got to a point where I wanted more. My first attempt at a monogamous relationship lasted 6 years. Her name was Diane. She ended up getting pregnant, and I honestly thought we would have a life together. Excited when I heard the news, I went out and bought $600 worth of baby clothes, toys, and merchandise. I went to the house to surprise her, and she began to weep. She kept saying she was sorry, then began to cry hysterically. I told her to calm down and speak."

Jon had a flashback of the incident…

"I am sorry Jon. I just couldn't. I…I…I just couldn't."

"Couldn't what?"

"I can't do this anymore. I can't. I am not made for this. I am sorry for hurting you."

"Diane, you are starting to piss me off. What is going on?"

"I am not pregnant."

"Not pregnant? What do you mean? Why would you make up a story like that Diane? You know how I feel about you."

"I didn't make up a story Jon. I was pregnant, I am just not anymore."

"Wait. I don't understand. What do you mean not anymore?"

Jon assumed what happened, but needed to hear her say it to confirm it. He felt a lump in his throat, and fought back the tears.

"I had an abortion baby. I am so sorry."

"Sorry? You killed a child, and all you can say is sorry? Why? I don't understand. Why would you do this?"

"Baby, I couldn't do it by myself."

"That is bull Diane and you know it so don't give me that crap! You know me. You need to explain to me right now why you did this to my child? Is there something you aren't telling me? Was there someone else?"

Diane began to cry even harder.

"Aw hell. I am sitting here and…all I do for you and you cheat on me? Then make me think I am having a child, then…whew."

Jon was so enraged that he punched a hole in the wall. He hit a stud, and scratched the skin off his knuckles. With drops of blood falling onto the carpet, Jon was numb to the physical pain because of the emotional damage Diane's words caused. He stared at Diane as if he was attempting to burn her with the rage within his eyes.

"So who was it? Who's child did you kill Diane?"

"It doesn't matter baby? I want you. I was wrong, but please forgive me. I need you!"

"Who Diane? Who was it? Someone I know, huh? I can't believe this ish."

"It doesn't matter baby. All that matters is we don't let this divide us. I was wrong, but I just couldn't go through with it if there was a chance it wasn't yours. I couldn't do that to you."

"You make it sound like you did me a favor. Like you risked your life for me, and I should give you a Congressional Medal of Honor. I cannot believe you would do something like this."

Jon stormed out the house and slammed the door. The blood from his hand stained the white screen door. Diane chased after and tried to grab his arm, but Jon snatched away. Feeling desperate, she ran to her car in the driveway, grabbed her gun from under the seat, and ran back over to Jon who was now behind the wheel of his car.

Diane stood in front of the car, and with the 9mm pistol pointed at the windshield she stated, "Baby, I love you, but don't make me do this to you. Now come back in the house and let's talk about this. I lost my baby, and I will not lose you. Get out the car now!"

Jon turned the car off, and thrust the car door open. He walked up on Diane, grabbed the nose of the gun, and held it to the left side of his chest. As he gripped the barrel with one tear refusing to drop from his eye, he looked directly into Diane. Jon's eyes told her that their relationship was over forever.

"You know what, go ahead and pull the trigger. You can't hurt me anymore than you just did."

Jon's demonstration showed he was not afraid of her bluff, but his eyes were what made her break down and drop the gun. Diane fell to her knees and began sobbing heavily. Jon took the gun out of her hand, and tossed it into the yard.

"You don't have anything else to say to me. Your actions have already said enough."

"Baby please. I need you," Diane said as she grabbed Jon's legs. "Please don't leave me. You are all I have. You are everything to me."

"And that is my story. I shut the door of my car, and smashed the gas pedal until the tires squealed. That was the last time I saw her."

April sat not knowing what to say.

"Wow baby. I had no idea. So what ever happened to her? Do you still love her? Did you guys ever hookup later on?"

"No April, I don't love her. Honestly I thought I loved her because I cared for her deeply, but I think I was more in love with the idea of a family than I was actually in love. And I told you after the argument that was the last time I saw her."

"A girl who was willing to put a slug in you because she was so in love just let you go? You are trying to tell me that she never once tried to reach you?"

"Yes, she attempted. Later that same night, Diane's mom called me. Soon as I pick up the phone, she said that Diane was no longer with us. I asked what she meant, and she said that after our fight, she was so hysterical that she jumped into her car and sped off in an attempt to reconcile with me. Along the way, she was side swiped by a pickup truck. They pronounced her dead on the spot. I was questioned because my prints and blood were on the gun. Long story, but apparently before the accident she let some rounds go in the driver's side of her car, and they thought I was the one that shot her car up. All water under the bridge now. It eventually all boiled over."

"Baby, I am so sorry." April tried to be sympathetic, but she couldn't hold back her reaction. "Boy you sure pick some crazy ones."

"She was not crazy, she was just misunderstood. I felt I was the only one that really knew her. I don't think I truly loved her like she loved me, but I definitely didn't want anything bad to happen to her."

"Whatever, that chick was crazy and you were in love with her. And what was she doing with a gun in the first place?"

"Why do most people get guns April?" Jon asked in a condescending manner.

April thought about the earlier conversation she had when her mother asked if April wanted to be right, or save her marriage. April knew she had issues being argumentative, so she decided to adjust her tone; even though her feelings were hurt hearing about Jon's ex girlfriend.

"I am sorry J, I am not trying to argue with you. I was out of line…I shouldn't have called her crazy. I just love you, and sometimes it is hard hearing about you with any other female."

"You are cool baby, I understand. I don't like hearing about your old boyfriends either. But to answer your question about the gun…in her case, she lived on the south side Chicago and it wasn't necessarily the safest neighborhood. She begged me to purchase her a pistol. I was reluctant at first, but eventually I went and I registered one under my name. I took her to classes at the shooting range so she could learn how to use it properly, and once I felt she had a handle on it, I let her have it. When the accident occurred, the 9mm was found in the automobile. I do not know what she was planning on doing with it…whether it was killing me or herself. God only knows."

"Maybe she just put it back in the car for protection. Sort of like how people don't leave home without their license…that is if her neighborhood was as bad as you say it was."

"I don't know, but what I do know is that the situation messed with my head. That is what prompted my vow of celibacy. I was confused and hurt. I needed to find out who I was as a man, and discover what I had done to make her cheat. I promised myself that if I found the right woman, I would never leave. I would do whatever it took to make it work."

"I am glad that I am that woman. I lucked up finding you."

"Yea, but I have a bag full of issues. That abortion hurt me April. I don't think I will ever get over it…regardless if it was my child or not."

"At least you are willing to talk about it. You will never experience deliverance until you admit what it is you need to be delivered from. If you never get those things that hurt you out, and continue to hold it in and deny it happened, you will never heal. You took the first step in trusting me. Most couples lie about their past to the point they convince themselves nothing ever happened."

April spoke words that ministered to herself. Now she just had to get the courage to practice the words she preached.

CHAPTER SEVENTEEN

Anonymous

Groceries

April and Jon declined the night out with their friends, and opted for a night home with each other.

"Baby, we are out of everything."

"What do you need Ape?"

"Everything. Eggs, sugar, flour, rice, seasoning. I want to cook for you, but we are running low."

"I will take you to the store. Come on."

Jon and April arrived at the local market, and browsed through the aisles.

"Baby, the game is about to come on pretty soon. How about you take half the list, and I take half. Cut our time in half."

April was annoyed at Jon's anticipation to leave, however after reflecting on the strides they made in their relationship, she was just happy to spend time alone with him; even if that meant watching the game.

"Ok, but only if you get my pads. You have to go to that section anyway to get your deodorant and other stuff. Pick me up some more lotion too please."

April took the cart and list, and Jon went to retrieve a basket to carry. He walked over to the toiletries section, and stood like a deer in the headlights overwhelmed with the selection of maxi pads. *Now what does she get again? There are so many brands. Overnight, heavy days, light days, long, short, wings, no wings, wishbones, hell I can't remember. Oh well, I will just grab one.*

Jon randomly chose a box of feminine pads, threw it into his basket, then headed towards the male products. While he inspected the shaving cream brands, another man in the aisle was searching for shaving cream as well. Jon noticed the can in his hand.

"Hey, I thought about trying that gel. Is it any good?"

The man adjusted his ball cap and smirked. "Yea bro. It has aloe and some other stuff in it, and it is good for your skin. My lady loves it."

"Good look man. I will try it out."

The guy adjusted his ball cap again and noticed the box of pads in Jon's basket.

"I see your old lady has you out shopping for pads, huh?"

"Yea man, you know how it is. The Mrs. runs the show."

"I can certainly understand that."

Jon looked at this man, and he thought he recognized him. Before the man walked away, he asked, "Hey man, you look familiar. Do I know you?"

"I don't know. Probably not. I am not from around here."

"I am not either technically, but moved here when I was younger. You just look like somebody. You play any ball? Maybe we played against each other in an AAU league or something."

"Naw, not me bro. I love watching bball, but I am not good enough to play it on that level."

"By the way, my name is Jon."

The man extended his hand to shake Jon's hand.

"My name is Brandon. So, you getting ready for the game tonight? What do you think we are going to do with them?"

"I don't know man. We are looking pretty good. I am hoping that we can come away with a W. Everyone is healthy and should be in the lineup."

Jon and Brandon stood in the aisle and talked sports. Meanwhile, April was completing her list, and realized that she forgot to tell Jon that she needed a new razor. She walked to the toiletries section to locate her husband, and soon as she turned her cart down the aisle, she saw Jon talking to a man…Charles.

Her heart felt like it imploded as she experienced a rush of anxiety. *Oh my God. What in the world is going on? I don't need this stress right now. We are just now turning stuff around. Whew, I feel light headed. I pray Charles wouldn't be that stupid to say something. No, he didn't say nothing because Jon would not be that calm. Jon would kill him. Just stay calm April.*

Even though her blood was boiling, April approached her husband and tried to keep a mild temperament. She took deep breaths to slow her breathing down hoping that it would slow down her heart rate.

"Hey Baby"

"Hey Ape. I was just talking to Brandon here about the game. B this is my wife April. April this is B"

"Nice to meet you ma'am."

April acknowledged his greeting with a tight lipped smile.

"Looks like you did well for yourself Jon."

Jon nodded his head in agreement. "Yea, this is my baby. I can't complain at all."

"You guys make a nice looking couple. Look Jon, it was nice to meet you. April, a pleasure to meet you as well. I hate to be rude, but I have jet. I need to run some more errands before the game. Have a good one bro!"

"You too."

As Jon leaned over to inspect another brand of shaving cream, April made eye contact with Charles. With a knifing smile, he began to snicker as he walked away.

"That guy was pretty cool. I should have invited him to watch the game with the fellas and me sometime. You know, something about that guy. I can't put my finger on it, but he looks familiar."

"I suppose. Hey, I am done with my shopping. I think I have everything. You ready to go so we can see your game?"

April and Jon proceeded to checkout. April was distant as she thought of Charles interacting with Jon. She attempted to put on a fake smile to not show Jon something was wrong, but the encounter with Charles bothered her.

The Letter

Monday rolled around and April couldn't wait to get to her office. Once she arrived she located Charles's business card, which was buried in her desk drawer, and gave him a call.

"Hello this is Charles."

"You pull a stunt like that again and it is over for you."

"What Kitten? What did I do?"

"You know exactly what you did Charles. Using your middle name Brandon. Real cute. You lucky you lost all that weight. If he looks at my prom pictures, he will put two and two together."

"I see you the same ol April. Just as feisty as you were years ago. Kitten trust me, I was not looking to start anything. This is a free country. I was just shopping minding my business. He initiated the conversation with me."

"Well remember I know you too, and you are the same ol Charles. You tried to be funny. Listen to me, do not threaten my house again. I haven't forgotten what you tried at the hotel. I should have reported you."

"Reported me and said what? Please tell me. I have to hear this. What would you have said Kitten? That I twisted your arm and made you come with me? Or no, tell them that I used chloroform or the date rape drug. Or how about telling the truth? That you were some lonely desperate ex-girlfriend looking for attention since your husband wasn't giving you any, and at the last minute you decided to get a conscious? How you were kissing me like you wanted me to ravage your body, then decided to stop last minute. If you didn't want it, you shouldn't have came at all. You knew what was going to happen. Don't act like you didn't."

April sat in silence on the phone.

"Kitten, look. I am sorry if I hurt you. It was not my goal. In fact, my goal was to please you. I apologize for what I did, but you have to admit that you led me on."

"It doesn't matter what the situation was Charles. I told you to stop."

"Yea, yea, yea. No means no. I have heard that before. It would be one thing if I threw you down, hit you, then ripped your clothes off. That is rape. What we did? That was nothing but a misunderstanding, or what we used to call a tease."

"I don't know who you are anymore. I don't think I ever knew. Your poor wife. No telling what you do to her."

"I do what I want. She knows the drill. I get what I want when I want, and she gets access to my money. She knew the agreement coming in."

"You are so sick. I do not know what I ever saw in you."

"You know what you saw in me. You know what I can do."

"Charles, please. I said my peace, so my stance should be clear. Are done now?"

"April, I just want to see you one last time."

"Charles, no."

"Well, that will be kind of hard now since I am standing right outside your door."

April reluctantly looked up and saw Charles leaning in her doorway. He closed his sleek cell phone and slid it into the inside of his jacket.

"Like minds think alike. We apparently were thinking about one another at the same time as I was en route to see you."

"Oh my Lord Charles, you repulse me. You need to reroute your tired butt back up I-90 to Seattle. It is over. Why can't you let go?"

"Just let me say my part, then I will leave."

Charles walked towards April, and sat on the edge of her desk. With one leg hanging off the side, he rested his forearm on his thigh and leaned towards April in an attempt to perform his charm.

"April, my love, my Kitten, I respect you more than you will ever know. My heart tells me that you were the one, and I know I messed that up. I know we were made for one another, but it is just taking you some time to see that."

"No, I am not the one for you. And let me tell you what I see. All I can see in front of me is a tired, washed up ex-boyfriend who refuses to grow up and wants to live in the past. One who took advantage of a young girl and exposed her to sex. One who lied to me, and put my body in harms way because no telling what kind of STDs were simmering inside him. One who had me defending his behavior to my family and friends like a dag on fool. And oh, my favorite. One that let what was really in his heart be revealed…that I was just a piece of butt and he fantasized about my sister to get off? I am so glad God blessed me with a good man in Jon. If it wasn't for him, I'd think all hope was lost. When men like you exist, it just completely tarnishes the reputation of good men out there. You have no idea the damage you cause to the females you are with."

"April, I am so sorry. I was just immature, and didn't know what I wanted at the time. You were my number one girl though."

"Number one girl? What the hell? You say that like it is a prize and I should reverence my position. Was I supposed to be happy about that title? You know what, you are a trip. Funny how sometimes no matter how much some people grow, they stay the same. Charles, leave my office or I will call security."

"You are right April. Some things never change. My love for you never changed."

"Charles you are married. I apologize for any part I had in misleading you, but it is over. Go home to your wife. She doesn't deserve this."

"She doesn't deserve anything. I gave that woman everything she has."

"Don't say that. That woman birthed your children Charles, and she is sitting at home waiting for her husband to come home. A husband who she is trusting is out on business, and is being exclusive to her."

"Well that is about all she is good for. My children. The sex is boring. Nothing like what we had."

"Sex? Is that all women are to you? Be a man for once in your life Charles. If you don't want that woman, let her go. Don't rob her from the rest of her life. Free her from a man who doesn't want her, and allow her to live. Give her the opportunity to experience a man that truly loves her!"

Charles began to clap.

"That was real cute and sentimental. Sounds like a Hallmark card. Now let me bring you back to reality. She is not going anywhere. She is going to stay there until I say otherwise. I built all this. I introduced her to this lifestyle and I be damn if I let some two bit trick take me for everything I worked for. She was nothing before me, and I am not paying a dime to let her go. Besides, we have a prenup."

"You are so ignorant. A prenup, huh? That sounds like you. Well if you have that agreement, then what are you crying about? That is all the more reason to let her out of the relationship. It is apparent that you have cheated on her before."

"Well, that is the problem. I screwed myself. I was young, dumb and full of…well, you know how it goes. I thought I was in love so that was my excuse. I was adamant about this prenup to protect myself, but the only way she would sign was if I put in this infidelity clause that her attorney drew up. Basically, she would own 51% of my company, and a pretty hefty portion of my portfolio and Roth IRA."

"Smart girl."

"We are getting off track. Let's not talk about her. This is about you and I. Kitten, I am leaving town this weekend, but I want you to keep my number. I meant what I said on the back of the card…when I wrote that you were my first love. Do me a favor and just hold on to it. As long as you keep it, I know there is a sliver of hope for us. I never told you, but that is my personal cell phone number. Only two people know that number; my mother and my wife. If you ever change your mind about us, all you have to do is call. One call April, and I will drop everything for you."

Charles picked up the photo of Jon on her desk, and sarcastically sighed. He placed the frame down on its face, and he held his hand over it.

"I love you April. I truly do. I don't know what I can do to make you see that. I know you don't like that dude you married to. He don't know you like I do."

April was tired of arguing at Charles, so she just rolled her eyes and picked up the phone. "Can you send security in here please?"

"No need Kitten, I am leaving." Charles sat the photo back up, placed both hands in his pockets, then walked out with his normal swagger.

April thought about what Charles said, and opened her desk drawer. She grabbed his business card, then immediately threw it into the trash can. She sat there for a second, and rolled her chair over to the wire waste basket to pull the card back out. She flipped it over, and his cell phone number was written along with a note: *You are my first love, and my heart belongs to you. I will leave it all for you. Love Charles.*

April leaned back in her chair, and cracked a devious grin as she read his message. She picked up her cell phone and sent a text message to Jassmine: *Hey girl, I need a favor. What is your cousins mailing address?*

Within a few minutes Jassmine responded back with the information. April pulled up Charles's business loan application, and copied down some account numbers. These were accounts he confided in April that no one knew about; not even his wife. April typed the accounts on a blank sheet of paper, along with a sentence saying - *These are accounts you don't know about.* She then pulled out a blank white security envelope, and addressed it to Charles wife. She folded the paper with the account numbers, and placed it in the envelope, along with Charles's business card with his personal cell phone number and note in his handwriting.

April opened her billfold and retrieved her book of stamps. The letter was ready to go. With the return address being 'A Concerned Friend,' she walked out to the mailbox which was in front of her office building. She held the letter in her hand, and spoke to it like it was Charles standing in front of her.

"You hurt me, and damaged me for years because of what you did to me. I thought it was love you had for me, but it was obvious it was just lust. You were selfish, and only wanted to satisfy your own needs and desires. I gave you a piece of my innocence that I can never get back. What makes it so bad is I sat there and foolishly allowed myself to fall right back into your trap, then you misused my trust and tried to rape me. I meant what I said at the hotel, and I am a woman of my word. I told you if you came by the branch one more time that I would tell your wife. Goodbye Charles."

April felt dead weight released as the anonymous letter slipped through her fingers and dropped into the mailbox.

Obsession

J.C.

Jon was outside washing his truck when his son brought the phone to him.

"Daddy, telephone."

"I know, I heard it ring out here. Who is it?"

"Grandmommy."

Jon wiped his hands on his shirt, then grabbed the cordless phone.

"Hey Mom."

"How's Momma's boy?"

"Hey Momma. We are doing good. How are you guys doing? How's the weather?"

"Baby, it is wonderful. I keep telling your father you need to bring my grandbabies down here. We are not far from Disney World, so you wouldn't have to worry about hotel accommodations."

"I know Momma. We will try to get down there. Money is just a tad bit tight right now. Where's Daddy?"

"He went to the hardware store. Our patio screen door is slipping off track, and instead of letting the neighbor's son fix it, he is trying to be Mr. Handyman. You know how bull-headed your father is once he starts a project."

"Yea, I know. I got some of his genes."

"*Have* baby, not *got*. You *have* some of his genes. Baby, I didn't call to fuss at you or hold you up. I just wanted to check on you. I also wanted to tell you that some little hussy called my house for you the other day?"

"What are you talking about Mom?"

"Some little heifer. I promise these little hot tailed women think they are so smart. She called saying that she was a friend of yours from college, and after you left she hasn't seen you since. So I go on to tell her that is nice, but you are married now, and that is not appropriate for me to give that info out."

"Mom, stop playing."

"Jon, I am too old to play games. That is why I always warned you about these women. Years later you are still on this girl's mind."

"That is wild. I have no clue who that could be though. I only dated a couple girls before I dropped out and came back home to help out."

"Well, whoever it was, she was a persistent little thing. After I told her you were happily married, she went on to say she was in a relationship as well, and this was just out of friendship. Said that she missed your birthday, and you guys made some agreement that she would make you a cherry cobbler or buy you a cherry cobbler…or something. I really wasn't paying attention to her, I just know she sounded crazy. She also asked what your wife's favorite dessert was so she could make something for her. I told her once again I didn't think that would be appropriate, and she hung up."

"Did she leave her name?"

"I am sorry baby. You know sometimes I am hard of hearing. I believe it was Candice, or Carmen or something like that. Something that started with a C."

Jon dropped the trimmer he was holding. He experienced the same feeling he had in high school when he got caught by his parents doing something he had no business doing. He went from the feeling of butterflies in his stomach, to seeing straight red.

"Well Mom, I have to go. I will call back later and hopefully speak to Daddy."

"Ok. Tell April and the kids I asked about them and love them. Tell my mom and dad the same. Love you babyboy."

"More. Bye."

Jon hung up the phone and stared at the ceiling fan as he decided what to do. He picked up the phone and called Gordon.

"This is G"

"What's up Gordon, this is Jon. G I have a problem. What I am going to tell you I trust stays between us?"

"Aw hell, this sounds juicy. Yea J, you know I won't say nothing."

Jon proceeded to tell Gordon about the inappropriate relations he had with the young woman.

"All jokes aside J, I don't know what to tell you. I feel your pain bro. I have had quite a few stalkers. I tell you what. I can try to get some info on her for you. I got a friend who owes me a favor, and does a little private investigating on the side."

"Thanks bro, I appreciate it."

* * * * *

A couple weeks passed, and Jon went to pick Gordon up for a game of basketball.

"What's up bro"

"What's up J? What's been going on with you?"

"Nothing much man. You ready to go ball?"

"Yea man. I am going to take it easy though. The last time them young boys wore me out running up and down the court. Now you know ten years ago I would have given them the business. Guess I am just getting old."

"Me too bro, me too. But hey, we still play smarter though."

"True."

While Gordon was lacing up his classic Jordan's, Jon looked around his apartment.

"You must have had some young lady over here. House smells all good. It usually smells like Fritos and feet."

"Shut up J. Sometimes a little funk is good for the soul."

Jon walked over to the coffee table, picked up the ESPN Magazine, and started flipping through the pages as his friend went to the bathroom to relive himself. When he put the magazine back, he noticed a book.

"What's this? *The Best, Worst Father?* Man, what you have books for, you know you don't read. This to impress the ladies?"

The toilet flushed and Gordon walked out. "You know what, this guy at work recommended that book to me. It is pretty good. It is about this dude and the issues he has from his father not being in his life. His father dies, and writes these memoirs explaining everything. It is pretty good man."

"Yea man, I may have to check that out."

"Let me grab some water out the fridge J, then I'll be ready to go."

"Cool."

As Gordon approached the refrigerator, he saw a note he left for himself. Hey J, man I almost forgot. I called that friend of mines…the private investigator. They did some surveillance on Carmen, and I hate to tell you this, but she has been following you. She knows where you live bro."

Jon's smile on his face slowly diminished.

"That is not all I found out though. She is also stalking this other guy. His name is Jacen Cauldwell I think. Now I don't know if this is her ex, or another guy she is messing with. This is all the info they could come up with. They tried to do a background investigation, and they couldn't find anything under her name. It was almost as if she never existed."

"Man, somebody has to know something. How can your past not exist? People can't just disappear."

"Well bro, this is all they could find. Keep in mind this was done as a favor. I am sure if you came out the pocket, you could find someone else to do a thorough investigation."

"Naw man, that is cool. Thanks, I appreciate it. I don't want to sound ungrateful."

"I understand Jon." Gordon walked over to the table where his car keys resided, and opened the drawer. Within it were numerous receipts, and scrap paper. "Normally this is where I keep the ladies numbers. What I do is just reach in on my way out the door, pull out one, and that is the lucky lady for the night."

Recognizing Jon was not in a laughing mood. Gordon refrained from any more jokes, located the number, and handed the paper over to Jon.

"This is Jacen's contact info. Maybe he can help you out."

"Can I use your cell? Mines in the car. I want to call dude now if you don't mind."

"Here you go bro."

Jon dropped the basketball on the floor, and dialed the number. The phone rang then immediately went to voicemail, so Jon ended up disconnecting the call.

"Dude wasn't there. I will try back later."

Jon and Gordon jumped in the car, and the phone rang. Gordon looked at the caller ID, and it was an unknown caller. He handed the phone to Jon.

"Here bro, I think this is for you. All my broads numbers are programmed in."

Jon took the phone and opened it. "Hello."

"Hello, somebody just call here?"

"Is this Jacen?"

"This is him. Who is this?"

"Hey bro, you don't know me. My name is Jon. Look, I know this sounds crazy, but I really need to meet you somewhere. It is about Carmen."

Jacen didn't respond.

"You still there?"

"Yes, I am. I just didn't think I would hear that name again. Hey man, I don't know what she told you, but I am not like that, and her and I are a finished item."

"No no no. Man, it is nothing like that. I actually have a situation with her, and was wondering if we could chat. I also have some disturbing news for you. She has been following you around."

"Why doesn't that surprise me? Hey, I have a few minutes until my afternoon meeting. Can you meet me at Creamy's Coffee Café off West Oak? Say in 45 minutes?"

"Sounds like a plan."

"I will be wearing a blue sports coat."

Jon hung up the phone.

"Look G, I am going to have to cancel the game today. I am about to meet with this Jacen guy. Maybe we can hook up later on this evening."

"No problem man, handle your biz."

*   *   *   *   *

Jon arrived at the coffee shop, and saw a man in the corner wearing a blue blazer pouring packet after packet of sugar into his tea.

"Jacen?"

"Jon?"

The two men shook hands.

"Thanks for meeting me bro."

"No problem Jon. Can you tell me what this is about?"

"Carmen."

Jacen immediately paused from stirring the sugar into his drink.

"I am sorry, but that name just gets to me. That woman made my life a living hell. I thought I would never hear her name again."

"Do you mind if I ask what happened?"

"So you dating her?"

"Naw man, nothing like that. I met her at this diner, and we talked a few times, flirted, but that was as far as it went."

"Yea, that sounds like Carmen. I can hear it in your voice. She did something, didn't she? You don't even have to sleep with her for her to snap. It don't take much with her."

"Man, you have to tell me what is up. She told she broke up with her last boyfriend because he wanted to play for the other team. I assume that was you?"

"Yes, that was me. I am telling you, that girl is crazy Jon. She has been telling people that I came out the closet because she is trying to tarnish my rep. The truth is I had to file a restraining order against her."

"A restraining order? What did she do?"

"What didn't she do?"

"So, where did you meet her?"

"Her and some girlfriends came up to Chicago for the weekend. I saw her while shopping, made eye contact, and we exchanged numbers. We talked a couple times on the phone, and I went down south to visit her. She was younger, and it was flattering having her interested in me. She took me around the city, and introduced me to her friends as her man. A few weeks pass, and she ended up surprising me and moving to Illinois so we could be closer. That should have been my warning sign right there. Her friend even called me and warned me about her. She said Carmen had issues, but my nose was wide open. You know how bad Carmen is. I completely ignored her friend's warning. Our relationship progressed and things were going well. We got ready to do the do, and she makes me tell her I love her before I could put it in. I did, and boy do I ever regret that. Don't get me wrong. The sex was unreal. Carmen did things that I still can't get over. But in retrospect, if I could do it all over again I would have never even called that girl back. The older I get the more I realize beauty isn't everything. A chick can be beautiful on the outside, and straight ugly to the bone inside."

Jacen began to stir the sugar in his ice tea. "Man, why don't they have sweet tea up north? They act like sugar dissolves in this cold crap."

Jon sat there, and the more Jacen talked, the more his curiosity grew. "So what happened man?"

"Well we were doing good, but I noticed little possessive things she would do. She would go through my cell and home phone records, show up at places I didn't tell her I was going, and just argue about anything. She always accused me of stepping out on her. Then when my daughter would visit, she would refer to herself as mommy."

"Mommy? What do you mean?"

"Bro, one time I made the mistake of letting Carmen spend the night the same night my daughter was there. We were watching a movie, and she slipped and said, *Brittany, do you want Mommy to make you some popcorn?* I didn't think anything of it because she laughed as she corrected herself, and went on to say how she was just in love with my daughter." Jacen continued to stir his ice tea. "Man, I should have saw through her."

"So how did you end it with her?"

"After a while I got tired of her being possessive, and I felt she was growing too attached to my daughter. I told her that we needed some time apart. That is when she went on this tirade talking about how I said I loved her, and now I am trying to leave her and our daughter. How I am trying to ruin our happy home. Yes, she was crazy man. She straight acted like we were a family and that was her daughter. I stood my ground and demanded distance. I thought that was the best way to cut her loose. Yea right. That is when she really started acting crazy. She slashed my tires several times. She poured soda in my gas tank. The chick even broke into my house and put that stinky woman hair removal cream in my lotion. You know the stuff women use on their legs?"

Jon began to laugh.

"I am serious bro. It is not funny at all. This broad is crazy. I noticed my lotion smelled different and didn't use it. She has done everything you can think of. Lipstick on the mirror. Bricks through the window. Heck, she even called my mother acting like she was an old sweetheart of mines."

Jon thought about her calling his mother, and all the muscles in his face restricted and became tight. "Jacen, how did you get it to stop?"

"Prayer. Heck, I don't know. I think the last straw was when I saw her at the park playing with my niece. You see I was supposed to take my daughter to the park to play with my niece. My sister didn't know about Carmen and I breaking up. I had previously warned Carmen to stay away from my family. Well I pull up to the park and my sister is getting a cooler out her trunk. I ask her where my niece was, and she said she was over there playing with my girlfriend. When I saw Carmen over there, smoke came off my skull and I blew a gasket. I mean, I was fuming to the point I don't even remember how I got over there. She was telling my niece that her uncle was a homosexual and liked boys. I grabbed her by her elbow, and cursed her out something fierce and threatened her. So I am at home later that night, and the police show up. She told them I beat on her, and she had all these bruises which didn't exist."

"Whoa."

"Oh believe me bro, it got worse. After that died down, I filed a restraining order on her…that is when the fun started. She took my credit card number, and charged everything you could think of. The thing is she was so slick. She didn't go out and buy items full price…she did those payment plans. I had all kinds of infomercial stuff charged to me…from cookware to exercise equipment. This chick even signed me up for a $400 monthly agreement with one of those feed the kid programs. It took me forever to get my credit and bank account situated after her. She put my job in jeopardy calling me 20 times a day. She would find girls I was trying to date, and tell them all kinds of nonsense about me. Man, I could go on and on about all the little things she kept doing to me."

"I don't even know how I would react to all that. What did you do?"

"I wanted to kill her, just being honest, but I took my lumps. What else could I do?"

"You go to the cops?"

"And tell them what? Don't be naive bro. They don't care about us. We say this is a man's world, but the truth is women have all the leverage in the legal realm. Think I am lying? Call the police station and say a woman hit you and see what they say. Now flip that and let a woman call, and they will drag a man out of work in the middle of the day. I had to jump through all kinds of hoops just to get a restraining order."

"I feel you man. I have had my share of dealing with the law. So how did it end with her? Aside from following you now, appears that things cooled down a little."

"I had to learn my opponent. I approached her like this was war Jon. Soon as the dust settled, I did some research on her. Come to find out she never obtained a degree. She had been lying on her resume, but that was not all she lied about. She told me that her parents died when she was younger. The truth was Carmen's father left their house when she was seven. Sad thing was it was her birthday. He left to get some ice cream for her party, and never came back. Carmen's mother was hurt as well as Carmen, but instead of helping her daughter heal, she selfishly focused on dating and looking for another man. After numerous men, she remarried. The problem was this man used to rape Carmen, and her mother knew about it. It was almost like she was prostituting her daughter out to keep a man in her life. And check this out too. When I tried to perform a search on her, I could find nothing. Come to find out that her father had a love of operas, so her real name is actually Giselle…which you won't find on any of her records. Carmen is her middle name, or the one she goes by."

"I don't even know what to say."

"Even deeper. Let me take a wild guess. Your last name starts with a 'C' right?"

"Yea, it does. Why do you ask?"

"She goes after men with the initials J.C. That was her dad's initials. Jacob Cooley. I know bro, crazy. Telling you, this chick is psycho. Like those broads you see on those movies."

"What ever happened to her dad?"

"Nobody knows. Rumor is he moved out to Portland or Arizona. Can't be sure. One thing I do know is when I told her I knew about her past, she broke down like a little girl. I ended up calling her girlfriends because I actually felt bad for her. The girl needed help. I don't know what they did or said to her, but they got her off my back…or so I thought until you told me she has been following me."

"How did you find all this out?"

"The same way you did. I found her old boyfriend in Georgia. I also called her friend who initially warned me about her. Look, I don't know how you got involved with her. That is none of my business. I really don't know what to tell you other than protect your family, and yourself bro. Or find a way to take care of her permanently. Maybe you will get lucky and she will get hit by a train or fall off a building or something. I will keep you in my prayers man. Just speaking of her gives me the chills. Now I know she is aware of my new home, I have to change the locks at my crib. Hey, it's been real. Sorry to bounce so soon, but I really have to go."

"I understand bro. Thanks for meeting me man, I appreciate it."

"No problem. Hey, take my email address." Jacen wrote his email address on a napkin. "Shoot me a message and let me know how it turns out. If you need anything…witnesses, alibi, whatever…let me know. Somebody has to stop her!"

Jon watched as Jacen walked out the coffee shop. *Man, what have I gotten myself into?*

Miss Cooley

It was a Wednesday evening, and April and Jon were joking around with one another after dinner.

"You are in a playful mode today. Must have had a good day at work."

"Yea, it wasn't bad. I actually had quite a few people come in today. One in particular stood out. It was this young woman, and she invested quite a bit of money. She received a life insurance check, and wanted me to help her invest it. She was really easy to talk to…reminded me of one of my girlfriends. We ended up talking about hair, clothes, and of course men. She said our kids were cute, and reminded her of her son."

"That is cool. You should have gotten her number. Maybe you could replace Jassmine with her?" Jon said jokingly.

"No, I like to keep business and private separate."

"Understood. Hey, I was thinking…why don't you treat yourself today? Go get your hair and nails done. Here, take my card. I will clean this mess up, straighten the house, and maybe cut the yard if I can beat the sunset."

"Are you serious?"

"Yes Ape, go. You need some time to yourself. Go now before I start looking at what needs to be done and change my mind."

"Thank you baby!"

April kissed Jon, grabbed her keys, and left for her quick retreat. Jon continued to clean the kitchen. Once complete, he went to the garage to grab his tools, and proceeded to do some yard work. Thirty minutes into his work he spotted a car slowing down; the driver resembled April. *Now I know April didn't go out and buy another car in this short amount of time. That better not be her, but hey sometimes you can't put nothing past that girl.*

The vehicle stopped, and Jon slowly stood up while removing his gloves. As he walked closer, the woman placed the car in park and exited.

"Carmen?" Jon was stunned.

"Hey baby, what do you think?"

"Why did you do your hair that way? What is all this? And more importantly, what are you doing here?"

"I was trying to style it like April. Whatever it takes to keep your love. You don't like it? Just tell me what you want, and I will do it for you."

Jon noticed that she wore the exact same outfit that April wore that day, and it clicked that Carmen was the woman that came into April's office earlier that morning.

"Carmen, what is wrong with you? We are not together. I am married. Happily married with children. What are you doing?"

"You must not have been too happy. I saw how you looked at me those times in the diner. The words you said to me."

"Words? What words? I never told you anything other than I was dedicated to my wife. I told you that day one."

"Well, that is not how you acted. You told me how beautiful I was, and how if things worked out a little differently, maybe if our timing was right, then we would be together. Your eyes were telling me you loved me too.

Stop fighting it baby."

Jon couldn't believe that flirting with Carmen was taken in such a way. He figured it was harmless. As he tried to absorb what was going on, he thought back to his grandfather scolding him about the power of his words, then he realized the magnitude of the situation.

"No. I do not love you, and I am sorry if you took it that way. I apologize for the things I said to you. It was wrong."

Carmen was intent on gaining Jon's approval, so she ignored his resistance and convinced herself that he was just confused.

"I understand you have a wife and kids. Don't worry, we will figure all this out. Once we take care of her, then I am sure the kids will adapt to me, as you have. Look, I even got 'J.C.' tattooed on my chest. Now all you have to do is just get yours removed and put my name there. Or I can make it easy for you and get my name changed to April. It is kind of cute. I am sure I could get adjusted to it."

"Carmen, I said stop!"

"Stop what? We can't fight this."

"Carmen you have to stop this. I know about you. I know your real name is Giselle, and I know about your past."

She walked closer and stroked his chest. "I see you been doing your research. That's ok baby. That just means you care. I knew you loved me."

Carmen rubbed her hand down the side of Jon's face, and he caught a whiff of a fragrance which resembled the same perfume that April wore. Jon's body became full of rage. He grabbed Carmen by the arms, and shoved her against the car.

"Carmen, if you harm my wife, or anything of mines…on everything I love I promise I will kill you!"

Carmen began to cry, and pushed Jon away. As she jumped back into her car she yelled out, "You don't have to worry about that. Trust me."

As her car peeled off, Jon interlocked his fingers on top of his head in frustration. He turned to walk back towards the house, and noticed the neighbor covertly peeking behind their window. When Jon made eye contact, the neighbor let the drapes fall back in an attempt to be inconspicuous.

* * * * *

The next day, Jon and April were watching a medical show on the learning channel in the family room.

"Baby, I am exhausted. I think I am going to head up for bed and lay down."

"Ok hun. I am going to finish watching this show, then I will be up when it is over."

Jon staggered up the stairs, and flipped the television on to illuminate the dark bedroom. He left the channel on the evening news, and walked into the bathroom to brush his teeth. Through his vigorous brushing, he overheard the news anchor.

"The Bulls look to replace their head coach, the CTA expansion project, and a 24 year old woman jumps off a south Chicago building."

Jon stopped brushing, and placed his toothbrush on the counter. Something compelled him to go back into the bedroom. No sooner than he walked back into the living room, the phone rang. By the time it got to the second ring, the phone stopped. Jon walked around the bed and saw Gordon's name on the caller id, so it picked up the phone to hear a conversation taking place.

"Hey Gordon. You may have to call back tomorrow. I think he may be sleep."

"I got it Ape."

"Guess not," April replied. "J, Gordon is on the line for you."

"Thank you baby."

Gordon waited until he heard the click from April hanging up.

"Thanks April."

"I think she is gone G."

"I thought she was, but I was just trying to make sure. Bro, are you watching this?"

Jon immediately knew what he was talking about.

"You talking about the news? Yes man. This is crazy."

"Do you think?"

"I don't know man. May just be irony they were both 24, but we will see. Hey, I will call you back later."

"Alright J."

Jon grabbed the remote and turned the volume up as the news was coming back from a commercial break.

"Good evening I am Terri Ingram."

"And I am Steven Foster. We'll start with our lead story. Police this morning were investigating how a young woman fell from the roof of a South Chicago office building to her death. We have team coverage tonight beginning with Kristen O'Conner. As she reports, this was no surprise to the family."

A photo of the scene appeared over the shoulder of the lead anchorman. The video clip started, and the voiceover began.

"This was the teary scene today as co-workers paid tribute to a lost worker."

The scene was daytime and by the automobiles whizzing by in the background, you could infer it was possibly lunchtime traffic. The interview of a co-worker started without introduction.

"I only worked with her for a little bit. She was a sweet beautiful girl, but the rumor is she has been suffering from depression and bipolar disorder for a few years now. This is just sad. Anytime anyone loses someone, it is tragic. She was so young, and had so much life to live. I know we all have our time when we will pass, but people aren't supposed to die like this. Not in this manner. This just isn't right."

There were several co-workers hugging and consoling one another as they placed flowers on the ground. The camera then focused on news reporter Kristen who was reporting live from the scene. The only breach through the nighttime darkness was the illumination from the camera lights; which attracted numerous mosquitoes that kept swarming in front of the camera.

"This is the actual site where this tragic event occurred. Literally feet from me you can see the memorial of flowers left from friends and family coming to show their support. The unknown woman, who has now been identified as Carmen Cooley, was found on the road by a taxi driver around 3am Thursday."

Jon's lower jaw hung open, and he temporarily muted the television with his thoughts. *That was that dream I had. The flowers. The mosquitoes. What is happening here? What is going on with me? Was it a premonition?*

Jon focused back on the television as another video began. Underneath the man being interviewed, the title read: *James Martinez - Local construction worker.*

"We were working on the roads, and saw something fly by. There was no screaming or nothing, and it was dark, but we definitely heard something hit the ground. We walked around and saw a Taxicab parked with his hazard lights on and he was standing outside of his car. We got closer and couldn't believe it. It is a sad thing, but I am just happy it happened at night where no kids were around because it was very disturbing."

"The police have not released the official report from the autopsy so we don't know if she was under the influence of medication at this point. Per their preliminary investigation there were no signs of foul play, therefore this has been ruled a suicide. Kristen O'Conner reporting for WKTB News at 10. Back to you Steven."

The camera shifted back to the news anchors in the studio.

"Thank you Kristen. Our thoughts and prayers go out to her family. Today in Washington, a congressional hearing for…"

Jon shut the TV off.

I can't believe this just happened. Is this my fault? If it isn't, why do I feel so guilty? I wonder if Jacen pushed her off? What did take care of her permanently mean? No, he wouldn't do that. Why do women that get close to me die? Well, no…she was not my woman. I have to stop blaming myself. I truly did not want anyone to be harmed. And what is up with my dreams? I am so confused. Lord, I pray you forgive me, and help me to move forward in my marriage. I am sorry for my sins and I repent. I am sorry for what happened to Carmen, and pray you help her family heal from their loss. Give me clarity Lord. I feel so lost at times.

Jon fell to his knees and continued to pray.

CHAPTER NINETEEN

Spiritual Ties

Religious Show

April and Jon attempted to mend the troubled areas of their marriage. It was a rocky road at first because there were still some unresolved issues. Both deeply regretted the line they crossed with others, but were determined to make it work.

One evening on the way home from work, April brought home some buffalo wings from Jon's favorite restaurant. Jon converted their coffee table into a temporary dining table full of drinks, wings, and paper plates. The couple sat on the couch and proceeded to eat their wings while watching the remaining portion of the game.

"Thank you for my wings baby."

"You're welcome."

"I am amazed I got you to sit down and watch the game with me."

"Why are you shocked? I like basketball…I just can't understand the point in football. Football just seems barbaric."

"Football is not barbaric Ape. It is one of the most complex, strategic sports out there. It really is a chess match. I try to explain it to you, but you are not interested."

"I think the only thing interesting about football is looking at their butts."

Jon ignored April's comment and continued eating. While alternating dipping his wings in ranch and blue cheese, he glanced over at April's plate.

"Girl, I need to teach you how to eat wings. You leave so much meat on the bone. It is like you just take a bite, then you move on to the next piece."

"That is just because you are a caveman and like to eat bones. I don't like to get that close…that is gristle."

"That is not gristle, that is meat. Besides, gristle is good for you. It gives your booty that round shape. That curvature. It puts that sexy on it."

"Curvature? So what you trying to say? My booty doesn't look nice? I don't hear you complaining when you are all up on it."

"Hey, I am just trying to help you out my sexy lady," Jon responded with a smirk on his face.

April threw one of her bones at Jon, then lunged at him. She wrestled him into a headlock, then playfully demanded an apology.

"Now say you sorry for talking about my butt!"

"April quit playing," Jon stated now laughing hysterically, "I was just teasing you because you were talking about those football players. Stop, I can't breathe because you making me laugh."

"You can't breathe because you are a punk and your wife is beating you up."

Jon maneuvered out of her headlock, pinned April down, and tickled her until her screams were heard throughout the house.

"J, quit playing. Ok, ok, ok you win I quit. I am sorry."

The two continued to play with one another for a few minutes, then readjusted themselves to become comfortable on the couch. April straightened her clothes and used her hands to groom hair while Jon flipped through 300+ satellite channels of nonsense until he ran across a familiar program.

"Ape, you know my grandparents watch this religious station faithfully."

"You might as well keep it on. Not like anything else is on TV."

April snuggled next to her husband while he set the station and turned up the volume so they could hear the program. There was a well dressed couple, and under their names, the heading displayed the subject - *Spiritual Ties*. Jon tuned in just as the husband was in the middle of praying. After his prayer, he took his glasses off, placed them on the podium, and began to tell a story.

"You know, my grandmother used to knit blankets on the back porch. She would sit there and knit for hours sometimes. I would watch as she took her crochet hook, and intricately weaved each strand of yarn together strategically. When she was done, the end result was this sturdy blanket. Because of how the strands intertwined, you could tug, and pull, but not easily tear them apart.

"When a man and woman consummate their marriage through sexual union, their souls knit together this same way. I am sure you have heard of married couples becoming one flesh. This is ordained by God, and a good thing. Well just think about this for a second. If sex cleaves two married people as one, what do you think happens when two unmarried people have sex?

"I want to speak about spiritual ties today. Specifically, the ties which are formed through sinful acts or relationships. The ties formed when a man and a woman lie down together. I know this is not a popular subject, and most Christians don't want to talk about anything they did prior to being saved. The truth of the matter is we have all fell short, and if it weren't by His grace, many of us would be just like those people we have criticized.

"The first point I want to make is that sex is not just physical, but it is emotional and spiritual. The problem we are experiencing now are couples entering marriage with multiple partners. When I was a teenager, we had to take sex education. I remember vividly this video we were required to watch for the class. They placed a young lady and a young man on the edge of the bed. The narrator made a comment that every time you lay down with that person, you are laying down with all their partners. Through movie magic, they provided us with a visual representation by adding people the teens had slept with into the room. They did this effect until the bedroom was populated with partners. I remember our class laughed because there was no elbow room left in the bedroom, but believe me this is no laughing matter.

"This is how our souls are when we sleep with multiple people. You leave a little bit of your soul with each person you lay with. This affects married couples as well. Don't you realize there are married people who have a bind with someone outside of their marriage? I know people don't want to talk about their past, but sometimes the actions of your past affect your future. What we need to realize is there are consequences for all sexual sins. It could be an old lover, a fling, or a high school sweetheart. No matter whom it was, these ties can be as strong and as binding as those formed through the marriage covenant. These ties can cause all kinds of problems from obsession to addiction. It can also cause emotional and spiritual scarring.

"Let's go to the Word. Turn to your Bibles to Genesis 34:1-3. It reads - *And Dinah the daughter of Leah, which she bare unto Jacob, went out to see the daughters of the land. 2 And when Shechem the son of Hamor the Hivite, prince of the country, saw her, he took her, and lay with her, and defiled her. 3 And his soul clave unto Dinah the daughter of Jacob, and he loved the damsel, and spake kindly unto the damsel.*

"Ok, now in this passage, Shechem saw Dinah, and raped her. When he did this, the word says his soul clave, or adhered to her. If you read on, in Genesis 34:8 it states - *And Hamor communed with them, saying, The soul of my son Shechem longeth for your daughter: I pray you give her him to wife.*

"I believe this is what you young people call being sprung, or lusting after someone, but this is much deeper than these terms. Shechem longed for her soul. He was spiritually attached to this woman after one encounter. And for my brothers out there, you need to know this affects you as well. There is no such thing as casual sex. Let's go to the word again. In 1 Corinthians 6:16 it states that if you lay with a harlot, or prostitute, or whore, then you become one with her body, and the two become one flesh.

"I want you men out there to open your ears and allow this Word to pierce your heart. The Word tells us if you lay with a hooker, then you become one flesh. When you address it that way, that means it is impossible to have a one night stand. I know your pride is blocking you from receiving this, and you are probably rationalizing your behavior right now. *It is not that serious. I can have sex with no attachment. I have slept with plenty of women who I don't have feelings for, and I don't feel anything.* That couldn't be farther from the truth. You may not feel anything physically, but there is something spiritual that happens when you participate in intercourse with a female. The consequence for sexual sin is greater than you can imagine.

"Where are my men that have children by women they are not in a relationship with? I think your generation refers to them as babymomma's. I know men who can't be in the same room with their child's mother without fighting, but still end up sleeping with them, or impregnating them again. I know men who are married with children outside the home, and they get into arguments with their wife because they are taking sides subconsciously. These things happen because a spiritual tie was formed. Because of sexual sin, situations are birthed which can lead to spiritual confusion.

"Let's go deeper. This is directed to that player out there whose goal is to conquer as many women as possible. I need you to understand that your life will not always be the way it is now. Eventually, you may fill that void in your life, and locate the woman that God created just for you. Say you straighten up, and you are blessed to have this beautiful woman who is everything you wanted in a wife. Now you have to deal with your past. The sexual encounters of your past embed thoughts in your head until it pollutes your current marriage or relationship. You could find yourself fantasizing about an ex or old experiences until it leads to situations like infidelity, or even pornography. Some guys, by being promiscuous, take bits and pieces from each woman they slept with, and measure the woman they are currently with by this fantasy woman who doesn't exist. These things can kill any opportunity that you will ever have at a healthy relationship.

"There are numerous examples we can give. I am trying not to be negative, but the reality is we need to stop acting like these issues don't exist. We as men need to start being accountable, and realize that there are indeed consequences for sexual sin. I will touch on that a little bit more in depth later. Right now, I would like my wife to come and address the ladies."

Jon was really feeling what the speaker taught. He never had anyone break down spiritual ties to him before. An uncomfortable feeling came over him as he felt exposed, and convicted. He tried to adjust his mannerisms so April would not see how uncomfortable he was. What he didn't know was April felt the same exact way. The two continued to listen to the broadcast.

The audience applauded as the speaker's wife came to the podium.

"Thank you baby. You know women, I am sure that some of you are sitting there telling me I can't relate because I am married and have a husband, but trust me when I say that I know what you are dealing with. These ties affect married and unmarried ladies. Can I be transparent and tell my testimony?

"Within the first few years of our marriage, I had an old boyfriend that continued to call my mothers house to check on me. I didn't understand how I had this perfect husband who I loved deeply, but still felt sick in the pit of my stomach when I saw my ex, or heard he called. I know this is a subject most male egos cannot handle. No man wants to think about their woman being tied to another man, but can I be real here? And ladies, I can speak on this honestly because I have a good understanding husband who helped me through severing these ties.

"Let me back up and briefly explain my story. I dated my ex throughout high school, and a little in college. This man hurt me tremendously. When he hurt me, I felt like a complete failure and that it was all my fault. He cheated on me numerous times, and I stayed right there rationalizing his behavior wondering what did I do wrong? Was I not pretty enough? Or was it my body? What did these other women have over me? I did not understand at the time that the reason I felt compelled to stay was because our souls fused together.

"I was raised in the church, so I knew right from wrong. I think a major problem with me was that I had no real male role model in my life. You see, I didn't have a father to hold me and kiss me. I knew sex was wrong, but I justified my acts thinking that sex was a good trade off for my boyfriend's attention. I had no clue what damage it was doing to my soul. Because of the sexual acts of my youth, I had some deep emotional scars that I didn't heal from until later in life. I literally went years without being delivered. It affected my marriage and I didn't even realize it. Some of my ex's old mannerisms and behavior I still compared to my husband. Ladies, I know you understand what I mean. The best way I can explain it is relating to Mr. Potato Head. I wanted to take all the good parts and experiences I had with my ex, and transfer them to my relationship with my husband. I was subconsciously doing things that pleased my ex boyfriend because I was still under his influence. For example, my boyfriend loved to sprinkle Tabasco sauce on his pizza. When my husband and I ordered pizza, I always placed the Tabasco sauce out with the other condiments. Even though I never used this on my pizza, I continued to do this by habit years after I was with my ex. That was until my husband spoke up one day and said, *"May I ask why you always bring the Tabasco sauce out when we eat pizza? I don't like it, and you never use it either."* Right then I realized there was a connection bigger than I cared to admit. It was bigger than just a habit. I didn't understand why I did this because I truly didn't love him anymore. Why did he still have this influence over me?

"I talked with my husband and explained everything to him. We sat down and studied the Word regarding spiritual ties. There are good spiritual ties in the Bible in the form of marriage and friendships, but we focused on the ties formed as a result of sexual sin. After we studied, we came to agreement in prayer that the ties that he created in his previous relationships, as well as the ties I created, be broken.

"I pray this word sinks in with my sisters out there, and touches something in your spirit. I go a bit more in depth with my book *ROSE: Raising Our Standards & Expectations* and discuss alternate ways to validate yourself and walk closer to your purpose. I know women have a desire for attention and stability, but don't lease out the temple God gave you for his temporary gratification.

"Let me leave you with one last thought. Like my husband said to the men, the same applies to woman…there is no such thing as casual sex. When you lay down with a man, a bond is created, and sometimes they are very hard to break. We were not created to have multiple partners.

"A few months ago, my husband and I went to a Lawn and Garden store. We went crazy and purchased a dozen beautiful and exotic plants. After a month or so passed, I noticed that our plants started to die. My feelings were hurt, and I was confused why this happened. How something so vibrant and alive could just die? Determined to find out what happened, I performed some research and discovered it was the soil. Me never having a green thumb, I was ignorant to the fact that right under my nose, soil depletion was occurring. Soul depletion occurs when the components which contribute to fertility are removed and not replaced. This soil which was once rich in nutrients and necessary for basic plant nutrition, now lacked the ability to produce.

"Ladies, each time you allow a man to enter your body, you are allowing your soul to be depleted in this same manner. Women start out as being fertile soil, but as we walk outside of God's will and engage in sexual sin, we are left as depleted soil unable to produce what we were once able to. Like my husband said, there is no such thing as casual sex. By sleeping with multiple men, you are depleting your soul, and damaging any chance of having a real relationship.

"We are running out of time, but tune in next week and we will continue this series. Joining our show will be renowned relationship therapist Dr. Robyn Milburn. She will address the hormone Oxytocin and it's emotional and neurological effects. Until then, be blessed!"

Jon turned the TV off, and stared at the blank screen. The couple sat there for a second before he broke the silence, "Whew, that was pretty deep."

"I know baby, I was thinking the same thing. I definitely want to buy that R.O.S.E. book. Some of the things she said really ministered to me."

"You ready for bed?"

"Yes baby."

"I will bring up the strawberries. You want fudge or whipped cream?"

"Boy, you are so bad."

"Me bad? Never! I was strictly talking about dessert."

"Yea right."

April fell victim to Jon's eyes and when he opened his mouth to speak, her body gravitated towards him.

"Now I am open to other things, so what exactly did you have in mind? Were you going to show me that curvature of yours?"

April laughed as Jon nibbled on her ear, then wrapped her arms around her husband and kissed him intensely. He leaned down, placed his hands under the back of her thighs, and picked her up. Once secure in his arms, he carried his wife up the stairs to their bedroom.

Bills

The next morning Jon woke up early. Still drained from his night with the Mrs., he forced himself to go into his office to pay bills and balance his checkbook. When he shuffled through the mail, he thought about the show he watched about spiritual ties. The message he heard stirred something inside of him. He began thinking about his situation.

I never thought about the accountability on my part. Maybe I haven't cut the ties with Diane? Could that be part of the reason why we went through so much? Maybe my fear of being inadequate with my relationship with Diane, leaked into my marriage? Maybe that was why I was seeking validation with Carmen?

As Jon sat there, he thought about what he just went through with April and how he almost lost the most precious gift God gave to him. He took the words of wisdom from his grandparents, as well as the lesson he learned on spiritual ties, and began to meditate.

Lord, I don't know why I did some of the things I did. Please sever the ties that I created prior to my marriage. Sever the emotional ties I created with Carmen. Teach me about marriage. Teach me how to be a better husband.

After Jon prayed, he decided to study his Bible. He opened up his drawer, and pulled out the old weathered Bible that his grandfather gave to him.

Lord, please give me wisdom. Teach me how to study. Speak to me.

When he opened the Bible, an old piece of paper fell out. Jon opened the paper, and noticed it was his grandfather's handwriting. Written across the top was - *The Covenant.*

How did Grandpa know?

Jon smiled and shook his head in amazement as he admired his grandfather's foresight.

Housecleaning

It was Saturday morning, and April woke up to an empty bed. She knew that Jon had a side project to do, so she decided to prepare a nice breakfast for him.

Jon heard the sizzle of meat cooking in the cast iron skillet, and gravitated towards the kitchen.

"What's all this?"

"Well, I woke up to an empty bed and needed something to do. I see how you do me. Just make me pass out, then leave."

"April shut up," Jon said jokingly. "No seriously, what is all this?"

"I don't know. I am just in the mood I suppose. I saw the light on in your office, and I figured since you were working, I would make breakfast for my baby. Since I had all this stuff out, I started making a cake for us for this evening as well. Your favorite…Jello Cake."

"Aw baby. What got into you?"

"You know what got into me," April said flirtatiously. "You got into me. Got me up in here cooking and cleaning. Shoot, after last night, you can have whatever you want."

"Come on, you can't talk to me like that. You are going to make me stay at home."

April walked over and kissed Jon on his chest. "Just call them and tell them you can't make it."

"I wish I could baby. Hopefully it won't be that long."

"Ok hun. Hurry home soon. I miss you already and you haven't even left."

April prepared her man a plate of his favorites – grits, scrambled eggs with cheese, fried apples, bacon, sausage, and buttermilk biscuits. She smiled as her husband moaned in delight satisfied with the dishes his wife prepared. *He is so freaken cute how he eats with the fork upside down. I love this man so much I can't even feel my feet touch the ground.*

Jon finished his breakfast, kissed his wife, then left for work.

* * * * *

While April was cleaning the house, she thought about the message she heard about the spiritual ties. She sat down and thought about some unresolved feelings she had.

I love Jon, and I wish I would have never been stupid and hung out with Charles. What was wrong with me? You know, when I first saw Charles, it felt like someone punched me in my stomach. I didn't understand why I felt that way, but now it makes sense. It is not that I love him, but now I can see how I put myself into that position of familiarity with him again. Sometimes I feel like I am so jacked up. Not only was a tie created with Charles, but the situation with my uncle, and then you have that fool I fell for in college at OSU. I am an emotional basket case, and sometimes I don't think I can hold it together.

Lord, I repent. Please help me to get delivered from my past because I need these strongholds to be released. Help me to forgive these men, and move forward. I hate to even mention their names, but I need to be delivered because this is affecting my marriage. Please sever any ties created with them, and help me to bury the resentment I have regarding how they treated me. And Lord if you don't listen to anything else I ask, please, in the name of Jesus, break the tie that I created from walking outside Your will with Charles. I want to be a good wife to Jon and good mother to my children. Show me in Your Word how I should live. Guide me. I submit to you.

April started working on cleaning the office, and noticed an old Bible sitting on the edge of the desk. She grabbed the Bible from the desk, and plopped down in their comfortable leather office chair. As she browsed through the stale smelling pages, an old piece of paper was securely tucked in. Assuming it was a bookmark, April began to read the passages on that page. Not finding any revelation from them, she closed the Bible. When she closed it, the bookmark caught a wind current, and fell onto the floor. April picked the paper up, and opened it to reveal the writing.

The Covenant? Wow, this looks good.

When she read it, she realized how valuable the information was, so she took out a notepad, and started to recopy the contents of the page into her personal journal.

Chapter Twenty

Truth or Dare

Three months had passed since the miscarriage. During the time of healing from their loss, Jon and April decided to perform a marriage renovation. They started by implementing a few new home rules. One of the rules was that they had to eat at least one meal together daily as a family. They were amazed how much of a difference that made. Another huge change was dedicating date night to being a real date night; mommy and daddy time alone. During these date nights they took walks, went out to dinner, went to the movies. Jon even took her to The Peninsula. The two companion plants started to mature and blossom. April enjoyed Jon's attention, and in turn, he allowed himself to relax and enjoy her. The couple felt like they were remarried. By making a decision to change, exercising patience, and being consistent, through time the glow they once had was restored. They talked like they used to, they laughed, and their intimate moments were filled with uncontrollable intensity.

Sex Education

April and Jon's passion was stronger than ever because of their newfound honesty. It was hard at first, humbling, and ego bruising; but once everything was laid out on the table they pleased one another like they never have before. The initial sex education conversation started with Jon driving home from work and calling April from his cell phone.

"Hey baby. What are you doing?"

"Nothing, just waiting for my sexy husband to get home. What do you want to eat tonight?"

"You."

"Boy, you are so bad. No, I am serious."

"It doesn't matter. I am sure you will pick something good." Jon paused as he attempted to switch lanes. "This traffic is ridiculous. I will probably be here for a while. Make me laugh. Better yet, want to play truth or dare?"

"How can we do that over the phone J? Without you getting into an accident?"

"We just have to be creative."

"Ok, I am game handsome. Truth or dare?"

"Truth" Jon said confidently.

"Tell me a secret. Something you never revealed to me before."

Jon searched his memory bank for a moment.

"Wow, you paused for a second. What is the silence for? You have that many secrets? It must be bad."

"Whatever Ape. Ok, I have something, but you have to promise not to be mad."

April felt that nauseating feeling in her stomach. She felt she asked something she probably didn't want to know the answer to, yet she still responded, "Sure, I promise I won't get mad."

"When I proposed, that was not a real tattoo. It was an outline. I went back to get it done later, but I was scared you might turn me down."

"You have no sense at all boy."

"I know. I was praying it didn't rain."

April and Jon both laughed. Anticipating her husbands potential dares, April cut off the television and went upstairs to the bedroom.

"My turn April. Truth or Dare"

"Truth."

"Wow, a brave woman. Ok, truth. Do you honestly like sex with me? Am I your best?"

"Wow baby, skipped the appetizer, and went straight for dessert, huh?"

"I am serious April. Answer honestly. It won't hurt my feelings. Well it might, but I will get over it. I just want to know if I am pleasing my wife."

"Honestly?"

"Yes Ape, honestly."

"Well, sex used to be great. Right now it is good, but we are getting back to where we used to be. What made it great was your attention to detail and intensity. You were so into me, and into pleasing me. That made me highly orgasmic."

"I am into you. What do you mean intensity? Explain."

"It was just everything. Back when we first got married, you reacted to me differently. It is hard to explain, but it was a combination of various things you did. I loved feeling your hands on me, how you have such a strong, yet gentle touch. You took the time to notice what parts of my body required more pressure as you handled my delicate frame, and what parts to kiss. There was just a special way you ran your fingers through my hair while you kissed me and looked passionately into my eyes as if you could see straight into my soul. How your beautiful brown eyes seemed to glow. I loved the sensation of your fingers embedded in my back. I just loved how you were so attentive to my needs."

"Whoa. Man, I need to get back on the ball. So I am that bad now? April, I don't want you to lay there and fake. I get off knowing I please you. That is part of being a man…knowing you are pleasing your wife. That you can make her body feel like nothing else. That gets guys off, or should I say it gets me off."

"J, I really don't like talking about my past, but to answer your question, yes you are the best. And trust me, I am not just saying that because we are married. I love how you make me feel. I wish I could have glimpsed into my future. I would have kept myself for you. I was just young and stupid and seeking attention. I didn't have anyone to guide me, or teach me about spiritual ties. Teach me about having sex before marriage, and how much heartache it could lead to down the road."

"Baby don't worry about it. Everything you did in your past made you the woman you are today."

"I know J, and I love you for loving me. There are just things about women that you just can't understand. Men just don't get it. I know you say you love me, but it seemed like after these babies, you lost interest. I already felt self-conscious for how these babies altered my body."

"Baby, I am always into you. I love having sex with my wife. It is just that sometimes, guys don't like to spend a lot of time on foreplay. It is ok, but not all the time. Sometimes you just get the urge to be one with your woman immediately. Women like how men are at the beginning of relationships…how much attention we give. Well, we like how women are at the beginning as well…how spontaneous you are. The curiosity and the drive where you are ready and willing to do whatever, whenever. Women change too, but try to blame it all on us. My desire for you has never diminished. I look at you sometimes, and I am so attracted I just want to lie down and go to work. I still get excited about you like I did when we were first married."

"It doesn't seem that way sometimes Jon."

"I just don't understand women, nor really understand the changes you go through. And when it comes to sex, we guys like to think we have all the answers, but the truth is we really don't know. Trying to figure a woman out is like those Rubix Cube things we had back in the day. Those cubes where only certain people can do it. Then you have the guys like me who used to take the stickers off, and just place all the colors on the right side. I suppose that is what I do with us. I can't figure you out sometimes, so I take shortcuts and makeshift, or move the stickers where they should be…versus taking the time to move around and put things in the right place."

"Well why don't you hurry home and flip me around and find out what goes where."

"Girl, you going to make me wreck talking to me like that."

"Seriously J, you are a good lover. You have made my body feel like no other. I can't even begin to describe what you do to me. You are so considerate, and that is sexy to me. Like that thing you do where you won't let us stop until I have an orgasm…most guys are not like that."

"Well since this is a tell all, explain to me how most guys are then. How was your ex?"

"I have had bad experiences in the past. My ex used to think it was all about size and force, and I truly believe he got off by trying to hurt me. After we were done I used to cramp extremely bad. I don't think he had one clue about the female anatomy."

"Ape, I don't like that fool, and I wish that he would just dive off Niagara Falls head first. Sometimes I have visions of pushing him off. But speaking from a male perspective, most men equate power and depth with pleasure. It is hard to explain, but when you are a man there is something about having a submissive woman in bed. Now hear me out. I am not saying we want a super freak, and not saying that we want someone to lay there like a board and just do whatever we say either. We like an active woman, and one to surprise us and counter what we do. When I say submissive, I mean the way you give your bodies to us. Goes back to what I was saying about me getting off pleasing you. When you enter your woman, and her body reacts like it is just the best thing she has ever felt, and she is making all these erotic sounds, that is a turn on…hence the reason some guys could care less if a woman fakes because their goal is just to get off. Then you got other men who think those moans mean she had an orgasm. Those are the ones that run back to their boys bragging about what they did to her."

"Jon to be honest with you, I bet the amount of women who don't have orgasms, or don't really know what orgasms are, is larger than you can imagine."

"Really?"

"Yes baby, trust me. And it is not like anyone will ever talk about it. These women will never admit it for various reasons. Maybe they don't want to put their husband out there like he can't perform? Or it may be that they feel inadequate about themselves.

"The thing you need to understand is that most women just like the presence of a man, so they will use whatever means to keep him around. And heck in my situation, I didn't know what an orgasm was for a long time. I thought I did, but I had no clue. You give them to me on a consistent basis, but that is just because you are not selfish. It is just different with us because we just have a special connection."

"I am glad that you feel that way about me. What I don't understand… if sex is so bad for these women, why do they continue to do it?"

"Well baby, most women just do it to keep their man happy because they know if they don't, it will cause problems. Y'all will start whining and crying like a little girl."

"Very funny, but true. Yes, we have been known to whine a little when we don't get our way, but that is because y'all don't realize how it feels. That is wild. I will be honest with you, from a male perspective it is hard for most men to digest what you said. It is like trying to teach an old dog new tricks. Since most of us started having sex early, we have allowed women to feed into our ego for so many years that now it is hard for us to be retrained. Well that, and a combination of pride. When it comes to being with a woman, the louder the scream must mean that we are doing something. Well, how I used to think anyways. When we first got married, I studied your body and mannerisms, and tried to analyze what felt good to you. I made mental note of what you liked, and what you didn't seem to react to. I thought I knew what you liked, but maybe you are dropping hints. Tell the truth, are you one of those women who are hiding the fact sex is bad at home? I know sometimes you throw in a little extra audible on the moan to get me there when it is stubborn, but overall I'd like to think that I am satisfying you."

"No, you are not terrible, and no I am not hiding anything. And yes, sometimes I throw a little extra on there, but I like my baby to know that it does feel good to me. Just like a man, you tell the truth and he can't handle it. Y'all start whining like a little punk." April couldn't get her sentence out without bursting into laughter.

"Hey woman, watch it."

"You are good Jon. You just took my words and ran with them. Let me break it down for you baby. First of all, women are emotional. Sex is more than a physical interaction for us. It could be about the time you took preparing the environment, or something sweet you did or said. That sets the mood. Once inside, we feel so connected to you. I can't speak for the other cave women you were with, but with me stimulation occurs by contact to my clitoris. So if you move right you can stimulate it, thus causing me to have an orgasm. That is why sometimes I prefer to be on top…that way I can control the angle, speed, and how much of it goes in. Like I said, all women are different and what it takes to climax varies. Hitting the g-spot also can make us climax…that is if you can find it. If you stimulate it the right way…well, let's just call that indescribable. Then you have to factor in that all women are shaped different, therefore we have our own favorite positions. I like to be on top, but heck it all depends on my mood too. Sometimes I like you on top because I love the way you move, sometimes I like it on my side, and sometimes I like it on my stomach. Heck, sometimes I just like feeling you in there plain period. I could try to get deeper and more technical with it, but I am sure you took sex education before."

"Yes I did, but I never had an instructor as sexy as you. I wish I was there so you could show me while you describe. Maybe you can put on your glasses, and pretend you are my teacher?"

"We can try later J."

"No seriously, hearing you talk about it. Visualizing my wife. You don't understand what you do to me. Man, you just made it speak."

"J, you are so bad."

"I know, you like?"

"You know I like the way you talk to me baby. I like the way you move. I love everything about you. I love your face. I love how you smell. I love your body. I love your size. I love the faces you make when you get there. I love how your body gets tense and how you hold me prior to releasing. I truly enjoy sex with you. Don't get me wrong. It is just sometimes, it happens too fast. It is like we kiss, then immediately in the act. Sometimes I need to unwind first."

"Wow April, there is irony in that statement. You need to unwind, before sex, and I need sex to unwind."

"Explain."

"It is hard to explain how guys think. I love you, I truly do. It is not like I don't like touching and holding you, it is just, like you said, life's demands weigh heavy on you. Everything in society is rushed. Men have the burden of all the expectations of being a good leader. People scrutinize us and judge us as a man by how we take care of our family. Then we have our own guilt about the direction our family is heading. We get older, and feel the effects of time constraints. You are so desirable to me. It is not like I am some horny teen, it is just that by the end of the day, I don't want to go through 20 minutes of motion. I just want to cut through the red tape, and be inside of you...the same way we used to."

"If that is the case, they why don't you ask? You have not because you ask not."

"It is not that simple April. Everything is conditional with you. The room has to he the right temperature, you have to be full, but not too full. The wind can't blow southeast on a Tuesday."

"You are just being silly."

"No, I am being honest April. I don't think women sometimes understand the mixed signals they send. I don't know baby. I am not trying to argue, I just want to learn how to please you. Teach me how to make love to you again."

"You already know how J. Just observe me like you used to. Listen to my body like you used to."

"Ok, if I do that, you have to meet me halfway. Trust me when I say you are sexy, and my body desires you. You have to release and let go. I wouldn't even ask you to make love if I wasn't infatuated by you. And look at my genes? You see how my grandfather is...and that is with no Viagra."

The Touch

Arriving home from the hour long commute, Jon grabbed his wife, kissed her, then asked her to join him in the shower. He headed upstairs to prepare to bathe, and April advised she would be up shortly after. After a few minutes, April finally walked to the edge of the bathroom door and peeked in. Through the steam fogged glass shower doors, she saw the physique of her beautiful husband, and began undressing so she could join him. The couple washed each other, and talked about the events of the day. The hot water rolled down Jon's chest and splashed into April's face as she stroked the hairs on his chest. She took her index finger, and sensuously traced the letters of her name tattooed on his chest. When her body calligraphy was complete, she looked up and told her husband how much she loved him, and how glad she was God sent her such a wonderful man. Jon told April he loved her more, then the two slippery bodies embraced and began to excite one another with kissing and touching. Jon lifted his petite wife in the air to kiss her. Her legs wrapped around him, and he felt her warmth through the steam. He gently lowered April until her feet touched the floor of the shower, and the couple began intimate relations. Jon took a rag, and used it to tie April's wrists together. He then positioned April back's against the wall and pinned her arms above her head. As the water continued to bead off their bodies, Jon began kissing his wife on her neck. He slowly moved down her body, covering every inch, until he was on bended knee. April broke the rag bondage, and grabbed the back of Jon's head as he serenaded her body.

Once the shower scene was over, Jon wrapped a towel around his waist, and while still dripping wet, walked over to the one of the dual vanity sinks, and started to brush his teeth. April took her time to dry off. Still wrapped in her towel, she walked behind her husband and hugged him.

"Jon, I love you, but there is something I have to tell you. Something I never shared with anyone."

"Go ahead babe."

"I think we need to sit down first."

April grabbed Jon's hand, and walked him over to the edge of the bed. She guided him to sit down, then laid her head in Jon's lap as he played with her hair. She laid there for a couple minutes without saying a word.

"April, you ok baby? What are you thinking about?"

"Yes, I am ok." April did not know how to get her thoughts out. "Jon, I don't know how to even articulate what I need to say. Since we were on this Truth or Dare kick today, I just wanted to get this out."

"April, you can tell me anything. What's up?"

"I don't know how to say this, so I will just be direct. When I was little, my mom would take us over my uncle's house to play with my cousins. My uncle used to let the kids play in the basement. We'd be down there playing hiding-go-seek having a ball."

Jon started to feel April's body tense up while she was speaking.

"Sometimes when my cousins were playing, he would take me up to my aunt's room to play dress up. He told me how pretty I was." April broke down crying. *Oh my Lord, please let him understand. I need him. Please don't let him look at me differently. I need to be healed from this.*

"I was so scared Jon. I thought he would hurt me if I told somebody."

"It is ok baby."

"He kissed me J. At the time, I didn't know how to feel about it. It felt wrong, but he told me it was ok. He would put his nasty old tongue in my mouth, and sometimes would kiss my body. I would go up to the room, and he would have me try on my aunt's clothes. While I undressed, he sat there with his hand in his pants moving it around. I heard him growling under his breath, but had no idea what was going on. As he pleased himself, he kept complimenting me and telling me how grown I looked. After I changed he'd start wrestling and tickling me, but by the time he was done, he'd end up lying on top of me. My uncle never hurt me physically, but he would rub my breasts and inside my thighs. I blocked these thoughts from memory never to resurface…like it never existed, or was a bad dream. I would silently cry on my pillow, wishing someone would hear me. I can't explain the trauma of being that young and trying to keep a secret that you don't fully understand. Part of me felt I needed to protect him. I was frustrated, angry and confused. I didn't understand why this was happening to me? Being touched at such an early age really distorts a woman's view on men and future relationships. How can you clearly see yourself in a successful relationship when every experience you have with a man has been clouded by either your bad judgment with relationships, or how you were treated by your father, uncles and other men in your family? Does that make sense?"

Jon held his wife to comfort her. His face was filled with concern, yet he couldn't muster the words to convey what he felt. As he tried to sort through his thoughts, he said the first thing that came to mind.

"Yes, it makes sense April. My love, I am so sorry."

Tears began to stream down April's cheek.

"Sometimes I wonder if I welcomed it? Was my body subconsciously surrendering to him? Did I send the wrong signals? In a perverted sort of way, I convinced myself that he truly did love me. One time he removed my shirt, then he took his old hand and rubbed them inside my panties. As he explored inside of me, he continued to tell me how pretty I was and how much he loved me. He also told me that we couldn't tell people about our little game, and that when you love someone you will keep secrets for them. I felt something hard between my legs as he began to rub himself inside of me. My eyes glossed over with fear as my innocence was slipping away. I didn't understand what was going on, but it didn't feel right. He paused as he wiped the tear which dripped in my ear, and told me that it wouldn't hurt and I had nothing to be scared about. There was a knock on the door, and he quickly got up and told me to put my clothes back on. I felt sticky between my legs, but I didn't understand why or what the fluid was. I don't think I truly understood the magnitude of what just happened. Jon, I would feel so dirty afterwards that it seemed like I was naked even when I had clothes on. I would scrub myself so hard in the shower when we went home, and it seemed I never could get clean enough. I can't even imagine what he would have done to me if Alicia didn't knock on the door that day. She noticed that I felt uncomfortable around him when we visited, so she became overprotective. Alicia has been there for me more than she knows, and that is why I am so close to her. We never talked about it, but somehow I think she knew what was going on and tried to protect me from him. If he took me away, she would come knock on the door to get me, or wouldn't let me out of her sight when she was with me."

Jon was taken back by this info. *I can't believe I lived with this woman for 9 years, and I have not provided an environment where she felt comfortable in sharing her past and thoughts. What kind of husband am I?*

Jon immediately felt bad after hearing April's story.

"I don't know what to say baby other than I love you…and this is real love. I don't want you to let this man's perversion coerce you to believing that you did anything to warrant his advances. You did nothing wrong at all. That man was sick April! It pains me when you hurt. I am partially mad. Not at you, but at him for violating you. Makes me want to go over there and…"

"No Jon. I do not want that. This stays between you and me. I don't want to cause any drama. Not now."

"But baby, you have to say something. There are little girls in your family he could still be doing this to. If not to him, at least address it to your mom. I am sure she will take care of it."

"I don't know J. If it will keep you from hurting him, then I will."

Jon tried to hold his anger in.

"Why are you protecting him? As big as your family is, and how many little girls there are, how could you not say something. You can't let this slide. I can't let this slide. This is just not right. I knew something was not right about him. I have been saying it for years. Next time I will just follow through on my instincts."

"Jon, please don't do anything stupid. See, this is why I feared telling you because you are a hot head. Promise me you won't do anything crazy. I need my hubby, and I am not trying to see him get locked up over some stuff that happened to me when I was little."

Jon sighed. "You have my word, but only under one condition. You at least have to tell your mom, if not anyone else."

"I just don't know what it would change. I don't understand men and their obsession with sex. And women…well our views are distorted as well. Women are taught, by peers, media, magazines, that sex keeps a man. I did that in high school with Charles. I gave myself to him and what does he do? Turns around and sleeps with one of my volleyball teammates. I don't know Jon. I just have some issues with men. You are a rare breed, and I trust you. You please me, you are unselfish, and actually care about me. The problem is most guys are not like you. I wish I met you when I was younger. Heck, I wish I had a dad like you. I rarely saw my dad. Seems like he was more concerned with what happened with my brothers."

"All guys are not like that Ape. Just like Pastor was teaching in Bible Study about the prodigal son, we just have to come to ourselves. It is not in our nature to be out there sleeping with multiple women, but we too fall victim of negative peer pressure. There are women who can't be trusted, as well as men. It doesn't matter. That was in the past. You can trust me baby, and I definitely trust you."

"J, before you say anymore wait…there's more."

"Baby, it is ok. You don't have to do this."

"No, I want to get this out. Baby, please don't be mad at me."

"Mad for what April?"

"You have to promise Jon."

"Ok, I promise."

"I was pregnant before."

Jon stopped stroking her hair at this point. He tried to hold his emotions in, but was confused. April sensed his body change.

"Jon, please don't get mad. It was a long time ago. When I was in college, I told you I dropped out because of a medical condition. Jon, I was pregnant."

"Pregnant?"

"Yes baby, pregnant. I went to Ohio State for one year. While on campus, I met this local guy from Columbus who appeared to be different from the other guys I had dated. He was smart, respectful, and had his head on straight; or so I thought. He was older, so he took the time to escort me around campus and show me the hot spots on High Street. This guy always got us good seats at the Horseshoe and box seats for basketball games. I should have recognized the signs. When I visited his apartment prior to, it was too nice for a college student."

"Too nice? What do you mean?"

"Meaning expensive items…Italian leather couch, huge tropical salt water fish tank, big screen TV. I can go on and on. I knew in the back of my head that he was getting his money illegally, but continued to see him since he was treating me right. Well, one night we ended up going out for dinner at Outback Steakhouse, and I suppose I drank too much. We went back to his apartment and ended up sleeping together. The condom broke, and by his reaction I could tell I had made a grave mistake. A few weeks passed and I took a pregnancy test. I told this guy I was pregnant, and he went on and on about how I was a gold digger trying to ruin his life and all he had worked for. He pretty much made it clear that he was not going to be there for me, so since I was in a situation with no support system and I saw no other options, I dropped out and moved back to Illinois. Shortly after being home, I had a miscarriage."

Jon breathed deeply as he wiped both hands down his face.

"Baby, please don't be mad at me. I need you!"

"April, I am not mad. This was just a lot of information. Just like when I told you about my past with Diane, or about my sister's rape. You loved me unconditionally with all my faults. I am not saying you have faults, I am just trying to make the point that I don't look at you any different. I love you even more actually because you trust me enough to share with me. And as head of this family, you are putting me in a position where I can cover you in prayer more effectively."

"Thank you for being there for me baby, and not judging. I know it is uncomfortable talking about past relationships, but I wanted you to understand why I was so standoffish when we first met. I have had a history of choosing bad men, and you seemed too good to be true."

"I actually thought it was cute how spunky you were. It intrigued me. I bet when I helped you with that car you would never have thought we would be sitting here years later half naked with two kids under our belt. Man, time is flying."

"Jon, I truly meant what I said in the shower. God knew exactly what I needed, and sent him my way. You are such a blessing. I am so grateful."

"I think the same way. I know I am the man created for you."

April laughed. "Thank you for being here for me. Thank you for just being silly and making me laugh."

"No baby, thank you for making me happy. For trusting me, and allowing me to trust you. Whatever happened in the past happened. Right now I am focusing on what God joined together. Let no man break this apart. I am ready to focus on my life with you, and making every day meaningful. I love you dearly my April."

"I love you too baby."

CHAPTER TWENTY-ONE

Sowing

Jon's Seed

It was the day of their 10th anniversary. April attempted to leave work early to surprise Jon, but he beat her to the punch. She walked into the kitchen and noticed a mini-cassette recorder with a message attached instructing her to listen. April leaned against the counter and pressed play:

My dearest April, I sometimes find it hard to capture the words to describe just how much I love you. As I sat at my desk, I was so overwhelmed with these random images of you, and the things you do for me, and the reasons I love you that I decided to write you a love letter. There is a catch however. Instead of handing the letter directly to you, I felt it would be more fun if I made you search for it. I have a little game that I want to play with you. I will leave you clues, and…well you are a smart woman so you will figure it out. Go look at the living room television for your first clue.

April was excited about the scavenger hunt. As she walked into the living room, she heard her favorite home and garden show playing through the television speakers, and like Jon promised there was a clue taped to the screen. She pulled it off and it read: *Clue 1 - We use this to water your flowerbed.*

With the clue in hand, she made her way out to the garage and located her favorite watering can. Jon had purchased it for her at a flea market when they were dating, and she has held on to it ever since. She looked inside and there was an envelope attached to the inside of the container. She retrieved the envelope and ran her fingers across the words "Clue 2" which were written in calligraphy. When she flipped the envelope over, she noticed a wax seal and monogram embedded with April and Jon's initials.

"Nice touch," April thought. "This boy went out of his way."

She placed two thumbs on the seal, and using the pressure from her index finger on the opposing side, she broke the seal. She pulled out the paper and it read: *Clue 2 - Congratulations! You located the instrument, now it is time to look for the resource. What do you need to fill this instrument?*

April opened the garage door, and walked to the side of the house where their vintage brass water faucet was located. There was a string wrapped around the water spigot with an envelope encased in a plastic sleeve to keep the moisture out. April ripped open the plastic and retrieved her third clue: *Clue 3 - Now you have the instrument, and the resource. There is one last thing needed; the light. Find the place where we receive the most light.*

April immediately knew what Jon was talking about. They often joked about the location of their back deck, and how the sun beamed down so hard that it felt like the inside of a charcoal grill. April would place plants on their deck because they receive the most light.

Now holding the clues and envelopes, April walked along the side of their house and opened the wooden gate to the back yard. She stepped onto their wood deck, and there were 5 Tonka Dump Trucks lined in a semi-circle with their buckets full of rose petals. Surrounding the toy trucks were multiple Barbie dolls and GI Joe action figures. April noticed the middle of the table was occupied by a layout of pamphlets and applications. On top of the pile there was an envelope with "Your Love Letter" written across it. She broke the wax seal and opened the envelope to discover a beautifully written letter on what appeared to be antique paper, and a packet of rose seeds.

The first line read: *I couldn't arrange for all the family to be here this time, so I had to makeshift.* Realizing their children's figurines were supposed to resemble the crowd, April began to laugh as she thought about how cute it was that he tried to recreate their proposal. She continued to read her love letter:

I know this is not the traditional gift for a 10 year anniversary. I believe I was supposed to give you tin, or aluminum, or maybe it was diamonds…I can never remember. In any case, I don't care what society thinks. The only thing I care about is you, and how you perceive me, and what you need from me to grow.

April, I thank God for every year I have with you. I was praying the other night, and asking God what could I give you for an anniversary gift? And you know what, God spoke to me and told me to sow back into you. These seeds are a visual analogy for the beautiful woman waiting to blossom inside. These seeds without proper nourishing, watering, and cultivating yields nothing. I realized that all these years, I have not cultivated you. I have not watered you with the Word. I have not even sowed into you. I always knew your potential yield, but didn't realize my part as a man, and your husband, in helping you grow. Well today that stops. Everything in this scavenger hunt represents the process of sowing.

On this table you will find information and applications for nursing schools in the area. North Park University, DePaul University, and The University of Illinois (which is ranked in the top 10 colleges for nursing in the U.S.). I have also obtained a copy of your transcripts, and on the table you will find another envelope with an enclosed check for $8,000. I have been saving that money from overtime and those side jobs, and what better way to invest it than in my wife. I know this is not much, but it is at least a start, and I want to sow this into you.

Now you are probably wondering how will all this happen? Well, I have a game plan. I had our home appraised a few weeks back. I found out that if we sold right now, we would pocket a $67k. I have been searching, and I believe I located the idea house for us. I am almost 99% positive you will love it. It is smaller, but we always complained about this house being too much for our family. This home I found requires little a work, but has a nice size back yard, and it is closer to your mother's house and our children's school. With the profits from the home, and the side jobs I do, I have prepared a comfortable budget so that you will be able to quit your job, and go to school full time.

I love you April, and want to do what I can to help you reach your goals.

Happy Anniversary!

P.S. - Look under the table.

April looked under the table, and saw a manila envelope. She opened it and turned it upside down to dump the contents out. Onto the patio, a Teach Yourself Salsa At Home DVD fell out. She immediately began to cry.

While April was participating in the scavenger hunt, Jon hid discretely behind one of their trees in the backyard. Once he saw April found the DVD, he revealed himself and walked up on the patio to hug his wife.

"I love you baby. Happy 10th Anniversary!"

"Happy 10th to you too baby. I love you so much. I don't even know what to say."

April held on to Jon and squeezed his waist while tears outlined her nose. Jon kissed her on her forehead, then stepped back to look at his wife. He handed her a handkerchief, which he anticipated she would need.

"Clear that pretty face of yours. I have something else for you."

"Jon!" April said in a loving, yet scolding tone. "You are cutting up."

"You deserve it. Now you ready to find it?"

"Find what? What are you talking about Jon? What did I miss?"

"I am actually here to help you with the rest. See when I proposed I was able to give a signal and have the Bobcat buckets pour roses on the ground. Well since I don't have that luxury here, it has to be done manually.

Jon extended his hand like an usher inviting someone so that his wife would take the initiative. He stood back and watched as his April approached the 10lb Tonka Trucks. She went to the first toy truck, grabbed the handle, and lifted the bucket until the rose petals fell out. Once the bucket was empty, she saw a Polaroid taped to the bottom of the dump bed. The photo was of a picture frame, and at the bottom was a message - *This man's best friend.* April walked to the second bucket, and dumped the contents out. The second photo was of, what appeared to be a lump of coal, with the message at the bottom - *A girl's best friend.* She didn't really know how to interpret either photo, so she moved on to the third bucket. The photo appeared to be a shopping bag. At the bottom was written - *Something to replenish you.* April was completely lost, but kept quiet. She dumped out the fourth bucket, and there was a photo of a Mariachi hat with the message - *Something to replenish us.* April did not understand the meaning of any of the photos, but she suppressed her frustration and moved on to the last bucket. Instead of a photo, there was a mini-cassette attached.

With the vigor of a youthful child, April ran into the kitchen where she left the cassette player, and popped the tape in. She caught her breath, then pressed play: *My April, I have one last surprise for you. The photos you are looking at are visual clues for your last gift. In order to find the location, turn over all the clues I gave you and align them. They will reveal a map to your gift. I love you!*

April pressed stop, and took the clues and letter, which were still firm in her grasp, and spread them across the kitchen counter. Jon Jr. had a gift for drawing, so Jon had his son draft a map on the back of the clues with an "X marks the spot" showing her where her treasure was located. After deciphering it for a minute, she realized the location was their master bedroom. She immediately ran up the stairs, and as soon as she opened the door she screamed.

Jon slowly walked up the steps and greeted his wife at the door, who was now jumping up and down like a little kid.

"Jon, what is all this? Tell me, tell me. Can I pull the covers back?"

"Be patient. First, let me first apologize because I was dead tired and some things may not make sense. Come here so I can show you."

Jon took his wife's hand and walked her to the bed. The bed had four piles with sheets covering each.

"Look at the photos in your hand. The first photo, is supposed to symbolize you…because you are this man's best friend. I had a portrait drawn from one of your favorite photos."

Jon pulled the first sheet back and handed the framed portrait to his wife. She was astonished by the detail.

"This is amazing. I mean, he captured everything from my dimples to how my hair falls over my face. This is beautiful Jon. Thank you baby."

"Let's continue. The second photo asked what is a woman's best friend? What else but diamonds?"

Jon pulled back the sheet to reveal two jewelry store boxes.

"When I saw this in the store, all I could do is picture how sexy my woman would look wearing it."

April opened up the black felt covered boxes to reveal a 14K white gold diamond necklace, with 1 carat diamond earrings to match. Suspending from the necklace were 7 Leo diamonds which increased in size, totaling 1 carat. She walked over to their cherry cheval mirror and held the necklace against her chest to model it.

"Baby, this is absolutely gorgeous. My, you have good taste. I don't know what to say."

"Not through yet baby. I have something to go with your necklace and earrings. The third photo said to replenish you. This was meant to represent your wardrobe. I know things have been pretty tight lately, so…"

Jon pulled the cover back on the third pile.

"I bought you this dress I think you will look so fly in. I also got you this Visa gift card that you can use on whatever you like. Clothes, accessories, whatever."

April picked the dress up and held it to her body. "Dang boy, this is nice. This is my style. How did you know my size?"

"Well I pay close attention."

"But baby, how can we afford all this?"

"Don't worry about it. I worked a pretty big contract a while back, and as soon as we were funded, I took a portion and immediately invested it in something I could pull out in a few months. I picked up on some investment tips from you. See, I do listen to what you say."

April grinned.

"So anyways, I had been planning to do something nice for you for a long time now. April you are my everything, and I know I have not been the most supportive husband. When it came to our finances, I have been acting like a miser because of my fear of going back…back to that period of time when we had to do without. That was real rough for our family, and I vowed it would never happen again. I suppose I went a little overboard, and I am sorry for that. It came to me one day that life is too short to hoard, and if I am not enjoying it while I am here with you, then what is the point? We will be fine baby. We are no longer in debt and with upcoming contracts, along with the sell of this house, we will be more than fine. Now you have one last gift, but you have to open that one yourself."

April was confident of their future after Jon spoke to her. His reassuring tone always made her feel like everything would be alright. She loved his plan to sell the home as she had been begging him to move into a smaller home for years now, and the pros definitely outweighed the cons. April smiled with excitement thinking of returning to school and the plan he made for their family. After all these years, her dream was finally being fulfilled.

April was also glowing from the gifts Jon bought her. As she pulled the cover back on the last pile, it revealed a beautiful 3 piece Hartmann luggage set.

"New luggage? This is a very nice set baby. Now we have something to use if we ever decide to go somewhere."

"There is something inside for you. Open up the big one."

April unzipped the suitcase, and there was an envelope with "To Replenish Us" written on the outside.

"What is this?"

"Just open it and see. Maybe we can decide to go somewhere…say within the next three hours."

"Next three hours?" April was puzzled, but giddy with anticipation. She broke the wax seal and opened the envelope to discover two airline tickets to Cozumel, Mexico.

"Mexico? Jon, baby."

"Yes hun. Mexico. Figured why not go to a Latin country and check out a real salsa club?"

"But what about the kids? There are only 2 tickets?"

"The kids are already packed and staying with your sister. We have three hours to pack and get to O'Hare."

"I don't know Jon. This is so fast. Three hours? I can't pack in three hours."

"Don't pack then. Let's just go right now. We can buy new clothes when we get there."

"I have to at least take some clean draws. I don't play that."

Jon was amused at the animated reaction of his spicy wife.

"Well pack me some too. Let's hurry so we don't miss the flight."

April was exhilarated about her time away with her husband. She gazed at Jon, and thanked God for blessing her with such a beautiful man inside and out.

April's Seed

During the next few weeks, April and Jon began to take time to invest in each other's interests. Jon helped April determine a school, and assisted her with filling out the lengthy paperwork. In turn, April expressed a desire to receive carpentry lessons from Jon. Everything they did, they now did as a family. They both matured in their walk, and slowly started to sever ties with friends who were holding them back, and connected with people moving forward

It was Thursday; date night. April wanted to surprise Jon with a relaxing night. Jon walked through the door, and was greeted with a pleasant aroma. April grabbed his hand, and walked him over to his favorite chair. As he sat down he asked, "What are you doing?"

"Nothing baby. Just sit back and relax. Allow me to please you."

She slowly took off both of his work boots, and allowed her hands to crawl up his leg as she reached his belt buckle. April slowly untied them as she stared into his eyes. Once the buckle was loosened, she grabbed his hands, stood him up, and continued undressing him by unbuttoning his shirt. April pulled Jon down to her height, and kissed him on his cheek. Holding his hand gently, she walked her man up the stairs. As she opened the bathroom door, Jon was surprised to find a bathroom full of candles, and masculine Bath and Body Works fragrance.

She took the rest of his clothes off, and instructed him to enter the bath. Jon obliged stating, "Would you like to join me?"

"No hun. This is time for you." Before she left, she gave him the remote to the flat screen TV mounted on the wall, and the newest issue of

ESPN magazine.

"Take your time. I will prepare dinner when you are finished."

Jon sat in the tub and allowed himself to relax. It had been years since he actually had the time to sit and enjoy a good hot bath. After an hour or so, he emerged from the bath, and walked into the bedroom with his bathrobe on. April had a box lying on the bed.

"What is that April?"

"It is for later tonight. Open it up and find out."

"Jon opened it to discover a nursing outfit with some stiletto boots."

"Oh my Lord," Jon shouted out with excitement.

"This is the itinerary. We go downstairs and eat. Then you can have the night with your friends. Once you get back, I will be up waiting for you; ready to prescribe you some medicine."

"Friends? Man, bump them. Heck, we might not even make it through dinner."

April looked back at Jon with a playful, seductive look.

"Seriously April, I have no desire to hang out with them tonight. I want to stay right here with my baby."

Jon kept his robe on, and followed April into the kitchen.

"Since you were being nostalgic for our anniversary with the little proposal recreation, I figured I would try to take us back too."

April opened the oven, and pulled out two deep dish pizzas from Adriano's pizza parlor. She walked over to the kitchen radio to instruct the CD player to play.

"Girl, you are outdoing yourself. You even have Domenico Modugno playing. Wow."

"Well don't get too excited. I only have one song, so we have to listen to it on repeat."

April and Jon laughed, then sat and enjoyed their pizza via candlelight. The couple continued to eat and have good conversation. After dinner and a session of flirting, they enjoyed each other's company. Jon was excited to receive attention from Nurse Carter, and she was happy to take care of her first patient.

*   *   *   *   *

That following Saturday evening, April watched as Jon wrestled with their son on their master bed.

"Be careful Jon. Don't hurt my baby."

"Careful, here is your careful." Jon grabbed his son, and twirled him in the air like a helicopter as his son laughed hysterically. His daughter heard the commotion, and ran in their room full speed to defend her brother. As she pounced on Jon's legs, he grabbed the children and pinned them down; tickling them both repeatedly using his nose. After they tapped out and admitted Daddy was the champ, he kissed both kids on their foreheads, and sent them off to bed.

"I will come to tuck you in bed in a second boy. Now who's the champ?"

"I'm the champ daddy," he screamed as Jon lunged towards him. While his son and daughter ran down the hallway laughing, April grabbed Jon and wrapped her arms around him.

"I love how my kids look at you. Their eyes light up everytime their daddy comes around. You are such a good man. What can I do for you?"

"Baby, I am not young like I used to be. You already wore me out with that physical. I need a day to recoup Nurse Carter."

"I am talking about your dreams baby. How can I help you? Baby you are so gifted and talented. You speak well, and have a good rapport with co-workers. I have watched you grow over the years; as a husband, a father, and a man. You can do anything if you put your mind to it, and I admire that in you. I don't understand why you don't move forward with your business aspirations? I admire ambition, and you are a proven visionary. Why don't you follow through on it?"

Frustrated at the conversation, Jon replied, "The timing has never been right."

"You have entrepreneurial blood. Your dad, your uncles."

"Yea, and you see how that turned out."

"True, it did not turn out as everyone expected, but from what you said all the times were not bad times either. Yes, the business went belly up, but you are not them. Call them. Use them as a resource. Siphon info from them, and make your company stronger."

April grabbed his face to turn his head towards her. "Don't let your fear of failure prevent you from achieving your goals. I don't want to be a burden. I was created to be your help. What do you need from me? I can be your note taker. I can be your secretary. I can help you to organize your thoughts into a structured business plan. I was studying my Bible, and it said in Habakkuk 2:2 that you should write down your vision. I truly believe that God laid the provision for us. It is just up to us to walk into the blessings which are stored up for us. You have resources. I can get you info on SBA loans, and there are a ton of grants out there for what you want to do. I know a grant writer that can assist you in…"

Jon leaned in and kissed April before she could get the next word out.

"I am so glad your car stopped."

"What?"

"That day I met you. I am glad your car stopped. I told my co-workers I felt something different with you. God sent a gem my way. I am so thankful for you!"

Jon and April intertwined legs while kissing and knocked several papers off their bed. Halfway into their embrace, April jumped up.

"Wait. I got something for you."

"I bet you do. Stop playing girl. Come back here."

"No seriously babe, I have something for you. Get up real quick and follow me."

April grabbed Jon's hand and walked him down the stairs towards the garage.

"I apologize this is a few weeks late, but they couldn't get it done in time for our anniversary."

"Get what done April?"

April opened the garage where their '69 Stingray was parked. "Go over there and take the cover off."

Jon pulled the car cover off, and his jaw dropped to the ground as April arranged to get the Corvette painted pearl white.

"Oh my. I can't believe this. April!"

"You like baby?" April said with a grin sensing her husband's approval.

"Do I like? Are you kidding me?" Jon walked around the car to inspect it. He crouched down and ran his hands along the silhouette of the vehicle. "Man, they did an awesome job. Babe, how did you know I wanted white?"

"Because I listened to my baby. You mentioned it on our first date. I know that you have not had the time to invest in it like you want because you always had to put the needs of your wife and kids before yours. I just wanted to give something back."

Jon jumped behind the wheel circulating his hands on the steering wheel.

"This car is so sentimental. I declared on our first date sitting right here in this car that you would be my wife. Jump in. Let's take it for a ride for old times sake."

"What about the kids?"

"You're right. Ok, why don't you just close the garage then, and let's pretend that we are at that one recreational park. You remember? It was the first year we were married."

April remembered the passionate scene from their younger days and began to smile. She shut the garage door as he instructed, sat on her husband's lap and allowed herself to reenact the intimate moment with her man.

Chapter Twenty-Two

BBQ

Aaron

It was a sunny weekend and the aroma from backyard BBQ's throughout the neighborhood assimilated with the warm Midwest spring breeze. While Jon was boasting with friends about his grilling skills, he opened the lid of his huge smoker allowing a billow of smoke to escape and dissipate. This particular weekend several neighbors were grilling because of the mild weather, but Jon was holding a BBQ for a special occasion; to celebrate April receiving her Bachelor of Science in nursing.

The coolers were running low on ice, so Jon walked to the garage to retrieve a new bag from the deep freezer. As he walked in across the driveway and inspected the street full of cars from relatives, friends and his employees, he stopped in his tracks and focused on the truck with "JC Construction & Development" painted on the side door. Jon smiled as he thought about the lucrative 4 year contract he just signed for his construction company. During those months of April's schooling, he took a leap of faith and got his company off the ground. With the help of his father, Jon developed a solid business plan and was able to obtain financing to cover his tools, materials and labor. His father also put him in touch with his former business contacts; a business attorney who provided a safety net for Jon's company, and old accountant who made sure Jon's books were in order. Once the company was structured, Jon had no problem attracting business. Since he had a good rapport with a few building inspectors, word got around and he was able to competitively bid, secure contracts, and build a name for himself. JC Construction & Development specializes in residential construction and custom home builds, but Jon has plans to expand to commercial within the next 5 years.

Music played, people laughed, and brisket sizzled on the grill. The kids were in the back yard playing volleyball while some of the parents sat on the patio playing Spades. Jon stood and immersed himself in the love of his family. He took time to thank God for where they were at that moment. He reflected back on how far they came, and how they almost lost it all. After giving thanks he reached into the ice filled cooler, grabbed a Coke, and headed inside towards the kitchen. April was washing utensils when Jon came behind her. He wrapped his arm around her waist until his big hands palmed her abdomen, and gently kissed her on her neck. April moaned, turned around, and returned the favor. With wet hands, she allowed them to drip on her man as she wrapped them around his neck, and kissed him with a fiery passion. Midway into their kiss, Aaron walked into the kitchen.

"Oh you two kids stop it."

Jon laughed. "Hey, I can't help it. We are just practicing…trying to catch up with your mother. We need a few more kids."

"So you and my baby sis are trying for another?"

"Yes, of course. April just doesn't know it yet."

April looked at Jon with a mischievous grin.

"It is refreshing seeing the love between you guys." Aaron sat down at the kitchen table. "Hey, I need to ask you guys a personal question."

"Shoot, big brother. Or is this a male only convo?"

"No, it is not male only. I would appreciate your insight as well April. I don't really know where to start, so I will just come straight out and be honest. We are not doing too good."

"What do you mean *we*?" April asked.

"*We* as in Yolanda and myself. Things are kind of tough right now."

"Ape and I been there before bro. You need a loan? How much you need?"

"Not financial problems J, our marriage. Things are not looking good for us."

April was taken back when she learned her brother was having marital problems.

"I had no clue. She always seems so fond of you when we speak."

"That is just for show sis. She is like that. Likes to paint this picture of how she thinks people perceive us to be. I don't know what is going on with us. How did you guys turn it around?"

"That sounds like how we were. Big brother, I don't know your exact problem…all I can do is speak on what we went through. With Jon and me, we went through a rough spell as well. Through a series of events, we came to recognize that the person we wanted was right there in front of us the entire time. We just needed to adjust our perception because it was skewed."

"Yea Aaron, I agree with April. It was like our words were lost in translation. By us not communicating effectively, and being completely honest with one another, we robbed ourselves of years of joy."

"That's pretty heavy," Aaron said trying to absorb it in. "Can you guys do me a favor and pray for me? I don't know what else to do. She has this image of a family…it is hard for me to explain. For example, we have to wear certain colors so our family looks a certain way. When we interact with people, we have choreographed statements. She has serious issues how people view us as a family. She is so wrapped up in this fantasy world that she created that whenever I try to bring anything to her attention, she immediately flies off the handle. I don't know what else to do."

"Of course we will pray for you. Have you guys ever thought about attending counseling?" April asked in a concerned manner.

"What is the point? I know her. We would get in there, and she would paint this picture of our life to conceal the blemishes. I am supposed to be the head of our family, but feel lost."

"Big brother, this is the most I have *ever* heard you talk. I love daddy dearly, but you have his mannerisms. You keep to yourself, and don't let your emotions out. You need to speak to her. Tell her how you feel. You can't go through a marriage assuming your spouse knows what is going on in your mind." April walked over and kissed him on the cheek. "I love you. You are a good man. I understand that people grow, and change. My point is if you communicate with your spouse, you are growing and changing together, versus apart. If you don't talk, then there will be distance. Believe me, distance invites all kinds of drama into your relationship."

"April is right bro. Our pastor was preaching on the storms we face in life. He used the analogy of a boat. He said that in the ocean, there are unexpected hurricanes and tornados that can come about from nowhere and can turn your boat upside down. But aside from those storms, even normal waves can move you if you are not rooted. Picture a boat at dock. If you park it there, without anchoring it, the everyday normal currents will eventually cause it to move."

"I think I understand," Aaron replied as he attempted to apply the metaphor to his life.

"Aaron, this is how it is in marriage. We get married, park our boat, but have no anchor. Without that anchor, we drift apart. The point is we need to be rooted, or anchored, in the Word of God. Everything you need to know about how to repair your marriage is right there in the Bible my brother." Jon felt the pain of his brother-in-law, and prayed internally that he said the right words to heal, and comfort. He found it ironic that this conversation was so similar to the one he had with his grandparents.

"I don't have the magic words to repair or mend, but I have a seed for you. I wish that I could have my grandfather here to spit some words of wisdom to you, but he just left a few minutes ago. He can articulate it better than I ever could. In any case, my grandfather gave me something a couple years ago I want you to have."

CHAPTER TWENTY-THREE

The Covenant

Bible Study

Aaron was curious to see what Jon had for him. "At this point, I am willing to try anything," he thought. While Aaron sat at the table pondering his future with his wife, Jon walked into his office, opened his desk drawer, retrieved a folded piece of paper, then inserted it into the old Bible his grandfather gave him. When Jon walked back into the kitchen, he handed the Bible to Aaron and gave him a hug.

"You are my family and like a brother to me, so I want you to have this. Open it up when you get home."

"I appreciate it man, but I already have a Bible at home."

"Just take it bro. My grandfather gave it to me. Inside there is a study guide that he put together that has some scriptures regarding marriage. Just check it out."

"Thanks J. I guess anything is better than nothing at this point. I just pray something changes. I stay there for the sake of my kids, but the love between us seems lost. She…"

"I don't mean to cut you off, but I am going to tell you something my grandfather told me. Sometimes you have to work on yourself, and not worry about what she is and isn't doing. You have to pick up this Bible and understand what marriage is, and what your role is. Be the man that God called *you* to be. Once you align yourself with this Word, then you will begin to see the big picture."

"That sounds good J, but the Bible doesn't have to live with Yolanda, I do. The Bible doesn't have to hear her mouth. The Bible doesn't have to deal with her mood swings. The Bible doesn't have to love a woman who doesn't love you back. So tell me, will the Bible take care of all that for me? What can the good book do for us?"

"It can do a lot for you bro. There is so much wisdom within the good book, and so many answers to situations that we go through. The problem is we won't pick it up and study it for ourselves. We want to pick up self-help books, or magazine articles, or watch these Dr. Phil type shows to get advice…when the answers are right here. We are conforming to the world, instead of following His Word. Then when we go to church, *if* we go to church, we want to sit there and be spoon fed instead of learning the Word for ourselves. To answer your question, yes the Bible can take care of all that for you. It has the power to transform you. If you get transformed being the head of that household, you will be amazed at the results that come about. Hey, check this out. I want to show you something."

Jon sat down at the kitchen table, and opened up the covenant his grandfather wrote. He began flipping through the pages of his Bible.

"Something you said struck me…when you mentioned love. I want to read you something my grandfather had in his notes. The dictionary defines love as a deep, profoundly tender, ineffable feeling of affection and solicitude toward a person, such as that arising from kinship, recognition of attractive qualities, or a sense of underlying oneness. However when the Bible defines love, it gives the characteristics of love.

"In I Corinthians 13: 4-8, the passage says that love is: patient, kind, does not envy, does not boast, is not proud, is not rude, is not self-seeking, is not easily angered, keeps no record of wrongs, does not delight in evil but rejoices with the truth, always protects, always trusts, always hopes, always perseveres, never fails. So what you need to do is take that passage, and every place it lists *love* insert your name to see if you have those characteristics. Aaron is patient. Aaron is kind. Aaron is not self-seeking. Aaron keeps no record of wrongs."

"I see what you mean J. You are absolutely correct. I have been doing some soul searching, and I realize that there are a lot of areas where I need to check myself."

"These notes go more in depth. You can take this home with you, but he lists Colossians 3:19 and Ephesians 5:25, 28 as scripture references for a husband's love, and Titus 2:4 as a reference for a woman's love."

"What other passages does he have on there J? Is it just a page of scriptures?"

"We can go over some of this stuff if you want. It is basically an outline with scriptures and notes attached. The way my grandfather broke it down, for a successful marriage you have to understand 7 Biblical components of marriage. That is commitment, submission, fidelity, love, sex, communication and roles."

"What does he say about fidelity? I mean, not like I want to step out or anything, but just curious. You know I have read my Bible before, but I can't call it. Maybe I just didn't study hard enough or something, but I'd start reading, and by the time I am done with the passage I'd be daydreaming about a Luau in Hawaii with a roasted pig twirling on a fire with an apple in it's mouth or something. I joke, but seriously my brain wanders all over the place."

"Bro, what you have to do is just take some time before you read and meditate. Say a prayer to God that he clears your mind, and reveals Himself to you through His Word. Trust me, it works.

"Now regarding your question…fidelity is defined as strict observance of promises and obligations; loyalty; conjugal faithfulness, or strict and continuing faithfulness to an obligation, trust or duty. In order to have a healthy, trusting relationship there must be absolute faithfulness. Total fidelity from the husband and wife is required. The Bible is uncompromising in its demand for sexual faithfulness. Then he listed the scriptures Proverbs 6:27-29, Exodus 20:14, Matthew 19:18, Galatians 5:19, Hebrews 13:4 and Malachi 2:14-15."

"Your grandfather really put some time into that, huh?"

"Well look how much life he has lived. I don't know, but it seems like we have been approaching this relationship thing our way for so long, why not try another way? People our age have divorces at an alarming rate. I refuse to be a statistic. When April and I went through that period of time, I would sit there and think to myself that there had to be something that led to longevity in the relationships our grandparents had. People in their era stayed together 50-60 years…until someone passed. After April and I began studying the Bible, and being proactive to protect and fight for our marriage, I started to get the answer to my question. I truly believe our generation goes through divorces like grade school breakups because we have become detached from this Word."

"I can feel that J. Ok, what does he say about sex? Not that it is a problem because you know how I get down, I am just curious."

"Yea bro, whatever." Jon said while laughing. "He basically just wrote that the husband and wife are to find sexual fulfillment in each other and that sex is a gift through marriage from God. He listed Proverbs 5:15-19 and went on to say that sex is enjoyable, and God designed it to bring continuing pleasure. Then he mentions that sex is expected and listed the scripture 1 Corinthians 7:2-5."

"I am definitely going to check those passages out when I get home." Jon laughed again.

"Why a brotha have to hear about sex before he picks the Bible up?"

"You know what I mean J. I didn't mean it like that, I meant everything. Just about love, fidelity, all that stuff. Speaking of which, what is the difference between his section on fidelity, and commitment? Isn't that essentially the same thing? What does he say?"

"Let me clarify first. This is merely a study guide. A page of notes and scriptures regarding marriage. My grandfather didn't write this, this is all in the Bible…well, aside from the dictionary definitions. That being said, commitment is defined as an obligation; a pledge or promise; something that emotionally impels you to do something. When entering the marriage, you should have a grasp on what the Word says concerning commitment. Marriage is a lifetime commitment…then he lists Matthew 19:4-6, 8-9 which is concerning divorce. He goes on to say that it is better not to vow than to make a vow to God and break it, which is Ecclesiastes 5:4-5, and ideally only death should dissolve marriage, which is Romans 7:2-3."

"I wish I would have read that before I got married. Lifetime seems like so long."

"It can't be that bad man. If you are willing to put the work in, I believe it could turn around and be a lifetime of happiness."

"I don't know J. You guys only see one side of that woman. You don't have to go home with her."

"True. But on the flip side, she could probably say the same thing about you. It is just natural for us, as men, to shift the blame to women. I am not saying women don't have issues…sorry April, I didn't mean you. I mean some women in general."

April had been relatively quiet while her husband and brother spoke. When Jon sat down to speak with Aaron she continued to clean the kitchen, but stayed close enough to add a comment if necessary.

"I understood what you meant, but you are digging yourself deeper into a hole. I'd like to see you Johnny Cochran yourself out of this one." April said while waving her hand in a joking manner.

"Like I was saying bro-in-law…" Jon began to laugh under his breath. "Man, your sister made me lose my train of thought. Well put it this way. You determine the mood of your house. If you come home from work, and you have a funky attitude, then that is the attitude you will receive from your wife and kids. If you come home with a different spirit on you…a spirit of thankfulness and happiness and praise…then that is what you will get in return. Men have lost site on the power of influence we have. Our household feeds off us. We just need to learn how to project what we want. If we want our wife to be more appreciative of the hard work we do, then we need to be more appreciative of the hard work they do. It is really simple. If we had a rough day at work, we need to learn how to decompress prior to walking through the doors of the house so we don't bring that into our home. Do you feel me?"

"I hear what you saying J."

"I am not saying women don't have issues, but what I am saying is somewhere along the lines, we lost sight of what we are supposed to be doing as men. What our roles are in the relationship."

"Roles, huh? Was that your official lead in to the next section?"

"I didn't intend it to be, but it happened that way."

Jon ran his finger down the page full of his grandfather's chicken scratch handwriting, and found the section on roles.

"The dictionary states that roles are a function. If you look up function, it is defined as a factor related to or dependent upon other factors. Another definition states a function is something closely related to another thing and dependent on it for its existence, value, or significance. Within the marriage, God assigned particular roles for the man and the woman. Without roles, you open the doors for dysfunction as these roles are dependent upon one another."

"What are some of the roles?"

"Let me break it down into male and female roles. I am not going to read all these scriptures, but I will list the location so it becomes familiar, and read his notes. For men, we first need to understand order, 1 Corinthians 11:3. We need to get a firm grasp on the responsibility that headship carries. Headship is to be provided in love - Ephesians 5:25, it is to be done with understanding - 1 Peter 3:7, we should love our wives, be affectionate and not resentful - Colossians 3:19, and it is to equal the love for your own body - Ephesians 5:28. It goes on to speak about spiritual leadership - Ephesians 5:22-33. A man is the spiritual head of the family, but a wise Christ-honoring husband will not take advantage of his leadership role. Real leadership involves service, and a husband should serve his wife in whatever ways he can."

"Sure seems like a lot of responsibility on our part. What do I get in return? You know it is always about her. What she needs, what I have to do with her. That just gets tired after a while. She is so self-absorbed it is like I don't exist. I love her, Lord knows I do, but sometimes she makes me not even care. It is like her actions make me not even want to step up and do anything for her."

"Bro, that is when you need to step it up even more. Women were designed to be a gift for man…a gift from God that we are supposed to love, treasure and protect. Did you know that the way you treat your wife has a direct effect on what happens to you and your family? The Bible speaks about how we can block our blessings by not being considerate and respectful towards our wives. In Malachi 2:13-14 it speaks of God removing His favor as a result of breaking the marriage covenant, and in 1 Peter 3:7 it warns that mistreating your wife could hinder your prayers. The first time I read those scriptures, the prayer passage hit home with me. That is pretty heavy when you think about it because prayer is our communication line to God. Maybe that is part of your problem?"

"Maybe J. Who knows?" Aaron stated in a stubborn tone while trying to ignore what Jon just told him.

"There is all this talk about what a man is supposed to do…what is the role of a woman?"

"I will just skim through some of this. A woman should submit to the headship of her husband - Ephesians 5:22, Colossians 3:18, I Peter. 3:1, Titus 2:4-5, Genesis 2:18 and I Corinthians 11:8-9. No woman should fear submitting to a man that loves her as the Bible commands. A woman should also never undermine the leadership of her husband."

"That is easy for you to say J, look who you married. April is more susceptible to fulfilling her roles. Yolanda on the other hand…let's just say she is a handful."

April drained the water from the sink, and took off her gloves.

"So what was that supposed to mean big brother? I am more susceptible?"

"I didn't mean it like that sis, stop being so sensitive. I just meant that Momma taught you how to be a lady, and a good wife. Yolanda came from a different type family. Her people have some serious issues. Nobody in their family has ever stayed married longer than 6 years…we are like the record at 5 and a half. Momma warned me about Yolanda when we were dating, but I didn't listen. She said we were unequally yoked, but the sex was so good that I couldn't see straight. Now it seems like I am paying for it. I tell you one thing I learned from all of this. Never marry someone because it is the best option at the time. If you don't 100% love that person, don't marry them just because you feel like you are running out of options. Don't marry someone because it feels like time and life is passing you by, and you just want that companionship. The decision to marry should be based off unconditional love, not cognitive deduction. Meaning, you shouldn't choose your spouse by rationalizing with thoughts like - *I might as well since this is the best thing I have ran across thus far.* I am living proof of that *I might as well* is not an excuse for getting married! It is better to be alone than to be trapped in a marriage you can't escape from."

"Aaron, you are acting up. As long as we have been siblings, I haven't heard you speak this much."

"I am just being real April. Right now I just feel like something died between us. Maybe it was just my fault for getting into something I knew didn't feel right."

"You can complain about marrying the wrong person till you are blue in the face, but the thing is you are in the marriage now, so what do you plan on doing? You have to decide if you are willing to fight for your marriage, or just give up. People do change Aaron. You ever thought about just sitting down with her and studying the Bible together? Not to point fingers or judge her for what she is not doing, but it may be helpful. Me learning what Jon's roles were in a marriage helped me to understand my roles better. Sit down and go over what the Word says about a man's character, versus a woman's. Maybe have an open discussion about what areas your spouse thinks you need to improve in."

"Her character. Now that is funny. You guys really don't know that woman, otherwise you wouldn't mention her and character in the same sentence. Sometimes I feel she is straight evil. She took everything I thought I knew about women and threw it out the window. Why are you women so complicated April?"

"We are not that complicated, men just don't listen. And if there is that much of a character flaw, why don't you man up and speak to her about it? Spouses are supposed to help one another grow. Stop being all timid and say what is on your mind. Sit down with her and read some passages about female character. There are scriptures regarding the virtuous woman - Proverbs 31:10-31, scriptures warning to not be contentious - Proverbs 21:19, and passages on honor and respect - Ephesians 4:31-32, Ephesians 5:33, I Peter 3:1, 5-7. The thing is, if you are willing to dish it, you better be willing to take it. Meaning, you have to step it up and be willing to change yourself. If you want her to be the woman she is called to be, then like Jon told you earlier, you have to step up and be the man God called you to be."

"Ok Ape. That sounds good in theory, but application? Man please.

You make it sound like it is that easy to tell her something is wrong with her. All it will take is me reading something about submission and that will be the end of the conversation. You know women in this day and age ain't trying to hear that."

"That is because there is a misconception about what submission really is. You are the lead of that home, so you need to water her with that Word. Submission is the condition of being humble or compliant; to yield oneself to the power or authority of another. The synonym for submit is agree. Submission is not slavery, but it is the ability to agree to be compliant, and humble yourselves. Both male and females have to submit within the marriage. To be submissive means to cooperate voluntarily with someone else out of love and respect for God and for that person.

"In a marriage, there should be mutual submission - I Corinthians 11:3-16, and submission and love go together - Philippians 2:5-8. You see, God created man and woman with complimentary characteristics, so there is not one sex better than the other - Galatians 3:26-28. The problem is we let society convince us that submission is a bad thing. Submission is functional. We submit on a daily basis to our employer, to our government… why has it become such a big problem to submit within our marriage? Do you understand what I am saying? We have to make sure that we don't let the rebellion of authority and submission become a wedge that could lead to the destruction of oneness within a marriage."

"Pretty deep J. Pretty deep. Man, I see I have a lot I need to work on. There is a lot we need to talk about."

"Speaking of communication, if the head doesn't communicate…"

"I know bro, I know, I know, I know. I hear that from Yolanda all the time. *Why don't you ever talk to me? Tell me what is on your mind.* Yada, yada. Why do women ask so many questions?"

"Bro, let me give you some advice. That is what we signed up for. That is part of being a good, supportive husband…listening. If you don't learn how to communicate with your wife, then you will push her into someone else's arms."

"Trust me J, they would take Yolanda for a few hours, and I guarantee they'd send her back…probably with cash."

"Come on man, you can't believe that. You are just lashing out because you are frustrated."

"Maybe so, but I tell you one thing…she has some issues she needs to deal with. Issues I don't even feel comfortable sharing. Then when you add her family to the equation, a family that constantly stays in our business, it makes things more complicated. Her family is just special, and they always do and say things to try to be destructive in our relationship. Yolanda is the youngest sister, and it seems like they are all jealous of her for one reason or another. The crazy thing is they hate on her, but constantly run back to her when they get in trouble, or want to dump all their problems on her. I understand that family is supposed to be there for each other, but there are times when they are mad at their own life and say negative things to try to tear Yolanda down. It has an effect on her, and our marriage. I don't want her to cut her people off, but they always have some stupid drama going on and try to get Yolanda tied up in the middle of their mess. Then sometimes after she has been communicating with her family, the way she treats me and talks to me changes. All the women in her family have problems with men because their relationships did not work out, so they plant these seeds in Yolanda. My fear is that she is slowly turning into those people in her family that I despise. I don't even know if I am making sense. It is really hard to explain."

"You don't have to explain. Let me just tell you straight up…you have to protect your home bro. You say you love her, and part of loving her is protecting her. Loving her no matter what the situation is. Something I want to read for you. Hold up."

Jon flipped through his Bible until he found a scripture he previously highlighted.

"I was studying my Bible one night and came across this passage. I had read it before, but something just hit me this one night, and it prompted me to do some research. I am going to read to you this verse from my Amplified Bible. It is 1 Corinthians 13:7 and it says *Love bears up under anything and everything that comes, is ever ready to believe the best of every person, its hopes are fadeless under all circumstances, and it endures everything [without weakening]*. Now that seems pretty straight forward until you start digging into the Greek translation of the verb *bears*. You see, *bear* is derived from the transliterated word *stego*. There are three definitions for the Greek word *stego*. One means to cover to keep off something that threatens. Another means to hide, conceal or cover with silence. The last means to protect or preserve by covering.

"Now this is my interpretation. Bro-in-law, there will be some things about your spouse that aren't perfect, but regardless how you feel about her or if you aren't getting along, it is your obligation to protect your spouse. Attacks will come, and you have to be there to keep off anything that threatens her. You have to provide a place for her to confide in; a place where she feels safe you won't judge her, or go back to tell her business to anyone else. And finally, you have to preserve her by covering her with this Word. Yes she may have faults, but if you love her…unconditionally… then you will continually defend and protect your woman…your covenant partner. That is part of the commitment you made to her when you married her."

Aaron sat silently and thought about his situation with Yolanda. He looked out the window at his kids playing in the back yard, and felt his eyes getting watery. He tried to divert the attention from himself.

"Why did your grandfather name it The Covenant? What does that mean?"

"Man, you making me work tonight. I guess I should have started with that first, but we just got so deep into the conversation. A covenant is a usually formal, solemn, and binding agreement; a pledge; the conditional promises made to God, as revealed by scripture. In those days, covenants were pledges till death. There was often a sacrifice, or shedding of blood, which demonstrated the gravity and binding nature of the covenant."

"So was I supposed to prick my finger and blot it on a contract? She already sucking the blood out of me now as it is. I don't think she needs anymore."

"See, you just being silly now bro. Seriously, if we did as the Bible instructed and saved ourselves until marriage, then the first time we have intercourse the breaking of the hymen would release blood…which represents the blood covenant. In ancient times, they would sacrifice an animal, split it into halves, then walk between the torn flesh to symbolize their commitment. It was a way of them saying - *if I break this covenant, let me die as this animal we just sacrificed.* Now how many people do you know approach marriage in that same way? People nowadays look at marriage as a social contract, versus a holy covenant. They get married and approach it like a live in boyfriend or girlfriend, or business partners…if it doesn't work out they just quit, split assets, and part ways. When you marry someone, you don't part, you become one…Ephesians 5:32 for reference. That means your family becomes her family, your desires become her desires, and your finances become her finances."

"Yea buddy, she definitely took my finances."

"You know what I am trying to say. In some marriages, money severs them. In others it is lack of appreciation and respect. There are numerous reasons why people divorce, but I believe that off the bat, many people don't grasp that concept of oneness in marriage. I know I personally didn't.

I loved April, but I truly didn't know how to be a good husband until I started learning this Word. I think we get stuck on the idea of romance… but romance is not the glue that bonds a covenant marriage. You have to learn how to love her with the love of Christ. You won't learn how to do that until you pick up this Word and get it in your spirit."

"You know J, I have to be honest with you…I really have dropped the ball. I haven't studied my Bible like I should, and I know there is a lot more I could be doing to try to repair our relationship. It is just sometimes you get tired. Life is tiring. But yea man, I really appreciate this bro. I haven't had a Bible lesson in years…well one where I actually learned something. I remember when we were little going to church, and they told that story about the rainbow. I thought that was so cool. It was actually the first time I ever paid attention in church. Funny the little things that you remember from your childhood."

"That was in Genesis 9:16 where God made a covenant to never flood the earth again, and the sign of this covenant was a rainbow. Funny you say that because you can tie that in to marriage…the sign of the marriage covenant is a wedding ring which serves as a constant reminder, or memorial."

Jon yawned, and wiped his eyes.

"Excuse me, whew. Hey bro, I could go on all night using these notes as a blueprint, but I am getting tired. I had a pretty long day. How about you just take this home, then you can study it at your leisure? I can read until I am blue in the face, but you will never learn how to eat with someone spoon feeding you. You have to take this home and digest it yourself."

"Sounds good J. Thanks bro, I appreciate your words of encouragement. I know I complain a lot, but seriously, just being around you guys gives me hope that things will be alright."

"You will be alright man. You just have to change the way you are approaching marriage. It is holy, it is precious, and it is a gift from God. When you get to the point where you reverence the sanctity of marriage, then you will take the necessary steps to make it work."

The Invitation

The BBQ ended, and people started to leave. Exhausted by hosting, Jon and April began the annoying task of cleaning up. Aaron's family was the last to leave. April and Jon exchanged hugs and kisses, and helped Aaron and Yolanda load the kids into their Tahoe.

During the quiet drive home, Aaron wondered if his marriage would ever change. *I don't know how much longer I can take of this. Maybe Ape and Jon were right and I just need to speak up. Problem is, what do I say? I don't know what to do anymore. I am so confused and tired. I feel like my back is against the wall, and God is the only thing that can save us at this point. Well, one thing I know is I need to start reading my Bible more. I am almost embarrassed to say, but some of those passages I never heard of before. Soon as we get home, I am going to allot some time to meditating and getting some of this Word in me. Something has to change. I refuse to keep living life like this.*

The family finally arrived home and pulled into the garage. Aaron told Yolanda he had some work to do and would be to bed later. He made sure his kids were secure in bed, kissed his wife on the cheek, and locked himself in his office. As he sat there thinking about his life, he noticed his SUV keys resting on the Bible Jon gave him. He tossed his keys to the side and picked up the old, tattered Bible. Aaron rubbed his hand on the surface, allowing his fingers to read the letters. He opened up the Bible, extracted the study guide that Jon's grandfather prepared, and grabbed a notepad and pen out of his desk. Aaron covered his eyes with both hands, and slowly dragged them down his face as if his hands were extracting stress from his body. As he sat there adjusting his vision, he sighed, then said a prayer over his family.

"Lord, I have strayed. Somewhere along this journey I became lost. It is like I go to church, but I am not getting anything out of it. I don't want to continue to live life like this. I am often confused and have some many unanswered questions regarding how to be a good husband and make this relationship work. I need You to break through this confusion and help set my heart at peace with who You created me to be. Help me to be a better husband and father, Lord. Teach me how to deal with this situation. Open up doors for our marriage to be restored. I get mad and frustrated at times, but I love Yolanda with all my heart. Lord, please forgive me for my actions and the words I have said towards her. Help me to understand this Word. Clear my mind and reveal yourself to me. I invite you back into our lives, Lord. I invite you back into our marriage. In the name of Jesus I pray, Amen."

Aaron's heartfelt prayer left traces of teardrops that smeared the ink on his desk calendar. He took the end of his shirt and wiped the liquid evidence of his emotional breakdown from his mahogany desk. When done, he placed his Bible over the damp blemish, and began studying.

ABOUT THE AUTHOR

Jerome J. McCarthy is an IT Professional and freelance Web & Graphic Designer (econsumerdesign.com). A native of Dayton, OH, he now resides in Dallas, TX with his beautiful wife and four sons.

As Director of Information Technology for In His Image Ministries (located in Keller, TX), founder of The Real Life Series Publishing Co., and an author, Jerome strives to provide reading and multimedia material to encourage and bless the lives of others.

BOOKS AVAILABLE BY
THE REAL LIFE SERIES PUBLISHING CO.

**R.O.S.E. Raising Our Standards & Expectations:
Transforming Your Ability To Handle Relationships**
by Marla A. McCarthy
Non-Fiction/Self-Help
ISBN-13: 978-0-9800083-8-8

The Best, Worst Father
by Jerome J. McCarthy
Fiction/Novel
ISBN-13: 978-0-9800083-7-1

Rose From The Basement
by Jerome J. McCarthy
Fiction/Novel
ISBN-13: 978-0-9800083-4-0

Inquires should be addressed to:
The Real Life Series Publishing Co., LLC
P.O. BOX 1896
Keller, TX 76244
www.TheRealLifeSeries.com
info@thereallifeseries.com